"

Jake's eyes were t

Nora didn't reali   in
cahoots with someon   coconspirator against the world. It had been a long time since
she'd had that with anyone, unless she counted the illicit
pizzas she ordered for Maya.

Jake ran a hand through his long hair. Heat pooled low
in her belly. It suddenly felt like something inside her was
waking from a long hibernation. Something she'd thought
had been dead was only, it turned out, dormant.

She sighed and glanced at Jake as she unlocked her door.
He grinned and waggled his eyebrows at her. He was only
doing it because, like her, he was enjoying the echoes of
their covert operation.

Right?

His eyes slid down her body, but he jerked them back up,
like he'd been caught doing something wrong. All the mirth
had gone from Jake's expression. His eyes were no longer
twinkling. But they hadn't returned to normal, either. They
were doing...something else.

Well.

PRAISE FOR JENNY HOLIDAY'S NOVELS

MERMAID INN

"Bursting with humor, grand (and small!) gestures guaranteed to make you swoon, Holiday elevates the classic small-town rom-com." —*Entertainment Weekly*

"Holiday enchants with the sunny second-chance love story that launches her Matchmaker Bay series...This sweet contemporary romance is sure to win readers' hearts." —*Publishers Weekly*

"A picturesque locale, delightful citizens and some smoking-hot love scenes give this book all the feel-good joys." —*BookPage*

"Entertaining, wonderfully funny, romantic as all get-out." —All About Romance

ONE AND ONLY

"The perfect rom-com." —Refinery29

"A satisfying iteration of the contemporary bridezilla subgenre." —*New York Times Book Review*

"When it comes to creating unputdownable contemporary romances, Holiday is in it to win it."
—*Booklist*, starred review

"Delightfully sexy and sweet, Holiday knows how to deliver the perfect combination of sexual tension and happily-ever-after."
—Lauren Layne, *New York Times* bestselling author

"*One and Only* is fantastic! A great start to a new series. Compelling characters, tons of heat, loads of heart. I highly recommend!"
—M. O'Keefe, *USA Today* bestselling author

IT TAKES TWO

"Jenny Holiday turns up the heat and the charm for a summer read more satisfying than a poolside popsicle.... It's hard to imagine finding a more delightful summer escape."
—*Entertainment Weekly*

"This is romantic comedy at its best, complete with clever, sexy banter, a vibrant cast of characters, [and] a wedding that is a character in itself." —*Washington Post*

"Holiday combines class and sass with a hefty dose of humor.... This winning hero and heroine will take up residence in readers' hearts." —*Publishers Weekly*

"[An] irresistible mix of lively, piquantly witty writing; sharply etched, marvelously memorable characters; and some completely combustible love scenes that are guaranteed to leave burn marks on readers' fingers."

—Booklist, starred review

THREE LITTLE WORDS

"A perfectly plotted emotional journey.... Intense, heartfelt, mature and sexy as hell."

—NPR

"Holiday adroitly combines all the requisite elements of a great rom-com—scintillating, witty banter and incendiary sexual chemistry—and a pair of protagonists whose emotional complexity and realistic flaws lend a welcome measure of gravitas to this brilliantly executed romance."

—Booklist, starred review

"Combines pure fun with surprising depth.... Leavened with witty banter, Holiday's sweet-hot tale captivates."

—Publishers Weekly

"[The] HEA is reached with warmth, humor, steamy interludes, excellent friendships and really delicious-sounding food."

—BookPage

Paradise Cove

ALSO BY JENNY HOLIDAY

THE MATCHMAKER BAY SERIES

Mermaid Inn

THE BRIDESMAIDS BEHAVING BADLY SERIES

One and Only

It Takes Two

Merrily Ever After (novella)

Three Little Words

paradise cove

A MATCHMAKER BAY NOVEL

JENNY HOLIDAY

FOREVER
New York Boston

Copyright © 2020 by Jenny Holiday

Cover design by Elizabeth Turner
Cover illustration by Allan Davey
Cover copyright © 2020 by Hachette Book Group, Inc.

Forever
Hachette Book Group
1290 Avenue of the Americas, New York, NY 10104
read-forever.com
twitter.com/readforeverpub

First Edition: July 2020

Forever is an imprint of Grand Central Publishing. The Forever name and logo are trademarks of Hachette Book Group, Inc.

The publisher is not responsible for websites (or their content) that are not owned by the publisher.

The Hachette Speakers Bureau provides a wide range of authors for speaking events. To find out more, go to www.hachettespeakersbureau.com or call (866) 376-6591.

ISBN: 978-1-5387-1654-0 (mass market), 978-1-5387-1655-7 (ebook)

Printed in the United States of America

OPM

10 9 8 7 6 5 4 3 2 1

For Estelle, with love and Illuminations.

Acknowledgments

I had a tremendous triumvirate of editors working on this book. Lexi Smail helped plan, Leah Hultenschmidt edited, and Junessa Viloria saw it through production. You ladies are the best! Thanks to Elizabeth Stokes for making this series shine (Canada never looked so good) and to Estelle Hallick for deploying a tidal wave of puns to make sure people read it. As usual, I'm indebted to my ladies Courtney Miller-Callihan and Sandra Owens. And thanks above all to my readers (hello Northern Heat!).

Chapter One

❧

The first time Nora Walsh saw Jake Ramsey, he was getting his hair braided.

He was sitting in one of the chairs at Curl Up and Dye reading a copy of *Field & Stream* while a stylist did some kind of elaborate Maria von Trapp cross-scalp braiding thing to his long brown hair. The image was almost comical: this giant, beefy man sitting on a chair that looked like a piece of dollhouse furniture compared to him. It was like Jason Momoa's paler twin had shown up to play beauty parlor.

"Can I help you, hon?"

Nora transferred her attention from Aquaman to the older woman behind the reception desk. "Yes. Hi. I don't have an appointment, but I was hoping to get my roots touched up. Or to make an appointment for later, if you can't take me now."

"Come on in." The woman led her to the salon's

unoccupied chair—there were only two in the small space. "Carol Junior can take you after she's finished with Jake."

"Almost done." The younger woman was a carbon copy of the older one, minus the wrinkles. "I'm just playing around." She grabbed a hair elastic from her workstation, tied off the braid, and stood back to assess. "Well, that's not going to win any awards."

The man lowered his magazine, leaned forward to examine himself in the mirror, and shrugged. "Looks fine to me."

The stylist patted him on the shoulder. "You're such a good sport, Jake. Take that out, and we'll get you washed." She turned to Nora and gave a little shriek. "Oh my God! I *love* your hair."

Nora had a pixie cut. A very short, very platinum pixie cut. She'd wondered if it would stand out in Moonflower Bay, and it did. Pretty much all the women she'd seen so far—though admittedly, she'd only been in town a day— had long hair. She was afraid she would come off like the city girl who thought she was all that. But it wasn't like she sported piercings or tattoos or anything. She just had really, really short hair.

Unlike the big dude next to her, who had started raking his fingers through his hair to undo his braid. She wondered why he bothered getting it done in the first place if he was just going to take it out.

He transferred his attention from his reflection to Nora, and as their eyes met in the mirror, there was a record scratch in Nora's brain. It was like there was the normal, unremarkable, white-noise soundtrack of life unspooling as it always did, and then it just stopped.

She wondered if he felt it, too, because he blinked a few times and paused in undoing his hair.

His eyes were green. A green so intense that, together with his long, dark hair, it brought to mind something not quite human. If he had told her that he was part wolf, she might have believed him.

Or maybe he *was* Aquaman? Some kind of sea god or something? They *were* on a Great Lake.

She examined the rest of his features, trying to decide if they were mortal or otherwise. His jaw was clean shaven, despite the thick, lustrous hair on his head. His lips were full and pale pink. A stark-white scar ran over his upper lip on one side, so deep it pulled the lip up a little.

The stylist laughed, and the record in Nora's brain started playing again. The man returned to dismantling his hairdo, and Nora willed her suddenly hot cheeks to chill out.

"Look at you two! We've got a long-haired boy and a short-haired girl." Nora was about to fire back—she was primed for these small-town folks not to approve of her—when the woman added, "Not that there's anything wrong with that." Standing between the chairs, she put her hands on her hips and examined both of her customers in the mirror. "Because you both have *totally amazing* hair."

Nora didn't know what to say. Maybe this town wasn't going to be as small-minded as she'd feared?

The stylist wiped her hands on a towel before sticking one out in front of Nora. "Carol Dyson Junior. Folks call me CJ, though, to differentiate me from my mom." She hitched a thumb toward the front of the salon, where the older woman had retreated to the reception desk. "I don't think I've seen you in here before."

"Nora Walsh. I just moved to town."

CJ's mom—that would be Carol Senior, Nora reasoned— suddenly reappeared. "Oh! You're the new doctor!"

"I am." Word sure got around. Four weeks ago, she had been a physician in the emergency department at St. Michael's Hospital in downtown Toronto, a job she walked to from a twentieth-floor apartment a few blocks away. Today, she was the doctor in the small Lake Huron town of Moonflower Bay and was renting a house twice as big as her old apartment at a fraction of what she used to pay.

Also: four weeks ago, she'd had a boyfriend named Rufus. Now she was single.

"We're so glad you're here," the older woman said. "It's been a real pain having to drive to Grand View or farther to see a doctor since Doc Baker retired." She leaned in. "Did you buy the practice from Ed?"

Nora had not bought the practice from Dr. Edward Baker. She'd responded to a classified ad in *Ontario Medical Review*, just out of curiosity, once she'd started toying with the idea of a total life reset. Before she could even blink, Dr. Baker had responded with a more-than-fair price to buy him out. But there was total life reset, and there was total insanity.

She hadn't *quite* crossed over into insanity yet.

So she had counterproposed that she lease the practice for two years, Dr. Baker had agreed, and here she was. New town, new specialty, new life. And, most importantly, the government offered medical school loan forgiveness to people who did time in places with doctor shortages. Worst-case scenario, she spent some time professionally unfulfilled, treating ear infections and writing referrals for joint replacements, but she'd make some money and be back in Toronto in a couple years, ready for the Walsh Sisters' Real Estate Adventure.

Moonflower Bay was a palate cleanser, basically. Once

cleansed, she could go back to Toronto with a mended heart, a clear head, and a little bit of cash.

She could go back to Toronto a woman in control of her own destiny.

"Dr. Baker and I worked out a rental agreement for two years," she said to both Carols.

"Why only two years?" Carol Senior asked.

"My sister and I are planning to buy a house together, but the Toronto housing market is through the roof."

"So I hear. What a world we live in when a doctor can't afford a house."

"Not even close. These days, I think you have to be a Russian oligarch to afford a house in central Toronto." She explained about the loan forgiveness program. "So my sister and I are both going to save aggressively and start shopping in two years. In the meantime, I'm going to try my hand at small-town doctoring." Wait. Had that sounded patronizing? *I'm just gracing you with my sophisticated, big-city presence for a couple years?*

Neither seemed offended. Carol Junior pointed at Aquaman. "This here is Jake Ramsey."

"I like your hair, Jake Ramsey." Now that it was down, it came past his shoulders. It was the kind of hair women coveted. Nora might even grow hers, if it was guaranteed to end up looking like that. A mixture of naturally thin hair and long shifts at the hospital had always meant short, low-maintenance hair for Nora, but it was even shorter than usual these days, because she and her sister had shaved their heads five months ago in solidarity with their grandma, who'd lost hers while in treatment for breast cancer.

Jake made a sort of noncommittal grunt. So maybe he wasn't part wolf so much as part pig? Aquapig? She smiled.

That sounded like it could be a spinoff of the British show about the pig family that her youngest nephew was obsessed with.

Carol Senior excused herself, saying she needed to make a phone call, and CJ ran a brush through Jake's hair. "I'm trying to learn more about updos and braids. There never used to be that much demand for them, but Moonflower Bay has gotten popular with tourists in recent years. I'm finding myself doing more weddings." She patted Jake on the shoulder. "Jake is nice enough to let me practice on him in exchange for a weekly wash and the odd trim."

He shrugged. "They do some kind of thing to it that gets the tangles out."

"Deep condition." CJ chuckled as she fastened a smock around Nora's neck and handed her a magazine. "Let me just wash Jake's hair real quick and get the conditioner in, and I'll start on you. Sound good?"

Nora nodded, suddenly not trusting herself to speak. Because the view in the mirror was all wrong. She had been going to the same salon in Toronto for years. Sitting in the same stylist's chair. Because her hair was so short, she'd logged a lot of hours in that particular chair, looking at that particular view. It had been nothing special—the busy, big-city salon had featured two rows of chairs parallel to each other, deep inside the space, so all she'd ever seen in the mirror was other people's cuts and colors in progress. Here she could see a slice of Main Street through the large plate-glass window at the front of the salon. The graceful, historic redbrick buildings contrasted sharply with the deep-blue sky.

This view was, objectively, nicer. But it was *different*.

She was ambushed by the notion that this was *it*. This was the view from the salon chair for the next two years.

She had actually done it. She was *here*. It was day one of the life reset.

The past month had been filled with logistics: quitting her job, doing the banking stuff required to get out from under shared bills, disentangling herself from the man she'd thought she was going to spend the rest of her life with.

There hadn't been time to stop and think. To feel.

But now that she was here, she realized how totally alone she was. Not just boyfriendless but colleagueless. Friendless. One hundred percent on her own.

But that was okay, she reminded herself. That was the *point*. She had let herself grow way too dependent on—and deferential to—Rufus. Somewhere along the way, she'd lost *herself*.

She was jarred from her maudlin thoughts when the door opened and two women came rushing in.

"That was fast," Carol Senior said.

Both the women were older, and in a flurry of introductions, she learned that they were Pearl Brunetta, who owned a bakery, and Eiko Anzai, the editor of the town newspaper. Pearl, who had blue hair—and not old-lady blue but screaming electric blue—wanted to know when Nora was going to open the clinic. Eiko wanted to know if she'd do an interview with the paper.

They peppered her with questions about her plans until CJ elbowed her way in. "Ladies. Don't overwhelm her. She just got here. And I gotta do her hair now, so skedaddle."

"Sorry, sorry," Pearl said. "You come by my shop for some pie real soon, Dr. Walsh. On the house."

"And you let me know about that interview, okay, hon?" Eiko said.

Nora agreed to both demands and smiled as she listened to them bicker on their way out.

"You shouldn't call her hon," Pearl admonished.

"I call everyone hon."

"Yeah, but she's a doctor. You should be showing respect. We want her to stay, Eiko!"

"Okay, I'll start calling her Dr. Hon."

CJ winked at Nora in the mirror. "All right, Dr. Hon, let's get started."

As Jake sat under one of the dryers with his conditioner-slathered, plastic-wrapped hair piled on his head, he listened to the women talking about the new doctor's hair. It was, apparently, a "pixie cut."

That seemed appropriate given that Dr. Nora Walsh could pass for a pixie herself. She was short, but not just that—she was small all over. She had small features—a wee, slightly upturned nose, a bow mouth, and small hands. Her grayish-blue eyes and almost-white hair added a kind of cool, supernatural icing on what otherwise would have been cuteness.

She was really something.

"You getting settled in okay?" CJ asked.

"Yeah. I traveled light, so...yeah."

It sounded like there was a story there.

"Where are you living, if you don't mind my asking?"

"I'm renting a house in Southbank Pines. I wanted to get something closer to downtown so I could walk to work, but to be honest with you, this whole move was kind of a last-minute thing, so I took what I could get on short notice."

"Oh, that must be Harold Burgess's place." CJ met Jake's eyes in the mirror.

"Yes. Harold is my landlord. I haven't met him in person, though."

Harold Burgess owned a few buildings in town, and they were, to put it frankly, shitholes. But maybe his own house would be okay. After twenty years of wintering in Florida, he'd recently moved there full-time.

CJ and Dr. Walsh started conferring over the hair-color plan. Dr. Walsh rattled off some kind of code, and soon CJ was shaping little squares of tinfoil around chunks of her hair. He chuckled to himself. He had plastic wrap; she had tinfoil.

After working in silence for a few minutes, CJ asked, "Your place seem okay?"

The doctor's brow furrowed slightly. "Should it not?"

"No, no!" CJ said—a touch too quickly, probably, because the furrow deepened.

"It's a bit musty, but I put that down to it being closed up for so long—I gather it's been empty for six months. Anyway, I'm sure it will be fine. I just need to get some furniture in there. And dishes. And everything." She laughed in a way that struck Jake as false.

"You didn't come with anything?"

Dr. Walsh huffed a sigh that seemed partly self-deprecating. "Nope."

"Why, if you don't mind my asking?" *If you don't mind my asking* was kind of CJ's signature phrase.

Dr. Walsh paused for a long moment before answering. "Have you ever looked around and suddenly thought, 'What am I doing? What *is* all this crap? This is not how I thought my life was going to turn out'?"

Yep.

CJ paused with one of the foil doodads in her hand, her head tilted. Jake could pretty much guarantee that CJ had never asked herself those questions. When you were Carol Dyson Junior and you loved doing hair, which

CJ legitimately did, and your mom, Carol Dyson Senior, owned the town salon, life unfolded pretty much according to plan, he suspected.

CJ laid a hand on the doctor's shoulder. "Honestly, Dr. Hon, I can't say I know what that's like."

Jake did, though. Did he ever.

Chapter Two

*Nora left the salon feeling lighter than she had in a long time. New hair always did that. And CJ had done a bang-up job. Nora had been a little apprehensive, but CJ had had the same brands of bleach and dye her much pricier Toronto stylist used.

She paused on the sidewalk and took a deep breath of the lake air. Toronto was on a Great Lake, too, but it didn't smell like this, like...plants and earth. Which made no sense because it was a *lake*. Water. She laughed at herself, the city girl trying and failing to describe nature.

All right. It was Sunday morning. She was going into the clinic tomorrow to start getting organized, so she should spend today furnishing her house.

She wanted to get the bare bones, at least. A bed, a table, a few chairs. Some dishes. She smirked. She was going to be living like a bachelor, at least initially. She kind of liked the idea. She didn't need a Kitchen-Aid mixer she never used, a shelf full of art books she never read, or an ugly, uncomfortable sofa that cost more than she made in a month.

No, *Rufus* needed those things. He needed specific things. The right things. He was forever throwing away perfectly good things—her ancient hand mixer that was more than sufficient for the one or two times a year they baked anything; her sofa, which, yes, was a little worn, but a slipcover would have done the trick—and replacing them with newer, shinier models. "Upgrading," he had called it, and because she didn't really care about mixers and sofas, she'd been happy to go along with it.

She had even let him talk her into "upgrading" during her residency from her planned specialization in family medicine to emergency medicine—which had added a year to her studies—so they could be colleagues in the emergency department at the hospital where he was already a staff physician.

And then he'd upgraded her.

And by "upgraded," she meant "screwed a first-year resident on the ugly, uncomfortable sofa that had cost more than she made in a month."

Tears prickled at the corners of her eyes, but she forced them back. She was done crying. He wasn't worth her tears.

Maybe if she told herself that enough times, she would actually start believing it.

He *also* wasn't worth losing the new-hair-don't-care feeling she was rocking—she *did* believe that—so she got in her car and went shopping.

Three hours later, she owned a bed, a sofa, and a kitchen table and chairs, all of which were being delivered later, and was schlepping bags of dishes and groceries inside from her car when a pickup truck came vrooming down the road.

It was going way too fast for this quiet, residential street. This was more her stereotype of small towns: dudes in trucks with something to prove. Probably the sizes of their trucks were inversely proportional to the sizes of other things.

To her astonishment the truck screeched to a halt at the foot of her driveway and Aquaman got out. His hair was in a messy bun now.

"Dr. Walsh, there's an emergency. A woman has gone into labor on the village green. She says it's too early."

Nora blinked, "Labor-labor?" *Labor-labor* being the technical term, of course.

"Seems like. She's screaming bloody murder. Someone called 911, but I remembered you said you were living at Harold's place."

She dropped her bags on the driveway. "Let's go."

"Do you have any more information?" Dr. Walsh asked as she scrambled into Jake's truck. "Who she is? How far along she is? If the pregnancy is high risk?"

"No. I don't think she's local, though." Jake hadn't recognized her, but he would freely admit that he wasn't the most social guy, so that didn't necessary mean anything. "I came out of the general store downtown, and she was writhing around on the grass on the village green. She was shouting about it being 'too soon.' There's a crowd, but everyone's milling around in a not-very-useful way."

"And here I thought practicing medicine in Moonflower Bay was going to be dull."

"Do you have a phone?" he asked as he peeled down her street.

"Yes."

"I'm going to give you a number. It's for the lift bridge operator. We have to cross the river to get downtown. We need to tell him to have it down." Dennis had called Jake in as backup so much in recent weeks that Jake had his number memorized.

Nora introduced herself to Dennis, and they had a brief conversation while Jake drove as fast as he reasonably could, his tires squealing as he hung a right on Huron. She disconnected the call. "He said he's heard already and the bridge is down. He also said that someone named Sawyer has shut down the bottom end of Main Street, so there won't be any traffic, so you can—I'm quoting here—'drive like you just told Pearl that cake is better than pie, and she's coming after you.'"

"That means drive fast."

"I gathered that."

Dr. Walsh was out the passenger-side door before he had fully screeched to a halt next to the town green. He could hear the sirens closing in on them. He'd reasoned that he could get Dr. Walsh to the scene before the ambulance from Grand View would arrive, and he'd been right but only just, from the sound of things.

Dr. Walsh was small, but as she strode toward the emergency, she took command. She started pointing to people and saying things like, "You. Find me some clean towels or blankets. As many as you can get." And "You. Get me some hand sanitizer."

He was following her, though he wasn't sure why. His contribution to this event—get the doctor—was done. He had the odd compulsion, though, to hang around. To stand by and watch over things. Like a bouncer. An emergency-birth bouncer.

"Make way, please," she said as she approached the woman. People shifted around, but they didn't know her yet, so they didn't really get out of the way.

"This is the doctor! Get out of the way!" he yelled. Several dozen startled faces turned toward him. Several dozen startled people got out of the way. He wasn't much of a talker, generally. An unintended side effect of that was that when he *did* talk, forget yell, people tended to listen.

He stopped walking alongside Dr. Walsh once he was satisfied she had a clear path. But after two steps without him, she turned. "Will you stay? Keep people away?"

So she *did* need an emergency-birth bouncer. "Yep."

As she approached the woman, who was lying on her back on the grass, Dr. Walsh's demeanor shifted. She'd been barking orders, but she spoke now in a low, gentle voice. "Hi there. My name is Nora Walsh. I'm a doctor. I'm trained in family medicine and emergency medicine. Everything is going to be okay. Can you tell me your name?"

"I'm only thirty-seven weeks! It's too soon. I feel like my back is breaking!"

"That's an unusual name, but it's nice to meet you, I'm Only Thirty-Seven Weeks." Dr. Walsh took hold of the hem of the dress the woman was wearing. "May I?"

"Colleen," the woman panted, and she nodded. She smiled at Dr. Walsh's joke.

"Okay, Colleen, thirty-seven weeks is a wee bit early, but it's nothing to worry about. Some babies just like to jump the gun. I need to ask you a few questions—"

A contraction hit, and the woman screamed.

"Just let them come. We'll talk between them." Dr. Walsh took Colleen's hand but looked at Jake and jerked her head toward the crowd of rubberneckers that was reassembling. "Can you get rid of these people? And it sounds like the paramedics have arrived. Can you get them over here?"

He swallowed the lump forming in his throat—now that Nora was safely in control of the scene, emotion was seeping in around the edges of his consciousness—and nodded. When he returned with the paramedics, Dr. Walsh was talking quietly to Colleen. Another contraction hit, and she turned to the paramedics. "Nora Walsh, MD. She's fully effaced, and I'm estimating nine centimeters dilated. So we're going to have to do this here. First baby. Water broke an hour ago. No known complications. She's thirty-seven weeks along. Do you have some gloves and sterile sheets and pads? And umbilical cord clamps?"

One of the EMTs nodded, and the three of them went to work getting things ready. Colleen wasn't freaking out like she'd been before, but she still seemed pretty agitated.

Jake had left Sawyer, the town's chief of police, doing crowd control. He jogged back over. "Give me your phone, and show me how to do that video call thing." Back at the birth, he crouched near Colleen's head. Waited through a contraction that sounded excruciating.

"Eighty-one seconds," one of the paramedics said.

"Colleen, my name is Jake. I was wondering if there's anyone you would like me to call or..." He couldn't remember the name of the app Sawyer had just shown him. "Facetalk?"

"Yes! My husband! FaceTime my husband! Thank you!"

"Good idea," Dr. Walsh said.

"You can use my phone! It's in there." Colleen nodded at a bag that was half-spilled on the grass. He scrambled for her phone and entered the code she gave him. "He's under *husband*—not very original." She cracked a smile, but only for a second before another contraction hit.

"He's under *husband*." Sawyer had just shown him how to use FaceTime, but he didn't exactly know what to do with "He's under *husband*."

"There should be a gray app called 'Contacts,'" Dr. Walsh said, apparently reading his mind. "Open it, and there will be an alphabetized menu. When you find him, there will be a little icon of a camera as an option—press that."

"Thanks. I'm not a phone guy."

After some fumbling he connected the call, and he soon had a strange dude on the phone in front of him. "Dale!" Colleen burst into tears.

"Turn the phone to me first for a sec," Dr. Walsh said. She introduced herself to Colleen's husband, briefly explained what was happening, and ended by saying, "Everything's going to be fine, and you're going to end up with one hell of a story to tell this kid when it's older."

"She," Dale said, and Jake could hear the emotion in his voice. "It's a girl."

It's a boy. Jake was abruptly pulled from his memories as another contraction hit Colleen. "Oh my God, my back!" she moaned.

"You're having back labor," Dr. Walsh said when the contraction passed. "Can you roll over onto one side? That might take some pressure off. And if it's okay with you, one of the paramedics can apply pressure to your lower back. Some women find that helps."

Colleen nodded as she hefted herself to one side. "But can this guy do it?"

Wait. Jake looked around. Was he "this guy"?

Nora raised her eyebrows at him. "That okay with you?"

"Uh, sure." It was weird that Colleen wanted him, and the last thing he wanted to do was touch some stranger's back, but he didn't feel like he could say no. He even kind of remembered some of this. Massage for labor. He and Kerrie had had a lesson as part of their prenatal classes.

He handed the phone to one of the EMTs, and they all shifted around. Every time Colleen had a contraction, he pressed down on her back. It seemed to help. And her husband had the ability to calm her, even through the phone. He spoke quietly to her between contractions, which were getting closer together.

Soon Dr. Walsh had her pushing. Like the other birth he'd been present at, it was awesome. In the literal sense of the word: it filled him with awe. Jake knew with his brain that childbirth was something that happened every day— thousands of times a day, probably. But to see the raw power this woman was harnessing as she tried to get a small person out of her body—well, it was awesome.

"I see the head!" Dr. Walsh said. "You're doing great." The next contraction came, and she said, "Push, push, push." She had a way of exerting authority without raising her voice. She was clearly in command, but she was calm about it. "Here she comes!"

Jake was not a crier, but he had to blink back tears. Because there was a baby. A slimy, wriggly, tiny human who hadn't been there five seconds ago, and now was.

It was funny how new humans came into this world, like it was no big deal—but at the same time it was a Big Freaking Deal for everyone around them.

Which was also true of how people left this world.

Dr. Walsh spent a minute examining the baby using a stethoscope and some tools the EMTs had on hand. "Everything looks good. First Apgar is nine." She clamped and cut the umbilical cord. "Let's get them onto the rig before the placenta delivers." She put the baby on Colleen's chest and covered them both with a blanket. "Colleen," she said, her smile lighting up her silvery-blue eyes. "You have a beautiful, healthy little girl. And you did such a great job."

Soon Colleen and her daughter were on a gurney, and she was tearfully thanking Dr. Walsh as the bystanders, who had returned, broke into cheers and applause.

Sawyer moved in to try to disperse the crowd again. He shot a glance at Jake, but Jake wasn't having it. This was not the time for that. Sawyer, thankfully, turned to Dr. Walsh. "Sawyer Collins, chief of police. Welcome to Moonflower Bay, Dr. Walsh. I think I speak for everyone when I say how glad we are to have you here."

Well, hot damn.

That had been far from a genuine emergency. It had been a low-risk, if early, birth. But Nora's adrenaline had been pumping all the same. Unlike at the hospital, she'd been on her own, with minimal equipment. And they'd been sprawled on the grass, for heaven's sake.

She waved to Colleen and took a deep breath as the ambulance doors shut. She could feel herself starting to crash. She needed...what? To figure out how to get home, for one thing.

"Hey, Dr. Walsh." Jake appeared. She was glad to see him. He had a steadying presence. He pointed across the street at a bar called Lawson's Lager House. "I'm thinking maybe you could use a drink?"

Yes. Great idea. That was *exactly* what she needed.

But...she was covered in amniotic fluid and blood and vernix. She gestured at herself.

His eyes slid down her body, and one corner of his mouth turned up. "Well, he probably shouldn't, but Law *does* let Tigers fans into the bar."

There was a blob of blood on the *s* in the Tigers logo on her T-shirt. "Even Tigers fans who are walking biohazards?"

"Come on. I'll take you home."

"I'm kind of gross," she said when he opened the passenger-side door of his truck for her. "I should have asked the paramedics for a clean sheet."

"It's okay. This truck is a piece of junk."

"And here I had this idea," she said once he'd come around to the driver's side and gotten in, "that men with trucks were really territorial about them."

"Nah."

She glanced around the cab. The upholstery on the seats had holes in a few spots, and there was a lot of crap lying around. Not garbage—tools mostly. But also map books and CDs—he hadn't been kidding about not being a phone guy. And the outside of the truck had been rusty and dented in a few places. "Not a truck guy, either?" she teased.

"Nope. This is just a means of getting myself and my stuff from point A to point B."

They lapsed into silence. She tried to think of something to say. Usually sitting in silence with strangers was awkward. Probably because in her boisterous family, someone was always talking. And Rufus. He had *always* been talking. And the emergency room at St. Mike's was all about talking—and shouting.

People talking: that was the default soundtrack to her life.

Or it had been. But maybe the Moonflower Bay palate cleanser could come with a new soundtrack—or a lack of one. Because silence, it turned out, was kind of nice. Or at least *this* silence was. It was companionable. Jake didn't seem like the type of guy who minded being quiet.

Which, ironically, made her want to know more about him. "So what do you do, Jake Ramsey? What kind of stuff do you haul from point A to point B in this truck?"

"I guess technically I'm a fisherman."

"Technically?"

"Well, my dad was a fisherman until he retired recently. I went into business with him when I graduated high school. I still have the boat and the license. I just don't go out that much anymore."

"Why not?" He darted a glance at her. It wasn't an annoyed glance but more of a blank look. "Sorry. None of my business."

"I also co-own a carpentry business with Sawyer Collins, who's the chief of police—you met him back there. It keeps us pretty busy, so I don't fish much these days. So mostly the stuff I'm hauling is wood and tools." He pulled into her driveway and turned to her as he cut the engine. "You were, uh, really great back there."

"*You* were really great." He had been. Solid and steady and thoughtful. "That idea to call her husband was genius. And you were cool and collected. Most people aren't like that in emergencies." Most bystanders, in her experience, fell somewhere on the spectrum of minorly panicked to utterly useless.

He looked out his window, so his face was turned away from her as he spoke. "I had a son who died. His mom was determined to have a natural childbirth, so we took a lot of classes, and I read a lot of books."

"Oh," she breathed. "I'm so sorry." That was the last thing she'd expected this gruff man to say. "What was your son's name?"

He turned to her, his eyes slightly wide—like he was surprised? That couldn't be right.

"His name was Jude."

They stared at each other silently for a long moment. "Do you want to come inside for a drink? I have bourbon." She looked out the window for her abandoned shopping bags. "I think."

He kept looking at her, his expression impossible to read. What if he thought she was hitting on him? That was the last thing she was going to be doing during her palate-cleansing sojourn in Moonflower Bay. He'd been the first to suggest a drink; she was just suggesting a different location.

Just as the previously easy silence between them was starting to morph into a more uncomfortable variety, he finally spoke.

"I can't."

Chapter Three

❧

On Friday, Nora hired a receptionist named Wynd. "Wynd with a *y*," the woman had said, coming in carrying the *Moonflower Bay Monitor*, in which Nora had run classified ads all week. She hadn't been sure that anyone actually read the classifieds anymore, but she'd figured it couldn't hurt.

Wynd with a *y* looked exactly like Nora would have expected someone named Wynd with a *y* to look. She was wearing a floral romper thing, and her blond hair was twirled into two messy buns on the sides of her head. She looked like a young Gwyneth Paltrow going for a Princess Leia–at–Coachella look.

But she was also an experienced administrator, having been the manager of a small law firm in Grand View, the next town down the lake. She was at the end of maternity leave for her second daughter, who was almost one, and her older child was starting kindergarten in the fall. "I liked the law firm, but I think a job right in town is going to be a better fit at this phase of life."

Wynd was also a certified yoga teacher and "energy worker," whatever that was. But she seemed genuinely interested in health and wellness.

In other words, Wynd was dippy but qualified. Though that wasn't really fair. Dippy was in the eye of the beholder. It wasn't like they had to be friends. Nora stuck out her hand. "You're hired, but there's a catch. I'm only planning to be here for two years. My hope would be to find someone to buy the clinic from Dr. Baker, which might mean you could stay. But I can't promise that this will be a permanent job. If you accept, we'll be signing a two-year contract."

"That actually suits me. My husband and I are hoping to move to the countryside sometime in the next few years to start farming. We have some land already, and we're trying to save enough to build a house there and get things going."

"Well, great. That sounds like an adventure. What will you farm?"

"Alpacas."

"Wow." She'd been expecting something more along the lines of sunflowers or organic heirloom tomatoes. "I didn't know there was demand for alpaca meat." She didn't even know what alpacas were, actually. Maybe they were tasty?

"You don't *eat* them." Wynd looked horrified. "You raise them for their wool. But we're also going to have retreats where people can come and commune with them."

"Ah. Of course." Well, she'd stepped in it there. Moving on. "When can you start? I've hired a nurse. Amber Grant—maybe you know her?" Nora couldn't quite believe her luck. Amber the nurse had been okay with the two-year clause as well. She was interested in surgical nursing, but she needed additional training for that, so she was happy to gain some general experience at the clinic while she went to night school.

"I know of her," Wynd said. "She used to work at Lawson's Lager House, I think?"

"Right. Part-time while she was in nursing school. She graduated this past spring." Amber had driven to Toronto for an in-person meeting with Nora after they'd had a great phone interview, and they'd clicked immediately. While on paper Nora might have preferred someone with a little more experience, it had been immediately clear that Amber was going to make a great nurse, and that she would be a useful link to the local community.

"I only drink biodynamic wine," Wynd said, "so I don't go to Lawson's. So I don't know her–know her."

"Well, you'll meet her soon enough. I'm aiming to open two weeks from Monday, but she's going to start next week, helping me get things ready. Maybe you could join us. We can learn the ropes together, basically. We also need to send letters to all of Dr. Baker's old patients notifying them that the clinic is reopening."

"That sounds great—in theory. I just have to get some care lined up for Parsnip."

"You'd be welcome to bring Parsnip in. Not once we're open, of course, but that would be fine in the run-up to opening. I love dogs." The thought of dogs made her heart pinch, actually.

"Parsnip is my younger daughter."

Oh. Nora coughed to cover a laugh. Wynd had talked about having day care already set up for her little one, so she'd assumed Parsnip was a nonhuman creature. "Right." She needed to stop putting her foot in her mouth here. "Okay. Well, same logic applies. I love kids, too."

"I have her enrolled at a day care center," Wynd explained, "but her spot doesn't open until after Labor Day. I wasn't expecting to get a job offer this quickly." She scrunched her forehead like she was thinking. "My mother is going to take Cicada in the afternoons after school in the fall, and I'm sure she could take her for this last stretch of the summer, too, but I think giving her the baby as well will be too much."

"Cicada is your older daughter?"

"Yes."

Don't laugh. Don't laugh.

The door opened and Nora turned, grateful for the distraction. It was the police chief. She'd met him after the birth yesterday. He wasn't wearing a uniform today, though, so he must be off duty.

"Dr. Walsh. I thought I'd stop by and see how you're doing. But I can see you're busy. I'll come back later."

"No, no! We're nearly done here." She turned to Wynd. "Let's say two weeks from today will be your official start, if that works for you. That will get you in here a bit before we open the day after Labor Day. No pressure, but if you're able to put in some hours before that, that would be great. Feel free to bring…" She couldn't say it. "Feel free to bring your daughter. I'll appreciate any help you can offer, and you and Amber and I can get to know each other. I have your contact info, and I'll text you mine. If you can bring in a social insurance card, we'll do the tax forms. Sound good?"

Wynd smiled widely, and Nora felt herself returning it. She waved goodbye to her receptionist—yay! She had a receptionist!—and turned back to the chief.

"Nice to see you again, Mr. Collins." Was that right? She wasn't sure what to call him. "Chief Collins?"

"Call me Sawyer. I have a feeling we'll be seeing a lot of each other."

"Sawyer, then." She hesitated. She wasn't in the habit of telling people to use her first name. She was young and short and female, all traits she had learned contributed to people sometimes not taking her seriously as a physician. At the hospital, she had learned from senior women colleagues to announce herself as "Dr. Walsh" and not even let her first name be known.

But what were total life resets for if not to shake things up?

"Sawyer," she said again, "call me Nora. What can I do for you?"

"Well, mainly I'm here to invite you for drinks. I meet a couple buddies on Friday nights at Lawson's Lager House, just across the street. My girlfriend and a friend of hers will be there tonight, too. You want to join us?"

"I'd love that, thanks. Now?"

"The others come around five, but why don't we head over now if you're ready? I have a few professional things I want to talk to you about."

A few minutes later they were settling in at one end of a large, gleaming wooden bar, and Nora was shaking hands with Benjamin Lawson, the proprietor, who seemed to be quite friendly with Sawyer. "Nice to meet you, Benjamin."

"We're glad you're here, Dr. Walsh. Call me Law. Nobody calls me Benjamin."

Should she tell him to call her Nora, too? It was an odd thing, living and working in a small community. She didn't know yet who she was going to be friends with. In the city, if she was friends with someone, she would never treat them. But as the only doctor in town, she supposed she didn't have that luxury.

"Glad you're here, but I *am* annoyed you stole Amber from me." His twinkling eyes telegraphed that he was kidding.

"She seems like she's bound for great things. I'll be lucky if I can hold on to her for the two years I plan to be here. So technically, I think *life* stole Amber from you." Nora smiled to show she was teasing, too.

Screw it. She was just going to go with her gut here. So what if she had to perform a testicular cancer screening on this guy at some point? She would worry about that later. "And you call me Nora."

"Well, kidding aside, we are truly glad you're here, Nora."

"Everyone keeps saying that. You all must really miss Dr. Baker." The clinic had been closed for almost a year, but it seemed that its former owner loomed large in town.

Sawyer answered as Law was hailed by another customer. "We miss having a doctor, anyway."

"But not him specifically? Hmm. The plot thickens."

"Dr. Baker was fine, but from the town cop to the town doctor, he was a bit old-school."

"What does that mean?"

"He refused to face the fact that we have a fentanyl problem, for one."

"Ah. You're not alone there, unfortunately." The emergency room back in Toronto had been well acquainted with that problem.

"Right. And I get that it's a wider public health problem. It's not like I expected Doc Baker to single-handedly solve it, but just last week we had a kid OD on some kind of street cocktail. Thankfully, the paramedics arrived in time to save him, but honestly, it didn't look good there for a while, and I could use some advice on naloxone. Should my officers and I be carrying it, do you think? Dr. Baker told me not to open the force to potential legal liability, but I'm not sure that's right. I can't keep just standing there doing nothing." His voice had risen, and he rolled his eyes. "Sorry. I'm getting intense."

"No, it's worth getting intense over. My first reaction is yes you should be carrying it, but let me look into it some more and get back to you." She'd read a bit about police forces across the country debating whether officers should carry the overdose-reversing drug. But there might be legal and liability issues she wasn't aware of. "And that's not me blowing you off," she added. "I've never had to think about the intersection of medicine and law enforcement. So give me a couple weeks to do a little research, and we can put our heads together?"

He smiled. "I'd appreciate that."

"You said a few things? What else?"

Sawyer glanced over his shoulder. Someone was approaching. She followed his gaze.

Aquaman.

He was wearing jeans and a weathered gray T-shirt, and he had his hair in a messy bun.

"Hey," Sawyer said. Jake gave a slight nod. Sawyer was sitting on the last stool on the long side of the bar, and Jake took the next stool over, the first on the short side, putting them at a ninety-degree angle from each other. "You know Dr. Walsh."

Nora gave a little wave. "Yeah, Jake turns out to be a talented birth attendant." *Also, is he or is he not some kind of man-god hybrid? Asking out of scientific curiosity.*

Sawyer chuckled, and Law showed up and set a beer in front of Jake. Jake remained silent.

Sawyer turned back to Nora. "We have meth, too. There are some dealers in town. Though it hasn't been quite as prevalent since a lab was busted in Grand View last year. But I'm not sure how long the reprieve will last."

"Oh. Right." She had assumed that since Jake had arrived, the professional confab would come to an end, at least temporarily. "Fentanyl and meth. Got it."

"I have one more for you, though maybe less dramatic: measles."

"Yes, I read about the outbreak around here, and I know it's a growing problem in a number of communities."

"I had to drive a kid to the hospital in Zurich a couple years ago," Sawyer went on. "He was having seizures."

"Encephalitis?"

"Yep. Never want to see that again."

"So," she said, "fentanyl, meth, and measles. You sure know how to make a girl feel welcome."

"Yeah, sorry." He winced. "We also have amazing sunsets, a main street covered in moonflowers—and the lake, of course."

"Don't forget the mermaids." A woman appeared behind Sawyer, and she wrapped her arms around him from behind.

"Evie." His voice went all low as he leaned back against her.

"Happy Friday," she said, her voice going husky, too.

Wow. These two were *into* each other. They were practically oozing pheromones.

"Nora, this is my girlfriend, Eve Abbott. She owns the Mermaid Inn—we both live there. Eve, Nora Walsh."

Eve greeted her warmly, and Nora said, "I hear this town is a little mermaid crazy."

"You heard right," Sawyer said. "Wait until you see the Mermaid Parade." He rolled his eyes. "There's some kind of collective insanity that takes over—maybe you can diagnose it."

"Oh, you *love* the parade," Eve teased.

Soon they were talking easily, but an idea was starting to brew in Nora's mind. She was going to honor her pledge to look into the issue of whether the local police force should carry naloxone, but beyond that, she wasn't kidding herself that one cop and one doctor could do much about meth or the opioid crisis. But measles? At least locally? That might be a different story.

Her attention was drawn by a woman settling herself on the stool on her other side. She was— Nora shot off her stool. The newcomer was covered in blood. What *was* it about this town and medical emergencies? "What happened? Where's the wound?" She turned to Law, who'd been drawn by the commotion. "Call 911."

"It's fake blood!" The woman held up her hands. "Oh my God, I'm sorry! It's all fake!"

Nora sat, though her adrenaline was still pumping. But yes, upon further inspection, the blood was not quite the right color.

"Are you the new doctor?" the woman asked. Nora, still buzzing, nodded. "I'm Maya Mehta. I'm the owner and artistic director of the Moonflower Bay Theater Company. I run a theater camp for kids. We did stage combat today— the final swordfight scene from *Hamlet*. So sorry." She waved her hand at the others. "These guys are used to me showing up in all kinds of disarray."

Law reappeared with a wineglass and set it in front of Maya. He uncorked a bottle of white wine and silently poured her a glass. She must be a regular. "Maya."

Her eyes narrowed. "Benjamin."

Nora wondered what had happened to "Everyone calls me Law."

"I need to talk to you about your monstrous pizza oven," Maya said.

"You have pizza here?" Nora asked. She loved pizza. Rufus had not loved pizza. Therefore, Nora had had very little pizza in the last few years. But Nora was the mistress of her own destiny now, and that destiny, she decided right then and there, was going to include a lot of pizza.

Law slid her a small laminated menu. "I just built a wood-burning pizza oven out back." He glanced at Aquaman. "Well, Jake built it."

"And it's belching smoke everywhere," Maya said.

"It is not belching smoke everywhere. It's properly vented and is one hundred percent to code."

"My costumes are in the back of my building. The kids are doing *The Lion, the Witch and the Wardrobe* next week, and Aslan's head smells distinctly like smoke. And Aslan has asthma." Then, seeming to forget her beef with Law, she leaned forward and slapped the bar. "Jake! Your stepmom found me a great old wardrobe, but I need to rip out the back of it for it to really work on the whole gateway-to-Narnia front. Can you help me?"

Jake answered without looking up from his beer. "Yep."

It occurred to Nora that that was the first word she'd heard Jake speak since he'd arrived.

The thing about the new doctor was that she asked good questions. After Maya was done talking at him about her wardrobe, Jake listened to the doc talking to Sawyer and Eve about the town's public health challenges. She'd listened intently and asked intelligent questions.

And the question she'd asked him last weekend was still rattling around in his head.

What was your son's name?

Also, a question he had been asking *himself*: What the hell had possessed him to tell her about Jude? He *never* talked about Jude, and Nora Walsh was a complete stranger.

It was just that she was so competent. She had reacted to the chaos of the birth, and to Colleen's fear, with the perfect mixture of detachment and compassion. Briskness leavened with dry humor. She seemed like the kind of person to whom you could say, "I had a son who died," and she wouldn't overreact. Usually people responded one of two ways. They made him feel like he was drowning in an avalanche of pity. They brought their casseroles and asked their hushed-but-entitled questions, as if they had a right to know what was in his soul. Or, worse, they stood there with their intact families and their not-dead children and told him that God worked in mysterious ways, utterly oblivious to the fact that he was often *this close* to punching their lights out.

But not Dr. Walsh. She just looked at him like a dead kid was a thing that happened—a sad thing, but a thing— and asked, "What was your son's name?"

Not "How did he die?" Or "How old was he?" Those were the things people seemed to want to know. The salacious details. The things that would allow them to answer their real question: "How tragic is this, actually?"

"What was your son's name?" though. That was a real question. Who was this person you had but now don't have? It was a question about *Jude* rather than the circumstances of his death.

"Oh, I have a question for you guys."

He jerked his head up. Was she including him in "you guys"?

"So I'm living in Southbank Pines. In Harold Burgess's house."

Sawyer glanced at Jake. "Yeah. How's that working out?"

"Fine, except the major draw was supposed to be a deck out back. I've spent the last several years living on the twentieth floor of a high-rise, and I was really excited about a deck. But it turns out that what I actually have is a vaguely deck-shaped collection of rotten wood that disintegrated when I tried to stand on it. I know it's just a rental, and it should be Harold's responsibility, but I'm going to be here for two years, so I'm ready to throw some money at the problem. Jake said you guys have a carpentry business. Any chance I can hire you?"

"Of course," Sawyer said quickly. Jake tried not to roll his eyes. They didn't do decks. They did fine carpentry. As in bookshelves. One-of-a-kind pieces of furniture. Canoes for rich people with more money than sense. "But no charge."

"You can't not charge me!"

"Consider it a welcome-to-town gift."

She started to protest, but Eve chimed in. "Sawyer and Jake are basically this town's fairy godfathers. Sawyer in a professional capacity, of course, but Jake is always fixing stuff or building stuff."

"Yeah," Maya agreed. "Like, if you ever need the back of a wardrobe surgically removed, Jake's your man."

Well, busted. He figured he had the time and he had the skills. And he hated seeing a job that needed doing sit undone.

Which was how he found himself signed up to build a deck for Nora Walsh, aka Dr. Hon, aka the pixie doctor.

It occurred to him that he sure had a lot of names for someone he barely knew.

As she unlocked her car, Nora's head was spinning. So many new faces and names. So much *talking*. Well, except for Jake. The interesting thing was that everyone accommodated his silence. It was like they expected it, like it didn't register as out of the ordinary. Maybe it wasn't. Maybe he'd just always been that way.

This head spinning was not necessarily a bad thing, though. Nora felt...not happy exactly, but hopeful. Like maybe she'd turned a corner. This week she'd made huge progress on the clinic, gotten most of the important furniture into her new place, and finished things by hanging out at a bar with a bunch of people who seemed like they might become friends.

And she'd discovered that Law and his smoky oven made the best pizza she had ever tasted. Even Maya, who clearly was not a fan of Law's, agreed, judging by how she'd kept stealing pieces off Nora's plate and making secret little moaning noises when Law wasn't looking.

Nora thought back to last weekend, after her haircut, when she'd been hit with a wave of loneliness.

What was loneliness, really? She didn't mind being alone. She often enjoyed it, in fact, and sometimes craved it. And if the alternative to loneliness was the kind of sublimation of the self she'd gradually done the last few years, eating sushi instead of pizza with Rufus, taking his shifts when he had a concert he wanted to go to, nodding in agreement when he suggested it was vital that they spend eleven thousand dollars on a sofa, she'd take loneliness any day.

All she knew was she felt better for her night of conversation at the bar. She was starting to wonder if what she'd missed, after a week of working around the clock, was caring about other people's stories. Having them care about hers. For example, she had listened to Maya talk excitedly about how a kid in her summer camp had overcome his stage fright. And Maya had laughed her head off when Nora whisperingly told her why she had decided to order the night's special pizza, which was prosciutto, ricotta, and...shaved parsnips.

"Usually I'm a sucker for Hawaiian pizza, which I notice is on the menu, but I couldn't pass on the parsnips," Nora had said.

Maya had made an exaggerated choking noise. "Oh no! I was starting to like you, and then you went and ruined it by wanting pineapple on pizza!"

Nora liked Maya. Her expansive theatricality was amusing, and she offered a kind of friendly intimacy that was sudden but seemingly genuine.

So yeah, maybe Nora was a little less lonely tonight as she was taking her first tentative steps into the next phase of her life.

Her phone, in her back pocket, buzzed. It had been on silent, but she'd set it to vibrate, and her butt had been buzzing a lot while she'd been at the bar. She slid into the car and had a look.

Rufus. A bunch of texts and a voice mail.

Nice. Just when she'd been thinking maybe she'd started to turn a corner.

The maddening thing about Rufus was that even though he was the one who'd nuked their relationship, he kept wanting to *talk* about it. And not even in a groveling I'm-sorry-please-take-me-back sort of way. Not that she would have. It was more him constantly wanting to explain how he felt. They'd met during their residencies—he'd been in his final year, and she'd been in her first. But now that they were staff physicians and had less demanding schedules, he felt neglected. He felt the need for a partner he had more shared interests with. He felt they spent too much time with her family. He felt, he felt, he felt.

And, worse, he wanted to explain how *she* should feel: "You deserve more than I can give you."

He wanted to regulate her reaction to the whole thing, was what it came down to. He wanted to get away with it, but he didn't want her to hold a grudge.

How had she *loved* such an insecure, manipulative man?

Because she *had* loved him.

Did she *still* love him? She didn't even know anymore. It didn't feel like she did, but she also questioned if it was possible to stop loving someone at the drop of a hat—even if they did something terrible.

But that wasn't even the worst of it. Hearts were vulnerable. People gave them to the wrong people all the time. It wasn't pleasant, but it happened. But she had done more than that. Done *worse* than that. She had gradually migrated her tastes, her interests, her free time, to align with Rufus's. Not on purpose. Mostly because she genuinely hadn't cared about the hand mixer or the sofa, so it had been easier to go along with what he wanted. So the whole "We don't have shared interests" thing was kind of rich.

But she *did* care about pizza. And about which medical specialization to go into, for God's sake.

If everything went according to plan, the Moonflower Bay palate cleanser would work on both broken hearts *and* subsumed selves. She surveyed Main Street as she got in the car. Most of the merchants had moonflowers growing in pots, and many of them had Little Free Libraries as well. It was almost too adorable.

She just had to work, enjoy the lake and the beach, and not die of cute overload, and, by the end of her time here, she would be herself again.

As if on cue, a text came through from her sister. I know it's too soon, but I went into this open house. Fact finding. Only $1.4 million, lol.

The text was accompanied by a picture of a typical Toronto redbrick semidetached house.

> *Nora:* Oh "only" 1.4, eh? How many bed-
> rooms?
> *Erin:* Four! Three on the second floor for
> the boys and me and a fourth-floor
> master that could be your retreat.
> *Nora:* I told you I don't need the master!
> I'll be coming into this with less money
> than you will be.
> *Erin:* Yeah but I'll be coming into this
> with more humans than you will. Anyway,
> you need privacy. What if you're enter-
> taining gentleman callers?
> *Nora:* Not happening.
> *Erin:* Oh, come on. It will happen eventu-
> ally. Maybe we should look for a duplex
> so you don't abandon me when you find
> a proper man.
> *Nora:* First things first. Let's talk bed-
> rooms AFTER we have a down payment
> together. Besides, we talked about this.

They had. They'd agreed that if Erin ever remarried and wanted to expand her family, or if Nora's domestic circumstances changed, they would sell the house and split the proceeds, each of them ideally walking away with a nice chunk of equity. That part had been important to Nora, despite the fact that she felt certain she was *never dating again*. But according to Erin and the therapy-industrial complex, eventually that feeling would go away.

> **Erin:** You and your logic. Sheesh. I gotta go pry the boys away from their screens. Night-night.
> **Nora:** Hang on, one more thing. How is Grandma?
> **Erin:** Pretty good! As stoic as ever, anyway. Her new fave topic is how she never liked Rufus.

Nora smiled and, buoyed by the exchange with her sister, deleted Rufus's texts without reading them and his voice mail without listening to it. Grandma was right. He was exhausting. Which, actually, was a relief. Being exhausted by Rufus, rather than hurt by him, felt like progress.

All right. She'd had a lovely evening with new friends, and the clinic would open in two weeks.

The reset button had been fully and firmly pressed.

She typed the last text she would ever send Rufus. I don't want to talk to you. Here's my mailing address in Moonflower Bay. If there's anything we *need* to talk about, legally or whatever, send me a letter. I'm blocking you now. Have a nice life.

That should do it. They hadn't been married. She had happily left him all the joint possessions they had accumulated. There was nothing left to bind them together. If she was overlooking something, and if it was important enough, he could send her a damn letter.

When she got back home, she went out back, gingerly poked at the rotten deck with her toes until she found a chunk that seemed like it might not collapse under her weight, sat on it, and listened. The ad for this place had said you could hear the lake from the yard.

And she could. Just barely, but yes, there was the sound of waves.

She was alone, and it was okay.

Chapter Four

❦

On Saturday, Nora hit the mall in nearby London to tackle the problem of household linens, and then she put in a long afternoon at the clinic. She was tired and a bit cranky when she got home, but the sight of Jake Ramsey's truck parked in her driveway made her smile.

And wasn't that interesting?

There was quite a racket coming from out back. She let herself into the house, dumped her shopping bags, and went straight to the sliding glass door that opened onto the backyard from what would have been the dining room had she had any actual dining furniture.

He was facing away from her, doing something with a power tool she was pretty sure was some kind of saw. He didn't notice her watching him through the door as he turned and laid a long, flat piece of wood into place.

He was fixing her deck.

Well, crap.

Her throat tightened.

She had spent too much time the last few days pondering the nature of loneliness. Which was the only reason she could think of to explain why this—a little bit of human kindness in the form of a guy building a deck—was going to make her cry.

No. No, it was not. She allowed herself one sniff and looked for something to distract her.

Jake was wearing grungy jeans and beat-up brown work boots.

And he was *not* wearing a shirt.

It was really hot out.

So that made sense.

Not wearing a shirt when you were working in the heat was a logical, normal thing that logical, normal people of the male variety did.

She, however, was wearing what felt like half a gallon of Benjamin Moore Black Satin. She had spent the afternoon painting the front desk at the clinic. It had been a whim. The desk that had come with the practice had been a 1970s monstrosity made of fake wood paneling. She didn't want to spend the money to replace it since she was only going to be in town for two years, but she had stopped in at Andersen's Lakeside Hardware to ask if, theoretically, a person could paint over fake wood paneling. She'd had an odd encounter with the owner, an older man named Karl, who had assured her that yes, she could paint over the paneling and had amassed the necessary supplies but then refused to take payment for them.

But something had gone wrong. The primer had seemed like it was going on funny, but then she'd thought, what the hell did she know about primer? So she'd plowed on. And who knew? Maybe the problem wasn't the primer so much as the fact that she was spectacularly bad at painting. She'd tipped over the can at one point, and in her attempt to right it, her entire left arm had ended up covered.

But whatever. She was standing in the kitchen staring at Jake, and it would be weird to keep doing that. It would also be weird to pretend she hadn't seen him. So she slid open the door.

He had returned to the saw or whatever it was, so his back was to her. His tanned, muscly back. A fact she noted with clinical detachment. Mostly.

He turned on the tool, but he must have sensed her presence, because he stopped it right away, turned around, and took off the protective glasses he'd been wearing. Slid them up on his head, actually, like sunglasses. His hair looked like it had begun the day in a bun, but enough of it had fallen out that the glasses were actually holding a fair amount of hair off his face.

"What are you doing?" she finally said, before her brain could catch up to what a stupid question that was. *What do you think he's doing? Practicing his ballroom dance moves?*

"Rebuilding this piece-of-crap deck."

"That was fast. When I asked if you could do my deck, I meant sometime in the not-too-distant future."

He shrugged. She kept waiting for him to follow that shrug with some words, but none came. "Okay, well, what do I owe you?"

"Eh, it only took me a couple of hours." He started putting his shirt on. She wanted to tell him not to do that, but that would be wildly inappropriate. *Clinical detachment.*

"It only took you a couple of hours?" she echoed dumbly. In her imagination, which admittedly was based on nothing—she didn't even watch home improvement shows on TV, as evidenced by her painting failure—building a deck was something you measured in days, not hours.

"Yeah. I'm just throwing a quick cap over what's here. It's a shortcut. If you owned this place, I'd pull out the old rotten stuff and start from scratch."

"You would?"

He squinted at her for a moment. Because she was acting like a simpleton, mindlessly repeating everything he said in the form of a question. Maybe he was onto something with all the silence. If you didn't talk to people, it probably cut down on the frequency with which you had to listen to them say idiotic things.

"Sorry. I guess I should have checked in with you before I started. I just had this pile of scrap wood"—he gestured at the deck, which looked like an honest-to-God deck and not at all like a pile of scrap wood—"and a free afternoon, and..." He shrugged.

Ugh. She was being weird. Coming across as ungrateful. She was just so surprised. It was like she had wished aloud for a deck one day, and the next day, voilà! Deck!

And for some reason, she was inherently skeptical when someone did her a favor. Instantly on the defensive. Wondering what the secret agenda was. How she was going to be made to pay later.

Was that the kind of person she wanted to be?

Okay. She smiled. Started over. "Jake. This is amazing. Thank you."

He smiled back. Which made her feel good.

So she said some more. "Honestly, I was out-of-proportion disappointed about the deck situation. And it's been a long day." She held up her paint-splattered arms, and he chuckled. "So this is a lovely surprise."

"Well, give me five minutes to lay this last plank, and you can inaugurate your new deck."

She was imagining pouring herself a drink and doing exactly that. Should she ask him to join her? He'd rebuffed her last time. Well, what the hell. "I plan to—with a bourbon. You're welcome to join me."

For a second she thought he was going to say yes, but then his face changed. Went blank, just like it had in his truck last weekend.

He said the same words, too. "I can't."

Jake had strong legs. He had strong everything, thanks to a combination of genetics, the physical aspect of both his jobs, and a penchant for canoeing, often with a portaging element. So he wasn't used to his legs crapping out on him.

But that was exactly what they started to do after he nailed the last board into place and walked across Nora's new deck with the intention of reversing his response to her invitation. With every step he took, his legs felt shakier, but for some damn reason he kept moving them in her direction.

His arms joined the weak brigade when he raised the right one to knock on the sliding glass door, which was open a crack. It sort of felt like it might keep floating up, farther than it needed to, up into the sky until he lost control of it altogether.

"Come on in."

If his arms were floating up into space, Nora's were firmly grounded—in the sink, where she was trying to wash off the black paint one of them had been coated with earlier.

They both spoke at the same time. He said, "Thought I

might take you up on that bourbon after all," and she said, "Had a bit of a painting disaster at the clinic today."

Then they did it again. She said, "Great!" and he said, "What happened?"

She laughed. If he'd thought before that she looked otherworldly, with her white-blond hair and her icy blue eyes, that laugh went a ways toward unraveling that interpretation. It was low and throaty and... earthy. Very much of this world.

It was an interesting combination.

"I'm glad. It's been a long afternoon, and I could use the company. But I hate to say it, but I think I need to take a shower first. This"—she nodded toward the sink—"isn't cutting it."

"You need soap."

"Which I don't have out here, because I am a monster. But I do have it in the shower!" She looked around. For a towel, maybe? There didn't seem to be any in the kitchen, but there was a roll of paper towels just out of her reach. He grabbed them, pulled off several, and handed them to her.

"Thanks." She dried her hands. "All I have is bourbon. I have bourbon but no dish towels. Imagine your stereotype of a gross bachelor pad, and this is it, except without the bachelor." She lifted her arms. The black paint had smeared into a midtoned gray, and somehow it was all over both arms now as well as one of her cheeks.

A laugh burbled up, but he stifled it—and when was the last time *that* had happened?

"Anyway, bourbon is in the cupboard over the fridge, glasses to the right of the fridge—I have glasses!—so help yourself. I'll be right back."

She disappeared down the hall, and he got down two glasses and poured a couple fingers of bourbon into each of them. Took a sip of his and took in the small, shabby open space that made up the dining-living area of the house. Or would have, had it contained any furniture.

What the hell was he doing? He should just go. He had trout marinating at home, and the deck here was done. Although what she needed more than a deck was a plumber. He went over and examined a puddle of water at the foot of the dishwasher.

He was surprised to hear the shower turn off. She hadn't been kidding when she'd said a *quick* shower.

"Jake?"

She was calling him from the bathroom. "Yeah?"

"I forgot I have no bath towels, either. But I *did* buy some of those today. There should be a shopping bag near the front door. Any chance you can bring it here?"

He retrieved the bag. The bathroom door was open a crack. Her hand snaked out. "I'm so disorganized with this move, I got in the shower without the new towels or any fresh clothing on hand. I had this one gross threadbare towel in here that I've been using since I got here, but I threw it in the laundry today, so now I'm stuck."

She had only opened the door an inch, but there was a mirror behind her. Her shower had been so fast, there wasn't any steam. The mirror was not fogged.

He could only see a slice of her, but it was a nice slice. The back of her body, from shoulder dipping down to lower back, then rounding out again to a small, pert ass fit for a pixie. Dr. Pixie.

He was going to hell. He averted his eyes and handed her the bag.

Five minutes later, she reappeared barefoot. She was wearing cutoff denim shorts and a Detroit Tigers T-shirt. Not the same one she had worn the day of the emergency birth.

He nodded at it. "You weren't kidding about being a Tigers fan."

"Nope. My grandma went to medical school at the University of Windsor, and she became a fan. I guess I got it from her. In fact, when I decided to leave Toronto and do a stint practicing somewhere else, one of the things that appealed about here is that it's two hours from Detroit." She snorted in a way that seemed self-deprecating. "I say that like I'm actually going to go to games."

"Too busy?"

She started to answer but paused with a contemplative look on her face. "I was going to say yes, I'm kind of a workaholic, but I don't actually know. This is supposed to be a new chapter."

"You should make this a chapter that includes Tigers games."

She smiled—really big, in a way that almost caused a hitch in his breath. Smiles like that also helped unravel the air of otherworldliness she sometimes had about her. They made her seem fully, viscerally human. "Yeah. I should."

He handed her a glass of bourbon.

"Thanks. I hope you don't like it on the rocks, because I don't have any ice." She spun slowly in place. "I don't have anything, actually. As you have probably observed." She was still smiling in a way that seemed at odds with her pronouncement.

He thought back to what she'd said at the salon, about looking at your life and all the crap in it and not recognizing it. He lifted his glass. "To new chapters."

She clinked her glass against his and strolled over to the door and peered out. "But now, thanks to you, I *do* have a deck. Honestly, I can't believe Harold was advertising that pile of junk as a deck."

"Yeah, Harold Burgess isn't known for..." He wasn't sure how to put it.

"Being house-proud?"

He chuckled.

"I was really bummed about the deck situation. Like more bummed than was probably called for. But then you fixed it. But..." She did a slow pivot. "This place is a dump, isn't it?" She kept turning. "I rented a dump."

She had. It appeared Harold hadn't treated his own home any better than his rental properties. The paint on the walls was peeling, and the cracked linoleum in the kitchen had to be forty years old if it was a day. To be fair, the house would probably look better if it wasn't empty. But there was a general air of shabbiness everywhere.

"Did you not come to look at it?" Toronto was over a three-hour drive, which wasn't nothing, but when it came to where you were going to live, he personally would have come to check things out.

"Nope," she said cheerfully. "I just looked at the ad. It seemed fine in the little thumbnail pictures. And I was busy quitting my job and tearing through a moving to-do list." She sighed and slid open the door. "But really, I took this place because Harold said you could hear the waves from the yard, and you can." She cocked her head. "Almost." She stuck her whole torso out the door. "Sometimes."

"The lake is calm today." He motioned for her to go out the rest of the way. "You want to go sit on your new deck?"

"I sure do." The deck was a platform without a railing, so she sat on the edge of it like you'd sit on a step. "Sorry, I don't have any chairs, either." She laughed. "I'm *such* a loser."

"Oh, come on." He was pretty sure losers didn't go to medical school.

"You should have seen me trying to paint my front desk at the clinic today."

"I did see the aftermath. Did any of that paint actually get on the desk?" He stepped off the deck and leaned against a post in the yard that had probably once anchored a clothesline.

She snorted. "Not enough of it. It looks worse than when I started."

He almost offered to stop in and take a look at it next week, but he stopped himself. Because why would he do that?

They sipped their drinks. It was a hot evening. Still, too. Not a trace of wind—that was why they couldn't hear the lake at the moment. The wind was supposed to pick up after sunset, but until then, conditions were ideal for canoeing, which was what he would normally be doing right now. He would go when he got home and just make it a shorter outing.

"What would Jude be doing if he were here right now?"

He was startled by the question. Shocked, really. It made him physically jerk a little, and he sloshed some of his drink over the edge of his glass.

But when he sat with the question for a moment, he found he didn't mind it. He didn't mind it at all, which was not a familiar sensation, when it came to questions about Jude.

The difference, he was pretty sure, was that it was another *good* question, another about who Jude had been rather than what had happened to him.

"There's a broken-down old lawn chair in the corner of the yard there." She pointed to a chair that was more rust than metal. "You're welcome to drag it over if you're brave enough. Is your tetanus shot up to date? I can tell you that I did order some furniture today. So I'm not a *total* heathen.

I just have this weird aversion to cluttering up my new life too fast, you know?"

He knew what she was doing. She thought he didn't want to answer her question. But instead of asking it again, or making it into a big deal by apologizing for asking it in the first place—that was another thing people often did when he didn't immediately answer their intrusive questions—she was changing the subject. Letting him off the hook.

He looked out at the yard. Paradoxically, the fact that she *wasn't* demanding an answer made him want to give one. "Jude would be lying on the grass on his tummy, babbling. You know how they give you all these lectures about how tummy time is important for babies?" He turned to her, and she nodded. "They make it seem like it's going to be this terrible thing you're going to have to force on your kid, but not him. He loved it. I would stick him on his belly and crank up the music, and he'd lie there laughing and kicking his legs and rocking out."

He huffed a shaky exhalation. That was the longest thing he'd said aloud about Jude in four years.

"What kind of music did he like?"

Another good question. A *great* question, actually. "Any kind. He wasn't picky. Music instantly made him happy. His mom used to play him kid music, like Raffi and stuff?" She nodded. "Which was fine. Nothing against Raffi. Raffi's a cool dude. But I was on this secret mission to get Jude to like the Beatles."

"The Beatles are *much* better than Raffi."

"Right? And I think it was working. His mom went back to work when he was three months old. I was doing the rest of the parental-leave year, so he spent more time with me than with her. I'd stick *Sgt. Pepper* on, and he'd get all squealy."

"Ha! Suck it, Raffi!"

He brought his glass to his lips only to find it empty. She noticed. "Let me get you a refill."

He should decline. He should go home. He had canoeing plans.

But he didn't want to go home. Because, to his utter shock, he wanted to keep talking about Jude. He headed for the door. "I'll do it."

"Bring the bottle out," she called after him.

He stood in the kitchen for a moment, contemplating what was about to happen. Taking stock of the physical sensations in his body. He had words inside him, words where there were usually none, and they were lapping against the edges of his physical self, like waves against the shore at the cove.

The interesting thing was these weren't the waves he was used to. In his experience, when the waves overtook him, they didn't *lap*. They weren't gentle. And they always won.

This was not that.

He was clumsy as he fumbled with the bourbon bottle, and he had to concentrate on his steps as he went back outside. This time, he sat down—next to her on the edge of the deck. His hand shook as he topped up her drink.

He waited for the waves—the bad ones—to crash over him. They did not. They just kept rhythmically but not punishingly lapping against his insides, seeking a way out. So he opened his mouth and said it.

"Jude died of the flu."

She did not react with over-the-top dismay as most people did. She nodded grimly and took a sip of her drink. Then she hit him with another of those questions that were apparently peeling him back like the lid of a sardine tin. "Did you name him after the song 'Hey Jude'?"

"Yeah," he rasped. He leaned forward and rested his elbows on his knees. He was starting to get a headache. It had been threatening all day. He'd gotten a lot of sun and hadn't drunk enough water. But a headache wasn't the waves. A headache was endurable.

"It's too bad life can't be like that, huh?" she said. "Taking a sad song and making it better? It's a nice thought."

It turned out that *not* asking the nosy, entitled, salacious questions worked like truth serum. Before he could even process what he was doing, more words tumbled out of him. "It was November. I was planning to take him to get his flu shot. Dr. Baker had closed his practice that past summer. We were planning a trip to London to get Jude a fishing pole. He was old enough that he could sit up and sort of pay attention, and I wanted to take him out fishing before winter really hit. He was way too young to actually fish, of course, but I was going to get him one of those kid fishing poles and sort of hold it for him. So I thought I'd get the shot done when we went to London. We'd do the shot, and the shopping would be the reward. We were gonna go on the weekend, so my ex could come, too, make a day of it, and—" Fuck. His voice was cracking. "I shouldn't have waited. I should have gotten it done in *October*."

"You mentioned still being on the parental leave year." Her voice was calm. "So this would have been his first flu shot, right?" He nodded. "Children between six months and five years who have never had a flu vaccine require a second dose, four weeks later, for the body to mount a proper immune response."

He knew that. And he knew what she was actually saying: it wasn't his fault. How many times had he heard that, in the early days? *It wasn't your fault.* Everywhere he turned, someone was saying that. They'd said it preemptively, too, like they *assumed* he was twisted up with guilt. That was what he hated, the presumption. The gall of these people who thought they knew his mind. Who thought they knew God's mind with their "Everything happens for a reason"s and their "It was his time"s.

It wasn't your fault. Kerrie had said it, too. Said it so often that he'd started to wonder if she was talking to him or to herself.

"Right. But he got sick on November tenth and died on the thirteenth. If I'd gotten him the first dose right when the shot was available, there might have been time for a second dose." He had done the macabre math in his head so many times.

"We never got our vaccines in at the hospital I worked at until late October," she said quietly.

So, what? It *probably* wasn't his fault? That didn't help. It wasn't even about fault. The fact was, he had been the adult. The parent. He had failed at the most basic of tasks: keeping his kid alive.

The waves were starting. The bad kind. How had he been foolish enough to think they wouldn't get him in the end? They always did. He stood, took the elastic out of his hair, and dragged his fingers along his scalp. His headache was intensifying. "I should go. Thanks for the drink." He congratulated himself on his calm delivery. Speech hadn't deserted him yet, but he could tell by the thickening in his throat that it would soon. Usually he chose not to speak. This, this *inability* to speak that was part of what happened to him when the waves came, was different. It was a symptom of a kind of helplessness, though *helplessness* seemed way too benign a word. *Paralysis* was a better one, maybe.

"No problem," she said, apparently oblivious to the storm that was winding up inside him. "Thanks for the *deck*. If you don't mind seeing yourself out, I'm just going to stay out here on my *amazing new deck* and try to hear the waves."

A sliver of something, something like satisfaction, worked its way into his chest, even as the white-noise cacophony of the waves started to overtake him. To think of her here listening to the lake on the deck he'd built, while he surrendered to the waves, brought him a certain kind of unfamiliar gratification.

"The wind's going to pick up later." He managed to get the words out. They were quiet but still audible. He gathered his hair back in a loose ponytail as he crossed the deck. "You'll hear the lake tonight." He wasn't sure that last bit had come out loudly enough for her to hear. He was being overtaken. He might not make it all the way home. He might have to stop at Sandcastle Beach, and he *hated* it when he had to endure the waves in public. He hadn't had to do that for at least a year. He had gotten good enough at recognizing the signs that usually he could get a head start, make it home so he could sit by the lake and let the actual waves deafen him. Wait for them to drown out the waves inside him.

He had one foot back in the house when she called after him. "I like your hair, Jake Ramsey."

It was a silly thing to say, a throwaway line meant to echo their first meeting at the salon. But it startled him enough that it paused his descent sufficiently to allow him to say, "I like your hair, too, Doc."

Chapter Five

❧

*L*ate Tuesday morning, Jake showed up at the clinic. Wynd had put some wind chimes—Wynd chimes?—on the door, and they heralded his arrival. Nora looked up from the computer at the reception desk, which she and Amber and Wynd were huddled around as they worked through a sample patient's entry with the new charting and scheduling software.

Jake took a step back. Like maybe he hadn't expected a crowd. And another step back when Parsnip, who a moment ago had been happily playing with a set of wooden blocks, started power-crawling in his direction.

But then, seeming to realize she was trying to make a break for it through the door he was holding open, he stepped all the way in and shut it behind him.

He looked at Nora. "I thought I would drop by and take a look at your painting situation."

Parsnip, belatedly realizing that Jake had blocked her

path to the open road, let out a wail and started pounding his legs. Jake's eyes darted back and forth like he wasn't sure what to do.

Nora stifled a laugh. As Wynd got up to peel her daughter off Jake's lower extremities, she said, "Jake, I suspect you know Amber from the bar, but do you know Wynd Lewisohn?"

He nodded, and Wynd murmured greetings at Jake and soothing words at Parsnip.

"And this"—Nora got up—"is Wynd's daughter." *Don't laugh. Don't laugh. Don't laugh.* "Parsnip."

Jake laughed. Or coughed. Or did some kind of combination of the two. Wynd didn't hear it, though, because she was singing "The Calm Song" to Parsnip. As far as Nora could tell from her week of acquaintance with Parsnip, "The Calm Song" did not work on her. Neither did "The Clean Up Song" or "The I'm Sorry Song."

Parsnip had a mind of her own.

Nora liked Parsnip. She felt like at the ripe old age of one, Parsnip was already not the kind of girl who would grow up to let anyone tell her it was time to clean up if she wasn't ready to clean up.

"Hey, Jake. Long time no see," Amber said. She didn't seem to expect Jake to answer, because she turned immediately to Nora. "Maybe this is a good time to run out for some lunch?"

"Yeah, why don't you and Parsnip take a break, too, Wynd?"

When everyone was gone, she pointed to the front desk. "This is the painting situation." Jake crouched and examined the botched paint job. "Which is not your job to fix, by the way. I'm going to take another run at it later this week."

Ignoring her, he ran a hand over the vertical surface of the front of the desk, which was mottled because the paint had only selectively stuck. Little bits of the fake wood were showing through black blobs of paint. "What kind of primer did you use?"

"The kind the guy at Lakeside Hardware told me to use for wood laminate."

"Ah. This is vinyl, though. You need a bonding primer."

"I need what?"

He straightened. "I can do it. But maybe I should come back tonight. The fumes probably won't be good for . . . Did you say her name was Parsnip?"

"Yep. And her sister is named Cicada."

He snorted.

"Seriously, though, Jake, you can't paint my front desk." But why? Why couldn't he? Who else was going to do it? Nora didn't even know what bonding primer was.

He shrugged. "It'll hardly take any time at all."

"Okay, but I'll help. And I'll bring dinner. And you have to charge me."

He didn't agree to any of her conditions, but he didn't reject them, either. He just said, "Five thirty?"

By five thirty Nora was on her way back to the clinic with two pies. The first was a mini key lime. She had finally visited Pie with Pearl, owned by Pearl Brunetta, whom she'd met that first day at the salon. Pearl, it turned out, did several of her most popular pies in mini format, which Nora could already tell was going to pose a problem for her. But if the warm-from-the-oven coconut rhubarb Pearl had forced her to sample while standing in the shop was any indication, it was going to be an enjoyable problem.

The second pie was a pizza with chanterelles, roasted garlic, and heirloom tomatoes from Lawson's. The pizza menu, she had learned, was new, the result of Law's trying to branch out beyond just booze. Nora was planning to support Law generously in this endeavor.

And speaking of the pizza, hadn't Law said that Jake had built the outdoor oven? Maya had called him the town's fairy godfather when it came to building, and in Nora's experience that was proving true.

Jake was leaning against the brick façade of the building that housed the clinic when Nora arrived. He was so big, it sort of looked like he was holding up the building, but that was ridiculous.

She unlocked the clinic and said, "You want to eat first?"

"Nah. Unless you're hungry, let's leave it till I'm done."

"*We're* done."

"What?"

"*We.* Because I'm helping you." When he looked like he was about to protest, she cut him off. "Humor a girl who's on a self-sufficiency kick. I clearly have no idea what I'm doing, but I'm a decent worker bee."

He handed her a paintbrush. "Okay, but we can only do the primer today. It will have to dry before the paint goes on. So it really *is* going to go fast."

They got into a rhythm, and he was right about it going quickly. After sanding off the biggest blobs of dried paint, he showed her what to do. As they worked, he told her about the town's three annual festivals. The upcoming Mermaid Parade she'd already heard about—the whole town seemed to be eagerly anticipating it. There was also a Raspberry Festival earlier in the summer that she'd missed, and a locals-only secret party the first weekend in October.

"They call it the Anti-Festival," he said.

"*Anti* as in 'against'?" she asked.

"Yeah, you'll see how the town sort of has a seasonal

rhythm. There are a lot of tourists and day-trippers in the summer, but it drops off pretty dramatically. Seasonal businesses close, and everyone sort of hunkers down for the winter."

"So this festival marks the transition?"

"Yeah. It started as a joke—hence the name. The idea is that the tourists are gone, and the locals have their own party. There are fund-raisers for local causes—cakewalks, except with pie, a bachelor auction. Maya stages a play."

That was awfully cute. It sounded like something out of *Gilmore Girls* or a Hallmark movie. "Where does this happen?"

"Out on the strip of parking lots behind the businesses on the north side of Main Street. Everyone shuts down their storefronts. They try to make it look like the town has been abandoned. It's actually kind of funny. They get really aggressive about keeping out anyone but locals."

"I wonder if they'll let me attend. I'm only here for two years."

"Yeah, I heard you're leasing the practice. They'll probably have to consult their bylaws, but I bet they'll make an exception for you."

She used her brush to point to the big can of paint nearby—not realizing they were only going to prime today, she'd brought it out. "You know, I think I bought too much paint, even with me spilling a ton of it the other day. That can is still three-quarters full."

"Yeah, you could have done with just a liter, probably."

"I'm thinking now that I'm a painting expert"—she made sure he saw her eye roll so he'd know she was kidding—"I might take what's left over and try to paint that horrible metal chair in my backyard. Which is dumb. I should probably buy new lawn chairs."

"Nah, that's a great old chair. You just need to sand the rust off before you paint. I'll help." He paused. "Unless that's a violation of the self-sufficiency thing." Another pause. "Which, for the record, I completely respect."

God, this guy was too much. *Everybody* here was too much. "Why is everyone in this town being so nice to me? Pearl wouldn't let me pay for my pie just now. CJ offered to do a house call when I need my roots touched up. And that's just today. There must be a catch."

"It's that two-year thing, probably. I think everyone just wants you to stick, you know? This town really needs a doctor."

"Oh, so I'm just a warm body with a medical degree?" she joked.

"No. I think Dr. Baker was the warm body with the medical degree, and now that you're here, everyone is realizing exactly how much that was true." He paused. "That sounds uncharitable. He was a nice enough guy. He was just...not getting right in there on the town green when a tourist was going into labor, you know?"

"The scientist in me needs to point out that my clinic isn't even open yet, so all these favorable conclusions are premature."

"Nah. You can just tell."

Well. She liked that assessment. "Speaking of tourists in labor on the town green, Sawyer told me that Colleen called the police station looking for both my name and your name—she said she'd forgotten them."

"Huh. I wonder why?"

"Maybe so she can send us thank-you notes? Name her kid after us?"

"Jake Nora?"

"Nora Jake!" she teasingly corrected. "It is a girl, after all."

"Nora Jacobina?"

She wasn't sure why she found that so funny, but she had to pause in her painting because she was cracking up. "Nora Jacobina sounds like a pilgrim."

He chuckled, and they settled into a companionable silence as they worked. They'd each started on one end of the desk and had gradually been making their way toward the center—toward each other.

"See?" he said as his left arm brushed her right. Goose bumps rose on her flesh despite the fact that it was a warm evening. "Piece of cake."

"Wow. That was anticlimactic. I guess it's time for dinner. I was prepared to work a lot harder than that."

He stood back and examined their work. "Let's take the food and paint to your place and do that chair."

She started to object. It was a reflex. But as she'd wondered the other day with respect to the deck, why? Someone offered to help her, and something inside her automatically rose up and said no? Wasn't she supposed to be not doing that anymore?

"Okay. We can eat on my glorious new deck and listen to the lake."

An hour later, her good-as-new chair was drying in the warm twilight, and they were sitting on the edge of her deck, eating pizza.

"This is so good," she said. "Even cold."

"Yeah, Law has been wanting to start serving food for a while. I think he's onto something."

"My favorite is the Hawaiian—he uses this ridiculous pancetta that melts in your mouth and grills the pineapple with this balsamic glaze. But I didn't know if I should inflict that on you. So many people object so vehemently to pineapple on—"

"Nora?"

Oh *hell* no. She shot to her feet and looked wildly around the yard. She had to have imagined that.

"Nora? Hello?"

Crap. She was too content, wasn't she, with her pizza and her chair and her deck? Apparently so, because the Ghost of Nora's Past was here to take her down a few pegs.

Yap, yap, yap! Despite her dismay, her heart did a happy little leap at *that* familiar sound.

It was coming from the front yard. She leaped to her feet. But as she made her way to the gate that divided the backyard from the front, she slowed, suddenly feeling clumsy, unsure of her footing.

"Everything okay?" Jake's voice came at her as if through a fog.

She must have looked as unsteady as she felt because suddenly he was at her side—which was a good thing. When Rufus appeared from around the front of the house, Jake had to physically hold her up. But just for a second. She ordered herself to get her act together and took a step away from him and toward Rufus. Generally speaking, *toward Rufus* was not her preferred direction these days, but she needed to assert her dominance. This was *her* territory. *Her* crappy house. *Her* new life.

Which did *not* include Rufus.

So she walked the last few steps to the gate, put her hands on her hips, and summoned her best ice queen tone. "What are you doing here, Rufus?" She tried to keep her eyes—eyes she hoped were radiating judginess and disdain—on Rufus, but she couldn't help dropping them for a second. As soon as she made eye contact with the little basset hound in Rufus's arms, he yapped happily at her in greeting. She suppressed a smile.

Which wasn't all that hard to do, because Rufus had started toward her. She held up a hand. She was the one regulating how much distance there was between them. "I asked you what you were doing here."

That galvanized Jake, who covered the short distance between them until he was once again at her side. He didn't do or say anything, though. He just stood there, his eyes moving between her and Rufus, assessing. It occurred to her that some men, in the name of honor or chivalry or whatever, would rush in and be all, "The lady asked you a question, asshole," but Jake merely stood there, his solid, wordless presence having the same steadying effect it'd had during the emergency birth.

But she wasn't going to lie. The fact that her silent support system was a gorgeous man-god was not going unappreciated here.

She turned and raised her eyebrows pointedly at Rufus.

"I need you to take the dog," he said quickly.

It was all she could do not to lunge for the little creature she had come to love so much. She forced herself to be cool. "Why?"

Rufus was clearly uncomfortable, alternately kicking the ground in front of him and eyeing Jake like a bratty little boy who'd been caught doing something stupid by a cool, older kid. "It turns out that basset hounds are one of the worst breeds for people with allergies."

Oh hell no.

She knew exactly what he was getting at, but she decided to play dumb. "But you're not allergic to dogs."

"It's not their fur so much as their dander, which I guess is extra potent or something."

"And you have that vacuum cleaner that cost as much as a used car. You *do* love that vacuum cleaner." It was one of the objects he'd insisted on. A top-of-the-line Miele even though all they'd had to vacuum were area rugs—the actual floor of the apartment had been hardwood.

"And basset hound drool is a factor in allergies, too. You remember how much he drools."

A wave of revulsion washed over her. He couldn't seem to find the strength or the balls or the *whatever* in himself to take responsibility for what he was actually saying. To *say* what he was actually saying.

Her sister had told her that there was a formula for how long it took to get over someone—a month for every year you'd been together. By that metric, it was supposed to take five months for Rufus to be in her wake. As much as she hated the fact that he had just shown up uninvited at her house, she also kind of appreciated that his doing so was putting her on the accelerated plan.

Okay, she was done here. "Rufus, I think what you're trying to say is that the resident you cheated on me with is shacking up with you a month after I walked in on said cheating, and that she's allergic to dogs?"

He turned bright red, which she enjoyed, but he didn't answer.

"Is that right?" she goaded. She felt a hand on her lower back. Jake's, resting lightly. A visceral reminder of his presence, should she need it.

"Chloe is allergic to dogs," Rufus mumbled.

She laughed.

Then she laughed some more, because she was happy that she could laugh about this so soon. She was *totally* on the advanced track here. She might be lonely, but she wasn't lonely for *Rufus*, which she was going to take as a win. "Hand him over."

Jake leaned over and whispered in her ear, "You want this dog?"

She nodded. She did want the dog. The dog was the only damn thing in the whole split she'd wanted, but she hadn't presumed to ask because he was Rufus's—from way before she came on the scene.

Although . . . even though she had just been thinking how she appreciated Jake's low-key approach, his silent but steadfast support, part of her wanted to see what he would do or say if she said no, she didn't want the dog. How fast would Jake have Rufus running away with his tail between his legs—pun intended?

But no. She was happy to play power games with asshole ex-boyfriends, but she couldn't do that to loyal canine companions.

Rufus edged forward and handed her the dog over the gate, keeping his eyes on Jake. Once the transfer had been made, he took a big step back and said, "I have a box of his stuff in the car. I'll leave it on the porch."

"Hang on," she called, and he paused in his retreat. "Repeat after me. 'I'll leave a box of his stuff on the porch, and I swear on Chloe's perfect, perky resident boobs that I will never contact you again, Nora.'"

Jake guffawed, and Rufus rolled his eyes.

"I'm not kidding, Rufus. Say it, or find someone else to take the dog." It was an empty threat, but she was banking on him not knowing that.

"I'll leave a bag of his stuff on the porch, and I swear on Chloe's perfect, perky resident boobs that I will never contact you again, Nora," he mumbled, not making eye contact.

She turned away from him for the last time. It *really* felt like the last time, and it felt…good. She smiled.

Jake whistled and took a step back.

"That," she said, "was Rufus. Species: disgusting ex-boyfriend who makes me question my taste in everything." She pressed her nose to the fur on the dog's head, inhaling his comforting, familiar smell. "And *this* is Sir Mick. Species: miniature basset hound."

"Sir Mick as in Jagger?" Jake asked, still reeling a little from watching Nora take down her ex in such spectacular fashion.

"Yep." She kissed one of the dog's long, floppy ears, and she must have interpreted Jake's snort correctly, because she added, "Named by Rufus long before I came on the scene."

"Not that there's anything wrong with the Stones," he said, following her around to the front of the house.

"I know, but they're not the Beatles—am I right?"

"You are right."

She eyed the box on the porch.

"Let me get that."

They went in the front door, and Nora set about unpacking the box and filling a water bowl for Mick.

After Mick had had a drink, they went back outside and sat on the edge of the deck. She looped Mick's leash around her ankle. He gazed pitifully at her pizza and started whining.

"You, my little friend, are supposed to be on a diet, but from the look of things, Rufus has not been prioritizing your BMI." She looked out at the yard. "I don't suppose you do fences? I suddenly find myself in need of a fence."

Not really. Like decks, fences didn't really fall into the

fine carpentry category he and Sawyer focused on. "Sure. And you know, your bathtub desperately needs to be recaulked. I can do that for you, too, if you like."

"What about dishwasher repair? Do you do that, too? Because mine is toast."

"I'm not an expert, but I can have a look. And you have some exposed wires in a corner of the living room. I assume they're not live, but we should make sure."

She snorted. "I was kidding. I figure a fence is my problem to solve, but all that other stuff is my landlord's job. I sent him a list."

"Which I can pretty well guarantee he'll ignore."

"So you're just going to do it for me?"

Pretty much. He shrugged.

"Well, that's nice of you. Freakishly nice. And I'll absolutely hire you for the fence, but let me at least try to get Harold to take responsibility for the rest."

Mick, who, once he'd given up on begging for pizza, had curled up and fallen instantly asleep at Nora's feet, emitted a loud snore. She looked at him affectionately. "I wasn't a dog person before I met Rufus, and Mick is a pain in the butt. He snores and drools, and he's got all kinds of geriatric ailments. But damn, I missed him."

"Dogs'll do that to you."

"You have one?"

"Used to, but it went with the ex-wife."

"That sucks."

"You know, I didn't actually want her. I mean, I like dogs. But Daisy—that was the dog—and Jude adored each other. Seeing Daisy without Jude was . . ." He didn't know how to explain it.

"Like a wound that never healed?"

"Yeah."

And *this* was why he was here. This was why he had built her a deck. Why he was going to talk her into letting him repair her dishwasher and caulk her bathtub. Because, for the first time in four years, he *wanted* to talk about Jude. With her. It was unprecedented and a little bit weird, but he was going with it. Even if it made the waves come. Because they came anyway, didn't they?

"You want to see a picture of him?" She nodded, and he pulled out his wallet. "This was the August before he died. His mom had this silly costume made for the Mermaid Parade."

She took the picture from him and examined it with a smile. "He looks like you."

"You think?" People said that a lot, but he also saw a lot of Kerrie in their son.

"Totally. The eyes especially. If he'd lived long enough to grow his hair, you could have had a mini-me."

He laughed. "My ex wouldn't have allowed it. She was always after me to cut my hair."

"Really? It sort of seems like your signature thing."

"It definitely helps me maintain my hermit image." He was gratified when she smiled. "I started growing it in high school because I had a fling with this older tourist one summer, and she was into long hair. Then I just got used to it."

"You grew your hair to please Mrs. Robinson!" she teased.

"Pretty much." She laughed, but he had no problem owning that. Hell, he would have done anything Sarah, his Mrs. Robinson, had asked him to, so profoundly had she blown his seventeen-year-old mind. He still thought of her with fondness.

"So you already had the long hair when you met your ex?"

"Yep."

"I don't understand people who get into a relationship with someone and then proceed to try to change stuff about them. Like, didn't you kick the tires? Didn't you know what you were getting?" She'd been speaking increasingly urgently and seemed to realize it suddenly. She flashed him a sheepish grin. "Sorry. Rufus hated my hair, too. He always wanted me to grow it and stop dyeing it."

"Does Chloe the Resident have long hair?"

"You'd better believe it. Long, shiny blond hair—which isn't any more natural than mine, but it's a less extreme shade—to go with the perky, perfect boobs."

Nora's boobs seemed pretty perky to him. Small, yes, but they were in proportion to the rest of her. Not that he was going to say any of that. He limited his commentary to her hair. "I like your hair. It suits you."

"I like your hair, too."

Which was something they'd said to each other enough times now that it was starting to feel like an inside joke. He smiled. It was a beautiful night. The sky was just beginning to turn a darker blue. They ate in companionable silence for a few minutes. Well, not silence. You could hear the lake. He glanced over at her.

She must have felt his attention. She said, "Jake?" though she kept looking at the sky.

"Hmm?"

"Thanks for everything today. For the painting help, of course, but also just for...being here."

"No problem."

"I don't want to freak you out or anything, but I think you're my first real friend in Moonflower Bay."

He nodded. He found he didn't mind that idea at all.

He was also pretty sure the waves would not come today.

Chapter Six

‿

When Jake got to the bar on Friday, it was packed with people, and not the usual crowd. Sawyer and Eve were at the bar, but so were Karl, Pearl, and Eiko.

He approached with caution. Jake respected the elders of the town, but they were trouble when they had a mission—and he was pretty sure, based on the way they were talking animatedly to Sawyer and Eve, that they had an active one. Some of the younger folks had nicknamed the town Matchmaker Bay after the machinations of the older guard. They said it like it was cute. It was not cute. He started to turn. He was going to leave before anyone saw him.

"Jake! Jake!"

Dammit.

Pearl was waving at him and pointing to his usual stool. He sighed and walked over, but he didn't sit.

"We're talking about the new doctor," Pearl said. "What do you think of her with Jason Sims?"

"I say this with love, but you should leave that alone," Eve advised. "She just got out of a five-year relationship. She told me last week she's here to clear her head, and that she's not looking for anything like that."

"Yeah, but I think Jason likes her," Eiko said. "Or likes the idea of her, anyway. I don't think they've met yet."

Eve curled her lip a little at the mention of Jason, perfectly summing up Jake's thoughts about the town lawyer. He had mild douchebag tendencies.

They all looked at Jake like they were waiting for his vote on the matter. Okay, then. "Her clinic isn't even open yet. Maybe let her get settled for two seconds before you start meddling."

Sawyer shot him a puzzled look.

"How cute would it be if the town lawyer and the town doctor got together?" Pearl said, apparently determined to ignore his vote if it didn't line up with what she wanted.

"She's only here for two years," Jake said, though he wasn't sure why he was arguing with them. They only heard what they wanted to hear.

"But plans change," said Karl. "Especially when the heart is involved. Which brings us back to Jason."

Sawyer caught Jake's eye and gave a small nod toward Jake's stool—he still had not sat down.

He shook his head no. This was not why he spent Friday nights at Law's, to get caught up in the maddening machinations of the town matchmakers. So he turned around and went home.

Nora was finishing up at the clinic when she got a text. Hi. This is Maya. I got your number from Sawyer.

Nora and Sawyer had exchanged numbers and had spoken a couple times during the week about the naloxone situation.

> *Maya:* Are you going to Lawson's tonight?

She'd considered it. She wasn't sure how informal the Friday-night thing was—did she need to be invited?

> *Maya:* If you are, any chance you can order a pizza and sneak me a piece or two? Or seven?

Nora laughed. Sure. Or, and I know this is going to sound crazy, you could just order your own pizza.

> *Maya:* I can't. It's complicated.
> *Maya:* But also, that pizza is so freaking good I'm having literal dreams about it.
> *Nora:* Understood on both fronts. I'm just about done at the clinic, so I can be there in ten.

When Nora arrived, Maya waved her over to a spot between herself and Sawyer. Eve was on Sawyer's other side, and Pearl was on the next stool over.

Nora looked around subtly for Jake, but he wasn't there.

Everyone made easy small talk, and when Law came to check on them, she said, "Can I order the mushroom pizza?"

Maya kicked her in the shin.

"Ow." She turned to her assailant, who shielded her mouth from Law's view but very clearly mouthed "Pepperoni."

"Actually, make that pepperoni."

"You got it," Law said. "Small?"

Maya coughed.

"Uh, no, I think I'll go for a large, thanks." She turned toward Sawyer. "I had an idea about your measles problem this afternoon. The Mermaid Parade is coming up, right? What if I set up a public information booth along the parade route? Does it go down Main Street?"

"That's a great idea," he said. "The parade draws lots of families with young kids."

"It's not just about kids, actually. Most adults born from the seventies to the nineties never got a second dose of the MMR vaccine. It wasn't standard practice then, but it is now. So there are lots of people walking around who need boosters to achieve full immunity. I was thinking we could distribute info sheets."

"Why not actually set up an outdoor clinic?" Maya asked. "Like, give the shots right there?"

"I bet seeing prominent people in town getting their shots would make an impression," Eve said. She swatted her boyfriend. "You should find out if you ever got a booster, Chief."

"I doubt I did." He turned to Nora. "My childhood wasn't full of a lot of, ah, oversight."

"Sawyer raised himself," Pearl said. "And his sister." She beamed at Sawyer like a proud grandma.

Sawyer shook his head, clearly uncomfortable with the topic. "Anyway, assuming I need the booster, I'd be happy to be your first customer."

"Oh! Oh! I have the best idea!" Maya exclaimed. "You could do it *on* a float in the parade."

Law, who'd been popping in and out of the conversation,

scoffed. "She's not going to give shots on a float in the Mermaid Parade."

"It would definitely be a great PR stunt," Nora said, not wanting to hurt Maya's feelings. "The problem is, I can't just randomly give people shots. I would need to take a medical history and all that." She turned to Sawyer. "If you're up for doing that in advance, I can definitely shoot you up during the parade." She made an apologetic face at Maya. "Maybe not *in* it. I'm not totally confident in my ability to jab people while on a moving vehicle. And the vaccines need to be refrigerated, so it gets complicated logistically. Maybe for now we just set up a table outside the clinic?"

"Works for me," Sawyer said.

"Okay," Maya said, "but you have to let me make advertisements. We can hang them on the floats and they can say, 'Watch Sawyer get stuck with a needle in front of the clinic.' Or some catchier version of that that I have yet to think of."

"We can decorate the information table, too," Eve said. "I have lots of paint left over from the renovation of the inn. Maybe we could make a big, colorful sign."

"Of mermaids getting shots!" Maya exclaimed.

"Yes!" Pearl said.

"Flu shots, on the other hand," Nora said, thinking out loud about this whole festival-vaccine connection that everyone seemed to be running with, "I *can* just give to people if I take down some info from them. Jake Ramsey told me there's this town-only festival in early October? It's a bit early, but I can see if I can order some vaccines in time for it."

Suddenly Pearl and Maya, who had been yammering about vaccine-and-mermaid-related decor, went dead silent.

After an uncomfortable moment, Maya finally spoke. "*Jake* told you about the Anti-Festival?"

Law had arrived with her pizza—well, with Maya's pizza—and he paused, holding it over the bar, his eyebrows raised.

"Yeah. Was he not supposed to? It's some kind of inside joke, I gather?" Maybe she was too new to take part in it?

"No, no," Eve said. "It's not a secret—at least not from you. It's just that Jake doesn't...talk a lot."

"I was actually thinking Jake could probably help me with a flu-shot clinic."

"He's the wrong person for that," Sawyer said quickly.

"On the contrary, he's the perfect person. There's an argument to be made that when you know someone whose life has been affected by flu-related complications or deaths, you're more likely to..." She trailed off, realizing that everyone was looking at her with some degree of shock. "What?"

"How did you know about Jake's son?" Eve asked.

Why was she getting the feeling that she was treading on forbidden ground here? "He told me," she said warily.

"He told you about Jude?" Sawyer's tone was a combination of skeptical and defensive. Nora glanced at Maya, who was openly gaping.

"Uh, yeah?"

"He just came out and told you?" Pearl asked. She seemed less gobsmacked than the others, but she was looking at Nora with an intense curiosity that made Nora nervous.

Why did Nora feel like saying yes was somehow a betrayal of Jake? She didn't have to answer, though, because Pearl got up. "I'm having an epiphany. I gotta go."

Eve turned to Nora. "Sorry we're being weird. Jake is

kind of famous for being antisocial, so we were just a little surprised."

"Antisocial?" Maya said. "Try *mute*."

That didn't accord with Nora's impression of him. Yes, he didn't seem like the kind of person who wasted words, or who hurried to interject himself into things—witness his silently watching over both the birth on the green and her confrontation with Rufus. But they had spoken easily, and, between the topics of his son and her loser ex-boyfriend, rather intimately.

"Anyway." Eve was clearly trying to move the conversation beyond Jake and what he had or had not told Nora, which Nora appreciated. "I heard you like baseball."

"You did?"

She smirked. "Pro tip: Do not utter a word anywhere in this town—or wear a Tigers T-shirt to Curl Up and Dye—that you don't want getting out."

"There's a group of town elders who have their noses in everything," Sawyer said. "They tend to congregate at the hardware store."

"Right," Maya said. "Except they don't really *congregate* at the hardware store so much as *plot* there. So beware of the following individuals: Karl Andersen, who owns Lakeside Hardware. Pearl Brunetta"—she pointed at Pearl's abandoned drink. "Eiko Anzai, who's the editor of the town newspaper. And, to a lesser extent, Art Ramsey, Jake's dad."

"What does that have to do with the salon, then?" Nora asked.

"I think Carol sort of reports to them," Eve said. "Last time I got my hair done, I thought I was making idle conversation about maybe starting a little vegetable garden, but the next day Karl was on my case about it."

"Basically, if you want your business to stay private, be very, very careful what you say in front of the elders of Moonflower Bay, regardless of location," Maya advised.

"Anyway, baseball," Eve said, apparently correctly intuiting that Nora's head was spinning with all these names. "There's a town softball league—*that* was my point."

"Oh, thanks, but I'm more of an eat-nachos-while-watching-other-people-exert-themselves sort of person than I am an athlete." Actually, though, that was another thing she was hoping to change while she was here. She needed to find a way to get some exercise into her routine.

"What about theater?" Maya asked.

"Like watching it? Sure."

"No. Like being in it. I'm putting on a gender-swapped *Death of a Salesman*—so it's gonna be *Death of a Saleswoman*—at the Anti-Festival this fall. You would make a great Wilhelmina Loman."

"You mean like *Death of a Salesman* where it's all grinding poverty and family dysfunction and he kills himself at the end?"

"That's the one!" Maya trilled. "Except with a she instead of a he. And I can *totally* see you in it."

Nora didn't know how to say that there was no way on God's green earth she was going to star in *Death of a Salesman*. Or -*woman*. But she didn't have to answer because Maya presented her with another option. "I don't suppose there's any chance you're into English Premier League football?"

"You mean like soccer?" Nora asked.

"Yeah. I got into it when I was doing a semester abroad in the UK. It turns out to be very dramatic. The rivalries, the arc of the season. You want to watch the next game with me? My team is Crystal Palace."

"Back off, everyone." Sawyer turned to her. "They're just trying to make you feel welcome, but you don't need to sign up now for a season of softball playing or soccer watching. What about a boat ride? A group of us heads out on the lake a couple of times a month on Law's pontoon."

"That sounds perfect."

Chapter Seven

❧

The next Friday afternoon, Jake was working on Nora's fence when she got home. They had argued about him working on her place—inside and out—but he'd won her over with a promise to charge her market rates for it all and with the assurance that he would fit her in between existing jobs. He did not intend to keep his promise about billing her, but he was fitting her in between other jobs, which meant he worked in little stretches, often at odd times. That, plus the fact that she was putting in long hours at the clinic getting ready to open, meant he hadn't actually seen much of her. They'd overlapped once and shared another pizza, but that had been it.

"Jake," she said when she appeared from around front. "I'm glad you're here."

Mick, who had been sleeping in the sun, got up at the sound of her voice and started wiggling his butt.

"I hope you don't mind that I let Mick out for

some...Well, I was going to say exercise, but that's not really his thing, is it?" She'd given him a key to the house so he could scope out repairs that needed doing inside, and he'd taken to letting the dog out to keep him company while he worked on the fence.

She laughed. "Of course I don't mind. The sun and the grass are good for him. Probably a shock for an old city dog." She glanced over her shoulder. "I have a semi-awkward favor to ask."

"Shoot."

"My grandma's here for a visit. She's recovering from a bout with cancer, and she's pretty frail. My sister and I—my sister's here, too—have been driving her around and showing her the sights, and we took her for lunch in Bayshore. But she wants to see my house before they hit the road. I thought we'd be able to help her up the steps to the porch, but she's in worse shape than I expected. I saw your truck in the driveway, and I was wondering if you could, like, hoist her up."

"Of course." He wiped his sweaty hands on his jeans and went hunting for his discarded T-shirt. "Let me just make myself presentable."

"She would probably appreciate it more if you *didn't* put that back on," Nora said, smiling as he pulled his shirt over his head.

"Yeah?" he said, not quite sure how to respond.

"Let's just say she's not your typical little old lady. She's been known to appreciate a hunky man-god from time to time."

"Did you just call me a hunky man-god?"

"*I* didn't call you a hunky man-god. I just said my *grand-mother* would say you're a hunky man-god." She rolled her eyes, but she was smiling. "Sheesh. Don't get a big head."

To his great surprise, Jake found he didn't mind Nora teasing him.

Or thinking of him as a hunky man-god, for that matter.

He followed her around the house, whistling for Mick, who came up to trot happily alongside him. The two women out front were clearly related to Nora. The sister was a carbon copy of her—except her hair was more of a strawberry blond—and the grandmother, though she had darker coloring, had the same small, almost elfin features as her granddaughters.

"Jake, this is my sister, Erin Walsh, and my grandmother, Dr. Penelope Walsh. Grandma, Erin, this is my friend Jake Ramsey."

"And my knight in shining armor," her grandma said.

"Oh, I don't know about that, Dr. Walsh." It tickled him that she was Dr. Walsh, too. "Maybe more like your pack mule, but I'm happy to be of service either way. You ready?" She nodded and handed her purse to Nora's sister. As gently as he could, Jake lifted her into his arms and ascended the short flight of stairs to the porch.

"I could get used to this," the elder Dr. Walsh said, a teasing note in her voice. He set her down, and she immediately took his arm, so when Nora opened the front door, he escorted her inside.

"I noticed you got furniture," he said to Nora. The living room was still spartan, but there was a small sofa and a side chair in it now. There was a table in the dining area, too.

Dr. Walsh surveyed the space with narrowed eyes. "What a dump."

"Thanks, Grandma," Nora said with affection in her voice. She turned to Jake. "My grandma is not known for suffering fools."

"When you suffer fools, you suffer," Dr. Walsh said. "And who wants to suffer?"

"Amen. And here's to not suffering any more fools," Erin said with a pointed look at Nora.

"Yeah, yeah," Nora said, and he could only surmise that they were talking about her ex.

"Don't worry, Dr. Walsh," he said, "I'm going to help your granddaughter get this place into better shape."

"I like him," she said, pointing to him but speaking to Nora, who was headed for the kitchen. "Just this morning the UPS guy called me Penny. Can you imagine? I had to correct him. I earned my title."

"Our grandma graduated from medical school in 1962," Erin said. "She was one of Canada's first female cardiac surgeons. There's even a procedure named after her."

"The Walsh repair," Dr. Walsh said. "It's a particular suturing technique for valve replacements."

"That's impressive. Clearly you inspired your granddaughter."

"Nah," Nora called from the kitchen. "Grandma is not impressed with family medicine. Real doctors cut people up."

"That's right!" Dr. Walsh yelled, even as she smiled at him and shook her head to show she was teasing. "My son—these girls' dad—is a doctor, too. So is their older brother."

"Wow. And what about you?" Jake asked Erin. "Did you go into the family business, too?"

"Heck, no," Erin said. "I'm an accountant."

"Every family needs its black sheep." Dr. Walsh patted her granddaughter's hand.

The affection among the three women was palpable, even as they razzed each other. It made Jake smile. It reminded him a little of the happy days of his childhood, when his mom had been alive and his brother still lived in town. They hadn't been as snarky-smart as this family, but they'd known how to have fun, passing long, happy summer days in the cove.

He had been so looking forward to Jude getting older, so they could have adventures, too. Inside jokes.

Sadness settled on him like a blanket. But in so doing, it made him realize that it *hadn't* been there earlier. He and Mick had passed an hour without him thinking about Jude.

He . . . didn't know how to feel about that.

Nora appeared from the kitchen with a stack of glasses and a container from the town's famous beachside lemonade stand. "Jake, you want to join us for some lemonade? We stopped at Legg's in our outings today."

He started to demur, but Dr. Walsh the elder patted the sofa next to her. "You might as well stay. You're going to have to heft me down those stairs in about ten minutes."

He sat and accepted a glass of lemonade from Nora.

"So," her grandma said. "Is this thing you two have going a romantic thing?"

Nora choked on her lemonade and started coughing. "Oh my God, no."

"Sexual?"

"Grandma."

"What? I'm just asking."

"Grandma, I *just* got out of a five-year relationship."

"With an asshole."

"What difference does that make?"

"Maybe you get over assholes faster." She shrugged. "I don't know. I never dated any assholes."

"Okay," Erin said to Dr. Walsh. "Down, girl."

"We're just friends, Dr. Walsh," Jake said.

He paused to consider that he hadn't made a new friend in years. And that he hadn't had sex since Kerrie.

He hadn't thought he was in the market for either of those things. But look at him now: he had a new friend.

"Anyway, I *told* you," Nora said, "I've declared a moratorium on boys. Dating, romance, all of it. The whole point of being here is to clear my head. Ponder my history of bad judgment."

"You've put yourself in a time-out," Dr. Walsh said.

He could see Nora gearing up to protest, but she cracked a smile instead. "That's actually exactly right. I've been thinking of it more as a palate cleanser, or a life reset, but time-out works, too."

"That's all fine and good," Erin said, pointing mock-sternly at Nora. "But don't forget the *other* point of being here. Saving money. Have your woo-woo feelings, but save your pennies while you're doing it."

"Right." Nora turned to Jake. "My sister and her kids and I are going to get a house together in a couple years."

He remembered that from the salon, from the first day they'd met.

"Now that she doesn't have to live with Doofus—oops, I mean Rufus—anymore, we're going to pool our resources," Erin said.

"My grandma lived next door to us when we were kids." Nora cuddled up to her grandma on the sofa. "So we're into the whole extended-family-in-close-proximity thing."

Dr. Walsh smirked as she kissed Nora's head. "This is the part where I should probably invite you girls to move in with me, but my condo is small, and honestly, I got the whole extended-family-in-close-proximity thing out of my system."

Erin shook her head affectionately. "I hate to be the party

pooper, but we should go." She turned to her grandmother. "You have your group this evening."

"Cancer survivors support group," Dr. Walsh said to Jake. She rolled her eyes. "Honestly. In my day they cut out your tumor, blasted you with chemo, and called it a day. Now, they want you to talk about your feelings nonstop."

"My mom died of cancer," he said. Because apparently the Walsh family had the effect of making him blurt out his tales of woe and dead relatives.

"What kind?" Dr. Walsh asked.

"Breast."

She nodded. "Same here. It's a bitch."

"It really is." He still remembered the cutting news of his mom's diagnosis, coming so soon after Jude died. Grief layered on grief.

"All right, Mr. Pack Mule Knight in Shining Armor." Dr. Walsh held her arms out to him. "Get me out of here. I have to go talk about my feelings about my missing boobs."

He chuckled and did as she asked. Erin ran ahead and opened the car door. Just as he was about to set Dr. Walsh on her feet, she tugged his head down so his ear was next to her mouth.

"She's not as tough as she seems. You take care of her, okay, Jake?"

"Yeah," he whispered. "You got it."

Nora jogged down the steps, and hugs and farewells were exchanged. Soon she was waving at the car as it backed out of the driveway.

"Sorry," she said. "My grandmother is a force."

"Nah, she's great."

"She is great. Honestly, I think I miss her more than anyone else in Toronto. She was widowed early—that's why she lived with us when I was growing up. So she was like a second mother. Except, you know, the kind who made you practice stitches on a banana when you were eleven."

The car disappeared around a corner at the end of the block, and Nora turned back to the house. "What do you say we splash some bourbon into that lemonade and sit for a bit?"

"I say that sounds like a great idea."

Once they were settled on the deck, she heaved a sigh. "Oh my God, I'm exhausted. I had no idea getting the clinic ready was going to be such a production." She suddenly perked up. "But you know what?"

"What?"

"I was telling Karl Andersen about the chair we painted, saying how well it turned out and how I wished I had another one, because *one* chair is sort of sad. Well, he shows up early this morning with another one! Like, not exactly the same kind, but same vintage, you know? Metal, with those swooshy armrest things. I left it at the clinic because I had my sister and grandma arriving, but I'm totally going to paint it to match that one"—she pointed—"now that I know how."

"You remember when you asked me why everyone was being so nice to you?" he asked, thinking back to his aborted trip to the bar a week ago. "You asked me what the catch was. The catch is that a large proportion of this town will be all up in your business the moment you give them an inch."

"Yeah, I heard. I also heard that one of these meddlers is your dad."

"My dad is like one of those old guys who retired and didn't know what to do with himself, so he started hanging out with this crew of old folks at the hardware store a couple years ago. A year after that, bam, he had a new wife." She shot a worried glance at him, and he rushed to clarify. "Which is a good thing. She's good for him and to him. I like her a lot. My point was just that yeah, they got to him and now he's one of them."

"You make it sound like zombies."

He barked a laugh. He wasn't used to laughing, but Nora sometimes had the most spot-on rejoinders. "It's exactly like zombies."

"Well, I've been warned about them already, but this chair thing made me think that maybe a meddling pack of old people could be exploited for good. I mean, can I just tell Karl or Pearl that I'm, say, missing my mom's chili, and voilà, I'll suddenly have chili?"

He smiled. "Probably, but you should remember that they'll be playing a long game. They might give you chairs and chili, but it will be in service of a larger scheme to trap you here. You're only planning to stay two years, right?"

While they drank, she told him she was taking advantage of a program that would help her get rid of her student debt and that since the cost of living was so much lower here, she was hoping to save a bunch of money to help with the down payment she and her sister would need. She smirked. "Well, it's partly that. There's *also* the part where I fled my entire life after it imploded."

"The new chapter," he said, thinking back to her using that phrase when they were talking about the Tigers.

"Exactly. Anyway, my point is that I've been very open with everyone, including Pearl and Karl, about the fact that I have a two-year lease on the clinic. I'm gonna get my head on straight, pay down my debt, and then I'm leaving."

"That's what you say now."

"What are they going to do? Tie me up?"

"No, but they'll try to make you put roots down however

they can, including, probably, by trying to matchmake you with someone." He didn't outright tell her that "someone" was Jason Sims. She'd figure it out soon enough.

"A hard no to that." She made a jokey retching noise. "I'm definitely *not* in relationship mode right now." Her eyes narrowed. "Wait. Was the deck part of this? Is the fence part of this?" She pointed at him. "Are *you* a secret agent of the town busybodies?"

"Nope. I stay out of it. We have an unspoken truce. They leave me alone. I think they think I'm beyond help with my tragic history and all."

"Oh, right. Of course. Sorry."

He shrugged. "Don't be. I'm basically the only person in town they don't try to mess with." He huffed a bitter laugh. "I guess that's the one perk of having a dead kid."

He waited for a hint that the waves were coming. For the feeling that he needed to get out of here, to go home and sit by the lake and be with his boy and try to hold off the waves—or at least anchor himself to endure them. He had become familiar enough with this feeling to know that certain sets of circumstances triggered it. One of them was heavier-than-usual doses of socializing. And Nora's family, for him, had been a heavier-than-usual dose of socializing.

The feeling—that warning bell of a feeling—didn't come.

Another one did, though. That feeling of communion he sometimes had at home, only occasionally, only when he was very, very lucky. It was a sense that Jude was here somehow, even though Jake knew, objectively, that was ridiculous.

But the point was, Nora's presence didn't preclude that feeling. Being here in her backyard, instead of by the lake, didn't preclude it. There wasn't a precedent for that.

Nora laid her palm on the back of his hand. "I don't think there are any perks to having a dead kid."

"No. No, there aren't." He paused and took in her small fingers, tipped with short, slightly squared nails. Everyone was always telling him that he needed to learn how to cope with his loss. They had all kinds of bullshit phrases that sounded nice but didn't actually *mean* anything. *Move through your grief. Let go.* What those people, suffocating him with their grasping and scheming, didn't understand was that he didn't need to move on. He needed to *hold on*, even if holding on came with a cost. Came with the waves. "Some people try to see silver linings," he said. "They talk about God's plan or God opening a window or some shit."

She moved her hand to pick up her lemonade. He kind of wanted her not to do that. He kind of wanted her to keep resting that small, capable hand on top of his.

She took a sip of her lemonade. "Well, fuck those people."

He smiled. Exactly.

When Jake got home late that night, Eve and Sawyer were swimming in the lake near his house. Jake lived in a little cottage on the beach in a small, hidden cove. His grandparents had built the place back when the town was a lot smaller than it was today. They, and later his parents, had treated it as a sort of getaway, visiting mostly on the weekends. Probably because getting to Paradise Cove was a bit of a production. The only way in was on foot, and you had to walk out and around a rocky outcropping that separated the cove from the lake proper.

He had followed in their footsteps initially, keeping a place in town and coming to the cottage with Kerrie and

Jude to watch the odd sunset. Kerrie had always been more of a people person, and the isolation got to her. The same way he needed quiet to feel okay, Kerrie had thrived off the energy of other people. But once she'd gone back to work, he and Jude and Daisy had come here almost every day, splashing in the shallows and retreating inside for stories and lunch when the sun got too strong.

Then, when Jude and Kerrie were both gone, he'd moved out here for good.

"Hey." Sawyer was wading in to shore.

"Don't mind me," Jake said, heading for the cottage. He, like his parents before him, didn't mind townspeople using the beach. Sawyer had taught Eve how to swim here last year, and he suspected the two of them had mushy feelings about the place—which he had no desire to know about. He was all for them taking a moonlight swim, but he didn't need to witness it.

"We missed you at the bar tonight."

Oh, shit. It was Friday. He'd completely forgotten.

Well, he hadn't *forgotten*. He'd known it was Friday— or he'd started the day knowing it was Friday, anyway. He'd finished installing some built-in shelves in Bayshore and had gone to Nora's place intending to finish the fence and head downtown to Law's.

But then Nora's family happened. *She* happened. And apparently, all his plans just evaporated from his brain.

"Yeah, I didn't feel like it tonight."

Which wasn't really a lie. What he had felt like doing tonight was sitting on Nora's deck, the deck he'd built for her, and listening to her say, "Fuck those people." They'd spent the whole evening out there, talking as they watched the stars come out.

"A bunch of us are going out on Law's boat tomorrow.

We thought we'd introduce Nora Walsh to some people beyond the usual Friday-night crew. Make her feel welcome.
I know you never want to come to this kind of stuff, but
you know I'm going to persist in inviting you."

"What time?"

Sawyer raised his eyebrows. "Four. At the marina."

Eve splashed up. "Are you coming?" She and Sawyer
shared a look Jake couldn't decode.

"Yeah, sure," he said. "I don't have anything better to do."

By the next weekend—the long Labor Day weekend—
Nora was beginning to think that there were two versions
of Jake. There was Friend Jake, who, although he was far
from chatty, was thoughtful and, she would even go so far
as to say, charming in his own quiet, low-key way.

Then there was Public Jake. Public Jake didn't talk
unless he was asked a direct question. On the boat ride last
weekend, for example, he'd been as silent and grumpy as
the one time they'd overlapped at the bar.

And today, the day of the infamous Mermaid Parade, he
was practically mute, to use Maya's characterization.

But to be fair, maybe that was because he was busy.
On the boat ride, he had agreed to be the brawn to Maya's
brains—Maya had been cooking up schemes for the vaccine
information table Nora was planning for outside the clinic.
She was really gung ho about designing it, and frankly,
Nora was happy to let her run with it.

The funny thing was that there were a few different
ways a person could interpret *vaccine information table*.
Nora had—call her crazy—imagined a table. With some
information. And yes, probably some pretty signs or maybe
even some balloons.

Maya, however, had interpreted *vaccine information*

table by sourcing a nearly dead used van from this guy Jordan who owned an auto shop in town. She had enlisted Pearl to help paint and decorate it, though the word *decorate* did not seem to do justice to what had occurred.

"Welcome to the Vaccine Machine!" Maya exclaimed, waving her arms in the air like a game-show hostess.

"The concept is based on the Mystery Machine from *Scooby-Doo*," Pearl said while Nora stood there with her mouth hanging open, "But with mermaids."

"Mermaids getting shots," Maya added.

The outlandishness of the van, they theorized, would attract attention. They were not wrong about that.

"Wow," Nora said. The van was painted aqua and lime green, like its *Scooby-Doo* namesake. But it was also painted with mermaids—mermaids getting shots, just as Maya had promised/threatened.

"Oh my," Eve said, laughter in her voice—the bar crowd was on hand for the unveiling. "This sure is...something."

Law snorted.

"Just wait," Maya said. "It gets better. It's not fully set up yet."

Jake appeared, dragging what appeared to be a wooden arch that had been painted a deep blue.

"Come check out the inside while Jake finishes getting it ready." Maya opened the rear door. "We removed the seats and built a little exam 'room.' Well, by 'we,' I mean Jake."

"Wow," Nora said again. It seemed to be the only word she could summon when it came to this crazy van. She glanced at Jake. He was attaching the arch to the top of the van.

"I know you're not going to give shots today," Maya continued, "but I thought in the future, you could drive it around."

"Hang on now. That might be a long shot," Pearl said. "It barely made it here."

"We can find you a mini refrigerator that you plug into the lighter, and you can be a mobile clinic," Maya said, ignoring Pearl. "Like the ice cream truck!"

"Except instead of dispensing tasty treats, she'll stab people with needles," Law said.

"Oh, shut up, *Benjamin*."

"Don't you need to go get ready for the parade, Queen Maya?" Law asked.

"No, *Benjamin*, because at this point I can do it in my sleep, thanks to you and your machinations." She turned to Nora. "This jerk has gotten me elected mermaid queen three years running now."

"And you don't want to be mermaid queen?"

"Would you, a grown professional woman, want to be mermaid queen?"

"I see your point," Nora said, although she wasn't the one who'd designed a mermaid-mobile.

"Okay, so one version of this thing is the mobile clinic," Maya said.

"Again, I just want to point out that mobility might be a little ambitious," Pearl said.

Maya continued to ignore Pearl as she led them back around to look at the outside of the van. "The other version is a display of sorts, for at events like this where you're just going to be parked. Jake installed brackets on the van and built this arch thing with slots in it. The arch is the base, and we insert event-specific signs on it as needed."

She pointed at Pearl, who produced two pieces of plywood. One was a brightly colored sign that said, "Get a booster." The other was a mermaid smiling atop a rocket.

"So this is for today, when you're going to give Sawyer his booster shot," Pearl said, "and hand out info about the MMR vaccine."

"But we can swap these out for other ones in the future," Maya said. "'Keep your health pristine, get your vaccines,' could be a general one."

"'Fight the flu, it starts with you,'" Pearl said. "For the Anti-Festival."

Nora glanced at Jake to see if the mention of the flu had made him uncomfortable, but he was just silently attaching the signs to the arch he'd already braced to the van. The result was . . .

"Amazing." Ridiculous, but amazing. She was certainly going to get people's attention.

Finished with the installation, Jake climbed down the stepladder he'd been standing on and winked at her. He found the whole thing ridiculous, too, she was pretty sure.

"Jake." Maya pressed her hands to her heart as she admired their creation. "You. Are. The. *Best.*"

Jake didn't answer—he hadn't said a word the whole morning—just started dragging the ladder away.

Nora had to agree, though. Jake was indeed the best.

Chapter Eight

❧

*J*ake didn't have people over to his place. Letting them use the beach—*ignoring* them while they used the beach— fine. And sometimes Law and Sawyer came over, but that was as far as his hospitality generally extended.

Which was why it made no sense that Nora was here with him. He pulled his truck into his usual parking spot near the intersection of Locust and Sarnia Streets, cut the engine, and turned to examine his passenger.

"We walk from here?" she asked.

"Yep." He was getting a weird, niggling feeling that he was making a mistake.

"Oh, I'm excited about this!"

But no. There. That was why he'd invited her over. She looked happy. She'd been running herself ragged in the month the clinic had been open, and she'd told him the other day that she was exhausted. He'd responded by impulsively inviting her over for a celebratory end-of-the-first-month dinner.

She set Mick on the ground and clipped on his leash. "I keep hearing about the mysterious Paradise Cove, but it's like it's a state secret or something."

"Yeah, this town *can* keep a secret when it suits them."

"Like the Anti-Festival thing next weekend?"

"Exactly."

"You going to it?"

"Nope."

"Not much of a festival guy?" she teased.

"Nope."

"You just build all the shit for them?"

He shrugged.

"You totally do. You're like the silent engine that makes this town go, as far as I can see."

"Nah."

"Face it, Jake. You're the strong, silent, heroic type."

"How's your grandma?" he asked, by way of deflection but also because he was genuinely interested. Nora had told him more about her family in the last few weeks, over a handful of dinners they'd shared while he'd been working on her place—she always insisted on feeding him. Since she wasn't actually cooking, he generally took her up on it. He didn't want her to go out of her way, but he'd happily eat a piece of pizza with her.

"Grandma says she's fine, but I don't know if I believe her. She's sort of stoic and silent. Like someone else I know." She bumped his shoulder with hers as they walked. "When anyone asks her how she's doing, she stonewalls."

"What do they say? Doctors make the worst patients?"

"Exactly. She's eighty-seven. The chemo really

weakened her. I know it takes a long time, but I don't feel like she's bouncing back like I would have expected. But I admit I might be guilty of believing she's invincible."

"I think maybe everyone thinks that about their parents to a certain extent. I remember when my mom got diagnosed, I thought, *Well, this sucks, but it will be okay.*"

"But it wasn't."

She hadn't phrased it as a question—that was Nora for you: good at not prying—but he answered it anyway. "Nope. It turned out to be stage four." They walked in silence for a few moments, crossing the grassy stretch that extended toward the lake. "The stupid thing is, I thought, *Well, Jude died a year ago, so my mom isn't going to die, too.* I honestly thought that. Like you don't win the lottery twice. Or *lose* the lottery, I guess. It's embarrassing to admit, because it's totally nonsensical."

"It is and it isn't. Having worked in an emergency room, I can tell you it's normal. Our human minds try to impose order, or patterns, on the randomness of the universe. Not to get too woo-woo, but I think it's what makes us human. We try to see meaning where there isn't any."

"Or justice where there isn't any," he said, thinking back to how ripped off he'd felt when they'd had to face the fact that his mom wasn't going to make it.

"Or justice when there isn't any," she echoed. "That's exactly right."

They walked on, Mick's wheezy breathing the only sound. He liked that she didn't mind silence. She didn't pepper him with questions. She asked questions, great questions, but in context and at the right time and in the right doses.

Soon they reached the beach. "I suggest you swap your shoes."

"You leave boots here?" she exclaimed.

He did. He had an old, cruddy pair he left here for himself, but in anticipation of her visit, he'd dug out Kerrie's old rubber boots and stashed them here with his on his way out this morning.

Was it weird to be offering Nora his ex-wife's boots?

No. Why would it be weird? It wasn't like she was his girlfriend.

"These will probably be too big." Kerrie had been a lot taller than Nora. "But they should do the trick." She donned the boots, and he shifted his shopping bags to one arm. "You want me to carry Mick?"

"Nah, I got him. He only weighs eleven pounds."

"I have to say, before I met Mick, I didn't know basset hounds came in miniature."

"Well, it's kind of unclear if they actually do. Rufus paid four grand for him from some guy who called him a 'designer dog.'" She kissed one of Mick's ears as they stepped into the lake. "And you were worth every penny," she cooed. "But the vet told us that it's not a distinct breed, and that they're made from breeding runts or breeding bassets with other, smaller breeds. Who knows? Who cares?" They followed the line of rock out into the lake until it ended. It was kind of fun to splash through the shallow water in boots. "It's just around here."

She stepped out from behind the outcropping and stopped while she was still in the water, blinking rapidly. She exhaled a breathy little sigh. And inhaled as a smile blossomed. "Jake Ramsey. Are you *kidding* me?" She swatted his arm.

He tried to see the scene through her eyes, through new eyes. It *was* pretty damn picturesque. The cove itself created a solid wall of rock that enclosed a small beach.

His cottage was on the far side, small but tidy, with a deck facing the lake. You could *definitely* hear the waves from his deck, though they were only lapping gently at the moment—it was a still evening. The overall effect was of being cozily tucked away with what felt like your own personal Great Lake.

"This is *amazing*!" Nora exclaimed—and Nora wasn't naturally the exclaiming type. She loped ahead of him, set Mick down on the beach, and turned in a slow circle, taking in the whole scene. "I can't believe you *live* here!"

Her approval felt good. Not that he required it. But he had a lot of respect for Nora, so it was gratifying that she liked his home. "Yeah, it can be kind of a pain to have to walk to your house, but I think it's worth it."

"Totally worth it," she enthused. "It makes it better, even. It's like you have to work for your payoff, which I bet makes you appreciate it all the more."

Exactly.

"Well, come on in." He led the way up the steps—the cottage was built on short stilts. "It's not much, but it's home."

"You want me to leave Mick out here?"

"No, no, bring him in."

"Holy crap!" Her reaction to the inside was as effusive as her reaction to the setting.

He grinned. "I think I told you that my mom was an artist."

"You did, but...holy crap."

Every available chunk of wall was covered with his mom's paintings. Some of them were the landscapes she'd made her name on, but there were also lots of less formal works, including portraits of Jake and his brother at various ages. The place was an explosion of art and color but not overly curated. Because the cottage hadn't been anyone's permanent home in his mom's era, she'd just thrown things on the walls willy-nilly. It had become the home for her "rejects," pieces she wasn't sure about or wasn't sure she was done with. The individual paintings were nice enough, but the aggregate effect was really something—again, especially when he tried to view the place through fresh eyes.

Nora walked right over to a big painting near the door to the deck. "Is this Jude?"

"Yeah." It was of Jude, but his mom had set him in outer space—she'd always played with themes of magic and eternity, especially closer to the end of her life, when she'd known her diagnosis was terminal but had still been able to work. In this one, Jude was grinning as he floated among stars and nebulae. "She did that after he died."

"It's beautiful. Not in a flowery, sympathy-card sort of way, but in a real way, you know?"

"Yeah." That was part of why he missed his mom so much. Like Nora, she had been able to face the horrible things in life with clear eyes. She had been a rock after Jude died, which was part of why her death had hit him so hard. He moved to the kitchen and had to clear his throat. "How do you feel about trout?"

"I feel great about trout."

He unpacked the big salad he'd bought from Sadie's Diner and got the fish out of the fridge where it had been marinating. "I caught these this morning, so they're fresh. I thought we'd grill them outside." He paused with the fridge open. "I have wine or beer. I also have bourbon if you'd rather." He didn't generally stock bourbon, but he'd bought some for her. He didn't generally stock anything, for that matter, unless Sawyer and Law were coming over, because he didn't drink alone at home. After Jude died and Kerrie left, he'd made a conscious decision to keep his drinking social, which meant mostly at Lawson's Lager House. It seemed like it might be too easy, otherwise, to let himself slip into oblivion.

"Wine would be great." She nodded at his full hands. "You want me to get it?"

"Sure. Thanks. I'll have a glass, too."

Soon they were outside, and he was firing up the grill. "I should warn you that this is an old-school charcoal grill, so it's going to take a while for the coals to be ready."

"I brought snacks!" She ducked back into the house after she'd set two glasses of wine on the outdoor table. She returned with a bag of nuts from Jenna's General and a cluster of grapes. "I think it should be fine to let Mick loose. He's afraid of water, so he can't really get in or out of the cove." As soon as she let him off his leash, Mick lumbered down to the beach and started snuffling around.

After Jake was done lighting the coals, he joined her at the table. He had designed the deck with a built-in bench that spanned one side. The table was arranged so that if you sat on the bench, you could look at the lake. Nora was sitting on the bench. He had chairs on the other side of the table—he supposed so that in theory, he could have people over for dinner and have enough seating. Sometimes he and Law and Sawyer sat around this table.

So he should sit on one of those chairs, across from Nora.

But he did not. He sat next to her on the bench.

"Here's to one month under your belt, Dr. Walsh." He lifted his glass and clinked it against hers. "How does it feel?"

"It feels exhausting." She toasted with him. "Though I guess that's good. We're pretty much booked solid most days. And I pulled some stats. In the month since the

Mermaid Parade, I've done a dozen MMR boosters and seen two families who'd been hesitant but decided to bring their kids in to start the schedule. I totally put that down to you guys and your crazy van."

"Not my crazy van. Maya and Pearl get the credit. I was just the muscle."

"Well, I've come to understand recently—the hard way—that actions speak louder than words, so you're just going to have to live with some of the credit."

She was talking about that dirtbag Rufus. Thinking about what he'd done to Nora made Jake angry. But, simultaneously, being compared to Rufus and coming out on top made him feel good.

She was confusing.

Even more confusing? When she said, "Still. I'm beat," heaved a huge sigh, and let her head fall onto his shoulder.

It was not even remotely a sexual, or romantic, gesture. It was companionable. They had become genuinely close in the six or so weeks she'd been here. For some reason he hadn't bothered examining, he had clicked with her. She was smart and funny, and she didn't do false sentiment.

She was his friend. They were *friends*.

He allowed himself to consider the nagging feeling he'd had earlier, when they'd gotten out of the truck and started the trek into the cove, that he had a problem. He'd thought, then, that bringing Nora here was kind of unprecedented. He didn't do that.

So what did it mean that he had?

What did it mean that he wanted to put his arm around her? To encourage her to lean into him and rest?

She had woken him up. Woken his *body* up. He was intensely, viscerally aware of her at all times. Of where she was, and of how much distance there was between them. Like when he was working on her fence and she got home, he could tell she was about to appear from behind the house before she did. When she opened the pizza boxes she often brought home with her, he watched her small, efficient hands and imagined them pressing a stethoscope to a chest. Imagined them pressing against a chest *without* the stethoscope.

Sawyer and Law had tried to give him a phone a couple years ago. They'd staged an intervention and said it was time to get on some dating or hookup apps. He had shut that right down. He didn't want a phone. He didn't want apps. He didn't want *people*. He could take care of things by himself in the shower when the need arose. It was a mechanical problem to be solved dispassionately.

The problem that had been niggling, and that was now making itself more overtly known in his consciousness, was that Nora made him feel things that were *not* mechanical.

He didn't put his arm around her, but it was a close thing.

Nora had a problem, and that problem was that she wanted to jump Jake.

Her sister had told her, today in fact, that this *wasn't* a problem. "That is one fine specimen of human male, Nor," she'd said during a FaceTime. Nora had not brought this up; Erin had. "I mean, could you *do* better for a rebound fling? But you make sure it's just a fling, because I have a bunch of house listings to send you."

Nora had declared her Moonflower Bay time-out a "no boys" zone, but she hadn't actually thought through what that meant. Certainly it meant no boyfriends. And no dating, because dating was how a person ended up with a boy-friend. Just like she was keeping her house mostly empty, she didn't want to clutter up her life or her brain with other people's junk. She didn't want to have to please anyone but herself—and she was still figuring out what that meant.

One thing she hadn't really taken into account as she'd thought through the life reset was the concept of casual sex. Mostly because she hadn't really had much of it in her life. She was more of a serial monogamist.

She was pretty sure she wanted a husband and kids someday, so at some point she was going to have to get back on the horse. Just not yet.

But... did she have to take a breather from sex itself?

When her sister and some of her hospital friends had suggested she go out on the prowl and have some revenge sex, she'd laughed. The idea had actively repulsed her.

But then there was Jake. Sneaking up on her. Strong, steady, gruff, kind, gorgeous Jake who *also* did not want a relationship.

The thing about Jake, though, was that in addition to all that, he was damaged. He was hurt, perhaps irreparably, by all that had happened to him. That wasn't a recipe for a clean rebound fling. And, perhaps more to the point, he was her *friend*. He had never given her any indication that he thought of her as more than that.

So yeah, if there was going to be any no-strings-attached-ing, it wasn't going to be with Jake.

Which was too bad, because she really, really wanted to jump him.

So all she could do was lean against him—in a totally platonic way—and sigh.

But that wasn't nothing. And this cove felt like a perfect little secret the universe had deigned to reveal to her. She was sitting in maybe the prettiest place she'd ever seen, watching the October sun paint pink stripes across the sky, while her friend—a good, true man—cooked her fish he'd caught himself. She sighed again, but tried to make it a more contented one.

"You okay?"

"Yeah. I was just thinking that *this* is exactly what I imagined as a best-case scenario when I decided to come to Moonflower Bay."

"Yeah?"

"I mean, not *this* exactly, but I had this idea of getting out of my own head, right? I had this romantic notion of standing next to a Great Lake—living next to a Great Lake—being a curative, somehow. Like, it would be beautiful but also...I don't know, powerful. Capable of scouring me clean." She lifted her head from his shoulder and shook it. "Listen to me, all hippie-dippy. I sound like Wynd."

"No. I know what you mean. The lake can be pretty, like it is right now, but you should see it in a storm. It's raw, merciless power then. You look at it for long enough, in enough different moods, and you do sort of start to think of it as a force. As something with the power to change you."

"To heal you, you think?"

"No. Not that. It's a sort of temporary comfort *because* it's so indifferent. Whatever happens, the lake goes on."

"Even when people don't."

"Even when people don't," he echoed.

She stood and walked to the edge of the deck, picking up her wine along the way. "So you used to fish commercially?"

"Yeah, my dad and his dad before him fished this lake. I grew up on my dad's boat, and he formally cut me in when I graduated high school. I told you Kerrie went back to work when Jude was three months old?"

She nodded. She had wondered about that. Canada

offered a one-year parental leave program, and most women took the whole year.

"Once she went back, we agreed that I'd take the rest of the leave and look after him until he was one," Jake went on. "It just made more sense because she earned a lot more money than I did. So he and I were going to hang out until he was one, then he was going to go to day care, I was going to go back to work, and Dad was going to retire."

"And then Jude died and so much for that plan?" He didn't answer right away, so she turned back to look at him. "I'm sorry. That was too blunt."

He shook his head. "No. I like blunt. Everyone always walks on eggshells around the topic. I was just thinking about how to answer. All I know is I didn't want to go out on the boat afterward. I did, a bit, but when Sawyer and I started the carpentry business, it did well from the start. Also, when my mom died, she left her estate to me and my brother. You can't tell from this"—he waved a hand back at the cottage—"but she did really well. Financially, I mean. She lived a modest life, but she had dealers in Toronto and New York."

"Wow."

"And I don't have any expenses, really. I live here rent-free, though I keep trying to get my brother to take some kind of buyout."

"And you get your hair cut for free."

He chuckled. "Exactly."

He turned to stare at the last of the sunset. "I never really thought about it this way, but I think I stopped wanting to fish because I always imagined Jude and I would do it together someday. He loved the water. You know how some people stick a baby in the car and drive them around to get them to calm down?"

"Yes. I've heard lots of stories like that both from my sister and from patients."

He pointed to a rack near the foot of the deck that contained a canoe. "I'd take him out in the canoe. I rigged it so I could snap the car seat into it. We'd get going, and he'd conk right out. I'll admit I probably had a romantic notion of this unbroken line of Ramsey men fishing the lake. And then Jude was gone, and...I don't know." He shook his head like he was disgusted with himself.

"You lost your vision of the future along with your son," Nora said softly.

"I never thought about it like that, but yeah, I think so. And Kerrie didn't want me going out at first. She had this irrational fear that I was going to die, too, so she didn't like it when I was away all day, especially out on the lake. And for the record, I don't say 'irrational' like I'm dismissing it. We all reacted in our own ways. I respected it."

She wanted to ask what had happened with Kerrie. She knew, intellectually, that the stats on marriages surviving the death of a child were not great. But it sounded like Kerrie had clung to Jake, at least initially. She also found herself intensely curious over what kind of woman Jake would marry.

"I really only go out on the fishing rig—it's in a marina up the river a ways—once a week these days, and even that only because people expect it."

"What do you mean, people expect it?"

"My dad used to pull the boat up to the pier on the little beach every Tuesday afternoon and sell to the townspeople directly. So I do, too. I don't want to let people down."

Wow, this guy was honorable to a fault. "I think people would survive without your fish."

He smirked. "Yeah, but then they'd get their fish from the grocery store."

"Again, I'm going to go with: I think they'd survive."

He got up, went to the grill, and picked up a pair of tongs. "After you taste my fish, you'll see."

Chapter Nine

❧

$\mathscr{A}$ few days later, Nora pushed open the door to Lakeside Hardware before opening the clinic. Four sets of eyes swung toward her as she made her way into the dim, old-school store stocked floor to ceiling with all sorts of hardware.

"Good morning," she said, wishing she'd changed first. She had taken to getting up early, driving to the clinic, and going for a run before starting her workday. She was suddenly aware of how hot and sweaty and unprofessional she looked.

"Nora." Karl greeted her. "Nice to see you. I know you know Pearl, but have you met everyone else?"

"Eiko Anzai." The woman next to Pearl waved. "We met at the salon your first day in town."

"You're the newspaper editor."

"And you're the new doctor who was supposed to contact me about an interview."

"Right. Sorry about that. I hit the ground running trying

to get the clinic ready to open, and things have been busier than I expected now that I am open." But actually, maybe now would be a good time for an interview. She and Amber and Wynd were starting to hit their stride, and work was feeling slightly less all-consuming. And the exposure a newspaper article would provide would be good.

But, thinking of Jake's warning about the town busy-body network, she kept her mouth shut.

Karl gestured to the other man sitting on the patio furniture display the group was occupying. "This is Arthur Ramsey."

"Oh! You're Jake's dad!" He looked a little like Jake. They had the same green eyes and big build.

"You know Jake?" Art's brow furrowed in a way that made Nora wonder if he didn't approve of her.

"Um, yes. He's doing some work on my house." *And my clinic. And my ridiculous vaccine-mobile.*

And I was totally platonically cuddling with him at his house Saturday night.

"What can I do for you?" Karl asked.

"Well, I'm not here for hardware. I'm actually here to ask you a favor. I understand this is sort of the unofficial community center in town?" Karl flashed her a huge grin—he seemed to like that interpretation. "I'm planning a flu-shot clinic at the Anti-Festival, and I was hoping I could leave some flyers here to let people know about it."

Karl started to take the stack of flyers, but Pearl laid her hand on his arm and halted his progress. "Dr. Walsh, did you know there's a town bachelor auction as part of the festival?"

"I heard something about that."

"This year it's going to be a bachelor and *bachelorette* auction," Eiko said mildly, but she looked at Karl while she spoke, and he retracted his hand without taking Nora's flyers.

"*Oh*," Pearl said. "And she's a *catch*."

Uh-oh. "It's nice of you to think of me, but I'm not really looking for—"

"It's very casual," Eiko said. "Entrants have lunch with the suitor who wins them. So you don't have to do anything but stand there and watch the gents compete for your favor. And then they feed you!"

"Suitor"? "Gents"? Had she time-traveled back to the nineteenth century?

"Or ladies," Pearl said. "You tell us which, and we'll do our thing."

So maybe *not* the nineteenth century.

"The auction is how I met my wife," Art said.

"I'm so glad we took Maya's advice and widened the proceedings to include bachelorettes," Pearl said. "She was right last year when she said we were being sexist."

"I totally agree, Pearl," Karl said. "And I happen to know that Dennis Bates is already working on his lunch hamper."

"*I'm* not going to be in the auction," Pearl said. "I'm *running* the whole festival. I don't have time to be in the auction. Anyway, I've told you a thousand times, I will *never* date anyone in this town."

"Dennis Bates has an enormous crush on Pearl, but she continually rebuffs him," Eiko explained matter-of-factly to Nora.

"Dennis Bates who runs the lift bridge?" Nora asked, though she wasn't sure why. Her aim here was not to get sucked into the town gossip network, merely to leave her flyers. "Anyway," she said before anyone could answer, "could I leave these here?"

"You can leave those here if you stand in the auction," Karl said.

Uh, *what*? She blinked. Was this sweet old man *bribing* her?

"He's bribing you," Art said helpfully. "He does that."

"You really won't let me leave these here?" Nora said.

"I will let you leave those here if you stand in the auction," Karl said.

So much for a simple favor.

"It's for a good cause," Art said. "It raises money for the town library and food bank."

"Still, I—"

"Who doesn't love a picnic?" Eiko said. "You could meet some nice local boy."

"Or girl," Pearl said.

"I'm *really* not looking to get involved with anyone. I'm only planning to be here two years."

"I'll give you a free ad in the newspaper if you stand in the auction," Eiko said.

Oh, for God's sake.

Although she was a little bit impressed. She'd thought she was playing these people. That she would come here and exploit their goodwill and their desire to keep her in town and get them to give away her flyers.

But who was playing whom here? Jake had been right to tell her to watch her back.

"It's just lunch," Pearl said.

Nora sighed.

Pearl, correctly interpreting it as a sigh of capitulation, clapped her hands. "Yay! You are going to be our crown jewel."

"Well, thanks, I guess, but I think you overestimate my

draw. I just got here. No one knows me. Who's going to bid on me?"

The chimes on the door tinkled, and in walked Jake.

Everyone said hello to Jake, who raised his hand silently in greeting and gave his father an extra nod. "I was hoping one of you knew how to get in touch with Harold..." He trailed off when he noticed her. "Oh. Hi."

"Hi."

"Hi," he said again.

Nora's skin started to prickle. She could feel everyone's eyes on them—she felt like they were zoo animals. She just couldn't figure out why. All they had done was greet each other politely.

"Harold Burgess?" Karl finally said. "Was that what you were asking? How to get in touch with Harold Burgess?"

"I know how to get in touch with Harold Burgess," Nora said slowly, feeling like she was missing something. "Assuming we're talking about Harold Burgess my landlord?"

"Right." Jake shifted his weight from one foot to the other, none of his signature steadiness in evidence. "I actually need to talk to you, too."

"You do?" Eiko asked, glancing at Pearl, who coughed.

"Yeah, it's about your house." Jake stopped shuffling, but his eyes darted around like he was looking for an escape. Maybe he had the in-the-zoo feeling, too?

"Well," she said, "I have my first patient in thirty minutes. I have to get out of these gross running clothes. You want to walk with me to the clinic?"

He nodded and held the door for her. As she followed him out, Pearl called after them, "Be good, kids."

*   *   *

"Gross running clothes" was not how Jake would have described what Nora was wearing. She had on form-fitting, black running tights and a bright-green tank top. She looked like an ad for an athletic magazine.

"I didn't realize you were a runner." He'd known she was getting up and out early these days—he had been seizing the opportunity to do some early-morning work on her house before other jobs, so they sometimes said a quick hello as he was arriving and she was leaving—but he'd thought she was just going to the clinic.

"I'm not. I'm doing this couch-to-5K training system that's supposed to train you to run a 5K. But I'm so out of shape, I'm winded after like five minutes."

"Out of shape" was another phrase he would not have used to describe Nora. Her legs weren't long— she was short enough that nothing about her was long— but he was pretty sure he could span the entirety of one of her thighs with his hands. Theoretically. And he was going to hell, but as she strode up the sidewalk ahead of him, her ass, which was small and round and perfect, bounced.

"I have good genes, and I'm petite, so I pass for a fit person. But I'm actually not. One of the goals in the whole life-change thing was to work less so I could exercise." She wrinkled her nose. "I hate running."

"You should take up kayaking, or canoeing, or something that involves the lake. You like the lake, right?"

"I was thinking that. Or even walking on the beach."

"What happened to the Tigers?"

She paused in unlocking her clinic, her brow furrowed. "What do you mean?"

Yeah, that had been a non sequitur from her point of view. "I was just thinking that had also been one of your goals in moving here. You wanted to go to Tigers games. But isn't the regular season almost over?"

"It's totally over. I dropped the ball on that one."

Well, crap. In his quest to fix Nora's house and build her vaccine van monstrosity, he'd forgotten about the Tigers. He would happily have driven to a game with her.

Whoa. He would *happily* have driven to a game with her?

That was more than a little weird. He didn't follow baseball. The last time he'd been to the States had been before Jude was born, when he'd tagged along with Kerrie to a law conference in Cleveland. He hadn't even been as far as Toronto in recent memory.

She ushered him into the dark clinic, and he followed her to the back, where she had an office.

She rummaged through a bag and pulled out a dress. "So you want to get a hold of Harold? Why wouldn't you just ask me?"

Right. "I have some bad news."

She paused, holding a stick of deodorant she'd unearthed from her bag. "Okay."

Nora struck him as the kind of person who didn't like things sugarcoated. So he just came out with it. "There's black mold all over your bathroom. And probably beyond. I knocked out the tile in the tub this morning to see how far it went, and I think it extends past the bathroom. The only way to be sure is to start taking down walls."

She blinked rapidly as she set the deodorant on her desk. "I thought you were just recaulking the tub."

Yeah. Even though he'd worn her down on the topic of interior improvements in her house, he'd only done so by downplaying how much he was actually doing. "I'm sorry. I should have called you. But there was a cracked tile. I found a stack of spare tiles in the basement, so I was just going to replace the one. I pulled it up, and..."

"And now I have no tub."

"Yeah, but more to the point, now you have a house that is not habitable. I think it's behind the wallpaper in the hallway and your bedroom, too." She seemed like she was going to argue with him, so he said, "Come on, you're a doctor. You know you can't live in a house with black mold."

She deflated. Actually physically slumped forward in place. It pained him. Probably more than it should have. It wasn't the end of the world. It was just a rental. But he felt bad that she was going to lose her yard where she could sometimes hear the lake.

"So you were just going to call Harold and not tell me?"

"No. I was going to tell you." He *was*. He was just..."I don't know. I wanted to speak to Harold myself." He wanted to punch Harold's lights out, actually.

She flashed him a wry smile. "Well, I guess the upside is I don't have much to pack." She looked at her watch. "I have to kick you out now. I do this poor man's shower in the mornings here now that I'm a 'runner.'" She narrowed her eyes. "And, Jake, you're the best, but I'll battle Harold myself." He nodded and had begun to leave when she called after him. "Actually, there is one thing you *can* do, if you don't mind."

He turned. Held himself back from saying, "Anything."

"Let me know if you have any ideas on places to stay short-term. Though maybe I should just go back to the hardware store and ask them." She rolled her eyes. "They seem to have an answer for everything."

They would have an answer, but God knew what it would be. He didn't trust them not to mess up her life. He wanted to invite her to stay at his place while she looked for a more permanent solution. He would clear out his mom's studio, even, make it into a second bedroom. But that was too weird. He cleared his throat. "Don't go back to the hardware store. Let me ask around a bit."

"Thanks. And I'm not picky about anything except that I need a place that's pet-friendly."

"About Mick. I actually took him with me on my way out of your place. He's in the truck. I thought I'd keep him for the day if that's okay with you? I felt bad leaving him there—the little dude wheezes enough as is."

"You sure he won't be in your way?"

"Nah. I'm out at a job site today. Big house with a fenced yard. He'll have fun."

"Jake. You are the best. Thank you."

Her praise warmed him. "No problem. I'll meet you back here at the end of the day. I actually have an idea regarding your housing situation."

An idea that was not her becoming his roommate.

Which bummed him out more than it should have.

Black mold.

Nora had managed to mostly put the whole disaster out of her mind—minus a very annoyed lunchtime voice mail to Harold—because the day had been packed. She had not allowed herself to imagine a scenario in which the clinic got going so quickly. But it turned out that the town was hungry for local medical care. Almost everyone she saw gave a little speech about how happy they were not to have to drive to Grand View or even to London to see a doctor. She and Amber had been run off their feet all day, and every time she'd popped her head into the reception area, Wynd was taking a call—and that was how it had been for weeks.

She had wondered if a family practice clinic in a small town was going to be boring. And while it wasn't the heart attacks and broken bones that had gotten her adrenaline pumping at the hospital in Toronto, she was digging the variety and the ability to get to know her patients. In the emergency department, her job had been to address the immediate problems she was presented with and either admit patients or patch them up and send them on their way. Here, she was going to be able to follow people over time— or, rather, over two years. She had seen a pair of newborn twins the other day and was looking forward to seeing them again at their next checkup.

Wynd stuck her head into Nora's office, drawing Nora from her thoughts. "Hey, Nora. Eve Abbott and Jake Ramsey are waiting for you out front, and I'm headed home."

She glanced at her watch. She'd been catching up on charting and had lost track of time. Amber had long since left. "Yeah, okay, thanks, Wynd. See you tomorrow." Jake she wasn't surprised about, but she wondered what Eve was doing here. "Actually, hang on a sec, will you?" Wynd came back. Nora didn't know how to say this. She honestly wasn't sure it was any of her business. But she'd ordered the flu vaccines for the Anti-Festival earlier in the week, and it had been on her mind. "I wanted to ask you a question. You don't have to answer it if you don't want to. But are your kids vaccinated?"

"Oh my gosh, yes."

Well, that was a relief. Wynd had a little postcard taped to the wall above her desk that said, "Mindset is Everything," and Nora hadn't been sure if she meant it literally.

"I don't think there's a single person in this town who went to Jude Ramsey's funeral who wouldn't vaccinate their kids," Wynd said uncharacteristically vehemently.

"I'm sorry for asking." And sorry she had made assumptions. "It's just that flu season is rolling around, and I've been thinking about this stuff."

"It's okay. I get it. I'm a hippie. But my kids have all their shots." She flashed Nora an irreverent grin. "Mind you, if you want to talk about fluoridated toothpaste, I will fight you. But they have all their shots."

"Nah." Nora smiled. "Let's fight about fluoride later. You go home now."

She followed Wynd into the waiting room, where her friends were waiting. "Hi, guys. What's up?"

"Hey, Nora. Jake says you're in the market for new housing."

"I am indeed. I apparently have a black mold situation."

"Well, I happen to have a room at the inn I don't know what to do with. It's yours if you want it. But fair warning: you might not want it."

"Why not?"

Jake gave a sort of snort-guffaw, and Eve said, "Seeing is believing."

A few minutes later, they were climbing the stairs to the third floor of the Mermaid Inn. "When I was a kid, I spent summers here with my great-aunt, who owned the inn before me, and this was my room," Eve said. "It's too small, and, frankly, too bonkers to rent out. Sawyer and I lived in it for a bit, but we've since moved downstairs to the owner's suite."

She swung open the door, and Nora stepped into a one-room Barbie Dreamhouse. Both the walls and the tile floor were pink—baby pink on the walls and fuchsia on the floors. "Wow."

Eve followed Nora inside. "Yeah, my aunt let me decorate it myself when I was nine."

Nora wanted to ask why the room hadn't been remodeled as part of the renovation Eve had done last year, but she didn't want to be rude.

"I should just redo it," Eve said, reading Nora's mind. "Or knock down the wall and expand the room next door, but I'm sort of weirdly emotionally attached to this room, even if I don't want to live in it anymore."

It really did look like someone had decorated with a cotton candy machine, but Nora wasn't in a position to be picky. And, hey, she could definitely walk to work from here. It was all of fifty feet to the clinic across the street. Except...

"It's great of you to offer, but I can't live here. I have a dog."

"I can take him until you find a place," Jake said.

Damn. Were there no limits to how great this guy was? She turned to face him. He was lurking in the doorway, the room itself being too small to accommodate two normal-size adults and one man-god-size adult. He must have read the skepticism on her face, because he said, "What? I like Mick. He's low maintenance. He napped in the shade all day today."

"I can't just ask you to take my dog."

Could she? Then again, what choice did she have? A hotel, she supposed, but could she find one that would take Mick?

"What are you asking for it?" she asked Eve.

"Oh, nothing. It's just sitting empty anyway."

"What is it with you Moonflower Bayers refusing payment?" It was slightly maddening. She twisted around to shoot Jake a look.

"How about this?" Eve said. "I've talked Sawyer into taking our first-ever vacation—in a couple weeks. It's hard to get away because of both of our jobs. I've got one of the cleaning staff lined up to manage the place during the day, but I haven't yet figured out what to do for the evenings. I need someone here. It probably won't be any actual work beyond checking people in if they arrive late in the evening and just being around if there are any issues. I was going to hit up Maya, but if you're here anyway…"

Nora still didn't feel like that was a fair swap, but she wasn't in a position to argue. "You got yourself a deal. I'll look for a new place and try to be out of your hair as soon as I can, but either way, I'm happy to cover your holidays."

"Great. Let me give you a quick tour. Bathroom is shared and down the hall, unfortunately. I'll show you the kitchen, and laundry is in the basement." She walked over to a small window. "This sticks a bit. You have to really lean into it if you want to open it."

Jake stepped into the room to peer at the window, which put him right behind her. She could have sworn she could feel heat radiating from his body, but that was crazy.

"I'll fix this," he said.

Of course he would.

Chapter Ten

❧

*I*t turned out Nora liked living downtown. She could even see the lake from her tiny window.

She couldn't hear it like at the old house, but she could see a thin slice of it if she craned her neck, and that seemed like an even trade.

And she'd gotten her wish about walking to work. In fact, she could walk to get pretty much whatever she needed. Since she wasn't a cook—Eve had told her to treat the inn's kitchen as her own, but she had yet to take her up on that offer besides by keeping a stash of Diet Coke in the fridge and a box of granola bars in the cupboard—she had taken to walking around town and cobbling together meals from Jenna's General and from Law's.

And she could walk to the little beach, which she was planning to do this evening, in fact, with Maya and Eve, to take part in the town tradition of throwing moonflowers into the lake on a full moon.

Yeah, it was weird, but it was Friday and it had been another satisfying but long week, so she was just going to go with it. Apparently it was some kind of rite of passage: you couldn't really be a Moonflower Bayer until you threw a moonflower into the bay—which made an odd sort of sense, she supposed.

There was only one thing she missed about her old house: Jake.

Without a falling-down dump, she had no need for his handyman services.

It wasn't like she didn't see him, though. They had fallen into a habit whereby if he was on a job in town or wasn't working or out on the boat, he would bring Mick by the clinic at lunch and she would step out for ten minutes. It was like supervised visitation with her dog. Although she missed Mick, neither he nor Jake seemed to mind the new arrangement. They seemed genuinely fond of each other, and it had become normal to see Mick lumbering along behind Jake as he strode through town. Whereas Nora always kept him on a leash—he tended to wander off on her otherwise—Jake didn't seem to need to. She supposed that was one of the perks of being a man-god: small dogs instinctively obeyed you.

Her ten minutes at lunch were sort of like supervised visitation with Jake, too. They'd walk Main Street or sit in the gazebo on the town green, but there were always people around. They never talked about anything real like they had over the handful of dinners they'd had. They didn't talk about Jude or Nora's grandma.

She was surprised by how much she missed it.

On Friday night, she pushed open the door to Lawson's Lager House and there he was, sitting next to Sawyer at the bar, nursing a beer. Her stupid heart skipped a beat.

She made her way over and sat, leaving a few empty stools between them—she was meeting Maya—but he looked up and right at her.

"Hey, Nora." Sawyer gestured to the empty stool next to him. "Join us, will you?"

"Thanks." She slid over a few stools. "If you're sure I'm not interrupting. I'm waiting for Maya, but I'm early."

Law ambled over from behind the bar. "These two dudes have been warming those two stools every Friday night for I don't know how many years, so at this point, they're practically begging for someone to interrupt them."

"I don't know, Law, I'm pretty sure the bromance is a three-way thing." A young woman had come up behind Sawyer, and she did a thing to his shoulder that was a sort of half hug, half punch.

He grinned. "Clare Bear!" He turned to hug her properly. "Clara, this is Dr. Nora Walsh. Nora, this is my sister, Clara. Clara's home from school in Toronto. She's studying electrical engineering." The pride was positively radiating off him.

"Can't miss the Anti-Festival." Clara shook Nora's hand and went to sit on the other side of Jake. "What's up, Jake?"

Jake gave a half shrug.

"You don't say? That's so interesting." Clara kissed him on the cheek even as she teased him. Then she leaned up and availed herself of an over-the-bar hug from Law. The two men seemed to have an easy familiarity with Sawyer's little sister.

The conversation turned to what Clara, who was in her second year at the University of Toronto, was up to at school and why she had taken a taxi from the Greyhound stop instead of calling Sawyer to come and get her.

"Because it's Friday night!" Clara protested. "It's bromance night!"

"You know I would have thrown these two over in a heartbeat to come get you," Sawyer said to his sister.

"But Sawyer, it's not just Friday night; it's full-moon Friday!" She turned to Nora. "Do you know what that is?"

"I do! That's why I'm here. Eve Abbott and Maya Mehta are indoctrinating me in this weirdo tradition you all have. Eve is coming later—she's checking in some guests at the inn, but I'm meeting Maya here for a drink first."

"Wait no longer, my friends. Maya is here." She appeared on Nora's other side. She made a funny face. "And apparently Maya now talks about herself in the third person."

"Here we go," Law muttered.

"I'm sorry, what did you say, *Benjamin*?" Maya set her elbows on the bar.

Law set a wineglass in front of her and started filling it. "I said, 'Yay! Full-moon Friday!'"

Maya rolled her eyes—but subtly, so that only Nora could see. It gave Nora a little thrill. Nora had never really had close women friends, which was funny because she'd grown up in a house of women—she, her sister, her mother, and her grandma had outnumbered her dad and brother. But school, and then residency, hadn't left a lot of time for socializing. Then she'd met Rufus and, without really meaning to, integrated herself into his life.

Living at the Mermaid put her at the center of a certain social circle in town. Pearl, whose bakery was next door, was always poking her head into the inn. Maya lived across the street and seemed to pop up everywhere, often pleading for Nora to illicitly supply her with some of the pizza she couldn't admit to liking. Both women were usually in attendance at the cocktail hours Eve hosted a few days a week at the Mermaid for guests and friends.

Nora still missed Jake, though. She glanced at him only to find he was already looking at her.

Before she could think how to react—smile? Look away?—Maya was back to needling Law. Nora gathered that it was almost like a hobby of hers. "You should come with us. You could wish for a personality."

"I would, but Amber quit"—he looked pointedly at Nora and hitched his head at a young man manning the bar on the far side—"and I don't trust the new guy alone yet."

Nora winced. "Yeah, sorry about that."

He grinned. "Nah, I'm just giving you grief. She was only ever planning to be here through school. You said it yourself: she was never going to be a lifer."

Well, look at her. Not only did Nora have girlfriends, she was enough of a regular that the bartender was teasing her.

After Eve arrived and greeted Clara, Maya hopped up. "Let's get this show on the road. Everyone who's coming, drink up and let's go."

Nora slid off her stool.

"You're really not coming, Benjamin?" Maya asked.

"Nope. Some of us have jobs that prevent us from wasting our time on wishes."

"You wouldn't know a wish if it bit you in the ass."

"On the contrary. I just wished that you would leave, and look—it's coming true."

"Are they always like this?" Nora whispered to Eve.

"Yeah, it's kind of their thing." Eve shrugged. "We're all so used to it, it doesn't even register."

"Let's go!" Maya called. "Chop-chop!"

Jake swallowed the last of his beer and got off his stool.

Everyone stopped talking and swung to face him. He gazed back at them with no particular expression on his face.

Maya cocked her head. "You're coming, Jake?" He made a vague noise that sounded like assent, and everyone remained quiet. Nora wondered if maybe it wasn't normal for Jake to join their flower-wishing ritual.

"Well, great!" Maya said with a suspicious amount of enthusiasm. "Come on, everyone."

A few minutes later, they all were crowding into A Rose by Any Other Name, Maya's father's flower shop. The small store was packed with people, some Nora recognized and some she didn't.

"Hey, Nora, have you met my parents?" Maya introduced her to a smiling fiftysomething couple behind the counter.

"We're so glad you're here," Maya's mom said, echoing the refrain Nora had been hearing from everyone in town.

"On the house," her father said, smiling as he set a flower on the counter in front of Nora. Then he slid one over to his daughter and said, "Two dollars."

"I'm family!" Maya feigned outrage, but there was obvious affection in her expression.

"That's the friends and family discount." Her father's eyes twinkled. Nora could see where Maya got her sense of humor. "They're four bucks apiece retail. Amaryllises are expensive. Now if you wanted to, say, start working here, you'd get the *employee* discount."

"Nice try." Maya shook her head fondly at her father as she clapped her hands to get everyone's attention. "Cue up your wishes! We're heading out!"

Jake hadn't done this since before Jude was born. Kerrie used to like to come and make wishes every once in a while. He suspected that the last couple of times, she'd been wishing for Jude. She'd wanted to get pregnant so badly. She had just started her law career and had decided that "right now" was the optimal time to have kids, even though they were young. She'd reasoned that it was either that or wait until she made partner. He was game either way—he liked the idea of kids, and Kerrie was smarter than he was. He had trusted her judgment regarding timing.

But when the first few months of trying yielded nothing, she had started fretting that maybe there was something wrong. He'd told her that it was too soon to worry, that it was fun trying, and that it would happen in due time. And in an attempt to get her to relax, when she'd rushed home from work early one afternoon declaring that she was at peak ovulation, he'd refused to drop his pants and do it immediately—which had been uncharacteristic for him. In those days, whether they were babymaking or not, he'd generally been ready to go anytime. Instead he'd taken her out for dinner in Bayshore, and as they'd driven back to town, they'd realized it was a full-moon night. So they'd nicked some flowers and headed for the pier.

He'd never asked her what she wished for, but it had been pretty obvious.

And it had worked. Or his dinner-and-a-glass-of-wine relaxation method had. *Something* had worked, because three weeks later, there was the little plus sign on a pregnancy test. She had been so happy.

They both had.

"So these aren't actually moonflowers?" Nora, who was walking beside him, held up the flower she was carrying, drawing him from his memories. "Maya's dad said it was an amaryllis? I thought the whole point was moonflowers. This is *Moonflower* Bay, after all."

"Yeah, that's not a moonflower." She wrinkled her forehead. It *was* kind of confusing. "You've seen the moonflowers everywhere downtown? Or at least you did in the summer?"

"Yeah, they're lovely. And once I moved into the Mermaid, I was able to appreciate them more, since I was often walking around in the evenings."

"Yeah, but have you noticed the plaques?"

"Directing people *not* to use the flowers for wishing? I wondered what that was about."

"The wishing thing became really popular a few years ago," he explained. "Tourism has really taken off around here, what with the Raspberry Festival and the Mermaid Parade. People started stealing the moonflowers. There was one year when by the start of August, there were just all these sad vines with no flowers. So the city council installed plaques directing people to buy flowers at A Rose by Any Other Name. Imported flowers also allow the wishing to go on year-round. It used to just be a summer thing—it only lasted as long as the moonflowers did."

"Hey, are you guys coming?" They had fallen behind the group, and Maya was calling back to them. Sawyer shot Jake a quizzical look over his shoulder.

"Sorry!" Nora caught up with Maya. "Jake was just explaining the reason you don't use actual moonflowers anymore."

Sawyer raised his eyebrows at Jake. Yeah, yeah, whatever. He was having a conversation. Honestly. He wasn't as bad as they all made him out to be. But he didn't need any grief, so he stayed at the back of the pack. He eyed a display of moonflowers in front of Curl Up and Dye. It was late in the season, and most of the town's signature flowers had already died, but the salon had somehow kept theirs looking great.

"So why don't you just import moonflowers?" Nora asked Maya. Even though Jake wasn't walking next to Nora anymore, he listened in as the women spoke. "That would seem like the obvious thing to do."

"You can't retail moonflowers," Maya said. "They're flowering vines, so it's not like you can cut the blossoms off and ship them somewhere. So we import amaryllises and call them 'wishing flowers.'"

"The town conspires to ruin everyone's wishes, basically," Eve laughingly declared.

"No, the town conspires to protect its heritage," Sawyer said.

"The only way to do it *right* is to steal one," Maya said. "But that's illegal. There's an actual town bylaw."

"And if you're friends with Mr. Goody Two-Shoes," Clara said, mock-punching her brother in the shoulder, "or *related* to him, stealing is out."

Nora laughed as she listened to everyone explain. "No offense, but this town is really weird."

When they got to the pier, everyone fanned out. Nora was on the far side by herself. Jake made his way over and stationed himself at the railing next to her. "Hey. Use this instead." He passed her a moonflower like they were doing a drug deal.

She gasped quietly. "Where did you get this?"

"I stole it from Curl Up and Dye."

She glanced over her shoulder toward Sawyer, who, as far as Jake knew, had never actually booked anyone for grand theft moonflower.

"Just take it. You should have a real one your first time."

God. Listen to him. "You should have a real one your first time"? Had he sustained a head injury?

Very possibly, because when she held out her amaryllis and said, "Okay, swap," he switched flowers with her.

He should just tell her to use them both and make two wishes. But that would usher in a whole conversation about why he didn't want to make a wish.

"I have no idea what to wish for." She extended her palm out over the lake. But then, seeming to think better of it, she quickly retracted it. "I guess I shouldn't be displaying my contraband so overtly."

He chuckled. "It's fine. No one's paying attention." It was true. Sawyer and Clara were chatting, having done their wishing already. Maya and Eve were laughing and leaning out theatrically over the water.

"Just so you know," Sawyer called to them, "I wished that nobody would fall in this evening, so watch yourselves there."

"Make a wish," Nora mused, waving to acknowledge Sawyer's warning. "It's so vague. Like, I should wish for world peace, right? Or at least comprehensive vaccine coverage?"

"In my experience," he said slowly, formulating his thoughts as he spoke, "you should wish for something personal, and it should be small." He always used to do that. For example, the last wish he'd made here, that night he was pretty sure Kerrie had wished for Jude, had been for some hot, non-chore-like sex—given Kerrie's focus on conception, things had become a bit mechanical in the bedroom. "If you keep it specific, and within the realm of possibility, it's more likely to come true."

"But is it actually a wish then, if it's already likely to come true?"

He smiled. "You got me there, Doc. I'm never going to win any philosophical arguments with you. Or anyone else. But especially you."

"Are you saying I'm a snob?"

"No! I'm just saying you're smarter than I am."

"No, I think you might be right." She extended her arm again, this time with her palm over the flower to obscure it. "Okay, a specific, within-the-realm-of-possibility wish. Let's do it together."

Well, crap. He was not prepared for this. He had only planned to come along to...why? He had no idea.

Regardless, the path of least resistance was to just drop the flower into the lake. She would never know if he made a wish or not.

"On three," she said as his own words echoed in his head. Specific. Within the realm of possibility. "One, two, three."

It popped into his head just before his flower hit the water.

I wish Nora could find a place to live where she can hear the lake.

Chapter Eleven

❧

$\mathcal{T}$he Saturday morning of the Anti-Festival dawned clear and cold. It was one of those falls when it felt like someone had flipped the switch from "summer" to "not summer." Jake didn't mind. Fall meant the town would slow way down and shed its seasonal tourists. The lake would become less welcoming and make you work harder to love it. He didn't mind that, either.

He had never actually been to the Anti-Festival other than to attend the plays Maya directed, and only when Sawyer's sister Clara was in them. Generally he would spend the days leading up to the weekend building whatever sets or stages were needed for the play or other events like the bachelor auction and the dunk tank, and then he would get the hell out of there until the play on Sunday afternoon.

But not today. Today, he was installing a giant sign on the Vaccine Machine that said, "Do No Harm; Stick Out

Your Arm" and a companion one that showed a mermaid fighting off a giant cartoon flu virus.

Because that was apparently what he did now.

He was unloading the signs Maya and Pearl had made from the back of his truck when the van wheezed around the corner. It was sputtering like a dying old man.

He jogged to get ahead of it—he didn't have to jog very hard—so he could remove the traffic cones that had been blocking off a spot for it in the parking lot behind the Mermaid.

Maya hopped out of the driver's seat, and Pearl and Eiko emerged from the bakery. Pearl generally left the back door open on account of how hot it got in there with the ovens going—but maybe also so she could eavesdrop on everyone.

"I'll get the new signs installed for you and get out of your hair," Jake said.

Pearl laid a hand on his arm. "Thank you for helping with this. I know it can't be easy."

It was and it wasn't. Yeah, helping with the flu-shot clinic made him think of Jude, but thinking of Jude wasn't as gutting as it used to be. And he certainly didn't want anyone else to lose a kid to the flu. So here he was.

"All right." Pearl, back to her chairperson-of-the-festival persona, spoke brusquely. "I have to find Law and get him to release Amber from her bartending duties to cover the flu clinic while Nora's in the auction."

Wait. *What?*

"I thought Amber quit the bar when she finished school," Maya said.

"She did, but now that Law is doing pizza for the festival, he needs more help. Amber agreed to work the outdoor bar while he mans the pizza oven, but that was before Nora agreed to stand in the auction."

Once again: Wait. *What?*

"Anybody can bartend," Pearl went on, "but only Nora and Amber can give flu shots, so I need Amber over here for the auction and aftermath. That was the only way Nora would agree." She threw her hands up in the air. "Logistics!"

"I have to admit, I'm a little surprised you got Nora to agree to be in the auction," Maya said, voicing a severely understated version of Jake's sentiment.

"Yes! And isn't she going to be a catch?" Eiko said happily. "Jason Sims told me he's been working on his hamper all week. Isn't that adorable?"

Adorable. That was not the word Jake would use. Jason Sims was not Nora's type. He was boring, and he had bad hair.

But whatever. Nora was probably just doing a good deed. And with Pearl on her case, she probably hadn't stood a chance. It was just lunch.

With Jason Sims.

He started setting up the van. Pearl was still hovering, so he asked, "When you said Jason was working on his hamper, what does that mean?"

"Oh, well, you know, the lunch hampers that are part of the auction."

He didn't know. He had never attended or apparently paid any attention when it was talked about. He hadn't known, for example, that they'd added bachelorettes to the lineup.

Pearl must have interpreted his silence as her cue to explain. "The idea at the beginning was that the person doing the bidding would pack a lunch for the person they won in the auction. People have started getting really creative with their lunches. It's become part of the theater of it all. You announce your monetary bid, but you also say what's in your hamper. And I have to say, last year, a lot of people got really creative about presentation. We had some crystal goblets and fine-linen picnic blankets." She paused. "And you know Jason."

He did not know Jason, not really, on account of the whole as-boring-as-watching-paint-dry thing. But he gathered that Pearl was saying Jason was going all out. Which sort of went with Jake's impression of him, and of his profession in general. He would fuss over details that ultimately didn't matter and be rewarded for it.

He never would have said that to Kerrie, who was also a lawyer. And of course he understood the principle of people needing lawyers in certain circumstances, but it wasn't like lawyers were out there, say, saving lives. Or delivering babies on the town green.

He had finished installing the new signs. He stood back. "Well, there you go."

All three women started oohing over it.

"Do you know where Nora is?" he asked. She was the one he was doing this for.

He'd thought he was talking to Maya, but Pearl answered. "Oh, she was on her way over, but I sent her out for some chocolate chips." She smiled. "I had a little chocolate chip emergency this morning."

Nora felt like she'd lived an entire life before she got to the flu clinic just as it was set to open at nine. First she'd encountered Pearl in the lobby of the Mermaid freaking out over chocolate chips, which she'd apparently not ordered enough of for the massive batch of chocolate chip cookie pies she was making for the festival.

She'd been in such a panic that Nora had offered to go buy some, but Pearl had needed so many bags that she'd had to drive not only to Grand View but up to Bayshore because she'd bought out the store in Grand View. She'd texted Maya, who assured her that she and Jake were fine getting everything set up without her.

Then Eiko had cornered her on the street and insisted that the interview she kept putting off simply *had* to be done. Nora wasn't clear on why it had to happen at that exact moment, but she acquiesced, reasoning that it would be good exposure for the clinic—and also that actually doing it would be faster than arguing with Eiko about it.

Then she had to go back to the clinic to get her supplies and the cooler of vaccines. By the time she had lugged everything to the van, a small line of people had already formed.

She paused and took in the current incarnation of the van. As before, her response was *Wow*. There was a mermaid sucker punching a green flu-virus cartoon with three eyeballs and another mermaid getting a shot from a smiling but slightly demented-looking doctor Nora sincerely hoped wasn't supposed to be her.

"Wow," she said again, this time out loud.

"It's really something, isn't it?" Karl Andersen, who was the first in line, asked.

"It really is." She shook her head. "Just give me five minutes to get set up and we'll get started."

"Thanks. I've got emcee duties at the Pie Walk, and then I need to move the prizes for the three-legged race and the egg toss from the store to the Mermaid—we're staging the awards ceremony out of the kitchen there."

Nora worked at a steady pace all morning. She would have been stressed by the size of the line if it hadn't seemed like everyone was happy to chat while they waited. When Law, who was manning the outdoor pizza oven behind the bar, noticed, he started taking orders for slices and shuttling them over to people.

She probably should have lined up a helper, someone to do the paperwork and bring her water and stuff like that. She could have asked Wynd if she was free, but it hadn't occurred to her. Probably because she wasn't used to needing helpers.

Because usually, if she needed something done, Jake was just there doing it. Before she could even verbalize anything.

But of course, he wouldn't be here today, at a flu clinic of all places. And she would never ask him to be. She kind of wished he had a phone so she could text him and ask him if he was okay. But anyway, what was she going to say? "Hey, how's it going? I'm thinking about you and your dead kid as I slide into hour three of jabbing needles into people's arms"?

"Hey, Dr. Walsh, nice to see you again."

Speaking of Jake. It was his dad. "Hi, Mr. Ramsey."

"Call me Art. Have you met my wife, Jamila?"

They greeted each other, and soon she was gloved up and preparing to inoculate Art.

"I had a grandson who died of the flu," he said softly as he sat.

Something twisted in Nora's chest. She'd been so focused on Jake's pain, but of course Art had experienced Jude's death as a terrible loss, too. "I know," she said softly. "Jake told me."

His eyes widened. "He did?"

"Yes. It sounds like Jude was a great little guy."

She pressed a cotton ball against the injection site

and for some reason felt compelled to leave her hand there.

Jamila put her hand on her husband's shoulder. "There's been so much loss in this family."

Art looked up at his wife with such love in his eyes that it almost took Nora's breath away. It seemed all the more amazing knowing that Jake's dad and Jamila were only together because Jake's mom had died. But if there was one thing she had learned in her time as a doctor—on the job, because they didn't teach this in medical school—it was that the human heart was capable of holding conflicting emotions at the same time. Real love, which it was clear these two had, was expansive. It did not demand exclusivity across time. It made room for grief.

She realized with a jolt that she had never had that kind of love with Rufus, even in their earliest, allegedly happy, days.

Jamila must have sensed Nora's unease, because when she sat for her shot, she started talking about furniture. "I hear you're living temporarily at the Mermaid but looking for a new place? I gotta tell you, I have a serious antiquing habit. You want any help with furniture, you come to me, okay? You'll make my day."

"Lord knows she has enough in storage, she could start a lending library for antiques," Art said.

"You better watch what you say, my love, because I might just start a shop when I retire."

"No way. We're hitting the road when you retire." It was Art's turn to aim an aside to Nora. "We're buying an RV."

"Well, we'll see about that."

The two of them bantered while Nora finished up

with Jamila. Soon it was noon, and Amber showed up to take over.

"On the one hand, thank God." Nora took off her gloves and shook out her hand. "I think I have carpal tunnel. I feel like the whole town has been here." She eyed the line. It was down to two people. "Actually, maybe they have been."

"Well, I'll do these two and stay open for any stragglers." She sat in the chair Nora had vacated. "You said, 'On the one hand, thank God.' What's the other hand?"

"On the other hand, now I have to go stand onstage while people bid on me like I'm a racehorse on the auction block."

Amber nodded. "Now you see why I was happy to help out here this afternoon. If I'm here, I can't be there. They could pry me from the bar, but they wouldn't dare mess with the vaccine drive."

"You are smart. I'm not sure how I let myself get talked into this."

"It's probably not your fault. The key with Pearl— and Eiko and Karl, too—is to learn to recognize a certain look they get in their eyes. When you see it, you have to avoid them at all costs. Like, even if it means you have to physically run away."

"Noted." Nora chuckled and went off to face her fate. She took a seat in one of the reserved chairs in the front row as she'd been previously instructed.

Eiko was emceeing. She made a big deal about how they were doing bachelors *and* bachelorettes this year, and she started with Jenna Riley from Jenna's General, which Nora had learned was a cute, semi-high-end general store on Main that sold maple fudge and homemade dog treats along with the usual Gatorade and newspapers. Nora had no idea what the going rate for a bachelor or bachelorette in Moonflower Bay was, but everyone oohed and aahed when Jenna "went" for eighty bucks to a guy Nora didn't know who reported that his hamper contained homemade macaroni and cheese made from his mom's famous family recipe, Greek salad, and lemon bars.

Next up was someone named Charles, who Nora didn't know but who was apparently a teacher at the elementary school. A merry bidding war broke out between Maya and Elena Gardner, whom Nora had seen at the clinic. Elena won him for 120 bucks and "Pesto and grilled chicken pressed paninis, asparagus, and, for dessert, peak-of-season fresh Niagara peaches, which you can't argue with because I have type 1 diabetes." Everyone applauded, including Nora, who, as Elena's doctor, heartily approved. She thought again how nice it was to actually be able to follow the same patients over time, to keep tabs on their progress and their lives.

"And now we have Moonflower Bay's newest bachelorette," Eiko said. "Please join me in warmly welcoming Dr. Nora Walsh to her first Anti-Festival."

Nora's nerves fired as the crowd cheered. What if no one bid on her? Maya, who was sitting on an aisle near the front, let out a wolf whistle as Nora walked by.

"We're so glad to have you in town, Dr. Hon," Eiko said to Nora as she ascended the stage, and not into the microphone. She seemed to really mean it, and Nora couldn't help returning her warm smile, even though she was still wary about this whole thing.

Well, it was only lunch. It wasn't like whatever happened in the next few minutes was going to alter the trajectory of her life.

That's what she told herself, anyway. In truth, she was

suddenly so nervous, her heart felt like it was about to beat out of her chest.

Eiko lifted her microphone. "All right, my friends! This one is a catch, isn't she? Let's open the—"

"Five hundred bucks and a Hawaiian pizza."

What. The. Hell?

Jake. That was what the hell. Who else would it be? Hadn't she *just* been thinking he was always there when she needed him?

She got over her confusion faster than the crowd, which was rippling with murmurs and exclamations. He was standing at the back of the seating area, so everyone had to twist around to see him.

She had a clear sight line, though. She could see him, and he could see her. He was staring at her, in fact, and, unlike her, he appeared completely unruffled.

When Eiko raised her mic again and said, "Well, my goodness. We have five hundred dollars on the table. Do I hear any other offers?" the crowd went dead silent. You could hear the seagulls cawing. Nora felt like she could hear her own heart beating. It was still going faster than it should have been, but from a different kind of nerves from before.

The silence went on.

Nora had come to understand that Jake was an almost-mythic figure in town. He was the damaged hermit who never spoke. That didn't accord with Nora's experience with him, but she'd watched him in social settings and had heard people talking about him enough to understand that he occupied a certain role in the collective imagination.

So she supposed that was why, when he suddenly appeared at the auction with a too-high bid—when he suddenly appeared at the auction *at all*—it literally struck people dumb. They didn't know what to make of this version of Jake Ramsey. They hadn't known this version of Jake Ramsey existed.

Certainly none of them were going to bid against him. He hadn't needed to bid five hundred dollars. He could have said *five* dollars, and that would have been that.

Nora had the idea that Jake didn't like public scrutiny. She didn't blame him. Who did, really? Or maybe it was more that he didn't like public *pity*, and for him, scrutiny always came with pity. He had once told her he liked that she didn't walk on eggshells around him.

"Going once..."

As Eiko stretched out the last few moments of the bidding, the silence intensified, became painful. Nora was a little afraid she might expire on the spot before Eiko finally said, "And Jake Ramsey is our winner!"

There had been no instructions regarding what to do after one's auction. The other "couples" were gathered near the front watching the proceedings, and presumably they would go off and eat their lunches when it was all over. But Jake didn't move from his spot at the back of the crowd. So she should probably go to him? Even though Eiko had moved on and was in the middle of singing the praises of Dennis Bates, Nora still felt like she was under a microscope. She was a bug trapped on a glass slide, and on the other side of the lens was the entire damn town.

Or maybe it was just Jake, who continued to watch her intently.

As she passed Maya, she heard another low whistle. Except instead of being a good-natured *hubba-hubba* whistle from a friend, this one was more like *Girl. Holy shit.*

As she approached Jake, she raised her eyebrows and

shook her head. Smiled despite herself. He answered her with one of his own—also, she thought, despite himself.

She held up her palms. "Dude. What are you *doing*?"

He shrugged, and his grin became self-satisfied. "Saving you from Jason Sims."

"The lawyer?"

He stepped closer and looked around, as if to make sure no one was watching or listening.

Of course, everyone was watching and listening.

He took her elbow and steered her away from the crowd, speaking under his breath as they went. "Yeah. Word on the street is he was gonna feed you foie gras."

"Ew," she said instinctively.

He held up the pizza box. Her stomach growled. He smirked and hitched his head at a backpack he had slung over one shoulder. "And there's bourbon in here."

None of that explained why he'd bid five hundred bucks, but she decided not to overanalyze it. "Well, thanks, Jake. I owe you." She looked over her shoulder. People were still twisting their necks and looking at them. That feeling she'd had in the hardware store the morning she'd agreed to stand in this stupid auction, of being an animal in a zoo, was back with a vengeance.

"Let's find somewhere to eat this where everyone's not watching us," she whispered.

"Gazebo around front?" he suggested.

"I feel like that's the first place people will look once this breaks up."

"You think people will be looking for us?"

"Uh, don't take this the wrong way, Jake. I know what your intentions were—and weren't—but you made quite the splash back there. You bid way too much, and...well, you showed up to begin with."

Something changed on his face—realization dawned. She wasn't sure about what, just that he looked like he had solved a long-standing mystery. "Oh my God. I played right into her hands."

"Whose?"

"Pearl's. She set me up!"

Nora laughed and patted him on the arm. "Poor Jake. Outmaneuvered by an octogenarian. Come on. Let's eat at the inn."

They went in through the back door, which opened onto the kitchen. She'd been thinking they'd eat at the island, but Karl Andersen was sitting at it with his back to them, doing something she couldn't see. He'd said earlier that he was staging the awards ceremony from here, so he was probably getting ready. *Dammit.*

They were trying to get *away* from innuendo. Being spotted sneaking inside for a cozy, private lunch was *not* going to help their cause, especially when the spotter was Karl.

Apparently they were due a stroke of luck, though. Karl hadn't heard them come in. Nora had been leading the way, and she turned and put a finger to her lips. Jake nodded and carefully—and silently—shut the door behind him. They moved excruciatingly slowly across the room, like the air was molasses. It felt like it took forever to get even halfway across the kitchen—at which point she made the mistake of looking at Jake.

His mouth was clamped shut in concentration, and his eyes were open wide—almost bugging out. There was something about giant Aquaman trying to tiptoe lightly that struck her as funny. He must have felt her attention, because he looked over and met her eyes. Soon they were both shaking with silent laughter. He looked like he was trying not to throw up. His chest heaved and his shoulders rose before he got himself back under control. She pressed a palm over her mouth, looked away from him, and kept plodding forward.

The kitchen was connected to the dining room via a swinging door. When they reached it, they stopped as if by silent agreement. Nora wasn't sure how they should handle this. Should they try to maintain their stealthy but slothy pace or should they push through as quickly as possible and run for it? She tried to remember if the door squeaked when it opened and closed.

Jake decided for them. He grabbed her hand, but only for a second. Once he had her attention, he dropped it and made a quick one-two-three countdown motion with his fingers, his eyebrows raised. *We go on three?*

It was too bad. She liked his hand. It was big and warm and pleasingly rough.

She nodded in answer to his silent question, but, choking back laughter, she held up a finger of her own. *Yes, but hang on a sec.* She had to turn her head away for a moment to get herself back under control. She was glad they seemed to be able to communicate via ESP. When she felt like she wasn't going to burst out in hysterics and undo all their painstaking progress, she turned back to him and nodded.

To her surprise, he took her hand again. He'd taken it to begin with as a nonverbal way to get her attention—she'd thought. And his other was stabilizing the pizza box he had balancing on his forearm. He was standing between her and the door. Wouldn't he need a hand free to push the door open? Or to do their countdown for real?

Apparently not. He turned so the shoulder of the pizza-box arm was angled toward the door. Winking, he mouthed, "One, two...three."

A burst of happy adrenaline surged through her as they

clattered through the door. "Keep going!" she whispered as they tore through the dining room and skidded around the sharp turn they had to make to mount the staircase.

"Go, go!" he urged, and she let loose a peal of laughter as they raced up the stairs. She couldn't keep it in anymore.

She hadn't been thinking about where they were going other than away from Karl. But of course they were going to her room on the third floor. It was the only place they would be guaranteed privacy. They laughed all the way up. Jake had a low, rumbly chuckle that scratched not unpleasantly against something tender inside her.

When they reached her door, she had to drop his hand to fish her key out of her pocket. Well, she had to drop his hand because their little caper was over. Because that was the only reason she'd been holding it in the first place.

Wow, though, she missed it. Like, already. But also in the broader sense. She missed physical touch. Affection. She should probably wonder how much of it coming from Rufus in recent months—years?—had been genuine, but going down that road wasn't going to be productive.

"Well, we showed him," Jake quipped, his eyes twinkling. "We should be spies."

That was another thing she missed: being in cahoots with someone. Feeling like it was you and your coconspirator against the world. It had been a long time since she'd had that with anyone, unless you counted the illicit pizzas she ordered for Maya.

Jake ran his liberated hand through his hair. Which drew her attention to both that damn hand *and* his ridiculously attractive hair.

Heat pooled low in her belly.

She had thought she was going to be dead inside for a long time. Or at least for the five months Erin had informed her was her allotted get-over-Rufus window. But in fact, like on that night on Jake's deck when she'd laid her head on his shoulder, it suddenly felt like something inside her was waking from a long hibernation. Something she'd thought was dead had been only, it turned out, dormant.

She sighed and glanced at Jake as she unlocked her door. He grinned and waggled his eyebrows at her.

He was only doing it because, like her, he was enjoying the echoes of their covert operation.

Right?

His eyes slid down her body, but he jerked them back up, like he'd been caught doing something wrong.

She looked down at herself. She'd tried to spiff herself up for the auction, so she was wearing a dress. It was a wrap style that closed in front like a robe. It was low cut—lower than the dresses she wore at the clinic—but she was pretty flat chested, so the cleavage effect wasn't as dramatic as it would have been on someone else. But things had gone a little askew during their dash upstairs, and the V had shifted so she was showing quite a bit of side-boob on one side—one of the downsides of small breasts was that there wasn't a lot of terrain there to keep the necklines of dresses like this one from shifting out of place.

All the mirth had gone from Jake's expression. His eyes were no longer twinkling. But they hadn't returned to normal, either. They were doing…something else.

Well.

"Jake?"

He went into the tiny room and set the pizza on the dressing table. "Yep?"

She wasn't really sure how she had the guts to ask what she was about to ask. Maybe because he wasn't looking at her. He was unloading a thermos from his backpack—that must be the bourbon.

She followed him in and closed the door behind her. "You know how you don't have room in your life for a relationship?"

He froze with his back to her, the thermos in one hand, its cap in the other. She thought back to the first time she'd laid eyes on him, at the salon. She'd thought of it then like a record scratch, a sudden interruption in the normal soundtrack of her life. This felt like that, too. Like the record of their friendship had been playing as normal, the needle traveling in an orderly fashion along its groove. But now she was going to ask him a question that would jostle the needle, and somehow they both knew it, even though she hadn't actually said anything yet.

The room shimmered with tension as he slowly set the thermos and cap on the dressing table and turned. "Yeah?"

She swallowed hard. "What about sex? Do you have room in your life for sex?"

He looked at her for a long time. Another thing she'd thought earlier about Jake was that he did companionable silence well.

This silence was not companionable.

Crap. She had majorly effed up here. What the *hell* had she been thinking? Clearly she *hadn't* been, otherwise—

"Yes. Yes, I do."

She blinked, unable to move anything besides her eyelids as those four words, delivered in his gruff baritone, unleashed a tsunami of exhilaration, fear, and lust inside her body.

She was so focused inwardly, on tsunami abatement, that she hardly even perceived his approach until he was there with a hand on one of her cheeks and his mouth on the other.

The hand was familiar. As when she'd had it in her own downstairs, it was warm and a little bit rough. It was big, too. With his palm at her jawline, it covered the whole side of her face, and his fingers extended up past her hairline.

His lips were warm and a little bit rough, too. He'd pressed them to the middle of her other cheek and was now dragging them down her throat. Her pulse was so strong there, she worried she was coming across like a lust-addled idiot.

He took a step closer. He'd been touching her face with his hand and his mouth, but now their bodies were aligned. His free hand snaked around her waist and pulled her against him.

He was hard. He was *really* hard. It was unmistakable, right there against the soft center of her belly. She could only surmise that he'd done that on purpose, that he *wanted* her to feel him.

"Now?" she croaked. "We're doing this now?"

He pulled away, and she immediately regretted the question. Because it had made him pull away. She'd lost the lips and the hand and the heated hardness.

A slow, semiwicked smile blossomed on his face. "Did you want to schedule it for later?"

"No. I mean, maybe. I mean maybe *also* later." His brow knit. She was making a hash of this, sending mixed signals. She cleared her throat. "Jake. Let's have sex now, but maybe also later, if that ends up being something we both want to do."

He got the trying-to-hold-back-laughter look from before as he pressed his lips together and raised his eyebrows.

"Do you have a condom?" she asked.

"Why would I have a condom?" He did laugh then, as if the idea of his being in possession of a condom was so preposterous, the only reasonable response was to laugh.

She rolled her eyes but she laughed, too, and it went a long way toward easing her nerves. "I don't know. Don't you have a bunch of them in a bag made of leather you tanned yourself from a deer you killed yourself?"

"Do *you* have a condom?" he countered.

"Why would I have a condom?"

"I don't know. Because you're young, hot, and single?"

"You think I'm hot?"

He raised his eyebrows and glanced pointedly down at the rather impressively sized bulge at the front of his jeans.

She couldn't have wiped the grin from her face if she tried.

He came back to her. Placed his mouth back on her throat. Used his other hand to pull her against his body again, except this time, instead of placing it on her back, he splayed his palm over one ass cheek. *Oh dear God.*

His lips started moving. He wasn't kissing her exactly, just dragging his mouth against her too-sensitive flesh.

She let loose a shaky sigh. He made her feel like she was melting and tensing up at the same time—the two sensations were at war inside her body. "What about the condom, though?"

"We don't need it," he whispered against her skin.

"Uh, *yes* we do." She stiffened. She was on the pill, but there was no way she was having casual sex without a condom. She never would have thought of Jake as one of those guys who would try to suggest otherwise. She was shocked, frankly.

"No, I mean we don't have to do stuff that requires

a condom." He was still speaking with his mouth right on her.

"*Ohhh*," she breathed, her body surrendering to the melting as she contemplated what "other stuff" might mean. "Okay."

"Although…" He pulled back again. "I could go downstairs and ask Karl if he has one."

She laughed and shrieked at the same time. The idea of Karl finding out what was going on up here was both mortifying and amusing. He took a step away, and she tried to reach for him to get him back. That was the wrong direction. He was supposed to— Oh. *Oh.*

He was taking off his shirt.

She sucked in a breath. It wasn't like she hadn't seen his chest. He'd been shirtless a couple times in her yard, back at the old house. But that had been a look-don't-touch situation. Now, by contrast, she was going to get to put her hands all over him. She was— All right, then.

He was shucking his jeans, too.

He was taking the efficient approach, which she could appreciate. The *idea* of seductively peeling your bed partner's clothes off was always sexier than the reality of it, when legs got caught in pants and bra clasps were hard to figure out.

And either he wasn't wearing any underwear, or he was good at multitasking, because when he straightened, he was naked.

He was a naked man-god.

Muscular and beautiful and…he was a big guy, and every part of him was in proportion. In proportion and at attention.

"Well," she said. "You get right to the point, don't you?"

His eyes darkened, and she worried she'd offended him. "I don't do romance, Nora."

There had been a warning in his tone, but she didn't need it. "I don't want romance." She meant it. She wasn't cluttering up her life with furniture right now, while she found her feet, so she *certainly* wasn't going to clutter it up with romance.

She pressed a hand to her throat. She'd been worried before that her fluttering pulse would give away her lust, but now it was thundering so hard it physically hurt. So did the juncture between her legs, where she could feel her pulse equally strongly.

"I mean it. I like you, Nora. And obviously I'm attracted to you. But I had my run at the whole relationship, white-picket-fence thing, and I'm done with that."

She must not have answered fast enough, because he took a step back and something shuttered in his expression. "And before you try to tell me that time heals all wounds—"

"I would never tell you that." She'd spoken more sharply than she'd intended, but honestly she was a little offended. "I would *never* tell you that."

She'd thought maybe that was going to be the start of an argument, and/or the end of the proceedings, but he surprised her by smiling. "And *that's* exactly why I like you. You don't speak in platitudes. You don't *think* in platitudes."

She sucked in a breath. That might be the nicest thing anyone had ever said to her. "Well, I mean it, too. I'm supposed to be figuring out my life these next two years. Being kind of selfish. I can't do that chained to a guy."

His smile deepened—he liked that answer—and something twisted in her belly. "I also like your hair."

Okay, apparently they were still on the listing-things-they-liked-about-each-other section of the proceedings. "I like your hair, too. Will you take it down?" He started to do so, and she worried suddenly that she should say something else, lest he think she regarded him merely as a hot body with a great head of hair. "I also like the way you...get stuff done. You don't talk about doing things. You just do them." She laughed at herself. Then she laughed at the whole situation—turned on and cracking up was not a combination she had experience with, but she liked it. "Is it weird that we're listing off things we like about each other while we're naked?"

"Well, *I'm* naked. You, on the other hand"—his eyes made a slow journey down her body—"should *get* naked."

"You wanna help?" It was out before she could think, and she'd said it automatically, like it was the next line in a script. It was what she would have said to Rufus, but hadn't she just been thinking that undressing a lover was never actually as exciting or sexy as it was supposed to be?

He must have agreed, because he said, "No. I want to watch."

Well. That was a good answer. An answer that went straight to the knot of tension between her legs and twisted it a little tighter.

She reached for the tie of her dress, which was at her waist. He started toward her from where he'd been standing near the door, but as he passed, he held his arms up in a no-hands sort of gesture, making a show of not touching her as he slid past her and sat on the bed.

She pivoted to face him. He rotated his hand to signal that he wanted her to get on with it.

As she started undoing the knot, he asked, "What kind of dress is that?"

"A wrap dress?" She wasn't sure why she had answered

with a question. She just wasn't sure what he meant. Was he referring to style? Type of fabric?

"A wrap dress," he repeated. "So now you're going to unwrap yourself?"

She was going to try. The dress had holes you fed ties through, and one of the ties was absurdly long when it was undone because it had to go all the way around her waist and through a hole on the other side of the front. It looked like a simple dress from the outside, but it was actually kind of complicated, structurally speaking.

She might have gotten self-conscious as she started pulling the long tie out, but he, Mr. Mute, started performing a monologue. "I gotta tell you, that neckline has been doing a number on me since I saw you up on that stage."

She paused. "I think it would be racier if I didn't have such small breasts. I don't even need a bra. This dress would be a lot sexier if I had perfect, perky breasts like—"

"You are *not* about to invoke the Intern."

"Well…"

He lifted a finger. "I swear to God, if you say her name, I will get up and leave." She made a show of closing her mouth. He shook the still-raised finger at her. "All right, then. Now unwrap yourself."

She did. She even managed all the ties and holes without feeling too awkward. Which left her standing in front of him in her panties. Black, bikini-style, functional cotton panties, which, although they might not have been her first choice if she'd known Jake Ramsey was going to see them, were at least not as bad as they could have been.

It didn't seem like he was looking at them anyway. Her nipples started to…buzz? There was a distinct tingling sort of sensation happening in each of them. He was definitely looking at her breasts. In fact, she might say he was *leering* at her breasts.

"See?" he rasped. "Perky."

"Yeah, but they're so small, they can't help but be perk—"

"And *perfect*." The bed was shoved up against a wall, and he scooted back on it until his back hit the wall. Then he curled his index finger at her.

Nora did not have bad self-esteem, generally speaking. But she'd meant what she said when she told him she was skinny but unfit. Yeah, she was petite, but she had jiggly bits.

He curled the finger again, and his eyes sparked in a way that suggested he did not see the jiggly bits the same way she did.

So she went. Crawled across the bed until she was kneeling in front of him.

He reached immediately for the breasts they had just been discussing. In another context she would have used the word *groped*, except his touch made her jaw go slack. An involuntary moan slipped out.

"*Perfect*," he said again just before his mouth made contact with a nipple.

She was kneeling up between his legs, so his head was at nipple level, and he went to town. Holding, kneading, working the flesh up into a handful that he would scrape his fingernails over before gathering it again and putting it in his mouth.

"Jake," she breathed.

He hummed with his mouth still on her. "Hmm?"

She hadn't meant it as a question he needed to answer, had just been mindlessly saying his name as pleasure beat through her like a kettledrum being struck, over and over, too fast, so fast she couldn't catch a breath. "I think I might come just from this," she gasped.

"Why don't you?" he said lazily, but even as he made the lewd suggestion, he let go of her with one hand, which he then shoved down the back of her panties. He squeezed her butt briefly and then came back around front and burrowed through her folds.

"Ahh!" She arched her back instinctively, and it had the effect of shoving her torso forward far enough that it hit his.

Which, in turn, had the effect of reminding her how much she had wanted to touch his chest before.

With her breasts, though. She wanted to touch his chest with her breasts.

So she kind of rudely removed his hand from her panties. He started to say something, which she was pretty sure was an apology. That wasn't called for. But instead of telling him as much, she straddled him. Mashed her chest against his and ground down on his lap.

"Oh, damn, *Nora*," he bit out.

She wanted to laugh. Not at him, but in triumph. He thought he was playing her so expertly, being the Minister of Sensations while she was the...ministeree. But two could play at that game. She writhed shamelessly until she got herself into a position where she could rock back and forth on him in a way that perfectly stimulated her clit.

"Oh, shit," he growled. "I'm not going to last very long this time. I'm sorry."

She laugh-moaned. "This time?" How much did she love that phrase? Because it implied that there was going to be a *next time*.

"Yeah, next time I'm going to beat off like twenty-five times before I see you."

"Oh my God." That was so...flattering. Filthily flattering. She rocked harder. "It's okay. I'm not going to last much longer, either."

They rutted against each other, and just when she was starting to get frustrated, when the pleasure was starting to tilt into get-it-over-already irritation, he kissed her.

On the lips. Which they had not done yet.

It was just a simple kiss. No tongue, even. But it tipped her over the edge.

It had been a long time. She came long and hard.

He came, too, with a growl and a great big buck of his hips.

Eventually she slid off him, her panties all sticky with her wetness and his come. She'd been vaguely intending to get all the way off the bed and find some clean clothes, but he lay down and tugged her down with him, arranging her against his chest.

Apparently whatever this was, this "I like you and we're having sex, but we're never going to be a couple" thing, it came with cuddling.

She was down with that.

They were quiet for a long time as their breathing slowed. The companionable silence had returned.

"You never took your underwear off," he said, stroking her back.

It was true. She'd done all that grinding with a layer of cotton between them. She was playing with his hair, combing her fingers through it. He didn't seem to mind, so she didn't stop as she said, "So?"

"In retrospect that seems like a lost opportunity."

She huffed a laugh. "Over the panties. Is that third base? Or just second?"

"I don't know. You're the baseball person. You tell me."

"I've never actually known. First base is kissing, I think? But maybe that's wrong? I really have no idea."

"Well, everyone knows first base is rolling around nearly naked in a pink room. So we can check off first base. Good job." He raised his hand for a high five, and she laughed and slapped it.

She wasn't sure if she could or should return to playing with his hair, so she left her hand on his chest and forced it to remain still. "What's second base then, do you think?"

"Sex on the beach. With condoms."

She laughed again. She was doing *a lot* of that here. "In October? Brr."

"Sex in a room overlooking the beach," he said without missing a beat.

"Sex in a room overlooking the beach with condoms?" she clarified.

"Of course." He paused. "If you want to."

She smiled. "I want to." She sighed happily. "Does friends-with-benefits second base come with grilled trout?"

Even though she wasn't looking at him, tucked up against his chest as she was, she *felt* his smile. "Of course it does."

Chapter Twelve

Oh, for God's sake.

Jake hadn't been kidding about his plan to beat off twenty-five times before he next saw Nora. Well, maybe twenty-five had been an exaggeration, but he had gotten in the shower an hour ago, after he'd cleaned both the cottage and the fish in preparation for her arrival, to take the edge off. Yesterday he had lasted all of forty-five seconds after she'd started grinding on him, and that was not a statistic he could live with on an ongoing basis.

But as he and Mick sat on the deck waiting for her arrival, it only took one glimpse of her as she rounded the outcropping in the boots he'd left on the other side for her earlier in the day—he'd picked up one of her discarded shoes to check the size before leaving her room in the inn yesterday and bought her a new pair this morning—for him to pop a semi.

Mick barked.

"I know, dude. I know."

He got up, adjusted himself, and walked out to meet her. He'd instructed her to bring nothing, but her arms were laden with bags.

He wasn't sure how to greet her. Should they kiss? He wanted to kiss her, but that was probably uncalled for. He'd meant what he'd said about not doing romance, and he genuinely believed they were on the same page about that. So he gestured for her to hand over her bags. "What's all this?"

She picked up Mick, who was yipping happily at her feet and wagging his entire butt, and started kissing his head and... Was he jealous of a *dog*?

"A pumpkin chiffon pie from Pearl's, a bottle of wine, some doggie treats, and..." She nodded toward the bag in his right hand. "Look in that one."

He pulled out a box of condoms and chuckled. "Extra large. You flatter me."

"Oh, come on."

He shrugged. He had bought some, too. The same kind, in fact.

"I'm actually a little scared of that thing."

Was she talking about his dick? He furrowed his brow.

"I mean, I'm kind of shrimpy." She laughed, but not like she had yesterday. This laughter seemed a bit forced. "And you're kind of...not shrimpy." She grimaced jokingly. "And it's been a while."

"*Nora.*" He stepped in front of her so he could look at her. *God.* He would attend the Mermaid Parade every day for the rest of his life and make small talk with the whole goddamn town before he would want Nora to do something she didn't want to do. "You're here for dinner. Nothing else has to happen."

"I know." She rolled her eyes as she came to a halt— he was blocking her path. "I mean, I'm here for dinner and for ... everything else. I really am. I'm just ..."

He didn't like this. The Nora he knew was decisive. She didn't let sentences trail off. She wasn't afraid to speak her mind. "What?" he said, as gently as he could. Then, realizing that staring at her super intensely probably wasn't helping the cause of getting her to feel comfortable talking about what was bothering her, he continued walking toward the cottage.

He wanted to grab her hand, but that was another thing that wasn't called for. They'd only done it last time as a practical means to keep together as they'd run away from Karl. They were friends who were sleeping together—or friends who had slept together once, past tense, because he wasn't going to push her here—and there was no reason to hold hands.

"What's wrong?" he asked, as gently as he could.

She blew out a breath. "I'm having a crisis of confidence, to be honest. I was with Rufus for five years." She snorted. "And unlike *him*, I never slept with anyone else in those five years."

He held up his free hand, but in a joking way, because he thought it would lighten the mood and that she might appreciate that. "Do not speak her name. You are *way* perkier than she is."

She smiled. "Anyway, yesterday just sort of happened, but this is ... premeditated. Which has left a lot of space for me to ponder the idea that I haven't slept with anyone else besides Rufus for five years, and you know ..." More trailing off. He *hated* that. But he had to let her finish. "In retrospect, I guess I wasn't doing it for him."

Oh God. Someone should just reach into his chest and

pull his heart out right now. Stomp on it and throw it in the trash. Because this woman thought she was not sexy. He tilted his head and his neck cracked. Which seemed appropriate because he felt like he was going into battle.

"Yesterday aside, I haven't slept with anyone since my ex-wife." He wasn't sure what his point was. Unlike her, he wasn't feeling insecure so much as incredibly turned on, but he wanted her to know that this was a big deal for him, too.

Even though it *wasn't* a big deal. Because they were just friends.

It had been a while for him, was the point. A long while. "And we didn't sleep together in the six months between when Jude died and she left. So it's been almost four years for me."

"Really?"

"Really."

"How come?"

"How come we didn't sleep together the last six months, or how come I haven't slept with anyone since?"

"Either. Both." She stopped walking, so he did, too. "Sorry. None of my business."

"No, I'll tell you the whole sordid story if you want to hear it."

That seemed to cheer her. She smiled and started walking again. "Can we grill fish and talk about our sexual insecurities?"

"We can." The answer was immediate and instinctive, which was weird because if you had asked him to make a list of things he wanted to talk about with Nora or anyone else, sexual insecurities would have been dead last.

"I mean, is that allowed? Even if we're going to be friends with benefits, we're still friends, right?"

"Yeah."

"And friends talk about this stuff."

He shrugged. He didn't talk about this stuff with Sawyer and Law, at least since the ill-fated get-a-phone-so-you-can-get-on-hookup-apps intervention of two years ago.

"You're thinking you don't talk about this stuff with Sawyer and Law." She was reading his mind. He chuckled. She kept talking. "Yeah. Don't listen to me. I don't even know what the bases are."

"I already told you, first base is rolling around nearly naked in a pink room. Second base is talking about your sexual insecurities while grilling fish."

"I thought second base was sex on the beach with condoms."

He made a face. "Who told you that? That's not right. Second base is talking about your sexual insecurities while grilling fish. Everybody knows that." Mick, who had run ahead of them, circled back and started barking. "See, even *Mick* knows that."

If someone had asked Nora, yesterday morning during the Anti-Festival, what she would be doing the following evening, the last thing she would have said was that she would be grilling fish with Jake Ramsey and talking about how they lost their virginity.

"I had some girlfriends when I was younger," Jake said as he laid the fish on the grill. "Like, high school stuff. But really, it all started with Mrs. Robinson."

"She wasn't really named Mrs. Robinson, was she?"

He smiled. "No. Her name was Sarah. And she wasn't that old. I was seventeen, and she was thirty-four."

"That's twice your age! You were a child! Isn't that

technically statutory rape?" She sounded like a scandalized old lady, but she couldn't help it.

He shrugged. "All I know is I had the summer of my life. And then I took what I'd learned and became a slut."

Nora cracked up—so much for scandalized. "What does *that* mean?"

"She was here the summer before my junior year of high school. I met Kerrie the spring of my senior year when her family moved here. But before that, let's just say I put my Mrs. Robinson–instilled skills to good use." He came over and sat next to her. "To frequent use."

"You are terrible!"

"Well, maybe, but I never heard any complaints, if you know what I mean." He waggled his eyebrows. "Mrs. Robinson taught me well. I got kind of a reputation."

"So you were a playboy. A player." He smirked but didn't deny it. "A slut, like you said." She cocked her head. "Why do men get to be playboys, but women have to be sluts?"

"That question is above my pay grade, Doc."

She smiled. "So then what? Kerrie arrives and suddenly you're cured of your slutty ways?"

"Pretty much. I fell hard for her."

He got up to flip the fish. His back was to her, which was probably the only reason she had the guts to ask, "What was she like?" She was so curious about the woman who had captured Jake's heart.

"Out of my league."

That was the last thing she'd expected him to say. "What does *that* mean?"

"Smart. Driven. She wanted to be a lawyer—which she did end up doing."

"You're smart."

He snorted. "You need a 2.0 GPA to graduate from the high school here, or you did in my era at least. Guess what mine was?"

She chuckled. "I'm going to go with 2.0."

"Nope, it was 1.99, but there was a tornado that year, and it destroyed the outdoor stage they always used for graduation. I rebuilt it, and the principal rounded me up."

"Jake!" She hated hearing him run himself down, though he didn't seem that concerned about it. "There are lots of different kinds of intelligence."

"Don't worry, Doc. My self-esteem is fine. In those years I was just way more interested in being on the lake or snowmobiling or whatever than I was in being inside doing homework. And I have *lots* of other redeeming qualities." He did the over-the-top eyebrow-wagging thing again. "Thanks in part to Mrs. Robinson."

"So here we are supposedly talking about sexual insecurities, but it doesn't seem like you actually have any. It seems more like you had a dry spell by choice." A grief-induced dry spell, but she wasn't going to say that.

"I guess. Sawyer and Law bought me a phone a couple years ago because they thought I should get on one of those hookup apps, but I wasn't feeling it."

"I seriously cannot imagine you with a phone."

"I know. They were like, 'Well, you can use it only for this.' But no thanks, man. To the hookup apps but also to the phone more generally. I don't need my brain turned to mush."

"See? You *are* smart."

"So what about you, Doc? Hit me with those insecurities." She paused, and he got up and went to the grill. "If you want to. This is done. You want to eat out here or are you too cold?"

"Out here, please." She was cold, but she didn't want to go inside yet. "I'm still not over the fact that your front yard is literally Lake Huron."

"Okay, sit tight for a sec. I'll be right back."

She appreciated what he was doing, which was breaking up their heavy conversation. She suspected that when he came back, he wouldn't prod her. He would leave it to her to decide if she wanted to tell him anything. Which she did. Even though it was slightly embarrassing, given that he apparently had no sexual hang-ups to speak of. But his absence afforded her the opportunity to gather her thoughts as she stared at the lake.

She was starting to see that the lake had moods, for lack of a better word. The stillness of her first visit here, back when it was still warm, was nowhere in evidence. Tonight, there was a decent wind, and the water was choppy and gray, crashing against the shore in big, foamy waves. But it was still soothing, somehow. What had he said before? *The lake goes on.* It was oddly comforting. The lake didn't care about her tale of woe.

But you know who did?

He came back out with a tray laden with dishes. He winked at her as he set it on the table. "One more trip. Be right back."

Jake did. Jake cared.

A startling thought hit her: Jake was pretty much her best friend these days. Yeah, she had friends in Toronto. She had a couple group texts going, and people had checked in on her since the move. She'd issued vague invitations for them to come visit "once she was settled." But most of them were friends from the hospital who knew Rufus, too, and she felt awkward about that. Anyway, she'd always been closer to her sister—and her grandma, for that matter—than to her friends.

But what made a best friend? Someone you liked hanging out with? Someone who was always there for you? Someone you had inside jokes with? By all those metrics, Jake fit the bill, though maybe if there was a long-standing-history requirement, he didn't pass that.

Also, what about "Someone you have sex with"? Ha. She should probably be freaking out a little more over the prospect of sex messing up their friendship. People in books and movies were always worried about that. But for some reason, it didn't bother her. She wasn't having any problems compartmentalizing, and she was pretty sure Jake wasn't, either.

He came back with a bottle of water, a bottle of wine, a lantern-style flashlight—it had been late when she arrived, and it was getting dark now—and a big, heavy quilt that he draped over her shoulders before settling himself next to her on the bench.

"This is the softest quilt I've ever felt." It was like a cozy, cottony hug. She eyed as much of it as she could see, tucked as it was around her. "It's gorgeous, too." The design was subtle but complex, made of tiny triangles that varied only slightly in color or pattern. You had to look closely to see the variation.

"My mom made it. She always said you shouldn't treat quilts like pristine works of art. That you should wash them a lot so they get nice and soft. Use them, and not just inside. She was always dragging them around to use as picnic blankets or camping bedding." He served her a piece of fish as he spoke and nudged the salad bowl toward her.

"Oh my God, this is good," she said after her first bite of fish. "It's different from before, I think?"

"Yeah. This is pickerel. It's also good lightly breaded and panfried. I'll do it that way next time, but I'm trying to make the most of the last days of grilling season."

Next time. She loved the way he kept saying that. And the amazing thing was, she was pretty sure there *would* be a next time regardless of whether they ever got around to sleeping together this evening. It ratified her feelings that things weren't going to get weird. Jake was a person who could roll with the punches.

And, slightly surprisingly, she seemed to be, too.

Look at her. The life reset had yielded a new, flexible personality and a man-god best friend with benefits.

"I had a string of failed relationships before Rufus," she said, steering them back toward the topic at hand, even though he'd given her an out. "Going all the way back to high school. They almost always ended with the guy complaining that I didn't have enough time for him. Which I can't really argue with. School always came first, in high school and in undergrad, and then med school and my residency? I mean, forget it. You work a million hours a week. My last boyfriend before Rufus told me I was not cut out to be someone's girlfriend. He issued this ultimatum, saying I had to meet him halfway or he was going to leave me."

"What did that mean?"

"I don't know. I interpreted it to mean I should cook more, do more around the house. And to be fair, I really wasn't doing my share."

"What did this guy do? For a living, I mean."

"He was a junior high school science teacher."

"Well, that's just stupid. You're working more than he is—and he's not working at all in the summer—he should do the cooking."

"Well, isn't that enlightened of you?" she teased.

"I'm serious. You figure out what optimizes the collective well-being, maybe taking into account what everyone does and doesn't like to do, and you do that. That's why I was staying home with Jude."

Man. Jake Ramsey, if he could ever get over his perma-grief, would make someone a great husband someday.

"So what happened?" he asked.

"Despite my best intentions and my pledge to improve, I really *wasn't* doing half the housework. And then one time we had sex, and I fell asleep in the middle of it. And he left me."

He cracked up.

"In my defense, I had just come off a twenty-four-hour shift. The last thing I wanted to do was have sex."

He furrowed his brow and paused with a bite of fish halfway to his mouth. "So why did you?"

"I don't know. I was trying to meet him halfway?" She could sense that he was gearing up to object to this concept, and he wasn't wrong. Maybe post-reset Nora wouldn't have been so eager to please at any cost, but she didn't really want to get into it. "Anyway, my point is, then I met Rufus, and all of a sudden the scheduling stuff wasn't such a big deal, because he was as busy—and tired—as I was. He got it. None of my boyfriends before had been doctors. So I thought, *Hey, maybe my previous problems were just occupational hazards*. But then..." She shrugged. He could fill in the rest. He knew about Perky Chloe. "I guess it shook my confidence."

He rolled his eyes. "Fair enough, but I think the moral of this story is that Rufus is an idiot."

She liked that he said *idiot*. Everyone else had said something on the spectrum from *jerk* (Erin) to *asshole* (Grandma). *Idiot*, though, framed Rufus's behavior not as something mean so much as something stupid. Like his nuking their relationship showed a lack of intelligence. She smiled.

"What else you got?" he said, making a bring-it motion with his fingers.

"What do you mean?"

"When you said grill fish and talk about sexual insecurities, plural, I was imagining a longer list. Not just a story about a couple dim-witted ex-boyfriends."

Hmm. "I guess that's it."

"All right, then."

She laughed a little. Because she felt good. He'd earnestly listened to her fears, but ultimately dispatched them. Dinner, which they were almost done with, had been great. The darkening lake was enthralling. The stars were starting to come out. She was nestled in the world's softest quilt, bolstered against the cold autumn air.

Also, she was going to have sex. She glanced at him. Probably.

His hair was down. Windblown and slightly tangled and *God*, that *hair*.

She was going to have to make the move, she was pretty sure. He wasn't going to just swoop on in after she'd expressed misgivings. He wasn't that kind of guy.

He was wearing a short-sleeve T-shirt. Man-gods like him were probably immune to the cold. But maybe that was her in. "You must be cold." She could see him starting to disagree, but she did her own version of his exaggerated eyebrow wagging and held up a corner of the quilt.

He grinned, flicked off the lantern, and scooched in. They reshuffled themselves until they were both cocooned in the quilt, Nora tucked under his arm. She sighed. She was both empty and full. Full of another delicious dinner but also feeling like she'd shed a bunch of emotional junk in their conversation.

She tilted her head back. "You know, I thought the stars were impressive in town, but this is really something."

"Yeah, there's zero light pollution out here."

"I know I sound like a broken record, but it's still amazing to me that you get to live with all this"—she was too tucked into his body and their quilt to extract an arm, so she rotated her head, meaning to indicate the lake and the beach and the sky—"every day like it's not a big deal."

"I'm lucky."

She felt lucky, too. For the first time in a long time. She smiled into the cold dark. "Well, you're also about to *get* lucky."

"I'm lucky," Jake had said earlier. He'd said it unthinkingly. But he'd *meant* it, which was actually kind of astonishing. He wasn't the type of person who walked around marinating in self-pity, but no one could deny that he'd been through some shit in recent years.

But here he was in his cove under the stars, making out with Nora Walsh, who was straddling his lap.

So yeah, right now? Lucky.

God. He'd forgotten how good kissing could be. Or maybe kissing had never been this good. Either way, kissing Nora was pretty damn fantastic. She was *all* in, sighing into his mouth as their tongues tangled lazily. It was a slow, heavy, drugging kiss that sent desire pulsing through his body. He brought his hands up to cradle her face, letting his fingers wrap around and press into her scalp. He'd meant it, all the times he'd told her he liked her hair, but he *really* liked her hair. He liked being able to see the shape of her head, to span it with his hands. It was strangely hot. He slid his middle fingers farther around until they met at the base of her skull.

She moaned.

So he did it some more, dragging the pads of his fingers slowly but firmly against her scalp.

"Uhhhh."

She liked that. He made a note.

Her head got heavier in his hands, like she was having trouble holding it up.

Her jaw slackened some more, too, causing her mouth to open wider. He swept his tongue more deeply inside, licking into her slow and dirty.

He could feel it, too, the loosening of his body, the surrender of his limbs growing heavy.

She was still wrapped in the quilt. When she'd shimmied onto his lap, she'd kept hold of it, holding it around her shoulders like a cape. But as he pressed again into the tender spot at the base of her skull, she moaned again. Loudly—it echoed across the cove and pulled an answering groan from him. She let go of the quilt, slid forward on his lap, and wrapped her arms around him. Even boosted up on his lap like this, she was a head shorter than him, and it was impossible for them to be chest to chest like this and also kiss. She mashed herself against him, tucking her head under his chin and settling her core right on his erection. In keeping with the slow, languid nature of their previous making out, she didn't move. There was none of the grinding from last time. She just pressed against him— hard. Like she couldn't get close enough.

He felt like he was going to implode as he let his hands come off her skull so he could wrap his arms around her. Tight. So tight. She was small but solid in his arms. No one moved. And in the absence of any thrusting or writhing or friction of any sort, it should have been impossible, but his dick grew harder. They were fully clothed and fully still. How could he be this turned on? "Jesus, Nora," he whispered. "Fuck."

"Yeah." Her lips were against his chest, so her voice was muffled. "That."

"Huh?" he managed.

"Let's fuck."

He didn't need to be told twice. Without moving any part of his body besides his legs, he stood up, taking her with him. She clung to him, wrapping her legs around him as he straightened. She was light enough that he could spare a hand for the sliding door. He aimed for the couch, but she snapped her fingers and pointed at the kitchen island, on which lay her bags. He detoured there, and she grabbed the box of condoms.

With those in hand, he rerouted them to the couch, turned around, and sat on it, putting them in exactly the same position they'd been in before, except inside the warmth of the cottage.

But no sooner were they settled than she hopped off his lap. He was about to lodge a protest when he realized she was undoing her jeans.

He'd built a fire in the fireplace before she arrived, and it had burned down mostly to embers, but it was enough to see by. And she was something to see as she kicked off her jeans haphazardly.

"I'm coming right back there." Her voice was husky as she nodded at his lap. "So unless you want me to hump you over your clothes, I suggest you take your pants off, too."

Oh, crap. He pressed down on his dick for a second to get it to calm down before he did what she told him—but not before contemplating the strangely hot image of a naked Nora "humping him" while he was fully clothed. Something to remember for later, maybe.

The minute he sat back down, relieved of his pants, she climbed on top of him and immediately started on the buttons of her blouse. Following her lead, he pulled his shirt off. She slid closer on his lap until they were back where they'd been outside—minus the clothes. Which meant her nipples scraped against his chest, and she ground against his cock. She was wet already. So wet.

He hissed. He wanted to devour her. But he forced himself to be still, like she was. Closed his eyes and resisted bucking his hips up in time to the pulsing in his dick.

It was funny. This was exactly the same position they'd been in last night, in her room—her straddling his lap. But despite the mechanical similarities, everything was different. Before, they'd been teasing each other, alternately laughing and rocking against each other.

This was...heavy. Not in a bad way. But he had always thought of desire as something that escalated, ratcheting up and up and up until it exploded. This was the reverse. Like a coil spinning slowly inward, twisting inexorably tighter, like it was going to keep collapsing in on itself in a kind of slow-motion implosion.

"Jake." She invoked his name on a long, slow exhalation as she started moving her torso from side to side against his. He remembered how much she'd seemed to like having her breasts played with last night, so he slid his hands down to cup them from the sides, aiming to add to the sensation as she rubbed herself against his chest. Her nipples were sharp little nubs. It felt like someone was drawing on him. "Oh my God, Jake."

She pulled back with her torso, and he let his hands slide around to cup her breasts from the front. She hissed as she listed sideways. She was aiming for the box of condoms on the couch next to him.

The woman was good with her hands. In a matter of seconds, she had the box opened and a condom unwrapped. It was his turn to hiss as she unrolled it over him. She hadn't actually touched his dick with her hands last night. He'd come too soon, rutting against her like a teenager. And even though this touch—the condom-unrolling touch—was all business, it felt so good. The pixie hands *looked* so good, one of them steadying him as the other sheathed him.

She kneeled up on the sofa and placed her hands on his shoulders as she hovered over his length. "Okay?"

A noise came out of him he didn't recognize. It felt like a laugh—a laugh of incredulity because of course, yes, this was okay—but simultaneously like a groan of agreement. "Yeah," he bit out. "You?"

Her answer was a wicked smile—and a slow, tight slide down his dick.

He tipped his head back and closed his eyes. "Fuuuuck."

He had forgotten what this was like. Or maybe he'd never *known* what this was like. What *she* was like. She was tight and hot—and she was going to be his undoing.

She paused about halfway down and inhaled. He opened his eyes, righted his head, and examined her face. Her eyes were closed, and her face was screwed up in what he hoped was pleasure and not pain.

He let his hands settle lightly on her hips. Not to exhort her, but to remind her that he was with her. To facilitate their disentanglement if that was what had to happen. "You okay?"

"Yeah." She smiled but kept her eyes closed, like she was concentrating on something in her mind's eye. "I just need a sec."

He took the opportunity to examine her face. He'd thought of her as being tinged with the supernatural the first time he'd seen her. The pixie with the almost-white hair and the blue-gray eyes, she'd seemed cool, gilded with ice almost. But now, on his lap, in his cottage, painted with warm, orange light from the dying fire, she was positively radiating heat. It wasn't just the wet warmth that encircled his cock, a velvet vise—though it *was* that—it was Nora. She was warm. She was warming *him*, somehow, when nobody else had been able to for so long.

She opened her eyes wide, said, "Wow," and sank down most of the rest of the way.

All he was doing, on the surface of things, was sitting on his ass on the couch. He was no longer carrying her. He wasn't lifting anything or holding anything up. But sweat poured from his skin all the same. Had he just thought she made him warm? No, that wasn't the right word. He was *on fire*. The effort required to just sit there, while she *impaled* herself on him, looking at him the whole while with astonishment, like he'd invented sex or something, was almost unendurable.

"There," she breathed as she sank the last few millimeters.

Her eyes were warm, too, as they bored into his. Cool gray-blue but also *warm*, which should have been impossible.

There was so much pressure gathered at the base of his spine, in his balls, that all he could do was let loose a low groan. He fought to keep his eyes open through it. He didn't want to be the one to break the eye contact between them, which, oddly, felt like it was connecting them as much as their bodies were. He thought at first that they were going to take another pause, because she didn't move initially. Then he thought they were going to resume the same slow, languid, heavy rhythm from before, because she tilted her hips slowly forward, an inch or so maybe, like she was trying to work herself even deeper onto him.

"*Yes*," he exhorted, because that was a plan that suited him *just fine*.

But then she shocked him by running her hands, which had remained resting on the tops of his shoulders during her long, slow, exquisitely torturous descent, up the sides of his neck. His pulse thundered under her touch, but the pixie hands didn't stop there. They slid up over his jaw. Over his ears, squishing his earlobes as they dragged their way upward. Finally her hands were buried in his hair.

She made fists, tangling her fingers in his hair as she lifted herself a few inches off him.

Don't go. His hands instinctively tightened their hold on her hips. But he forced himself to let go, because of course he couldn't keep her there if she didn't want to be there.

But she wasn't going, not for good anyway. She slid back down and moaned. It felt like a reprieve, and it sent a bolt of lust spiking up through his chest.

And back up she went, tightening her grip, using his hair for leverage to help her thrust against him. She was establishing a rhythm, and once he got the hang of it, he put his hands back on her hips, letting them splay over her ass cheeks and help lift her up and encourage her down.

It was a rhythm that was going to kill him, though. Just end him right here and now. It was slow. So torturously, deliciously slow. He started lifting his hips up to meet her measured downstrokes. He couldn't help it, but she didn't seem to mind. She just opened her eyes wider and laughed. A single, disbelieving "Ha!" escaped her lips, but it morphed into a moan.

Suddenly she jerked and tilted her hips forward. Spread

her legs wider as her expression turned frustrated. He was pretty sure she was trying to rub her clit on him even as she kept bouncing up and down on his dick. Experimentally he let go of her ass with one hand and sought out the nub with his fingers.

She moaned again and bucked toward him. He watched her closely as his fingers slid through her wetness. "Yes?" he whispered.

She nodded rapidly and lost her rhythm, her hips stuttering up and down and forward and back, but with no predictability. He rutted shamelessly upward, making the shallow, punishing strokes that he needed.

"Oh! Oh!" She went still for a moment, every part of her small body tensing in his arms. With one final "Oh!" she shattered. Her inner muscles spasmed around him, and her hands twisted in his hair, the sharp pull on his scalp shoving him over the edge of his own release. He swallowed a shout and thrust up so hard he feared momentarily that he was going to buck her off him, but he steadied them.

Remarkably, they'd kept staring at each other the whole time—and they still were.

He didn't know what to say. So he just kept staring at her, panting.

Until the phone rang.

"You have a landline!" she exclaimed. She started to climb off him, but he banded his arms around her. He didn't want her to go yet.

"I do, but I ignore it most of the time." He was surprised his voice still worked. Surprised it hadn't been scorched into oblivion.

She shot him a bemused look as the ancient answering machine lurched to life. The beep was really long, because there were God knew how many messages on that tape.

Anyone who truly needed to find him knew how to do it, so he wasn't overly worried about it.

"Jake. It's Dennis Bates. Any chance you can fill in for me on the bridge for about an hour tomorrow evening? I have...something I have to do. Around six. Let me know."

Dennis, damn him, had ruined the moment. Nora was shifting on his lap, and he could hardly insist she stay there. He reached down to hold on to the condom as she slid off.

"Oh, crap. I didn't realize I was pulling your hair," she said as she disentangled her hands from said hair. "Sorry."

He winked at her as he tied off the condom. "You can pull my hair anytime you like, Doc."

She rolled her eyes as she grabbed another of his mom's quilts, one he had draped over the back of the sofa, and wrapped it around herself. He wanted to tell her not to do that, but that was not the kind of thing a person said in this sort of situation.

He watched her retrieve her clothes, and she hitched her head toward the small hallway that led away from the main room. "Bathroom?"

"First door on the left."

When she emerged a few minutes later, she said, "What happened to Mick? Oh my God, did we leave Mick outside?"

It took a considerable amount of effort to hoist himself off the couch. He was pretty sure his body was in shock. Going from four years of being on ice to *that*? It was a miracle she hadn't killed him. "No, he went in with me when I got the quilt and didn't come back outside." He pulled on his jeans, slipped past her, and flipped the light on in one of the two small bedrooms at the end of the hall. "I bet he's in here."

She followed him in. "Whoa."

"My mom used this as a studio. Well, mostly she painted outside, but she kept all her stuff in here." He pointed to a pile of old towels folded into a stack on the floor. Mick was curled up on top of them, snoring happily away. "She kept those towels there for quick cleanups. I've been noticing that Mick likes that spot."

"Wow. It looks like your mother was just here."

"Yeah, I haven't touched it." He moved past her. "Check this out." He pointed to a tiny unused easel on the floor next to her main one. "She got this for Jude."

"Oh," she breathed. He felt her looking at him. She was checking to see if he was okay, facing this memory of his dead mother and his dead son.

Oddly, he *was* okay. "He was too young to use it, obviously, but she had this whole plan to convert him. She always said my brother and I took after our dad too much to be any good at art, and I think she was right."

"Well, I don't know. All that carpentry. All those paint jobs. You have an eye for beauty."

Maybe so. Because Nora, her face flushed and her hair messed up, was surely a sight to appreciate.

"I mean, this place, too. The lake. You definitely have an eye, even if you're not an artist per se." She shook her head as if rousing herself. "I should go." She shot him an almost shy smile. "I should get out of your hair."

He wanted to tell her that she wasn't in his hair. Or that if she was, he was happy to have her there. He wanted to grab her hand and literally tangle it in his hair again.

But that was just his body overreacting to the end of the long dry spell.

He held her coat for her and went hunting for his shirt. "Hang on. I'll walk you."

"You don't have to do that."

"Nice try."

"Should we wake Mick and have him come with us so he can get some exercise?"

"Nah. He ran around all day."

"Jake Ramsey." She put her hands on her hips and adopted a mock scolding face. "You are going to spoil my dog. What's he going to do when I find a place to live and he has to go back to spending days by himself inside? What's he going to do when I move back to Toronto?"

"He'll be fine," Jake said firmly. He wasn't sure if he was talking to her or to himself.

As they set out across the beach, he was hit again with the strong desire to take her hand. Unlike on the way in, he even had an excuse. It was a moonless night, so it was pitch-dark and she didn't know this beach like he did. But they'd said no romance, so he needed to be disciplined here.

"So, uh, I have something to tell you."

The way she said it, all trepidatious, gave him pause. "Okay."

"I mean, I should have just said something earlier. I don't know why I didn't."

Oh, crap. Something was wrong.

"I'm, uh, actually on the pill."

"Okay?" He was trying to figure out where she was going with this.

"Rufus was super worried about pregnancy. Like, super, irrationally worried. Which was annoying in a way because it wasn't like it was *his* career that would have been threatened by an unplanned pregnancy. So I was on the pill *and* we used condoms."

"Okay."

"Which means I was always having safe sex, even though I was apparently sleeping with a lying philanderer for at least part of the time. And just to be sure, I had STI testing done and it all came back fine."

Oh. Holy shit. Was she saying what he thought she was saying?

"Have you had STI testing since Kerrie?"

"I have." He was glad it was dark. She couldn't see his face flush with pleasure. "So what are you saying, Doc?"

"Oh, crap, I forgot the boots."

They had reached the end of the beach, the spot at which they needed to wade out to get around the outcropping.

He'd forgotten his boots, too. She made him forget stuff. But no matter. He kicked off the flip-flops he was wearing and swung her into his arms. This was better than holding hands anyway.

She shrieked and laughed and said, "Don't do that! It's freezing!" But then she settled, wrapping her arms around his neck.

"So what are you saying, Doc?" he asked again, his pulse thrumming.

"I'm saying maybe third base is sex without a condom. Though I'm pretty sure that home base is, like, 'full sex,' as the kids would say. But anyway. My point is just that maybe we don't need condoms." She paused and laughed nervously. "If you want to do this again. And, you know, if that's okay with you. Because no pressure at all. I mean, we each just bought a box of condoms, so—"

"Nora?"

"Yeah?"

"Hush."

"Okay."

"Anytime you want to have sex, with or without condoms, you just let me know, okay?"

"So, just like splash my way into the cove and break down your door demanding sex?" She laughed.

"Works for me. Or call me."

"Are you going to give me your phone number?" she teased.

"I am. I might even start checking my messages."

Chapter Thirteen

❧

$\mathcal{N}$ora spent Thanksgiving with Eve, Sawyer, and Clara, and Jake, Art, and Jamila.

It was a little bit awkward.

Apparently Sawyer and Clara, who had been on their zown since Sawyer was a teenager and Clara was little, often spent holidays with the Ramsey family. And Eve had been folded into the flock once she and Sawyer got together.

Now they were folding Nora in, too. Because she was new in town and had no plans and they were nice people. Not because she was together with anyone.

Or at least not in the way they imagined.

She shot a glance at Jake. She had been trying not to do that.

He didn't notice. They were all clustered around the kitchen island at Art and Jamila's house, munching on appetizers while Jamila fluttered around, refusing any help to get dinner ready. Jake was staring at the counter and nursing a beer.

She didn't know if he was always like this—if this was part of the gruff, silent persona other people always remarked on—or if her presence was making things weird. She'd tried to refuse the invitation, but Eve and Sawyer wouldn't let her.

He wasn't just nursing the beer, he was sliding a thumbnail under the edge of the label and working it back and forth.

Oh God.

She had discovered this thing in recent days. Or Jake had discovered it. Anyway, it had been discovered. It involved her clit, which he paid a lot of attention to generally, but once, by accident, he'd sort of scratched it. She must have responded in such a way as to inspire him to do it again. And now there was a *move*, for lack of a better word. He would get her all worked up and then back off and play hard to get. After enough whining on her part, which he seemed to enjoy more than he really had a right to given that he was basically torturing her, he would gently scrape his nail—that very thumbnail he was now dragging back and forth over that beer label—over her clit. And she would blow. She would *detonate*. And he would smirk.

She hated it.

Aw, who was she kidding? She *loved* it. Just thinking about it made her squirmy.

"You don't do Thanksgiving with your family in Toronto, dear?" Jamila jolted Nora from her dirty imaginings. She was bent over basting the turkey as she spoke, which gave Nora a moment to get her act together. *Don't look at Jake. Don't look at Jake.*

"Well," she said, hoping her face wasn't reddening,

"my brother, my father, my grandma, and I are doctors. And my mom's a nurse. My sister is the only one who doesn't work in a hospital. It's impossible for everyone to get the holiday off, so we don't even try. We used to celebrate it on American Thanksgiving in November—my mom was born in the States, so there was a connection there—but everyone always thought that was too close to Christmas. So we do it on an alternate weekend, and now it's a full-on tradition." Which she wasn't going to say too much about, because their "alternate weekend" was always the weekend after Thanksgiving, which meant she was going to miss "Walsh-giving" this year. She was signed up to cover the inn for Eve and Sawyer's vacation—which she'd done without realizing the conflict. And she wasn't about to renege on the folks who were giving her free housing. Her family was mad at her, but they'd get over it.

"Sounds eminently logical," Eve said.

"So how have you been finding Moonflower Bay?" Jamila asked.

"Great," Nora said. "Everyone's been very... welcoming." *Don't look at Jake. Don't look at Jake.*

Jake had been very welcoming just this morning. And the day before that. And before that. They were doing a really good job with third base. Or home base, or whatever.

They were like teenagers in heat, basically.

In the week since their dinner at the cove, they had been jumping each other every chance they got. Going out of their way to jump each other.

Which was all fine. It was good.

It was *great*.

She just hadn't spent any time in proximity to him with other people around, much less his *dad*.

"Okay, everyone, I think we're finally ready." Jamila shooed them into the dining room. She started pointing to spots and naming who she wanted where. "Nora, you go there, next to Jake."

Nora obeyed, despite the fact that her body was mutinying. It was confused. It had been conditioned to respond physically to Jake when he was nearby. It had *not* been conditioned to sit quietly next to him through what, judging by the enormity of the feast laid out on the table, was going to be a very long dinner.

Nora laid her napkin in her lap and looked to Jamila for a cue to begin eating.

Jamila held up her hands and said, "Grace!"

Oh no. This wasn't a fold-your-hands-in-your-lap kind of grace. It was a hand-holding grace.

She tried to concentrate on Clara's hand, which was small and cool, rather than on Jake's, which was, as had been well established in recent days, big and hot and the perfect mixture of rough and gentle.

"Lord, we give thee thanks for what we are about to receive, today and every day. Bless those at this table as well as those who are absent from us, may they rest in peace. Bless this circle of family and friends. Bless our newcomer, Dr. Walsh, who is so very needed in our community. In thy name, amen."

"Thank you, my dear," Art said.

Everybody dropped hands. Except Jake didn't let go of hers. He was holding it under the table—so no one could see, which she supposed was a small mercy. She tugged as subtly as she could. He did not let go. He appeared unmoved as he picked up his fork with his left hand—he was seated to her left, so his right hand was joined with her left. The dude was right-handed. She knew that for a fact.

Completely unruffled, he speared a roast potato and popped it in his mouth.

Oh hell no. They were *not* going to spend the whole meal secretly holding hands. What happened to "I don't do romance"?

Forget subtle. She yanked.

Success! But it did cause everyone's attention to shift to her. Her not-subtle yank had had the effect of tugging Jake toward her before it managed to sever their connection, so they were face to face in a way that probably looked weird.

"Did you grow up in this house, Jake?" she asked, trying to make it look like she'd turned to him to ask him this totally innocent question.

"Nope." He picked up his fork with his right hand.

So he was going to retreat into his Mute Jake persona. She refrained from rolling her eyes, but only just.

"I moved here after my first wife—Jake's mom—died," Art said. "We lived just a block over. I wanted to stay in the neighborhood, but I didn't need that big a house anymore."

Jamila smiled at him affectionately. "We thought about upsizing after I came on the scene, but Art has this idea that we're going to buy an RV and live like vagabonds after I retire, which is at the end of this school year."

"You say 'idea' like you're not into it, but you *know* you're into it," Art teased. Nora thought back to the way they had bantered at the flu clinic.

"Oh, hush."

"She's even designed the interior," Art said. "She's a pretty serious antiques collector." He beamed with obvious pride. It was adorable. "This is going to be the best-looking RV in the history of RVs."

"If this place is anything to go by, I suspect you're right," Nora said. "Your home is beautiful."

"You have any luck finding a new place?" Jamila asked. "Don't forget I can lend you furniture."

Nora winced. She hadn't even started looking. She was too busy working to make time to go on the hunt. Okay, no, that wasn't true. She was too busy getting it on with Jake to go on the hunt.

"I haven't." She glanced at Eve. "I really need to get on that."

"Not on my account, you don't," Eve said. "It's been awesome having you at the inn. And you're making it possible for us to go on vacation."

"Well, thanks. You really saved me there."

"I like the idea that my old room is being put to good use."

Jake coughed. "Yeah, it's good to . . . put things to use."

She knew he was thinking of the same thing she was— hitting "first base" in that room the day of the Anti-Festival.

Everyone looked at Jake curiously, probably in part because it was a cryptic thing to say. But no doubt also because Jake was not one to make observations, cryptic or otherwise, unprompted.

He was messing with her again.

And it was working. Her cheeks heated. They were probably as pink as the room. And there wasn't a damn thing she could do about it.

"That was delicious," Eve said after they emerged from Art and Jamila's. She looked around. "Do you have your truck here, Jake? We can take you to the end of the beach."

"Nah, I walked, and I think I'll walk back, too, but thanks." Jake eyed Nora. She was still annoyed about the hand-holding, he was pretty sure. And she had come in the car with Eve and Sawyer and Clara. So this was probably goodbye for the evening.

Which was more than a little disappointing.

"A walk sounds good, actually," Nora said. "Walk off some of that dinner. If you don't mind company."

Jake had to tamp down a smile.

Nora waited until Sawyer's car was out of sight to whirl on him. "What the hell was that?"

He played dumb. "What the hell was what?"

"Oh, come on, Jake. Holding hands under the table?"

"Eh, it's fine." She did not understand how deeply ingrained his reputation was in town. People saw what they expected to see. "No one noticed."

Except maybe Sawyer. He was starting to worry that Sawyer was onto him. But that was more of a long-standing worry, predating the evening's renegade hand-holding.

But Sawyer aside, people did *not* expect Jake to be holding the new town doctor's hand under the table.

"What happened to not doing romance?" she asked. "Because I"—she stopped and smacked her chest. It was a quiet, still night, so it echoed across the dark street. "I am *not interested* in romance."

"That wasn't romance."

"Then what the hell was it?"

Good question. All he knew was that every once in a while—or, okay, a lot of the time—he was seized with the absurd desire to grab her hand.

He always resisted. Because she was right. They weren't doing the relationship thing. Grasping hands while they were having sex was one thing. While they were walking along the beach? No.

So he always managed to resist. But when suddenly

thrust into a situation where he was *already holding her hand*, he just...hadn't let go.

But Nora was right. What they were doing was *not* romance. Luckily, there was another explanation.

"That was me trolling you."

"Excuse me?"

"You said it yourself. We're friends with benefits, but we're also friends. Sometimes I like to prank my friends." Which had been true. Like fifteen years ago. "One time in high school when Law's parents were out of town and he was supposed to be minding the bar—he's a few years older than I am—Sawyer and I drained one of the kegs and filled it with water." Never mind that that was the last "prank" he could think of.

She shook her head. "You are the *worst*."

But she wasn't saying it like she meant it.

They walked on in easy silence until they turned onto Main Street. The inn was a few storefronts up.

"I'm fine from here," she said.

"You say that like you *don't* want me to blow your mind this evening."

She snorted.

"Well, okay then. If you're fine..." He started walking backward. "Good night."

"Jake." She stopped with her hands on her hips, shaking her head like she was a schoolteacher trying to cover her amusement by faking annoyance.

"Nora." He kept walking backward, but he slowed down. God, she was so easy to tease. She was *fun* to tease. Which was, for him, rather extraordinary.

"Come on, Jake." She crooked her finger at him.

He jogged back to her. "I'm not sure I understand. Your words aren't making sense. You might have to use body language." He held out a hand. "You might have to *take my hand* and show me what you want me to do."

"*Jake.*" With that single syllable, her tone shifted. Lurched, really, from light and bantery to low and needy.

He shifted to accommodate it. They were done playing.

This happened to him, with her. They'd be cruising along just fine and suddenly there would be this giant swerve. She would do something or say something, or even just look at him the wrong way—the right way?—and lust would just...slam into him.

It happened to her, too, he was pretty sure. She walked briskly and purposefully up the sidewalk, but she *radiated* need. He did, too, he suspected, because taking her hand or not taking her hand was suddenly the least of his worries. His entire body felt like it was pulsing to an unseen rhythm. It was an invisible force that was bigger than he was. All he could do was obey it. It wanted him to touch her, and not just her hand. It wanted him to be inside her.

"*Nora,*" he bit out as she kept going, past the Mermaid. He sounded like he was mad at her, which wasn't quite right, but where was she going? They hadn't talked about it overtly, but they seemed to have entered into an unspoken agreement to keep the fact that they were hooking up to themselves. Which meant no hooking up at the Mermaid, where they would risk Eve and Sawyer finding out. So they'd been spending a lot of time at his place.

"*Dammit,*" he muttered. It was a good twenty-minute walk to the cove from here. He should have driven.

She stepped into Main Street, cutting across it midblock. He followed her automatically—the pulsing inside him made it impossible not to—and his mind spun up, assessing the situation. The gazebo? No, too cold—the pixie doctor got cold easily—never mind too risky in their town full of busybodies. He eyed the street. Lawson's was closed for Thanksgiving, but Law lived upstairs. If he was home, maybe Jake could—

He'd overshot her. She'd stopped, and he'd kept going. He turned back to look at her.

"Jake."

There it was again, that yearning, borderline desperate tone. He was powerless against that tone. It lit a fire inside him. Lust burned, but also, alongside that, a fierce need to answer. To act. To do whatever she wanted.

She was standing in front of her clinic, pausing with the keys in her hand.

Her clinic. Of course.

What was the matter with his brain?

He took a deep breath. Clearly it wasn't getting enough blood or oxygen or whatever, because all the stuff required for rational thinking had flooded into his dick. His poor, beleaguered dick that hadn't seen this much action, this kind of intensity, in years. Maybe ever.

He worried momentarily that his legs wouldn't work. That in the continuing cascade of his body shutting down everything but his most animalistic needs, they literally wouldn't be capable of carrying him back to her.

But then she turned the key, clicked the door open, and looked at him. Just looked at him. Like her eyes commanded his legs or something. Whatever, he was *there*. Standing right next to her but not touching her, which was something somebody should give him a goddamn medal for.

She pressed her hand against his back and shoved him inside. As much as he wanted to press her up against the door as she shut it behind her, the front of the clinic was a waiting area with a big plate-glass window looking over the street.

She pushed him again. He might have laughed, had the whole thing seemed less urgent. Instead he hustled across the dark waiting area and through the open doorway next to the reception desk.

He'd thought they were heading to her office, which was at the end of the short hallway, but he'd overshot, apparently. She grabbed the back of his T-shirt and yanked, pulling him back and into the first exam room with her. Once inside she lifted the hem of her sweater over her head.

He slammed the door, and he did press her back against it this time. There was some kind of poster on it, though, and as he reached around to undo the clasp of her bra, it snagged on his hand or her bra or something, and ripped, and the sound ricocheted across the small room. And even though it was not, objectively, a sexual sound, it made his dick even harder.

It was like they were tearing the world apart to get to each other.

She shoved her hands up the hem of his shirt. They were cold, but it felt like they were burning him. She paused for a moment with her hands flat on his chest, panting, staring at him. He remembered, suddenly, that night he'd had her to the cove for the first time and his brain had glitched on the image of her hands, pressing against his chest.

Well, damn. Look at him now.

The hands weren't doing any caressing or anything like that, though. They were shoving. He loved the way she thought she could manhandle him. She was always pushing him or pulling his hair.

But maybe she *could* manhandle him, because he always did what she wanted him to do, went where she wanted him to go.

In that spirit he stepped back, let her push him away, but

it came with an involuntary growl that surprised him. Even though his higher brain understood that she probably had a plan he would end up 100 percent endorsing, his body was not down with the short-term sacrifice involved in severing their connection.

"Take off your pants." Her voice was all throaty and low, and she was shimmying out of hers, too, even as she commanded him. He about fell over trying to do what she said but also watch her. She was wearing skinny jeans, so she was doing a lot of shimmying.

Once free, she hopped up onto a step stool near the exam table, turned around, and hoisted herself up.

And spread her legs.

"Jesus, Nora."

"No foreplay, Jake. Just come over here and get on with it already."

He stumbled forward, tripping over his own feet to get to her.

She caught him, grabbed a handful of his T-shirt, which she hadn't managed to get off earlier, and wrapped her legs around him. This was the perfect angle, the perfect height. Taking her at her word, he guided himself to her entrance. She was radiating heat, and she was wet. So wet.

He slid in on a groan. Was he ever going to get used to how good she felt? It was obscene, almost, that he should be allowed to feel this good.

She grabbed his hair and forced him into eye contact with her. "If you make one crack about playing doctor, I swear to God, I will come, and I will murder you before you get your turn."

"Honestly..." He gave a long, hard thrust that physically scooched her farther back on the table. The paper lining on the table crinkled. She responded by letting go of him with one hand and putting it on the table behind her to brace herself. "That hadn't even"—he thrust again, and she moaned when he bottomed out—"crossed my mind." He thrust again and was rewarded with another moan. "But your threat is irrelevant, because..." One more punishing thrust, and he was shooting inside her. Too soon. "Goddammit," he nearly shouted as he came and came. "You have to stop doing this to me."

She wasn't listening. She'd closed her eyes and let her head fall back, which he had learned was something she did when she was close. So he put his thumb on her clit and his mouth on one breast and a few seconds later, she froze—and shattered.

"So no playing doctor, huh?" Jake said a few minutes later, after they'd caught their breath. He started to pull out of her, and she had the irrational urge to clamp her legs around him to prevent that from happening.

She let him go, though—of course she did. Once he found his feet, he grabbed her around the waist and lowered her to the floor.

"Yeah, pretty much every nonmedical guy I've dated—not that we're dating—has either genuinely wanted to 'play doctor' or else not been able to stop making jokes about the concept." He handed her her bra and sweater. "It gets old, and since it's my job, it's profoundly unsexy to me."

"Noted."

She tried not to ogle him as he bent over to retrieve his own clothes.

Well, okay, no she didn't. Because shouldn't that be one of the benefits of whatever kind of not-dating thing they had going here? In fact...She let loose a wolf whistle, which caused him to wiggle his ass at her as he stepped into his jeans.

"You're a lot of fun, Jake."

He pulled his T-shirt over his head. "You're a lot of fun, too, Doc." Stepping toward her, he reached out and smoothed her hair.

"Do I look like I just got laid in my own exam room?" she teased, making a mental note to come in early tomorrow to disinfect the table.

He tilted his head and considered her, apparently taking her question seriously. "You kind of do." He must have liked that answer for some reason, because he grinned.

Back out on the sidewalk, it occurred to her that they'd had sex twice today. And twice yesterday. And twice the day before that. It *had* been a three-day weekend on account of the holiday—during the preceding week they'd only seen each other twice—but still. "Do you think we're having too much sex?"

"Uh, no?" When she didn't say anything, he added, "Do *you* think we're having too much sex?"

"No, not really. I'm just thinking I've basically never had this much sex before. Or had sex at this rate, I mean. With this frequency. Whatever—you know what I mean." Even at the beginnings of relationships, in the flush of new love and new lust, she had never had this much sex.

He chuckled. "It's probably because we're both so sex-starved."

"Right." Although she'd had much longer dry spells between relationships. But no. He was right. They were in the right place at the right time. They were attracted to each other and shared the same outlook on what that meant—and didn't mean.

"But do you think we should cool it?" he asked.

She didn't *want* to cool it. But would it be harder to stop later, if they kept going at it this furiously?

They had arrived back at the Mermaid. She shook her head. She was overthinking this. What had happened to not letting her brain get bogged down with worries and junk? So she smiled at him. "No. I do not think we should cool it."

He smiled back. "Good." He saluted and started backing away.

For some stupid reason, this walking-backward thing he did was hella sexy. Like he knew it was time to go, but he wanted to keep looking at her? Or maybe that was overthinking, too. She ran a hand over her scalp, like she could physically calm her overheated mind.

His gaze followed her hand. "I like your hair, Dr. Walsh."

"I like your hair, too, Mr. Ramsey."

It wasn't until he got almost all the way home that Jake realized with a thud in his gut that he hadn't paid any attention to Jamila's prayer at dinner.

He wasn't sure what made him think of it now. He was just walking across the dark beach, still basking in the glow of the definitely-not-playing-doctor sex he'd just had. He'd forgotten to leave his porch light on, so it was darker than usual. He rounded the outcropping and looked up, and it hit him.

Usually the waves came with a warning, but not always. He'd grown familiar with the triggers, and with the subsequent little tells in his body. Seeing someone he hadn't seen for a long time. Hearing them say, "How *are* you?" Feeling his shoulders tense.

But sometimes they just came, like a freak storm from out of nowhere.

And sometimes, maybe, he *made* them come.

Because they were his due.

Because he *forgot* sometimes, and that was the worst thing of all.

He hated those fucking prayers. He *dreaded* them. He had to work hard not to punch the table during them.

He knew, with his rational mind, that Jamila meant well. Intellectually, he could even appreciate that she didn't try to paper over the past. She was kind. She loved his dad— and him. She understood that her happiness was conditional on their having lost Mom, and she didn't try to pretend otherwise.

But Goddammit, he hated it when she invoked Jude. She sometimes said something generic, something about missing loved ones who were gone. But sometimes she got rolling and got all specific. Her first year together with his dad, she'd made what felt like an endless speech, asking God to look after Jude, and he'd wanted to stand up and scream. Where had God been when Jude was alive? When Jude was hooked up to so many machines he looked more like a robot than a little boy? Or when Jake decided to wait until the trip to London to get him the flu shot? Where the hell had God been that day?

He'd calmed down somewhat in subsequent years, because he'd learned to anticipate it. He would do an internal version of plugging his ears and saying *La la la I can't hear you* as he said his own prayer of thanks. He thought about his boy and thanked the God he wasn't sure if he believed in for his nine months and thirteen days with Jude. It had become his own thing, his own little silent Thanksgiving ritual.

So what the hell had happened to him tonight? He'd been dreading the prayer, as usual. He distinctly remembered sitting in the kitchen, playing with the label of his beer, and fretting about it as dinner drew near.

But then...what? He'd been too busy holding Nora's hand like a schoolboy with a crush to even *notice* it happening right in front of him? He'd let his lust crowd out his tradition of remembering his boy at Thanksgiving?

Usually, when the waves came, he rushed home. Partly so he could freak out in private. But also because he had found that sitting by the lake, by the real waves, helped. Sometimes, when it was really bad, he'd go into the water. The waves there were stronger than the waves inside him. He could sync his breathing to them, and eventually they would overpower the storm inside him. He could sit until the only waves left were the ones *outside* his body. Until order was restored.

But that was assuming he wanted the waves to stop. That he *deserved* for them to stop.

He stopped walking as his face heated. Sometimes, when he thought back to laying his hands on Jude's forehead that first night, his own skin heated in some kind of macabre sensory echo. Jude had been like a little furnace as Jake got him out of his crib, gave him some Tylenol, and sat with him in the rocking chair waiting for the medicine to kick in.

Jake's breathing grew short, just like Jude's had that night as he'd gotten hotter and hotter.

Panic. Waking Kerrie. Calling Sawyer, who gave them a police escort to the hospital in Zurich.

He felt it now as though no time had passed. Stumbled forward as he fought the urge to double over on the sand. He needed to go inside. Sitting by the lake would help. Would lessen the attack. But if he was just going to fucking forget about his boy, his *child*, he deserved the full brunt of what was coming for him.

He dragged himself up the steps and into the cottage to hunker down.

Chapter Fourteen

Surprise! We're here!

The next weekend, Nora was having a lazy Sunday afternoon in the back parlor of the inn when the text from her sister arrived. She eyed it with suspicion.

She was about to text back something along the lines of *What are you talking about?* when the bell on the front desk started ringing nonstop.

Uh-oh. That couldn't be—

"Happy Walsh-giving!" Aiden, one of her nephews, shouted when she appeared in the reception area.

Holy crap. Her sister was here with her kids.

"Wow, when you said *mermaid*, you weren't kidding."

And her grandma.

Who was in a wheelchair?

Nora blinked as they all swarmed her with hugs and exclamations of "Happy Walsh-giving!"

"What are you guys doing here?" she asked after she had been passed around and hugged by all. She frowned at her grandma. "And what's with the wheel—"

"You didn't *honestly* think we were going to let you skip out on Walsh-giving, did you?" Her grandma swatted her on the arm.

Nora was on duty at the inn, covering Eve and Sawyer's vacation. She'd explained to her family why she couldn't attend Walsh-giving in Toronto this year, and after an initial flurry of objections, they'd acquiesced pretty easily.

Which, in retrospect, she should have found suspicious.

"Grandma thought it would be fun to surprise you." Erin made a *Sorry* face at Nora behind Grandma's back.

"I was hoping maybe we'd catch you in flagrante delicto with that large hunk of a man from last time," her grandmother said.

"Jake."

"That's the one."

Oh no. Jake. She had to call him. He was planning to come by with dinner, but hopefully he hadn't left yet. With Eve and Sawyer gone, they'd decided to "revisit first base," also known as "rolling around mostly naked in a pink room."

She hadn't seen much of Jake since actual Thanksgiving a week ago. She'd been a little worried about it, in fact. Had she come on too strong in the clinic? Was she inadvertently giving off let's-be-a-couple vibes? She didn't think so, but he hadn't shown up with Mick for lunch until the end of the week—that had been the longest stretch she'd gone without seeing him since they started sleeping together. To her relief, when he finally showed up, he seemed his usual self.

And when she'd reminded him that she was going to have the inn to herself and suggested a "change of venue," he'd done his eyebrow wagging and his backward walking and enthusiastically agreed.

She was bummed to have to put him off, but it couldn't be avoided. While she adored her family, they were a lot. Walsh-giving would last hours, and Jake didn't need the hassle.

She grabbed her purse and started rummaging through it to find his phone number—he'd written it down for her after they'd done "second base" at his place that time, but she'd never used it. "You should have told me you were coming. I would have made food." She would have tried, anyway.

"We brought leftovers from the big dinner yesterday!" Erin said. "It's in a couple coolers in the car."

"We have enough to feed an army," her grandma said. "So if you have anyone you want to invite...like, say, Hunky Jake..."

She had to call Hunky Jake and *un*invite him. "I'm so glad you guys are here. If you'll excuse me for just one moment, I'll—"

"Hunky Jake!"

Nora followed her grandmother's gaze to the door, the bells on which were jingling to announce the arrival of a visitor.

Hunky Jake. *Early* Hunky Jake. Filling the door frame entirely with his oversize self.

His eyes darted around. He was trying to make sense of the unexpected scene.

Oh boy. Sighing, she moved toward him. "Jake. Hi."

"Welcome to Walsh-giving, Jake!" her grandma said. She pounded the armrests of her wheelchair in frustration. "If I'd known you were going to be here, I'd have left this thing at home and let you do your knight-in-shining-armor thing. But you can help with the coolers. And dessert. We need to source some dessert. My heathen family ate all the pie yesterday."

Payback was a bitch.

Jake wasn't really sure how it had happened. He'd thought he was arriving for a booty call, but somehow here he was, seated around the inn's big kitchen island with Nora covertly feeling him up.

At least there had been no prayers at this dinner.

"Thank you so much for the pie, Pearl," Nora said sweetly as her hand slid up his thigh. After they'd gotten all the food inside, a discussion had ensued over where they would eat. The inn had a bunch of two- and four-person circular bistro tables in the dining room, where Eve served cocktails and snacks a couple of afternoons a week. But there were guests on the premises, and Nora didn't think they should take over that public space with a big family dinner.

So Jake had dragged one of the tables into the kitchen, and it was accommodating Nora's grandma's wheelchair and her two grandchildren. He and Nora were sitting on stools on one side of the kitchen island, and Pearl and Erin were on the other.

Thankfully, someone had found tablecloths to cover the surfaces. So at least there was something concealing Nora's groping.

"Thanks for letting me crash your party." Pearl beamed at the assembly—when Nora had gone next door to buy a pie, she'd come back with the bakery's proprietor, too.

"This crust design is so clever," Nora's grandma exclaimed. Pearl had developed a signature pie for the inn after Eve inherited it. It was a double-crust lemon pie, and the top crust was made to look like fish scales. "What kinds of tools do you use?"

"The scales are made with cookie cutters and laid over the finished pie. The edge of the crust is made with a pastry wheel."

"Maybe I should take up pastry making!" Dr. Walsh said. She turned to Pearl. "I'm a retired surgeon. You have no idea how much I miss cutting people up."

"Oh! Why don't you come over when we're done? I also have a pastry knife with a bunch of different-size blades you can swap out. It's basically a scalpel for dough." She looked at the boys. "Do you guys like video games? I have a brand-new Nintendo Switch."

"Pearl's not just a baker," Nora said to Erin. "She's a championship gamer."

A few minutes later, the old ladies and the little boys were trundling out the back door, leaving him alone with Nora and Erin—and a boner.

Nora hopped off her stool and smiled at him. "Want to help me with the dishes, Jake?"

He glared at her. But keeping an eye on Erin and making his move when she wasn't looking, he stationed himself at the sink. "Sure. You clear, and I'll rinse and load the dishwasher." Which he could do standing at the sink with his back to them.

She patted him on the shoulder, but she didn't give him any more grief.

"What's with the wheelchair?" Nora asked Erin as they shuttled dishes to Jake.

Erin sighed. "She's going to talk to you later."

"The cancer's back, isn't it?"

Erin didn't say anything, but she didn't have to. Even Jake could tell the news wasn't good.

"But why the wheelchair? If it's spread, isn't it in her lungs?"

"She'll want to tell you herself."

"Erin."

"It is in her lungs, but there's another tumor on her ankle. A new one."

Aww, shit. Jake wanted to turn and check on Nora, but he didn't. Not because of the boner. That was gone—nothing like cancer to take care of that. But because to do so felt too intrusive. He wasn't sure if they even remembered he was here.

"She says she's not going to treat it."

Something clattered as it hit the marble of the island. "What?"

He did turn then. Nora had her hands flat on the island, her arms straight, like she was bracing herself. He wanted to be the one bracing her. But he knew she wouldn't appreciate that. And she seemed to be holding herself up just fine.

"Yeah, I was hoping you could talk her out of it."

"I'll try. What does Dad say?"

"He says she's an adult, and—"

"Mom! Look what Mrs. Brunetta gave us!"

The sisters turned toward the younger of the two boys, who was clattering back into the kitchen. They pulled away from each other like they'd been caught doing something wrong.

The little guy was followed in short order by his brother, who was pushing Dr. Walsh's wheelchair.

Jake cleared his throat. "Hey, would anyone like to stroll down to the lake? This town has a tradition of folks making wishes by throwing flowers into the lake."

"Yes! Can we, Mom?"

Erin flashed him a sad smile. "That would be great.

Thanks, Jake." She turned to Nora, who gave a small nod. "I'll come with you."

Maya was working at A Rose by Any Other Name. Of course she was. Maya went out of her way to avoid working at the store. He wasn't really sure what was going on there, but he got the sense, from overhearing her at the bar, that there was some conflict between her and her father over her role in the family business.

But naturally, the one day he appeared with Nora's family in tow was a day she was behind the counter.

"Jake!" she said with surprise.

"Hey, Maya." She looked pointedly at Erin and the kids. He stifled a sigh. "This is Erin Walsh, Nora Walsh's sister, and her kids, Aiden and Brady."

"Well!" Maya stuck out her hand to shake Erin's, but she turned her head and shot him an exaggeratedly inquisitive look.

"We're here for some wishing flowers," he said, keeping his tone as neutral as possible.

"Of course!" She went to the refrigerated case and returned with a basket of them. Carefully she laid the flowers out on the counter one by one.

"We only need three," he said, after she'd laid the third and was reaching for a fourth.

"Nonsense," Maya said. "There are four of you. Or maybe you actually need five. Is Nora meeting you?" She raised her eyebrows. She was fishing for information, wanted to know what he was doing here with Nora's family but not Nora.

"Nope." She wasn't getting anything from him, though he suspected he would pay for this stonewalling later.

After a minor stare-down, she rang up the flowers—four of them, he noted with annoyance. Erin started to try to pay for them, but he pulled his wallet from his pocket. "No, no. I've got them."

"Hmm," Maya said as Erin murmured her thanks.

And so Jake found himself, for the second time in recent months, standing on the pier thinking about what the hell to wish for.

He was holding everyone up, too. After he'd explained the tradition to the Walshes, they'd all chucked their flowers in pretty quickly, Brady proclaiming his wish—a Nintendo Switch of his own—out loud and Aiden informing him it now wouldn't come true.

They were all waiting for him.

Why did he keep doing this? It wasn't like anyone would know if he threw the flower in without making a wish. He would just do that.

But then it came to him. Even though it was a stupid wish, one that, from the sounds of things, didn't meet his specific and likely-to-come-true criteria. But he made it all the same.

I wish Nora's grandma doesn't die.

Jake, God bless him, had come to Nora's rescue *again*, hustling her sister and nephews off so she could talk to her grandma. By the time they reappeared, she and the family matriarch had had it out.

She hadn't won. There was no out-arguing Penelope Walsh when she had her mind set on something. But at least Nora had found out what was going on and had said her piece.

"Thanks for being a good sport about the surprise, Sis." Erin hugged her harder than she normally would.

"Thanks for coming." Nora hugged Erin harder than she normally would. Erin hadn't shown her any real estate listings the whole day, which suggested how serious the situation was.

"Jake!" Grandma called.

"Yes, ma'am." He had been hovering in the kitchen doorway, but he stood at attention when she hailed him.

"I need some help getting into the car." She winked at Nora and Erin.

"You got it, Dr. Walsh."

They all went out to the street where Grandma, who had somehow managed to get out of the car and into her chair with only Erin and the boys, suddenly needed Jake to lift her out of the chair and install her in the passenger seat.

"Well, she's not dead yet," Erin whispered to Nora. As a family of mostly doctors, they'd always been comfortable with gallows humor.

"She's not going to die," Nora whispered back automatically, as if she weren't a doctor. As if she were a person who believed in the power of magical thinking.

Erin didn't correct her, though. She just squeezed Nora's hand, sniffed, and got into the car.

Which left Nora standing next to Jake on the sidewalk and blinking back tears.

"Jake!"

She turned quickly so Karl, who was crossing the street after locking up the hardware store, wouldn't see her. Jake puffed up his chest and stepped in front of her.

"I think I got you and Sawyer a canoe customer."

"Great, thanks." Jake shifted to better conceal her. It wasn't like he was actually hiding her, but he was giving her a chance to either flee or pull herself together, and did she ever appreciate it.

"You know Sadie from the diner? Her sister married some hotshot banker in Toronto. They live on the beach over there. You know where they have those three-million-dollar houses not even directly on the water?"

Jake made a vague noise of agreement.

"Oh, hi, Nora. Didn't see you there. I'm all out of your vaccine flyers, if you want to drop off some more. I heard you're actually going to get that van on the road?"

"Hi, Karl." Nora's voice came out sounding normal, which was a relief. "Yep. Pearl got Jordan to get the van fixed up enough so it's working."

"Really?" Jake said.

"Yeah. Obviously, I can't drive it with all your additions, but I reached out to the high school principal, and I'm going to do a flu-shot clinic there just before the holiday break."

"You are?" Jake said.

"Yeah, assuming the van actually makes it that far."

"What about the office here?"

"No appointments that day. Amber and I will do the flu clinic, and Wynd will hold down the fort for phone calls."

She wasn't sure why he was so interested, but she appreciated the distracting effect of the small talk. She felt better. Well, not better, but more in control. "Anyway, Karl, I'll definitely get you some more flyers, thanks."

Karl headed back across the street. Jake followed her back to the inn. Damn. "Jake. I'm really sorry, but...ugh. I can't believe I'm going to say this, but I'm not in the mood."

"That's okay, Doc."

"Sorry." Nothing like impending mortality as a libido killer. "I know it's only seven, but I'm full and tired, and I'm just going to go to bed and watch a zombie movie."

"A *zombie* movie?" He laughed out loud.

"Yeah." She shrugged. "I find them soothing. Anyway, sorry to uh...not deliver."

"Don't worry about it." He started doing the backward-walking thing. After a few steps like that, he started to turn away from her. But then he stopped. "Hey, Doc? You want some company with the zombies?"

She opened her mouth to decline. That wasn't in the friends-with-benefits script.

"Come on," he said, somehow anticipating her reluctance. "I watch movies with Sawyer."

"You do not." Jake was not a movie-night sort of guy.

"I do."

"Name one movie you've watched with Sawyer."

He paused for a long time but then said, "*Avatar*. I watched *Avatar* with Sawyer."

"The 3-D thing with the blue people?"

"Yep."

"That came out more than a decade ago! Like, before 3-D was really invented!"

He shrugged. "Yeah, okay, you got me." The backward walking started again. "G'night."

"Wait." It turned out she didn't really give a crap, at this moment, if watching a movie together was in the script. "I could use some company, actually."

He stopped walking and smiled. "I'm gonna go home and feed Mick and let him out. You cue up the movie, and I'll be back soon."

She did, and he was.

She plopped onto the bed and played with her laptop so it was at a better angle. "What do you think? A classic? *Return of the Living Dead*? Or something more comedic, maybe? *Zombieland*?"

"I leave this decision in your capable hands."

Soon they were lying side by side on her bed watching *Day of the Dead*. They were not touching. Which was fine.

She'd already told him she wasn't up for sex. So there was no reason for them to be touching. It wasn't like they were going to cuddle.

Wait. Was there a possibility he would think she'd cued up a scary movie so they could snuggle? He could not think that.

"So zombie movies, eh? What's with that?"

Good. Here was her chance to explain. "My whole family is into them. I grew up watching them. I'm not even sure where it started. Probably with my grandma. She always had this joking theory that zombies were actually just exhausted med students or residents."

He chuckled. "Remember when you compared my dad getting sucked into Karl's crowd to zombification?"

"Yeah. I have zombies on the brain a lot."

"Huh." He sounded thoughtful.

As the opening credits ran, she said, "She's not going to treat the cancer." She wasn't even sure why she was bringing this up. It wasn't like Jake could do anything about it. Jake would probably never even see her grandmother again. The thought caused a hitch in her breathing.

He glanced over but did not touch her—though she wasn't sure why she was even making note of the absence of a touch. Again, this wasn't a situation in which he *should* be touching her.

They looked at each other in silence for a moment, and he said softly, "I'm sorry, Nora."

She sighed and transferred her attention to the ceiling. "I mean, I get it. The prognosis is extremely poor. She's eighty-seven. Treatment would just be about extending her life, not about curing the cancer."

"How long does she have?"

"They're saying three to four months, but no one ever really knows."

She felt his attention, strong enough to pull her gaze from the ceiling. He was looking at her funny. Like he was mad at her? No, though his brow *was* furrowed. It seemed more like he suddenly didn't know her, which clearly wasn't right, either.

He recovered himself in an instant, though, making her wonder if she'd imagined that weird face.

"No one ever really knows," he echoed, and she realized that, crap, though she'd meant her comment in the sense that doctors could give an educated guess as to prognosis but a guess was all it ultimately was, it had made him think of Jude.

She opened her mouth to apologize for the insensitivity of the statement, but he grinned and hitched his head toward the door. "A herd of rabid zombie mermaids could come through that door right now, and that's it—we're toast."

She smiled. "Any regrets?"

He smiled, too. "Not really. You?"

"Well, if I got killed by rabid zombie mermaids right now, I would probably end up regretting that I didn't get to spend more time with my grandma before she died."

"You can do something about that."

"Yeah, I've been lying here thinking I might start going back to the city on weekends. It's a long drive, but...I could even take the odd Friday or Monday off and go for a longer weekend. I mean, shouldn't that be one of the perks of being your own boss?"

"You should do that. I'm not..." His voice cracked, and he looked at the ceiling and cleared his throat. "I'm not trying to make light of anything, but in a way, to *know* that you only have a limited amount of time left with someone is a gift." He turned back to her with a wry smile. "A shitty gift, mind you."

"Yeah." She had to clear her throat, too. "You're right."

"Oh, *shit*."

Jake wasn't sure what was actually waking him up, some kind of alarm—there was definitely an alarm going off—or Nora letting loose a string of curses.

"Shit, shit, shit. It's six in the morning. We fell asleep." She bolted out of bed, moved to the small dressing table, and started smoothing down her hair, which was sticking up in a way he struggled not to find adorable. He was sorry that he'd missed waking up with her, that she'd gotten out of bed so quickly. Despite the abrupt awakening, he was feeling pleasantly lazy. Content. Which was funny because nothing had happened between them except they'd watched a fairly epic zombie attack on a helicopter—who knew?

They hadn't even been touching, initially. They'd just lain there side by side watching as people's limbs got torn off and so on. He'd started to doze off at one point, and when he startled awake, he'd announced his intention to leave, even though leaving the ridiculous pink zombie cocoon to go home in the cold and dark was the last thing he wanted to do. But she'd rolled over, put a hand on his chest, and said, "Stay till the end?"

And then she hadn't taken her hand *off* his chest. She'd watched the rest of the movie with her head half-turned, nestled in the crook of his arm.

You couldn't have *paid* him to leave.

This morning, things were decidedly less cozy, judging by the way she'd shot out of bed. She met his eyes in the mirror and said, "I'm going to go for a run."

All right. He knew when he was being dismissed. He

levered himself out of her bed. "Thanks for ... Walsh-giving and zombies."

He'd meant it mostly sincerely, but it also made her smile, which had been his other aim.

"Do you have time to bring Mick over for lunch today? Poor guy spent the night alone because we were so sleepy."

"Sure thing."

He felt bad about Mick. As he made his way down the stairs, he vowed that Mick was going to get an extra-long lunch break, complete with a stop at Jenna's General for a fancy, handmade dog treat. Even though he had to roll his eyes at the peanut butter and bacon "Doggie Donuts" Jenna sold for five bucks a pop, Mick had—

"Jake."

Oh, *shit*. Sawyer.

Sawyer and Eve were due back today, he knew, but it hadn't occurred to him that *today* could mean six a.m.

He gave a moment's thought to trying to come up with an excuse. A reason why he would be coming down the stairs of the Mermaid this time of morning. He had nothing. He was fully busted.

Sawyer didn't even look surprised. Just stood there with his eyebrows raised.

Well, whatever. Sawyer might look like a dad busting a kid sneaking around, but Jake was not a kid. He didn't owe anyone any explanations.

So he just said, "Hey," brushed past Sawyer, and got the hell out of there.

He was going to pay for this later, though.

The payment came six weeks later. Karl really had gotten them an order for a canoe for the Toronto douchebag, so

Jake showed up at Sawyer's garage on a Saturday morning in early December.

Though they rented a warehouse space on the outskirts of town for most of their off-site work, they always worked on the canoes in Sawyer's garage, and they had an unspoken agreement that they only worked on them together. At first they'd worked in tandem because they'd been learning as they went—Sawyer had been building a canoe for Eve based on YouTube videos. But they had it down now, so he wasn't sure why they persisted, given that they were fine to divide and conquer on all their other jobs.

But whatever, it gave him something to do. Nora had made good on her plan to spend weekends in Toronto hanging out with her grandma, which was turning out to mean that he was bored out of his skull on weekends.

Which was a little bit odd. Also a little bit alarming. It wasn't like he used to require his weekends to be full of distractions.

It was all the sex, probably. His body had been jolted awake, and now it was no longer content with working on whatever project he and Sawyer had under contract, fixing stuff in town, or making his weekly fishing trip.

It was also not content with this whole weekend-celibacy thing. Back when they'd first started sleeping together, when Nora was still around on weekends, they'd had a lot of sex. So much that she'd asked him, that one time, if it was too much. But now that she wasn't here on weekends, they only managed a couple times a week.

Which felt like not nearly enough.

Which, in turn, was a slightly worrying sentiment. And if he avoided thinking about it by filling his weekends with tasks, so what?

Mick started whining from the passenger side of the

truck. Jake had gotten out but had been standing staring into the distance, pondering his newfound devotion to weekend plans, and Mick must have thought he'd been forgotten.

"All right, all right. Hang on." He ran around and lifted Mick out. He'd been noticing a slight limp. Nora had said she'd had it checked out a year ago and been told it was arthritis. And it didn't seem to be bothering Mick particularly. But all the same, Jake set him on his feet gently and gave him an extra head rub. "There you go, old man."

"Ahem."

Ah, crap. When he stood up, Law and Sawyer were there.

Law wasn't usually part of their canoe sessions. He only came around when he wanted to exercise his jaw about something. As if he didn't get enough time to do that at the bar.

Jake sighed and followed them around the house to the detached garage where they kept their canoes in progress.

"Are you dating Nora Walsh?" Law asked.

"Nope."

"What do you call it, then?"

He didn't answer, just sat and picked up a sanding block.

"Probably he's going to say they're just sleeping together," Sawyer said, and Jake shot him an annoyed look. "So I saw you sneaking out of the Mermaid at the crack of dawn that time because you *weren't* sleeping together?"

Jake ran his fingers over a rough patch near the boat's stern. "We watched a movie the night before, and we fell asleep. That was all that happened." Which was technically true. Also, this was pretty rich coming from Sawyer. They'd had a version of this exact conversation a year and a half ago when he was "not dating" Eve.

"So you're falling asleep watching movies in her bedroom," Law said.

"And fixing her deck," Sawyer said.

"*You* told me to fix her deck."

"And helping her with her vaccine thing," Law said cheerfully.

"I thought we were supposed to make her feel welcome. I thought we wanted her to stay."

"We do," Sawyer said.

Law smirked. "Maybe some of us more than others."

All right. He didn't need this shit. The Toronto douchebag could make his own damn canoe. He tossed the sanding block aside and stood.

"Oh, come on," Law said. "Don't run away."

"I don't need you guys to perform an intervention here."

"You know what?" Sawyer said. "He's right. He doesn't need an intervention. I think he's doing just fine on his own."

Jake wasn't sure why, but that pronouncement made him more uncomfortable than all their ball busting had.

"Still waters run deep?" Law said with a smirk.

Jake picked up the sanding block again. "Shut up."

Chapter Fifteen

❦

The morning of the high school flu vaccine drive, Nora, Amber, and Wynd met at the clinic early. It was a Friday, and they always had a staff meeting on Friday mornings to review the week behind them and look at the schedule for the week ahead.

They were in a nice groove. The three of them had gotten used to each other. They knew each other's quirks and accommodated them. For example, Wynd always brought Nora "coffee," and Nora always pretended to enjoy it, when in fact the chicory brew with almond milk tasted the way she imagined wood shavings mixed with dirt would.

"Mmmm, thanks," she said when presented with the vile concoction in a travel mug that said, "Nature is the Best Healer." She pretended to take a sip before saying, "We'll have to be quick today. What does the schedule look like next week?"

"We're pretty heavily booked," Wynd said, "but I did like you asked and kept two slots a day open."

"Great." Nora was finding herself getting booked up several weeks in advance, leaving no time for people who were unexpectedly sick, so they were experimenting with holding blocks of time for same-day appointments. "I have a couple more items, but we have to be at the high school at nine, so we'd better shelve them for next week." She turned to Wynd. "You okay here? Anyone comes in with anything urgent, send them to Zurich."

"I am, but can I, ah...talk to you before you leave? Just really quickly?"

Nora's favorite flower child looked decidedly less sparkly than usual. She glanced at Amber, who said, "I'll bring the van around and pick you up out front in a few?"

"Dr. Walsh..."

Nora had asked the other women to call her Dr. Walsh in front of patients but encouraged first names in private. Something was clearly wrong. "What is it?"

"Mike got laid off."

Oh no. "I'm so sorry. Do you want some extra hours?" It would be tight, but she could probably afford ten extra hours a week, come up with a make-work project.

"No. I actually, uh...want fewer hours. Like, ideally no hours."

Huh? Also: *Shit*. Nora and Wynd might never be best friends, but Wynd did a good job keeping the clinic running.

"I know I just started. I'm *so* sorry. But Mike's situation is the universe whispering to us about our next step."

"Are you sure? Because if it's whispering, you might be hearing it incorrectly."

"Well, we had a big chat about it, and I swear to goddess,

later that night we had a knock on our door from a Realtor who said he had clients in Toronto looking to pay cash for a place in Moonflower Bay, and were we interested in selling? So we're going to do it. We sourced a used RV, and we're going to move to the farm property and trust the process. If we work hard and we're lucky, we'll be hosting alpaca retreats by this time next year."

"Well, congratulations," Nora said weakly. She couldn't crap on someone's dream.

"I know it's a lot sooner than we planned, but sometimes that's the way things happen. When the universe gives you what you want, are you going to complain that it's too early?"

"No?" Though she didn't see why not. Didn't they say that timing was everything?

"No," Wynd said decisively. "Sometimes you just have to trust the universe." She patted Nora's arm. "Anyway, I wanted to talk to you today because I need my two weeks' notice to start now. We're moving this weekend, but I'll commute in for the next two weeks. Unless you can find someone sooner?" she added hopefully.

Nora sighed. She had to go jab teenagers now. Maybe one of them would be about to graduate and hear the universe whispering, "Become a medical receptionist."

She sighed again. Well, she could jab teenagers and contemplate her dilemma.

Sadly, this was a problem Jake couldn't bail her out of.

Speaking of Jake... "Hey, can you slow down?" Nora asked Amber, who was driving the Mermaid Monstrosity. "That's my dog!"

She rolled the window down as well as she could—it was manual and refused to budge after about the halfway mark—as Amber pulled up next to Jake. He had just come out of Jenna's and was bending over to feed something to Mick.

"Are you giving him treats?"

He looked up, surprised. "Doc." Then sheepish. "Guilty."

"Jake's keeping me in business." Jenna had emerged from the store with a piece of chalk to update her sandwich board with the day's new funny saying.

"He's supposed to be on a diet!" Nora protested, but she couldn't help smiling. Overall, Mick's time under Jake's care had slimmed him down considerably.

She hadn't told Amber yet about Wynd, but suddenly she really wanted to tell Jake, even though she'd just been thinking that this was a problem he couldn't solve. Sometimes it felt like she and Jake had ESP. *Wynd just quit, and I'm freaking out about it.*

It didn't work. "He really likes those bacon–peanut butter things," Jake said.

"Who wouldn't like a bacon–peanut butter thing?" Maya appeared on the scene—she lived in the apartment above Jenna's. "Hi, Nora! Are you on the move?"

"I am! Headed to the high school for a flu-shot clinic. You want to come?"

She wasn't sure why she was asking. Maya wasn't going to add any medical expertise, but she was really fun to be around, and Nora, still reeling from Wynd's news, could use the distraction.

"Sure!" She opened the passenger-side door. "Scooch over, though, cause I'm not riding in back."

The van had an old-school bench seat up front, so against her better judgment—the seat belt in the middle was only a lap belt—Nora scooted over.

"Sorry, Jake, no room!" Maya trilled, and they were off.

*   *   *

Though he would never admit it to anyone, Jake could kind of see the appeal of having a cell phone. If, for example, you knew someone who was running her first out-of-town flu-shot clinic and you had a cell phone, you could text that person and ask how it was going. You could ask that person to send you pictures.

If you were the kind of person who wanted to see pictures of flu-shot clinics.

For God's sake.

It was midmorning. He and Sawyer didn't have any active jobs. He and Mick had already been walking for an hour.

It was a beautiful day.

It was not a Tuesday. But what the hell. He wasn't even sure what he was going to do. He had basically bequeathed his traps to a guy who fished out of Port Frederick. But maybe he could get out his tackle and just . . . fish? Like, for fun? When was the last time he'd done that?

Half an hour later, he was waiting for Dennis to lift the bridge to let a bigger sailboat in front of him pass. Mick was perched on the stern of his trawler, a squat little mascot.

Twenty minutes after that, he'd dropped anchor in a spot about three miles north of the cove. He was using an ancient rod and lure, ones he'd had as a kid. Once he'd come on board with his dad, pleasure fishing had fallen out of his life. But he'd held on to all the stuff, because, like his dad had done with both Jake and his brother, he had planned on taking Jude out.

He never had gotten Jude his own rod, though. They'd never made it into London for that shopping trip.

The feeling of casting was both familiar and foreign.

Muscle memory kicked in, and within an hour he'd hauled in a dozen pickerel. He threw back most of them but kept a handful.

At a certain point he decided he'd had enough and sat back and stared at the horizon.

His boy was in this lake.

He and Kerrie had agreed on that, easily and immediately, even though everything else between them at that point had been fraught. They'd gone out in this very boat with no particular destination in mind. He had driven. Told her to let him know when she felt like they were in a good spot. She had nodded, so he knew she'd heard him, but she hadn't said anything, not for an hour. So he'd just kept going. It felt like they'd reached the middle of the damn lake by the time she signaled him to stop, though he knew with his rational mind that they had not even come close.

The weird thing was, they hadn't said anything. He'd racked his brain, trying to come up with words appropriate to the situation, but he kept coming up blank. She had been silent, too, but that was more unusual for her, the lawyer who always knew what to say. Maybe she had gone blank the same way he had. Or maybe she'd had lots to say but had been holding it in. Regardless, he hadn't asked her, and now it was too late.

But she'd held his hand as he'd held the urn out over the gray water. It had reminded him of the wishing flowers. A macabre, inverted version of the town tradition. Except there were no wishes here. Kerrie had wished for Jude, and Jude had come. But then he had gone.

He observed with mild interest that he was thinking about all this without losing his shit. More often than not when he went out on his Tuesday expeditions, he ended up doubled over and gasping for breath, and it was a toss-up whether he would stay out long enough to get anything to sell on the pier.

For some reason, today, he was able to look at the endless expanse of water and imagine Jude in a different way. He used to think of Jude buried beneath it, trying to get out. Like Nora's zombies, maybe. It was a nightmarish scenario, made no less so for its irrationality. He had told Nora, way back in her early days in town, that he'd stopped wanting to go out on the boat after Jude was gone. That was why. The waves so often came for him out here.

But suddenly, damned if he couldn't look at the lake and think of Jude with a sort of neutrality. Well, no, that wasn't right. Not neutrality. Definitely sadness. But not the doubled-over, hyperventilating despair from before.

It occurred to him that another reason to have a cell phone was that if you wanted to ask your ex-wife if she was silent the day you scattered your son's ashes because she didn't know what to say or because she felt like she *couldn't* say what she wanted to say, it would be easier to do that in a text than in a phone call.

When Nora got home from the high school, the Mermaid's cocktail hour was underway. The thrice-weekly event was, on paper, for guests staying at the inn, and they did attend, but so did some of the downtown denizens of Moonflower Bay. Nora spotted Maya and Pearl off in a corner, huddled over a phone.

"They're passing judgment on each other's Tinder matches," Eve said, reading Nora's mind.

"That's . . . actually kind of awesome," Nora said, smiling affectionately at her friend. Well, *friends*. Nora and Maya had slid easily into a close friendship, but Nora realized to her slight surprise that she genuinely thought of Pearl as a friend, too, despite her constant need to censor herself around Pearl lest the woman make an entire life plan for Nora.

"How was the flu clinic?" Eve asked.

"It was great. I jabbed seventy-seven kids and twelve teachers, and the principal is going to do some flyers for kids to take home about their parents potentially needing the MMR booster."

"Good for you!"

"Yeah, look at me. I've turned into a regular vaccine crusader," Nora joked.

Eve didn't laugh. "I'm serious. You've been here what? Four months? And you're really moving the needle on all these public-health challenges. And that's all *in addition* to actually being the town doctor! And by the way, Sawyer was saying that all his officers have been singing your praises on the naloxone question."

Aww. Nora was a little embarrassed by the praise but also by how happy it made her. She'd had her head down, working so much and so methodically that she'd never really stopped to consider her impact on the town.

A guest approached Eve. "Excuse me. I've been admiring that print." She pointed at a reproduction of a painting of a mermaid lurking in the water as she stared at a bunch of humans on a boat. "May I ask where you got it?"

Eve turned to Nora, murmured, "Excuse me," and led the guest to the painting. "It was my great-aunt's, but I have a similar one in the dining room that's by an artist in Bayshore—she has a studio there that's open to the public on weekends."

Nora had been listening to Eve, so she was surprised by Jake's stealthy arrival on her other side. Jake had never, to her knowledge, attended cocktail hour at the Mermaid before. She was happy to see him, even though seeing him made her remember the ESP conversation she'd tried to have with him earlier. Which made her remember her receptionist problem. Which took the shine right off the I'm-a-public-health-genius feeling she'd been enjoying.

"How did the clinic go?"

"Wynd and her husband are moving to the countryside and she just gave her two weeks' notice and I'm freaking out."

He blinked a few times—she *had* kind of ambushed him there. "Let's go see Mick, shall we? He's in the kitchen."

"What are you doing here, anyway?"

He paused, in both walking and speaking. "I thought you might want to see Mick."

Right. She did want to see Mick. "Should we take him for a walk?"

Winter had been late coming to Moonflower Bay. They hadn't had any snow, but the cold temperatures had arrived. Everybody said the lake moderated the winter here, made it less cold than it would be inland, but the dampness got into Nora's bones. She combatted it by wearing a ridiculous amount of winter outerwear—an ankle-length down parka, a wool hat, and mittens so big she had trouble with the leash.

Which Jake took from her with a laugh. "Maybe you should have done your life reset in Florida."

"Nah. I love it here." She started booking it down the sidewalk. "But we gotta walk fast, or we'll die."

"You love it here?"

He sounded surprised. She'd surprised *herself*. It had just popped out of her mouth. But it was true in that way that things said before you could think too hard about them often were. The lake, the quirky locals who had become her friends—even the meddling, blue-haired, septuagenarian gaming champs. The sense that she was making a difference. All that stuff had sneaked up on her.

They'd turned toward the lake when they left the Mermaid. "I mean, what's not to love about this?" She gestured ahead of them, at the little beach in the distance, as she picked up the pace even more. He followed her across the sand and onto the pier. When she reached the end of it, she rested her elbows on the railing and heaved a huge sigh.

"Okay, so Wynd quit," he said.

"Yeah, her husband got laid off, so they're moving to the country and starting their hippie commune."

"I thought it was an alpaca farm." Nora had told Jake about Wynd and her quirks.

"Potato-potahto." She sighed again. She sure was doing a lot of that today. Someone should give her a medal. "I mean, I get it. This is her dream. But...her dream wasn't supposed to arrive so soon."

He chuckled. "I don't think that's how it works."

"That's what she said." She tilted her head back and looked at the sky and ordered herself not to sigh again. To her utter mortification, hot tears started spilling out of her eyes. She was overreacting. But she couldn't seem to stop. "I was just starting to hit my stride with the clinic," she said, feeling the need to explain the uncharacteristic outburst. *Also, my grandma is dying.* She didn't need a psych consult to figure out that the tears were probably as much about that as about anything.

"Hey, now. Hey." Jake hunched down and leaned over the railing so he was in her line of vision.

She looked away from him. If he said, "Don't cry," she was going to punch him.

He maneuvered himself some more so he was back in her line of sight. "It's a setback, but we'll figure it out."

"I have a full day of appointments Monday."

"Did Wynd not even give notice?" He sounded gratifyingly peeved.

"She did. Two weeks."

"Okay, so you have two weeks to replace her. Piece of cake."

"Yeah, but unless I hire an unemployed loser, the new person will have to give notice at an existing job. Ugh, maybe I should just close the clinic early for the holidays and go to Toronto and be with my grandma." She'd been planning to close between Christmas and New Year's anyway, but that was still a couple weeks off.

"Is that what you want to do? Close up shop now?"

Was it? No. She couldn't do that to her town. "No. I don't want the clinic to close for longer than the holiday break we were already planning on. I have to figure out a way to stay open until then."

"Okay, then, that's what we'll do."

"'We'?"

"I'll help you."

Ah, Jake. He was used to solving problems, but this wasn't a problem that could be fixed with power tools and a can-do attitude. "What are you going to do? Answer my phones? I thought you weren't a phone guy."

He shrugged. "I'm rethinking that."

"And forget the phones, Wynd really is the only one who has truly conquered our stupidly complex scheduling software."

"I'll handle it."

She didn't want to make him feel bad, so she didn't say anything, but if Jake wasn't a phone guy, he *definitely* wasn't a software guy. But her face must have conveyed her skepticism, because he said, "Do you trust me?"

"Yes," she said automatically. Of course she did. He'd fixed her house, and then when her house proved uninhabitable, he'd found her another one. He had seen her at her most vulnerable, crying over her grandma and fighting with Rufus, and he was still here.

"Then let me handle this. Go to Toronto for the weekend. Hang out with your grandma, and I'll see you Monday morning at the clinic."

"But—"

"You wanna take Mick with you or leave him here?"

"You can't just—"

"I'll keep him, then. One less thing for you to worry about." He started the backward-walking thing.

"Jake!"

"Nora." He kept retreating.

"If you—"

"Be careful on the roads. You should leave soon, take advantage of the last of the light."

And with that, he turned his back and jogged off with her dog trotting along beside him.

Chapter Sixteen

c

"*S*he's coming!"

Jake chuckled as Amber stepped away from the window at the front of the clinic. Everyone was acting like they were throwing a surprise party.

And honestly, they might as well have been, given the size of the crowd that greeted Nora early Monday morning when she stepped through the front door, her eyes wide. He tamped down a smile. She was completely bundled up in a parka with the hood up and a scarf wrapped around her neck and covering the bottom half of her face.

"How's your grandma, dear?" Pearl was the first to intercept Nora. "Did she like the pastry cutter I sent?"

"She did, thank you," Nora said, her eyes darting around until she found Jake's. The effect was comical, given that her eyes were the only part of her face visible. "She had me make and roll out some dough just so she could cut it up, in fact." She shot him a look that was very clearly a *What the hell, Jake?* look, even though he could only see a small slice of her face.

He shrugged. Everyone else would fill her in.

"You know," Eiko said, "no one told me that your grand-mother was a famous surgeon. If I'd known, I might have written about it in the paper."

"But she doesn't live here," Nora said.

"I know, hon—Dr. Hon—but you do. Second-generation medical genius comes to town—that would have been a great angle. I still might do it. Do you have any pictures of the two of you together?"

Jake had known he was playing with fire when he walked into the hardware store after Nora left town and asked the old folks to help him. He *hated* their meddling, but this was for Nora. He'd suspected—and he'd been right—that they'd jump at the opportunity to help her.

"What's everyone doing here?" Nora asked as Clara approached from where she'd been camped out behind the reception desk with Wynd and Amber.

"We're your temps," Clara said.

Jake had *also* known he was playing with fire when he went from the hardware store to the inn to see if Clara was interested in earning some extra cash over her winter break. But Sawyer was already onto him. And even if that hadn't been the case, this was important. Clara was prob-ably a pretty reliable bet when it came to quickly learning complicated software.

Anyway, sometimes you had to do what you had to do, damn the consequences.

"What do you mean you're my temps?" Nora asked. Everyone looked at him, but he gestured back to Clara.

"Wynd is teaching me your software for scheduling and billing, and I'm going to be your receptionist until I have to go back to school in the new year. Hopefully you can hire someone permanently by then."

"And I'm backup for when Clara's busy with her girlfriend from Toronto," said Eiko with a twinkle in her eye.

"What?" Clara's jaw dropped, and Jake sighed. These people were impossible.

"Oh, come on," Eiko said. "Everyone knows your 'friend' who's coming to visit for New Year's isn't your 'friend' at all."

"I am going to kill my brother," Clara said.

"Well, I'm sure you thought—"

Jake cleared his throat to draw Eiko's attention and shook his head at her. Clara had only come out a year and a half ago, and as far as Jake knew, her holiday visitor was her first girlfriend. Honestly, there should be an age limit on the meddling the old folks did.

"Anyway," Eiko said, "I don't know about fancy software, but I can answer phones like nobody's business. I started my career in the 1960s as the secretary to the publisher of a newspaper. So whenever Clara can't be here, I can."

"I figure if someone prints the schedule on paper, she can handwrite in any appointments she makes, and Clara can enter them later," said Wynd from behind the reception desk.

"And I," said Pearl, "did some digging. The Clinton campus of Fanshawe College has a health care admin program. They'll have new grads at the end of the semester."

"Wow." Nora had started blinking rapidly. "Wow."

"And if that doesn't work out, I can fill in, too," Pearl said. "I mean, I am the two-time *Fortnite* champ in Senior Gamers of Southwestern Ontario, so how hard can medical billing really be?"

"And I can handle communicating with pharmacies," Amber said. "I help Wynd with it anyway when she gets busy."

Suddenly Nora's blinking looked like it was about to turn into blinking back tears.

"She just got here," Jake said, pushing through the crowd of women. "Let her put her stuff in her office and take her coat off before you all bombard her."

He grabbed her shoulder bag and started steering her toward her office.

"Thank you, everyone!" she called over her shoulder. "I should have said that right off, but I'm a little over-whelmed."

"Don't thank us," Eiko called back. "Thank Jake. It was all his idea."

He delivered her to the door of her office intending to leave her there, but she grabbed his arm, pulled him in with her, shut the door, and threw herself into his arms.

Her parka was so puffy, it was like hugging a marshmallow, but he'd missed his marshmallow over the weekend, so he went all in.

"Jake. I—"

Her voice was muffled by his chest. He reluctantly let go of her so he could hear her.

She looked startled—like, *really* startled. By the clinic still? He supposed it was a lot to take in. She looked at him a long time.

"You okay, Doc?"

I love you.

Thank God she hadn't said it out loud.

Because she didn't mean it like *that*. She'd just been so overwhelmed and relieved to find that Jake had solved her clinic problem. She meant it in the way you say, "I love you" when someone surprises you with something that makes your life easier or more delightful or when someone generally saves your ass when your ass did not expect saving.

Like last week, when she'd gotten a pizza to go from Law's and walked to Maya's with it. Maya had buzzed her up, swung open her door, taken one look at the telltale pizza box, and said, "I love you."

That was it. She didn't love-love Jake; she loved the way he made her life easier.

He also provided an interesting study in contrasts. Rufus had made everything harder. She hadn't realized it when she was in it, but it was true. Rufus was forever asking her to cover his shifts, which required her to cancel haircuts and coffee dates with her sister. He would insist they overshoot the movie theater a few blocks from them in favor of one a half-hour subway ride away because he liked the screens there better. She got it—or at least that was what she'd told herself. He cared about things like movie screens. She didn't, and it didn't hurt her to accommodate him, she had always reasoned.

And maybe it hadn't *hurt* her, but the little sacrifices had added up. The accommodations had accumulated until she'd forgotten what it was like for someone to have your back. What easy felt like.

Easy felt like such a *relief*.

"You okay, Doc?" Jake sounded concerned. She was being weird, and he was picking up on it.

"Yeah, yeah. Thank you for this."

"Eh, all I did was some wrangling."

Yeah, right. She knew full well he was the silent mastermind behind all of this, but she also knew he wouldn't want her to make a big deal out of it. "Well, thanks for the wrangling."

The week passed remarkably uneventfully. With Wynd still there and Nora's new army of helpers cycling in and out, everything was extra efficient. When the weekend came, she opted not to go back to Toronto. Her grandma had seemed stable the previous weekend. They were only open one more week, and then she'd take off for her previously scheduled holiday break.

Mostly she just wanted to catch her breath. Be still for a day or two—no work, no travel. Do some online Christmas shopping. Hang out with her dog. And maybe her pal the man-god.

"Hey, so sorry I'm late." Wynd rushed in. Their usual Friday-morning staff meeting was winding down. "There's terrible black ice out there. I just about bit it twice."

"Honey, you have to be careful," Eiko said.

"You know what?" Nora was feeling magnanimous. "If you want to just be done, I think we're on top of things enough that we can do without you next week."

"Really?" Wynd asked hopefully.

"I think so. Don't you?" She looked around at Clara, Eiko, and Jake. Yes, Jake. Even though he had no official role in the clinic's operations, he tended to stop by in the mornings to make sure everything was looking okay for the day ahead. He had even done a stint behind the reception desk at one point when Wynd had gone home early because of a storm, Clara wasn't around, and Eiko had to run off to cover the annual Polar Bear Dip in the bay.

Nora had come out from an appointment to find Mr. Not Much of a Phone Guy on the phone.

"Just because I don't like talking on the phone doesn't

mean I don't know how to do it," he'd said when she'd razzed him. He slid a stack of messages toward her. "And I *am* literate, you know."

"Yeah, we'll miss you, but we'll be fine," Clara said to Wynd. The members of Nora's misfit medical admin team all nodded in agreement.

And they were fine.

The next week presented a few minor problems, but everyone seemed to regard tackling them as a team effort. Patients got seen, even if things ran late. Appointments got made, even if people had to be called back later. Nora stayed late Monday evening to deal with the billing, which was okay, because Jake appeared bearing Hawaiian pizza and Mick.

They ate. And then they locked Mick out of her office.

They did it all over again on Tuesday.

The week was going great. And not just because of the locking-Mick-out-of-the-office part. In spite of the hiccups they'd encountered, she was full of gratitude toward everyone who was helping her out. Eiko and Clara and Jake, of course, but also Pearl, who was constantly showing up with pies. And Sawyer, who popped in from time to time to see if anyone needed anything. And Maya and Eve, who brought her dinner on Wednesday night, when Jake was at a job.

Even her patients were cheerful about longer-than-usual delays on hold or in the waiting room.

It felt like the whole town was coming together to support the clinic. To support her.

By Thursday things were humming along. Nora had a stack of résumés to look over for a permanent hire and an idea brewing to hire Clara this coming summer—if she was interested—to help her be more organized with her vaccine projects.

All was well.

When Nora came out of an exam room midafternoon, Eiko was waiting for her. "Your sister is on line one. I told her you were in with a patient and you'd call her back, but she wanted to hold."

Nora picked up the call in her office. "Hey! Did you guys get the tree up? I'm not going to be able to get out of here until about four tomorrow, so don't wait, but I'll—"

"Nora."

She knew, just from the one word, from the way Erin said her name. But she asked anyway. She wanted to be wrong. "What happened?"

"It's Grandma."

Oh, shit.

"She's much worse. We took her to the emergency room this morning because she was..." Erin's voice wavered before she regained control of it. "She was having a lot of trouble breathing. They admitted her. She's on oxygen, but she's getting all weirdly intense about making sure everyone knows about her DNR wishes."

"I'm going to get there as soon as I can."

"Now?"

This was the downside of the single-physician practice. She had been high lately on the feeling that she personally was making a difference in the lives of people in this town, that she had built something from nothing.

But it also meant that she personally was responsible for her patients. There was no getting someone to cover her shifts.

"As soon as I can." She had patients in the waiting room. She probably had one in each of her two exam rooms, too. Maybe if she just got through today, she could have Amber call everyone on the schedule for tomorrow and shuffle things around so the people who couldn't wait came first thing, and then she could be on the road before lunch?

"Nora. Come as soon as you can. Please."

After assuring Erin she would, she rose and walked out of her office feeling like she was floating outside her body.

Eiko was waiting in the corridor. "What's happened?"

"Nothing. I—"

"Don't take this the wrong way, Dr. Hon, but I once broke a story about the previous town council conspiring to siphon funds from the lighthouse rehabilitation fund. You can't fool me."

"My grandma's in the hospital. It looks like this is it."

"Oh no. I'm sorry."

Nora was about to brush off Eiko's words. Well meant as they were, she didn't want them. But Eiko was on to other things. She rapped sharply on the door of Exam Room Two. "Amber, can you step out for a minute?"

"What's up?"

"Nora's grandma is in the hospital in Toronto, and Nora needs to leave."

"Yes, if we can get through the rest of the day," Nora said, noting with amazement how calm her voice sounded, "I was thinking we could—"

"No. You go now."

"I can't just leave!" So much for calm. "There are patients here! We have a full schedule tomorrow."

"We'll take care of it," Eiko said. "Go home, pack some stuff up, and hit the road."

"What do you mean you'll take care of it? You can't—"

"We *can*," Amber said with the quiet sureness that made her such a good nurse. "We'll call everyone who's on the books for the rest of today and tomorrow and either reschedule them for after the holidays or, if it's urgent, send them to the walk-in clinic in Grand View. I can be here tomorrow in case there's anyone we can't reach. I obviously can't see them, but I can triage and either rebook them for January or send them elsewhere. And I can do that right now with the people in the waiting room."

"Are you sure?"

"Dr. Hon." Eiko emerged from Nora's office holding Nora's coat and bag. "We lived without you before. It wasn't pleasant, mind you, and we all like it a lot better with you here, but we can do it again. So just go see your grandma."

Her things were shoved unceremoniously into her arms.

"Okay," Nora said weakly. "Thank you."

"I'll call your sister back and let her know you're leaving shortly," Eiko said.

"Thanks," Nora said again.

"And if there's anything else we can do, you let us know."

"Could you let Jake know what's happened and ask him to keep Mick?" It was a stupid request. Jake was *already* keeping Mick. Mick was, at this point, more Jake's dog than Nora's, if you went by how much time he spent with each of them. Or the way he trotted along obediently after Mr. Dog Whisperer.

But she...just wanted Jake to know what had happened. It felt important that he know.

Chapter Seventeen

❧

The day after Christmas, Jake bought a cell phone.

Because he had lost his mind.

"Are you going to tell Sawyer about this?" he asked Clara, who was sitting next to him in the shuttered clinic using *her* phone to order him a phone.

Honestly, the modern world made his head hurt sometimes.

She shot him a quizzical look. "Would you prefer I didn't?"

He wasn't sure how to play this. Was she teasing him? He decided to just be honest. "Yes. I would prefer you didn't."

"So you're just going to have a secret phone that no one knows about?"

"I'm going to use it for weather reports when I'm out on the boat, but I don't want to make myself available all the time, you know?"

Except to one person.

God. Nora's continued absence was gutting him.

If only he knew her goddamn number, he could call her from his landline. But he didn't, and there was no way to get it without asking Eve or Maya or someone. Which he still might do. He just wasn't *quite* that desperate yet.

He had asked Eve once how she was doing, but there wasn't much news. "Sounds like she isn't doing well but is still hanging on," she'd said, as if that were specific enough. As if that told him anything of use.

And anyway, he wanted to know how *Nora* was doing. The "she" in his question had meant Nora.

"You might actually be onto something with that," Clara said. "I'm starting to think my phone is affecting my brain, and not in a good way. You want Android or iOS?"

"I have no idea what those words even mean."

"If budget is a primary concern, I'd say Android. But since—don't take this the wrong way—you're kind of a beginner, I'm going to say we should go with an iPhone. It's more intuitive."

"Just get me a phone." He winced. That had come out way too sharply. She hadn't done anything but help him. "Sorry."

"It's okay, Jake." She smiled affectionately at him. "I'm not going to tell Sawyer."

"Why not?" He wasn't sure why he was asking. He shouldn't look a gift horse in the mouth.

"Honestly?" she said as she tapped away at her phone. "Because you're one of the only people in this town who isn't giving me shit about Sunnie."

"People are giving you shit about Sunnie? What people?"

"Calm down. Not like that. Just, you know the way everyone in this town acts. They're being all wink-wink, nudge-nudge. Like, I just met the girl a few months ago. She's my first girlfriend. Meanwhile, Pearl has started emailing me pictures of wedding cake toppers with two brides. Even Sawyer is being kind of weird."

"Yeah, I can't help you there. I don't know how to make Pearl not be Pearl or make Sawyer not be weird."

"I mean, I get it. It's hard to be from Moonflower Bay and not let all this nosiness rub off on you. But why do people have to verbalize every thought in their head?"

"I ask myself that every day."

"Like, for example, even if I *suspect* that your suddenly buying a phone is related to your massive crush on Dr. Walsh, that doesn't mean I need to say it out loud."

He was tempted to protest. But what was the point? Clara was just a kid. She wouldn't understand the concept of friends with benefits. And the relevant point was that she wasn't going to tell Sawyer, who *also*, it seemed, didn't understand the concept of friends with benefits. So he returned the conversation to an earlier topic: "If anyone gives you shit—like actual shit about who you are—you let me know, okay?" People didn't just mess with Clara Collins.

She smiled. "Thanks, Jake. I mean, my brother is a cop and all, so I don't think I'm going to need to tap you for vigilante justice purposes, but I totally appreciate that I could. Now hand over your credit card so we can buy you a phone you're going to use to check the weather for all that fishing you don't do."

Grandma was slipping away. Every day she was awake less—overall and at each interval. And when she was awake, she was starting, sometimes, not to know where she was, or what year it was.

"You should think of medical school," she said to Nora

on the morning of Christmas eve, reaching out and flailing her hand. Nora grabbed the hand in her own. Her grandma's skin was thin and crepey and pale and studded with a line that was delivering fluids and meds.

"I did go to med school, Grandma," she whispered. "Remember how I'm patching up boo-boos in Moonflower Bay instead of cutting people up like real doctors do?"

They'd been joking around as recently as last night, but Nora didn't get the smile she'd been aiming for. Her grandma furrowed her brow. "I've seen you with patients. And more importantly, I've seen you with doctors. You already know as much as they do."

Hmm. Grandma had not seen her with patients—she'd been retired by the time Nora was in med school.

"She thinks you're me, honey." Her mom came up behind her and laid a hand on her shoulder. The family was rotating in and out so at any given time there were at least a couple of them here. "She always wanted me to go to med school."

"She *did*?" Nora twisted to look at her mom.

"You're wasting your talents, Pam."

Damn, she *did* think Nora was her mom. And, wow, that must sting. Nurses dealt with enough shit on the job.

"You know what, Penelope? I think you're right. I'm going to look into it." Her mom laid a hand on her grandma's forehead. "You try to get some rest, okay?"

Grandma nodded, seemingly relieved to have won the argument, and they stayed with her until her breathing, while still ragged, lengthened.

"Mom," Nora whispered. "What was all that?"

Her mom gestured for her to follow her into the hallway. "I was already a nurse when I met your father. Once it became clear I was going to stick, Penelope launched a campaign to get me to go to med school. She was really relentless about it in those early years."

"Did you...want to do that?"

"Not really. Maybe if I'd come from this family instead of my own, it would have been something I considered. It wasn't something anyone ever suggested to me until I met your grandma. But by then I was already so far into my nursing career, I wasn't interested in going back to school and making a big change."

"But it must have hurt your feelings." So many doctors thought of nurses as second-class medical professionals. She'd just never thought her grandma was one of them.

"Did it hurt your feelings all the times she tried to get you to specialize in surgery?"

"Maybe the first few times, but I eventually realized that's just the way she is—she likes challenging people. And I knew she was proud of me because I once overheard her bragging to her friends about how well I was doing in med school."

"Me, too. You remember when I won that award from the Canadian Nurses Association?" Nora nodded. It had been a big deal. They'd all gone to a gala and listened to the chief of pediatrics at her mom's hospital sing her praises. "Your father told me after the fact that Penelope was behind nominating me. She didn't want it to look like nepotism, so she strong-armed some of her friends into doing it for her."

Tears sprang to Nora's eyes, but she swallowed them back.

Her mom pulled her into a hug. "We were all so lucky to have her. You kids especially. You basically had a bonus parent who lavished love and encouragement on you." Her mom smiled, her own eyes growing watery. "With a good dash of nagging in there, too."

Nora nodded, grasping for facts. Facts would help her be stoic. "Is it going to be long, do you think?" Nurses always knew.

"No," her mom said. "Not long."

"Is it selfish to say I wish she recognized me?"

"Not selfish. But she does recognize you, honey. She recognizes you with her heart."

Jake sat on his couch for a long time hemming and hawing before he sent his first text. He wasn't sure if texting her now—now that *he* wanted to talk—was selfish. In the end he talked himself into it because when they parted, she'd said, "Let's not just...never talk again." He'd agreed. It had been surreal to watch her drive away and think, *Well, that's it*. He'd meant to keep in touch, and he'd even picked up the phone the first few times she'd called to "say hi," once the answering machine kicked in and he realized it was Kerrie. But things had tapered off. It was just...too hard. Also, he wasn't that much of a talker to begin with.

> Hey, it's Jake. Is this still your number? Is it okay to text you? You can tell me to fuck off.

> **Kerrie:** Jake! You got a phone.
> **Jake:** Hard to believe, I know.
> **Kerrie:** And yes, of course it's okay to text me. I'm happy to hear from you. What's up? How are you?

How was he? He had no idea. Confused. Maybe.

> **Jake:** I just wanted to say that I'm sorry about a lot of stuff. I didn't handle things

well at the end there. I know that's a lot to
dump on you in a text out of the blue. You
can just hang up on me. Or whatever the
text equivalent is. I just got this phone
and I don't know what the hell I'm doing.
Kerrie: Oh Jake. Neither of us handled
things well at the end. How could we
have? It was such a miserable end. I'm
sorry, too.

That was a huge relief, and more than he deserved.

Jake: I wanted to ask you a question.
You don't have to answer it if you don't
want to. But you know when we drove
the boat out to scatter Jude's ashes?
Should we have said something?
Kerrie: You mean like a prayer?
Jake: I don't know. Anything.
Kerrie: I didn't know what to say.
Jake: I didn't either.
Kerrie: What would you have said if you
could go back?

What *would* he have said? *I'm sorry I didn't protect you
better*, maybe? But that would open up another conversation
about how it wasn't his fault.

Jake: I don't know. Maybe just goodbye?
Kerrie: Yes. Goodbye to our boy.

There was a certain comfort in seeing those words that
she'd typed. Like they were saying them now. Too late, but

also not too late. Because who would they really have been saying them for?

> *Jake:* Anyway, sorry to ambush you. I'll
> let you go.
> *Kerrie:* I'm glad to hear from you.
> But . . . is there any reason you're thinking
> about this all right now?
> *Jake:* I'm never not thinking about it.
> *Kerrie:* Yeah. Yeah, I know.

Chapter Eighteen

 e

*S*he should have called first.

She didn't have his number, though. It had been written on the back of a receipt months ago and shoved into her purse. She had looked for it on Walsh-giving, to no avail. Anyway, that purse was in her room at the Mermaid, and she hadn't stopped there first.

Despite Jake's joke about actually checking his messages the day he'd given her his home number, Nora had never called him. They had an old-fashioned relationship. Friendship. Whatever-ship. He would show up in person, often at lunch. More recently at dinner, with pizza, while she was doing her billing. They'd make plans for the future, and they'd stick to those plans without having to text each other a million updates. It was refreshing.

Jake wasn't a phone guy. He really wasn't.

And after the past week and a bit, she needed one thing to stay the same. She needed one thing she could rely on.

She needed a place where she could fall apart. Someone who would let her do that and then prop her up afterward.

She hadn't been planning on coming back to Moonflower Bay today. The clinic was closed until after New Year's. There was no reason to hurry back. Her grandmother's funeral had been yesterday, and today was supposed to be spent opening sympathy cards and sorting through memorial donations. It was supposed to be about grieving together, just her family, without her grandma's legions of friends and former colleagues hovering. And it had been.

Until around dinnertime, when the weather reports started talking about a massive storm headed for Toronto.

They had all tried to talk her out of it. What was her hurry? It was dark. When the storm came, it might become dangerous. But once she'd heard the meteorologist on the radio say the phrases *significant accumulation* and *snowed in*, she'd become almost frantic. She *couldn't* be snowed in in the city for several days.

She had to get... back. Initially she'd thought *I have to get home*. But that wasn't right. She *was* home, huddling in a protective cocoon with her parents and siblings and nephews.

The problem was, it didn't feel that protective. It felt, suddenly, stifling. Everyone was crying all the time and that, paradoxically, made her extra committed to keeping her shit together. Someone had to schedule obituaries and select caskets and wash casserole dishes. So she'd just kept putting one foot in front of the other, kept *not* crying, a robot carrying out the administrivia of death.

Until she was faced with the prospect of being forced to keep doing it because she was *trapped*. Escape had become imperative.

Once on the highway, she calmed down a bit. As she

made her way along dark, empty country roads, and as the first snowflakes started falling, a word started to fill the silence, pulsing more and more insistently, like a weak heartbeat gaining strength.

Jake.

Jake.

Jake.

For some reason her mind kept landing back on the day—the moment—Rufus had ambushed her last summer. Jake had stood by her—literally stood by her—and lightly rested his hand on her back. He had not spoken. But he had been there, stalwart in his watchful silence.

That was what she needed right now.

She didn't even know if he would be home. His truck was parked in its usual spot at the corner of Locust and Sarnia, but that didn't mean anything. It was Friday night, and he always walked to and from the bar on Fridays. She'd given half a thought to stopping by on her way in. Even if he wasn't there, someone else would be.

But she didn't want someone else.

She could only hope it was late enough—it was just after eleven—that he'd be back home.

She parked behind his truck and began the cold trudge. She didn't have boots. In a warped sort of way, though, she relished the prospect of walking through the cold water. Maybe it would jolt her awake, get rid of this plodding, sleepwalking, robotic feeling.

She hissed when she splashed into the icy lake—there were literal chunks of ice here in the shallows. If she'd relished this, it had been theoretical. The water felt like it was made of tiny, invisible needles. This wasn't awake; this was hypothermia, or close to it. She rushed around the outcropping and stumbled onto the beach.

She cursed her way across the snowy sand to his front door, the cold air excoriating her wet ankles. She was so cold, she was panting. The cottage was dark. *Please be here.*

She took off her mitten and pounded on the door.

Mick started barking. *Mick.* Tears threatened.

He opened the door. *Jake.*

Jake.

Jake.

Jake.

Her refrain from the car kicked in again.

He was wearing flannel pajama bottoms and a holey T-shirt. His hair was all messed up, and he was squinting. She had woken him up.

He said her name three times, an echo of her mantra. The first was a question, like he didn't trust his eyes, was unsure whether it was really her. "Nora?"

She had made it. She was here. He was here. She was no longer a robot. She was a girl with a dead grandma. The tears came.

The second time he said her name was urgent, gruff, commanding, as he pulled her over the threshold and into his arms. "*Nora.*"

The third time he said her name, as her tears became actual, literal, *mortifying* wails, was gentle. Impossibly, acutely, exquisitely gentle. It was a whisper she felt as much as heard. "Nora."

Nora only let him hold her for a minute or so before she started trying to minimize her grief. "I don't know what's the matter with me. She was *old.* She was *eighty-seven.*" The sobbing of a moment ago had lessened, but she was still talking through tears. They were sliding out of her eyes silently and rapidly. "This is the natural way of things."

"Shh." He tried to get her back in his embrace, but she put her hands on his chest. She was keeping him at literal arm's length. So he laid his hands on her cheeks. It wasn't like he thought he could magically stop those tears that were still coming furiously, like a tap that had been left on, or even that he *should* stop them. But he did feel, irrationally, that even though his hands couldn't stop those tears, they could bear witness to them.

"I'm so sorry," she said. "This wasn't like Jude."

He shook his head. It wasn't a contest, or a zero-sum game. There was enough room for all their grief. *He* had enough room for it all. He would hold hers for a while, if she would let him.

But he found himself slow to speak. His throat was tight, and he couldn't seem to get the words from his brain to his tongue.

"I shouldn't be coming here like this. Waking you up, dumping this on you," she said in a rush.

He kissed her. It was the best way he could think to make her stop talking nonsense and to convey what he couldn't say. That he was so sorry her grandma had died. That he *wanted* her here. That he'd missed her and was glad she was home.

He went slowly, pressing his mouth gently against hers without moving it, so he could pay attention to the way she responded. So he could make sure it wasn't too much.

It wasn't too much, judging by the way she rocked up and down on her toes, gaining momentum, and, with her hands wound around his neck, hitched herself up and wrapped her legs around his waist.

He kicked the door shut with one foot and turned. He

gave a moment's thought to whether he should deposit her on the sofa or take her back to his bed, but he felt something wet on his hip. It was her foot. He slid one hand under her bottom so as not to drop her and the other down one leg. Her feet were wet. She'd walked through the lake.

So he went to the fireplace. He'd laid a fire earlier. It was down to embers now—he'd fallen asleep on the couch. He knelt in front of it and carefully laid her down on her back. Mick came over and stood guard.

She stared at him, silent tears still flowing as he tugged off her wet boots followed by her wet socks. Her jeans were wet up to the knees, too, so he unbuttoned them. She lifted her hips so he could get them off her, and as he did so, she shrugged out of her parka.

He'd only been intending to get her out of her wet clothing, but she kept going. She crossed her arms and reached for the hem of her sweater and lifted that off, too. When she got stuck, he helped.

She had not been wearing a bra.

Which was not the kind of thing he should be noticing right now. She was still crying.

But oh God, she was beautiful. The pixie doctor. The woman who fixed things. She was a healer who couldn't conquer death. Her hair was glowing almost silver, and the dying light from the fire was gold.

She was breaking his heart.

There were a couple of his mom's quilts on the couch. He reached for them and tried not to mourn the loss of her as he covered her up. Mick curled up next to her and whined. She turned her face into his fur.

Jake turned his attention to the fire. Spent a few minutes with some kindling getting it started again and fed it a log, then another, making sure it was really going.

By the time he turned back to her, she had stopped crying and was staring intently at him. One of her legs was sticking out of the quilt, so he moved to cover her better, but in the process his hand brushed her foot. Though dry now, it was still freezing. He pushed the quilt up a little and reached for her other foot with his other hand. He squeezed, and she sighed. He rubbed his palms briskly back and forth over the tops of her feet and slid up her ankles.

His intent had only been to warm her chilled skin, but she slid the quilt farther up, exposing her shins. So he slid his hands farther up and sent them around to massage her cold calves, staring at her the whole way.

She stared back, watching him evenly and with what looked like great concentration. He kept going, kneading up and down from her Achilles' heel to the backs of her knees, keeping track of her breathing as he went. It was slowing. It had been rapid before, shading into panting as she'd been crying. But now it was syncing itself to his, which he'd deliberately slowed as he'd been working on the fire. Or maybe that wasn't right. Maybe his was syncing to hers.

As he approached the backs of her knees on an upward pass, she tugged the quilt higher, exposing her thighs. She kept staring, her expression hard to read but the invitation in her gesture clear. It felt like more than an invitation, actually, it felt more like...what? Not a command exactly. An expression of need.

So he slid his hands slowly up past her knees, massaging the tops of her thighs. Her quads were tight, perhaps from all the running. He dug his thumbs in, watching her like a hawk, wanting to deliver exactly what she needed. Pressure, but not pain. Comfort, but not pity. Protection, but not constraint.

Her breath, which he was using as his gauge, kept slowing, shading into sighs.

But then, as one thumb brushed the crease where her thigh met her torso, there was a hitch.

His aim here was not seduction. It was something else, something he couldn't begin to name, but he knew, somehow, that it had to be delivered through his hands. That words, which had never been his forte anyway, were not sufficient.

But he would be lying if he said that hitch, that sigh interrupted, hadn't caused an echo in his own breath. A slight inhalation breaking through the rhythm he'd been weaving. He hadn't been planning to do anything about it, though, until the thighs he held, one in each hand, fell open.

He stopped the movement of his hands as his pulse kicked up a notch. It was diverging from his slow, measured breathing.

She pulled the quilt higher.

He did not move. He watched, frozen on the outside while storms raged on the inside, as she slowly, decidedly, gathered the quilt, which was now scrunched up around her middle, and set it to one side.

She rolled her thighs open some more, and he loosened his grip on them. While the legs moved, his hands stayed in place—maybe he *was* frozen—which landed them on her inner thighs. She had a tiny web of stretch marks on either side, and painted with the warm light from the fire, they looked like delicate, golden filaments.

He wanted to put his mouth on them, and judging from the way she had splayed herself open to him—the network of gold culminated in her pretty, pink center—she wanted that, too. He moved slowly. He had been kneeling, but now he moved back, transferring his gaze from her thighs to her eyes, assessing as he went. Slowly, slowly, he extended his legs, and then his entire body, along the floor. Her pupils, which he would have said were already blown out, dilated some more.

He raised his eyebrows.

She licked her lips.

Okay, then.

His first order of business was to move the now-snoring Mick. He picked him up gently and moved him to the couch before returning to exactly where he'd been before, lying between her thighs.

He lowered his head, and forgetting about the golden, gossamer threads that had initially captured his attention, he licked her seam. Just once. It was like pressing fast-forward, he knew, doing things out of order, but he wanted her most vulnerable skin under his mouth, under his teeth, and he thought she wanted that, too. She was salty and damp and quivering, and he was so fucking *sorry* her grandma was dead.

He checked in with her breath. It was slow again, but shaky. He'd kept his neck tilted back so he could watch her, and she'd tilted hers forward, so their gazes had remained locked.

Without taking his mouth off her, he slid down enough so he could taste her inner thigh. As he kissed it, he stroked the creases on both sides with his thumbs. Her skin was soft, but not perfectly smooth. That was the texture he had been admiring. It was like a map. No, like a key. The secret markings that made her her.

He must have been getting too moony over her thigh, though, because she grabbed his head. Jammed her hands into his hair and made fists. He loved that. He'd missed that.

She yanked his head back up.

In another circumstance he might have chuckled. But this wasn't that circumstance. The air between them was heavy. Serious. Shot through with grief.

But she was clearly communicating what she needed from him, so he put aside the mooniness. Enough with the gilded light and the golden filaments. He put his mouth back on her, and the way she bucked her hips at first contact and squeezed her thighs around his head told him she wanted him to get to the point. Good. He wanted her to use him for whatever she needed. So he went right for her clit, flicking his tongue over it the way he'd learned she liked. Usually he would draw things out, but she was already writhing and moaning and making fists in his hair, all signs that she was close. He switched to sucking, and she came within seconds, on a sob that sounded like it was half pleasure, half grief.

He stayed with her as she pulsed, resting his cheek on one thigh. He'd been so focused on her, first on admiring her like she was a painting and then on making her come, that he had lost touch with his own body. He was hard as iron. Of course he was. How could a man witness such a spectacle and not be? But it didn't matter. It felt not-urgent. A by-product of letting her use him to make herself feel... better?

That probably wasn't it. To make herself feel the way she needed to feel. He understood that.

When she loosened her hold on his hair, he glanced up at her. Her thighs were still splayed, and he was still resting his cheek on one of them.

She reached down and laid her palm on the other cheek, the upturned one, and something happened inside him.

He tried not to let it. He tried to swallow the tears

that were suddenly there, just below the surface. This was supposed to be about her. About being an anchor for her, a place to land. Being whatever she needed.

Her hand on his cheek felt like mercy where there had been none for so long.

Like her gold filaments were winding themselves around him, *knitting* something around him, something that bolstered him, made it easier to bear his own weight.

Slowly she sat up, which had the effect of dislodging him from the pillow of her thigh. She pushed him onto his back and started taking off his clothes. He let himself be manipulated. He lifted his arms up so she could work his T-shirt off and his hips when she tapped them so she could slide his pajama pants down.

He stayed passive as she climbed on top of him and used one hand to guide him inside her. As she sank down, he felt the wetness on his cheeks that wasn't supposed to be there.

He let it be.

The funny thing was that they hadn't said anything. She had been here, what? An hour? Two? More?

To say she had lost track of time was an understatement. As they'd...come together by the fire, time had stopped, it felt like. Nora wasn't one for flowery language. Normally she'd have said they'd had sex by the fire, but that didn't seem like quite the right phrase. But she wasn't going to say they'd made love. Because they weren't in love.

But something powerful had happened to both of them, and she didn't need to think back to her psych rotation to figure out that it had to do with grief.

And then she'd fallen asleep in his arms.

The fire was down to embers, and the cottage was cold and dark. He must have covered them with the quilt at some point, because they were both tucked under it.

However much time had passed, it had elapsed in silence. She'd tried to apologize at his door for her sudden, impulsive appearance, but that felt like a lifetime ago.

And he hadn't said a single word after he'd chanted her name those three times.

There were different kinds of silence. Everyone else always remarked on how Jake was so quiet. How he rarely spoke. Sometimes they even used the word *mute*. She, on the other hand, did not experience Jake that way. He said enough. He said the right things. When he didn't speak, it was generally because he didn't have anything to say— and what a rare thing it was, the ability to hold one's tongue.

But this silence from him was different. It was an active, almost reverential silence. An acknowledgment of something. She wasn't sure exactly what, except that again, she felt like it had to do with grief. With honoring it, maybe. Making room for it. Yeah, that's what this silence was about, making room for things.

It had been a silence so profound, she half wondered if her voice worked anymore. If his did.

But the silence couldn't go on forever. She didn't know if he was awake. He was spooning her from behind, and she couldn't see his face. She shifted a little, her intent to pull away enough to turn over, but he banded his arms more tightly around her.

"Jake, I'm—"

"If you're about to apologize again for feeling bad that your grandma died, you can just cut it out right now."

His voice, low and grumbly, was familiar, but it was also a surprise.

"I wasn't," she lied.

"If you have to apologize for feeling bad about your grandma, do I have to apologize for feeling bad about Jude?"

"No! That's my point. The two things are not the same." They weren't. They just weren't.

"They *are* the same." He spoke sharply, and he never did that. "They are exactly the same. We had people, and now we don't have them."

She didn't agree, but it felt disrespectful to keep arguing. "I should go."

"I got a phone."

"What?" She pulled against his embrace, and he let her go this time. She flipped over. "A cell phone?"

"Yeah. Which means I got Wi-Fi."

"You got *Wi-Fi*?" Holy crap. Had she fallen down the rabbit hole into Wonderland?

"Yeah. Which means if you have your computer with you, we can watch a movie."

"You want to watch a *movie*?" She was aware that merely repeating everything he said with the last syllable emphasized was not doing a lot for her reputation as an intelligent person.

"Yeah, let's watch one of your zombie movies."

"But...it's the middle of the night."

"You got somewhere to be?"

No. She had nowhere to be. The clinic was closed until January second. She had fled Toronto prematurely, so she had nowhere to be except her room at the Mermaid. And while she was fond of it, it was no accident that she'd driven right past it earlier tonight—on her way here.

"No," she said quietly. "Nowhere to be. My computer's in my car, though. In my suitcase."

"Okay, then." He got to his feet and extended a hand. He helped her up, settled the quilt around her shoulders, and pointed her toward the kitchen. "You make popcorn. I'll be back soon."

Chapter Nineteen

*Z*ombies are metaphorical, right?" Nora asked twenty-four hours later.

"You're asking me?" Jake rolled over to face her as the closing credits of *Dawn of the Dead* rolled.

"Yeah, I'm asking you."

"Well, you're asking the wrong guy."

"Come on. I mean, *Dawn of the Dead*—this one and the remake—are clearly about consumer culture."

"Clearly." He smiled lazily at her. He was making fun of her.

She rolled her eyes, but she secretly liked it. "And *Plan 9 from Outer Space*"—which they'd watched earlier in the day—"is clearly about nuclear fear."

"Clearly."

She threw a pillow at him.

"Yes. So *clearly* we can pick out a metaphor for individual movies—they reflect the fears of the era in which they're made. But what I'm really asking is, is there a super-metaphor? Like, beyond the scope of any individual movie. Is it apocalypse? Or is it not that complicated—is it just fear itself? What do zombies *mean*?"

"I thought zombies meant overtired med students."

Right. That was what her grandma had always said.

She swallowed hard. She'd forgotten for a moment. She was rolled up in the coziest cocoon of zombie movies— they'd watched four since last night—and sex, and she'd momentarily forgotten reality.

"Hey," he whispered, cupping her chin. He'd only referenced her grandma's interpretation of zombies as a joke, she knew, but thinking about her grandma was like a punch to the solar plexus.

"Hey," he said again, rolling over so he was on top of her. They hadn't bothered getting dressed since the last time they'd had sex—before the last movie. He was hard. Not just his penis, but all over. And even though he was propped on his forearms and holding most of his weight off her, he was heavy. Heavy in a good way. It felt like he was mooring her with his body. "You want to cry or you want..."

She smiled. First because this was how the past twenty-four hours had gone. He had let her lead. Which meant sometimes he held her while she stood at his front window and looked at the snow falling steadily over the lake and cried. And sometimes they...did other stuff.

And that was the second reason she was smiling. It seemed like her vocabulary failure of last night had infected him—speaking of zombie metaphors—too. He didn't know what to call it anymore, either.

And maybe she also smiled a little bit because she was happy. A little bit. Mixed in with all the sadness.

A steady diet of napping, sex, zombie movies, and snacks, it turned out, made her happy.

But she also didn't want him to get the wrong idea. She was leaning on him pretty hard right now, and she didn't think he minded, but she didn't want him to think she had any misconceptions about what was happening. So as a reminder—to both of them—she said, "I want you to get inside me, Jake." He groaned—he liked that answer—and she wrapped her legs around his waist. "ASAP, actually," she added, grinding herself on him.

He liked that answer, too, judging by the way a groan shaded into a growl.

He shifted his weight to one arm and grabbed his penis with the other. He met no resistance. She was soft, open. Maybe zombies were foreplay.

Or maybe lying next to Jake watching zombies was foreplay.

Regardless, he slid right in.

She sighed contentedly. She hadn't had sex without a condom for years. But there was something so delicious, so lazy about just rolling over and going at it.

And this *was* lazy. Not in an "I can't be bothered" way, but in an "I'm kind of spent from all the sex we've already had, but I still can't keep my hands off you" way. He ground his hips in slow circles against her, and because he was lying on top of her, pasting his whole body over hers, staying fully sheathed in her as he worked his hips, the angle put pressure on her clit. She moved against him lazily, too, keeping her ankles locked at his back. There was no thrusting, no athletic pumping, just small circles, just friction and want.

He came first, filling her with a low grumble that sounded like a mixture of pained and relieved. She wasn't there yet, and he kept moving his hips, but she'd lost the friction on her clit. He knew it, though, and peeled his body off hers just enough to press his fingers against her. He established the same rhythm they'd had with their bodies—slow and measured. She was wet, and his come was oozing out of her, and she loved the squishing sound they made when she rolled her hips in time with his circles.

"Come on, Nora," he whispered against her ear, his head buried in her neck. He wasn't hurrying her, just encouraging her. Sighing again, she let her head fall back. She'd been looking at where they were joined—it was so hot—but the weight of her head was too much now. "Come on," he said again, leaving his thumb on her clit but rotating his hand so he could insert a finger into her next to his now-soft penis.

Her muscles started fluttering around him. "There you go," he whispered.

If she'd thought about it, she would have predicted this would be a quick, serviceable orgasm. She was already so wrung out, both emotionally and physically. She'd had a lot of orgasms in the last twenty-four hours, *good* ones.

But holy crap, she had never had one like this. It started small, but then it just...didn't end.

"Yeah," he encouraged, keeping up the same rhythm with his fingers.

"Oh," she breathed as the contractions kept coming. It wasn't a hurried sensation, at least not at first. It started out measured, but it was expanding inside her. When she thought she was approaching the end, the whole thing would start over. It was a little bit scary, not knowing when the end would come, but not scary enough to make it end. "Oh!"

"Yeah, Nora. Keep going, baby."

A small part of her mind registered that it was a little absurd how he was cheering her on. But mostly his words, his low, sexy tone, just poured fuel on the flames.

Eventually, though, the sensations waned. As she came back to herself, vulnerability arrived. She was sweating and panting and sticky and crying a little—and not over Grandma. She wasn't generally one to get fussed over what she looked like while having sex, but that was because it usually didn't involve her partner watching her...do what exactly? Have multiple orgasms? Because that's what that had been, right? Or had it been one unending monster one? Her medical knowledge fell short.

Regardless, she'd lost herself there. She had no idea what she had looked like—or sounded like—from the outside.

He pulled his hand off her, and it almost hurt, she was so oversensitized. "Dear *God*, woman."

Dear God was right. Her already hot cheeks burned even hotter. Had she made a fool of herself?

He flopped onto his back like she'd slain him. "How can we make that happen again?"

She was magnificent.

That was the only word Jake had as he stared at the ceiling of his bedroom, his entire body turned to mush as if he had been the one who just had the five-minute orgasm.

Her stomach growled.

So she was hungry, too.

Magnificent and hungry.

He rolled off the bed. "We gotta eat something actually substantial." They'd been snacking since that first bowl of popcorn...whenever that was. He pressed the home button on his new phone to display the date and time—which was actually a pretty handy feature. Look at that. It was the last day of the year. He had a text from Clara inviting him to a New Year's Eve party at the Mermaid.

He had lost track of time as they'd dug in. It had been snowing for hours—days?—and that added to the sense of being unmoored from reality.

As did having every kind of sex every kind of way until he hardly knew his own name anymore, much less what time it was.

He rummaged around in the kitchen. Things were sparse. He did have dog food, though, so he set to refilling Mick's dish. Poor Mick. He had grown accustomed to a lot of exercise, but the poor mutt had gotten none in the last while. He'd had to settle for quick trips outside to do his business during breaks in taking care of Nora—in a few different ways.

She trailed out from the bedroom with a quilt wrapped around her. "Go back to bed. I'll bring you something."

She rolled her neck and kept walking toward him. "I think I need to, like, use my limbs."

"Okay." He pointed to the breakfast bar that separated the kitchen from the main living space of the cottage, and she sat. He opened a cabinet and peered in. He wasn't sure what he expected to see. It wasn't like there was going to be a Hawaiian pizza in there. "I need to make a grocery run."

"Jake Ramsey, are those *Lucky Charms*?" She sounded disproportionately delighted.

"Uh, yeah? You want some?"

"Yes!"

He needed to feed her something more substantial, but he got the box down. "I should probably say something about how these were left over from Jude—"

"He was too young for solid food."

"Or Clara likes Lucky Charms."

She rolled her eyes.

"What can I say? I'm a fan." He shrugged. "I don't know, those little dry marshmallows really do it for me." He passed her the box and collected milk, a bowl, and a spoon. "Help yourself, but you also have to eat something more substantial."

Which, at his house, meant fish. He opened his freezer.

"Is that fish? That you caught?"

"Yeah. I hate feeding you frozen fish, but I'm pretty much out of everything else. This is the emergency trout stash."

"Emergency trout stash!" She sounded delighted again.

The problem was, there wasn't very much of it. One medium-size fillet. He popped it in the microwave, and as it defrosted, he inspected the fridge again. Hmm. Did he have...Yes. There was still a hunk of gouda that had been part of a gift basket the Toronto douchebag had sent when they'd shipped the canoe.

"I'll go home tomorrow," she said through a mouthful of cereal.

"Tomorrow's New Year's Eve," he said, trying to project a casualness he did not feel. "Well, today, technically."

"It *is*? Man, I've totally lost track of time."

He had, too, which was why he was making trout melts at three in the morning. They'd been floating for who knew how long in a bubble of grief and sex and zombies.

"Eve and Sawyer and Clara are having a big bash at the Mermaid," he said.

"Oh. That sounds..." She wrinkled her nose.

"Horrible?"

She laughed. "Yeah. I mean, I love them. I just don't feel like a party." She cocked her head. "I feel like the opposite of a party, actually. I'll hide in my room, though."

He fired up the stove and plopped some butter into a frying pan. "You could just stay here."

He wanted to keep floating in the bubble a little longer, was the thing.

"I think I've imposed on you long enough."

Nora had a certain way of talking. She always sounded confident. Decisive. Even, he had learned, when she wasn't. Here, though, her *I think I've imposed on you long enough* was a little bit less resolute than the way she usually would have said it. You had to know her to hear it.

He knew her.

So he pushed back. Casually.

He *hoped*, anyway. It occurred to him that if he could tell when there was a chink in her decisiveness armor, maybe she could tell when his casualness wasn't 100 percent sincere.

"I don't want to go to that party any more than you do. Stay here. You can go back tomorrow. The clinic opens on the second, right?" He wasn't sure why he was asking. He knew that. He and Eiko had already conspired to cover the whole day, receptionwise, since Clara was headed back to school.

"Yeah. Back to the grind on the second."

"So stay. I'll run out for food tomorrow. I'll take Mick— he could use a walk. We'll do New Year's Eve here. Or not do it, more like. We'll eat and watch movies and..."

"See if that world's-longest-orgasm thing was a fluke?"

Yes. He had her. "Exactly."

She smiled as she nodded at the slices of bread he'd placed in the pan. "What are you making?"

"Trout melts."

"*Trout* melts? *Cheese* on *fish*?"

"It's like tuna melts, but with trout. Just you wait." She

flashed him an affectionate smile and, figuring that he'd won her over to both the sandwiches and staying for New Year's, he said, "Make a list of what you want, and I'll get it tomorrow."

"Will you do me a favor?"

"Of course."

"I'm parked behind your truck, so unless anyone happened by and recognized my car, no one knows I'm back in town. I'd like to keep it that way. I'm just...not ready for people."

"You got it." He was secretly pleased that he apparently didn't count as "people." He worked in silence for a while, breaking up the fish, scattering it on the bread and grating cheese over the whole mess. He glanced at her, wrapped in his mother's quilt. "You know what? We never decided what home base was."

She rolled her eyes. "If you're about to suggest that home base is multiple orgasms, don't."

"No? 'Cause that was pretty damn impressive."

"No. A base has to be a thing you know about in advance and you consciously decide to hit."

Yeah, he could see that logic—assuming logic even applied to their absurd bases thing. But he could still tease her. "You didn't consciously decide to do that?"

"No, I did not. That was a total surprise."

He plated the open-faced sandwiches and slid them across the island. "So it's not a superpower you were holding out on me."

"Nope."

"No idea how it happened?" he asked as he turned back to grab forks and napkins. He wasn't trying to push the issue. He was just really, really interested in having it happen again.

"If you're trying to suggest that it was you and your magical dick..." He whirled, and she winked to show she was kidding.

He made a face at her. "Not at all. My magical dick and I were just wondering if it was replicable."

They'd been teasing each other, but she turned thoughtful. "I honestly don't know what was happening there, but my best guess is that it was a function of being really comfortable and really primed. Like, we've pretty much been having sex nonstop, so it's kind of like there's already a perpetual level of desire humming along, you know?"

He knew.

"And you know, I think this friends-with-benefits thing we have going"—she waved her hand back and forth between them—"really works in the sense that I'm never on edge. I don't have all the usual crap going on in the back of my mind, like am I well enough groomed, is he going to think I'm too needy or too pushy or too slutty or too *whatever*." She picked up her fork and took a bite of the sandwich. "Oh my God. This is so good. I am officially sold on trout melts."

He wanted to ask her more about "the usual crap," and specifically what kinds of assholes inspired those kinds of fears, but she had moved on.

"How'd you get that scar on your lip? I've been meaning to ask you."

"Fishhook." She made a horrified noise, and he nodded his agreement. It *had* been pretty horrible. "I was ten. I was fishing with my dad and my brother—for fun, not on the boat. We were at the little beach. I'd run into town to get treats from the bakery, and my brother didn't hear me coming up behind him. He cast just as I was running back up the pier, and his hook caught my lip."

She winced. "That's like the worst pain I can imagine."

"Nah." It had been horrifically painful. He still remembered the shock tearing through him along with the hook, the ghastly feeling of his flesh splitting. But she was wrong. "It hurt like hell, sure, but only until it didn't. There are worse kinds of pain."

"Like what?"

"The kind you're feeling right now. The pain of absence. That kind of pain sticks around so long, it becomes part of you."

But enough. He was getting maudlin. He rolled his eyes at himself and smiled at her, hoping to lighten the mood.

She smiled back. "You are too much, Jake. Extended orgasms and midnight snacks aren't enough? You have to be the Yoda of grieving, too?" She put her fork down. "I'm about to say something, but I don't want you to freak out."

Uh-oh. Whatever she was going to say, he had a bad feeling about it. Maybe he'd gone too far with the caretaking. He didn't want anything to change. He had meant what he'd said to her all those months ago: he was not in this for romance or forever or any of that stuff. He couldn't face it if she—

"You're my best friend, Jake."

Oh. Okay.

That was *not* what he'd expected her to say.

He was her best friend. That was a relief.

Right?

"I think that was what was happening with the world's longest orgasm there. You're my best friend—don't let that freak you out. I know Sawyer and Law are your best friends. And I don't mean it in the BFF, let's-do-each-other's-hair way—though I *do* love your hair. And it doesn't have to be a mutual thing. Just because you're my best friend doesn't mean I have to be yours."

She was, though, he realized with a start. She was.

She was right that Sawyer and Law were close friends. He loved them, in his way, and he'd do anything for them. But they went way back. They'd always just been there. They were more like family.

But if you thought about friendship as the seeking out of people who weren't your default people, Nora *was* his best friend. It was startling.

"It's just that I'm totally comfortable with you," she went on. "You've seen all of me in a way no one else has. Like, *all* of me." She let the quilt fall a bit and made a face like she was mugging for a camera but quickly turned serious. "But also all my junk, you know? Rufus, my grandma, the whole life reset—all of it. Some people know about pieces of it, but you're the only one who knows about *all* of it." She huffed a laugh. "I'm not really sure how that happened."

That made two of them. Because everything she was saying applied to him, too. She had had the megaorgasm earlier, but he had *cried* in front of her and he'd barely thought twice about it.

She shrugged. "Anyway, my point is, you've seen all my junk and you're still here. And you still seem to like me fine, so..."

He grinned. He did like her fine.

Another shrug. "I don't know. It's possible I'm over-thinking this."

"Or it's possible home base is best-friends sex that leads to endless orgasms."

"Nah. I'm sticking by my assertion that the bases must

be clearly labeled in advance. They have to be aspirational. If anything, home base is sex followed by Lucky Charms and trout melts."

"But isn't that too close to grilled trout and talking about sexual insecurities, aka second base?"

"Touché." She smiled at him, and it hurt his heart a little, which was stupid because didn't he want her to smile? To feel better? She kept smiling through her next bite of food. "I guess home base will have to remain a mystery for now."

As Jake knocked on the door of Law's apartment—he lived on Main Street above the bar—it occurred to him that this visit might not be in the spirit of keeping Nora's presence in town a secret.

This was going to be a tough sell. Well, not a tough sell in the sense that Law would refuse to give him what he wanted. But he would probably insist on knowing why, and that would lead to another interrogation.

Still, it was worth it. And he was counting on Law keeping his mouth shut.

When Law answered the door, Jake could tell he'd just woken up. Law's eyes widened, and he stepped out into the hallway and shut his apartment door. "How'd you get in?" Jake had let himself in the bar's back door—it opened onto a small vestibule that contained an ancient pay phone and a flight of stairs that led up to Law's second-floor apartment.

"You gave me a key when I was building your pizza oven."

"Right." He ran a hand through his messed-up hair. Law slept late—part of being a bartender, Jake supposed—but it was ten thirty. The bar would open in ninety minutes—and it would be one of the biggest days of the year. "What can I do for you?"

"I know this is going to sound weird, but can you make me a pizza? Like, an uncooked one that I can finish at home?"

He braced himself for a tidal wave of questions, but Law just said, "Okay," opened his door a crack, reached inside, and extracted a pair of boots. "Let's go downstairs." He shoved his bare feet into the boots and took off down the stairs.

Huh. Was it possible Jake wasn't the only one hiding something—or some*one*—in his place? Jake had no idea who *someone* might be in Law's case. When he worked behind the bar, Law had no shortage of female attention, but he seemed more like a professional flirt than an actual player.

"This looks great." Jake looked around the small kitchen Law had carved out of one back corner of the bar. He'd seen it when it was under construction but not finished. Law's pizzas had been such a success this past summer that even though he'd envisioned them as a seasonal thing—hence the outdoor, wood-burning oven— he'd decided to put in a small kitchen with a gas pizza oven.

"Thanks." He opened the freezer. "I don't have any fresh dough, so a frozen crust will have to do."

"No problem. Thanks."

Law pulled containers out of the big industrial refrigerator that dominated the small space. "What do you want on it?"

This was the part where he'd out himself. He hesitated. It wasn't like she would care what kind of pizza he brought. He'd seen her eat pretty much all the varieties on the menu.

Still, he sort of felt, as stupid as it was, like this was their thing. "Uh, can you make it Hawaiian?"

Law paused in the middle of ladling sauce onto the crust and glanced up at Jake.

Here it came. Jake braced himself.

But Law just said, "Yep," and started scattering cheese. He worked quickly, going back to the fridge for pineapple and prosciutto. At one point there was a thump from above them. It drew both their glances up to the ceiling.

Ha. He *did* have someone up there. Jake smirked but said nothing. Law looked at him, and they held each other's gaze for a long moment. It was like they were daring each other to ask. Or, when no one said anything, like they were agreeing to keep each other's secret. For now, anyway, expediency was going to win out over curiosity.

"There you go." Law finished plastic-wrapping the pizza and transferred it to a box. He glanced up to the ceiling again. "Anything else?"

"No. Thanks, man."

"Lock the door behind you, will you?"

"Sure thing."

Law was halfway up the stairs by the time Jake even reached the door.

"Should we pause for a countdown?" Nora put down her pizza and picked up her phone to check the time—it was five minutes to midnight—and glanced at Jake. She was actually a little nervous about the whole New Year's thing. Not staying another night at his house—she'd only protested for show when he'd first suggested she stay. But the actual passing of the year. The countdown. Were they supposed to kiss? She had nothing against kissing him—

nothing at all—but kissing at midnight on New Year's Eve
was a very couple-y thing to do.

So they probably shouldn't do that.

Which meant she shouldn't have said anything, should
have let Wonder Woman carry on saving the world—
they were taking a break from zombies—and the year turn
unmarked.

But that had *also* seemed kind of weird, in a protesting-
too-much kind of way.

He sat up. "Let's go outside."

"Outside?"

"Yeah. Look at the lake. Breathe some fresh air. It's finally stopped snowing, so we'll be able to see the stars."

That sounded perfect. In addition to dodging the whole
should-they-kiss-at-midnight question, it just felt...right.

"But it's probably too cold."

"Not for me!" She slid off the bed.

"Everything's too cold for you."

"I'll man up. Woman up. Come on. We'll go outside,
and when we come back in, it will be a new year." She
wanted that now, so much.

They woke Mick, and a few minutes later they were
bundled up and trudging across the snowy beach to the edge
of the water. The Great Lakes, Nora had learned, didn't
usually freeze—apparently that was a once-in-a-decade
occurrence—but there were ice formations at the edge of
the water and some floating chunks bobbing in the cove.

It was too dark to see the horizon, but you could tell
where the boundary between lake and sky was because of
where the stars—they were indeed out in force—started.
The Milky Way looked like a band of snow.

There was no moon. That seemed right. It wasn't a night
for wishes.

The air was cold and sharp and cauterizing. Breathing it hurt her lungs, but in a good way. Like maybe it could scour her clean.

She looked at Jake, who was standing next to her but not touching her. Maybe it would work for him, too. Like she'd been a moment ago, he was staring at the sky. "Do you miss Jude more on holidays?"

He cleared his throat and kept staring at the sky as he answered. "Not really. He died before his first Christmas. But really, I miss him—" He turned his head abruptly to look at her.

"You miss him all the time?" she asked gently.

Her eyes had adjusted to the night, and the stars were so bright that she could see his face well enough to see that it was all crunched up. Like he was angry? Or maybe she *didn't* have enough light to read his expression, because she wasn't sure why he'd suddenly be angry.

He looked away suddenly. "Yes," he said with an odd sort of vehemence in his tone. "I miss him all the time."

They stood there silently. She wasn't sure what to say. It felt like something weird had happened there; she just wasn't sure what. Eventually enough time passed that she felt like it was safe to speak. "I bet it's after midnight."

"Yeah." His voice still sounded odd, but it was hard to say why. "Happy New Year, Nora."

"Happy New Year, Jake."

They didn't kiss. They didn't do anything. When they went back inside, he said he was tired and asked if she'd mind if he went to sleep. Of course she didn't mind. But then…he didn't go to sleep. She lay there in the dark next to him listening to his breathing. It never changed. Eventually she fell asleep, and when she woke up it was to a note that read "Happy New Year. I have a job this morning so I sneaked out. Didn't want to wake you. Let yourself out—boots are by the front door. —Jake."

But what had she expected? Breakfast in bed? The kiss they *hadn't* had at midnight? The orgasm-and-zombies bubble to last forever?

No, she told herself firmly. No. She had not expected any of that.

But if she was being honest, she had to admit it had been a close call.

Maybe she needed to pull back a bit. Not entirely. But enough that she didn't *start* expecting things from Jake that he wasn't able to deliver.

Chapter Twenty

Nora threw herself into work after New Year's. Because the clinic had been closed for two weeks, her schedule was jammed her first day back.

"I should have driven to the walk-in clinic," CJ Dyson said, presenting with chronic nosebleeds. "But I wanted to wait for you."

"You have a lot of broken vessels in there." Nora set down her scope. "Once they get this bad, they don't really heal. This cold weather, or even just jostling your nose, will set it off again. I recommend we cauterize it. I'll paint some silver nitrate inside your nose, and it will seal the vessels and prompt the formation of scar tissue. It'll hurt while I'm doing it, but then you'll be done."

"Yeah, that's what I figured. I had to have that done a couple years ago. And I know it's not a big deal, but I just thought, if someone is going to stick a probe up my nose and, like, fry the inside of it, I want it to be Dr. Walsh."

Nora chuckled. "I'm flattered. I think."

At her lunch "break," which was only ten minutes because Eiko had overbooked her due to all the demand, she looked at résumés for the reception job and emailed the top three candidates to set up interviews.

She was pleased to find that her first appointment after lunch was Eve.

"Hi! Happy New Year!" Eve said from the visitor's chair. She wasn't on the exam table, and she'd apparently told Amber she wanted to speak to Nora without the prescreening Amber usually did.

"Same to you. What's up?"

"I think I want an IUD."

"Okay. What are you using for birth control now?"

"Well, when Sawyer and I first got together, we were using condoms. Then I went on the pill..."

The pill.

Oh. Holy. Shit.

Nora's stomach dropped, and she had to force herself to pay attention to the rest of what Eve was saying.

"I just feel like I need a more long-term solution." Eve lowered her voice and leaned in. "We don't want kids anytime soon."

Focus. *Focus.* This was not a big deal. It was a little deal, and it could be remedied the moment this appointment was over. For now, her patient deserved her full attention.

"We might not *ever* want kids. That's why I didn't want to talk to Amber. You know what this town is like with its meddling. I mean, I know she would probably keep it confidential, but—"

"She would *definitely* keep anything you tell her confidential." Interrupting one's patients was bad form, but Nora had to set the record straight. "Or I'd fire her ass." Eve smiled. "But it's also fine to just talk to me."

"Clara just started university, and this is the first time Sawyer's been not on kid duty since *he* was a kid. And the inn is doing well, but it's still new. We're just so busy and we're kind of thinking if it ain't broke, don't fix it?"

"You know, you don't have to have a reason to want to prevent pregnancy. You can just not want a kid, either right now or ever, and that's okay. You don't have to justify yourself to me or anyone else."

"Right." Eve visibly relaxed. "Okay." She rolled her eyes self-deprecatingly. "I just have visions of it getting out and the old folks, like, dropping a baby on my doorstep in the middle of the night. But I'm being paranoid."

"No, I know what you mean. They can be very—"

Eve perked up. "Are they on your case? Why?"

"That would be something to talk about in our capacity as friends." She hadn't told anyone about her and Jake, but she suddenly kind of wanted to. Mostly because she hadn't heard from him since she'd left his place yesterday morning. Which wasn't all that unusual, she told herself. Anyway, she'd been planning to try to cool it a little with him, anyway.

"Right. Gotcha."

"So for an IUD, I'll need to give you a pelvic exam and test you for STIs. Then I'll give you a prescription for the actual IUD, you bring it back, and I'll insert it. Sound good?"

She pulled a curtain while Eve undressed, and they talked about the different models and how much pain to expect during and after insertion.

Nora gloved up for the exam. "Here we go."

"Is it weird to be friends with people and then have your fingers in their vagina?" Eve asked cheerfully.

Nora chuckled. "It's actually *not* as weird as I thought it was going to be."

"What about balls, though? *That* must be weird. You feel up someone's balls and then you run into him at, like, the farmers' market?"

She remembered how nervous she'd been about that very thing, about whether people should call her Dr. Walsh or Nora. All that junk had just faded away. "Not really. I think I've learned to compartmentalize." Even more, she sort of *liked* the whole feel-someone's-balls-and-run-into-them-at-the-farmers'-market thing. She felt like a mother hen to the town—in a good way. She handed Eve some tissues. "All done. I'm going to write you a requisition for blood tests. Get those done and get this"—she handed Eve her prescription—"filled and make an appointment to come see me. IUD insertion is generally easier when you're on your period because your cervix is dilated, so if you can, try to time it so you come back then."

"Great. Thank you so much. Dr. Walsh."

"Nora."

"Yeah, but we're compartmentalizing, right?"

Nora smiled. "Right."

"But do you want to hang out in another compartment soon? I haven't seen you since you got back, and— Crap. I never even asked you about your family, the funeral."

"It's okay, and yeah. Let's get together. Let's get together soon." She suddenly felt like she really needed to...be in another compartment with someone who wasn't Jake. "But can we do it not at the bar? Or the inn?"

"Oooh, the plot thickens."

Hopefully not.

Definitely not.

Or at least it was highly statistically unlikely that the plot was going to thicken.

"How about Maya's place?" Nora suggested. "I'll arrange it with her and let you know."

"Great!" Eve said. "Can't wait to have some drinks and talk about something other than my vagina."

Right. *We'll talk about mine.*

It was the second day of the new year, and Jake was still freaking out. It was the day Jude would have been four years and three days old. Because Jude's birthday was December thirtieth.

Jake always spent Jude's birthday by the lake. Sometimes on it, in the canoe, depending on how cold it was and how icy the cove was.

Regardless, he always spent Jude's birthday *alone*. The first year, Sawyer and Law had invited him to a movie, and when he'd demurred, they'd tried to elbow their way into his house. What he'd said that day, rebuffing them, was the most he'd ever said directly to them about Jude—about the Jude-shaped hole in his life. "I am only going to say this once. I know you mean well, but back the fuck off. December thirtieth is never going to be a normal day. I don't *want* it to be. Get the hell out of here and leave me alone."

And to their credit, they had. It hadn't come up again, with them or with anyone else. Probably because he made sure to spend every subsequent December thirtieth alone. Well, alone with his boy under the big starry sky next to the big black lake.

Until the year he *hadn't* spent December thirtieth alone with his boy.

Because he'd *forgotten* his boy.

His hands were frozen as he paddled back to shore. He'd spent most of today canoeing. Yesterday, too, after Nora had finally fallen asleep and he'd crept out of the cottage. His muscles ached from all the paddling, but it still didn't feel like enough.

He should have felt bad leaving her—she was mired in her own grief, and none of this was her fault. But what he had done—what he had *not* done—was too big for him to stay there.

It still was. Being on the move was the only way he could outrun his panic. Keep it even slightly in check. Give himself the space to think.

He had to cool it with Nora. What they had was supposed to be casual. Friendly.

But if it was making him forget his own child, his own *dead* child, how casual was it? If he was capable of being distracted from what was important to him by zombies and orgasms, it followed that he needed to arrange his life so it contained fewer zombies and orgasms.

So that was what he was going to do. He wasn't going to break up with her or anything. They weren't together to begin with, so that wasn't called for. He just needed to...cool things a bit.

After Nora emerged from her office—where she'd retreated after seeing Eve—Amber cornered her. "We're getting a little backed up. I have what I'm sure is strep in Room Two, and—"

"I need to step out for a minute."

"Uh...okay?"

Amber was surprised. Nora wasn't prone to bailing in the middle of a busy day.

"Just quickly." She was already on her way down the

short hallway to her office for her coat and keys. "I'll be back in ten minutes."

Nora hadn't counted on the fact that she and Eve would be going to the same place. Eve was putting on her coat in the waiting room when Nora rushed out—and ground to a halt. "Hi. I was...ah...I forgot something in my room at the inn."

"I'll walk with you." Eve was chipper, which must have meant Nora was doing a sufficient job disguising her internal terror.

"Everything okay?" Eve asked as they waited for a lone car to pass before crossing Main Street.

"Yeah, yeah." But actually... "No. Everything is not okay. Can you come up to my room with me for a second?" She had just decided, back in the exam room, that she was going to confide in Eve and Maya. She'd been thinking some evening this week. She'd buy a pizza and take it to Maya's place.

But what the hell—why not now?

"Of course." Eve's brow knit as they climbed the stairs to the top of the inn, and when she closed the door behind her in Nora's room, she said, "What's up?"

It was kind of funny the way the tables had turned. Ten minutes ago, in a room as small as—though considerably less pink than—this one, she'd asked Eve that exact question. She sighed. "I suddenly realized I forgot to take my birth control pill three days in a row, and they're in my suitcase somewhere." She started rummaging through said suitcase, which had gone from Toronto to Jake's to here and which she hadn't gotten around to unpacking yet.

"Okay, well, you're the doctor, but don't you just double up for the next two days?"

"Yes." She extracted the pill packet and popped two out.

They both looked around the room. There was a can of Diet Coke on the dressing table Nora knew was half-finished. She picked it up and took the pills.

"Okay, so that's fine, then?"

"Yes." It was fine. It *was*. That's what she would have told a patient in her circumstances. The chances that she was pregnant were extremely slim. It was just that... "I have had *so* much sex in the past few days." She buried her head in her hands and sat on the bed.

"You were getting it on in Toronto!" Eve sounded altogether too delighted. "Who's the lucky guy? Oh my gosh! Was this funeral sex?"

Nora sighed. "No. I came back on Friday."

"No, you didn't."

"I came back to town. I wasn't staying here."

"Ohhhh," Eve breathed.

"Yeah." Here she went. She squeezed her eyes shut. "I've been sleeping with Jake Ramsey for three months."

Eve started laughing.

Nora opened her eyes. "Thanks for your support."

"Sorry! Sorry! I just... *Jake*. Wow."

"If you tell anyone, I'll..." She didn't know what to threaten. She had no leverage here.

"Tell everyone I'm getting an IUD?" Eve supplied helpfully.

"No. No. I would never do that."

"Wow. You *are* hard-core."

Nora stood. "I have to get back to work."

"Hang on. You can't just drop that bomb and leave!"

"I have patients waiting."

"Okay, okay, but hang on for a second." The smile slid off Eve's face and she grabbed Nora's upper arms. "Are you okay?"

"We're not together. It's just a sex thing."

"Okay." She did not sound convinced.

"It is. I mean, it's a friend thing, too. But we're not together. It's a friends-with-benefits thing."

"I don't think those work in this town."

"What?"

"Sorry. Nothing. Your secret is safe with me."

That was one small piece of good news. "I have to get back to work."

She turned and fled, but Eve followed. "You were gonna tell Maya about this, right? That's why you were suggesting getting together at her place?"

Nora nodded.

"Okay, then. Maya's tonight. I'll arrange it. In fact, no, we'll pick you up."

* * *

Hey, happy New Year. Now that you have a phone I thought I'd wish you a great year and say that I was thinking of you on the thirtieth. I almost texted then, but IDK, it's a weird day.

Jake looked at the text from Kerrie for the millionth time. This was the problem with phones. People texted you shit, and you had to reply. What was he supposed to say? "Happy New Year. I wasn't thinking of you on the thirtieth or of Jude because I was too wrapped up in having meaningless sex"?

Or maybe—and this was the terrifying part—not-so-meaningless sex.

He went with It's a hard day, isn't it?

> *Kerrie:* Yeah. But it gets easier with time. Life goes on, I guess.
> *Jake:* Do you ever feel guilty about that?
> *Kerrie:* About life going on, you mean?
> *Jake:* Yeah.
> *Kerrie:* Not really. Maybe at first. But I saw a shrink who read me the riot act about that. I don't know if you've done that, but it helped a lot.

Clara had told him you didn't necessarily need to formally close off a texting conversation, that it was okay to stop responding when things wound down. He was going to take her word for it. Because he had no idea what to say to that. He didn't need a shrink to tell him to stop feeling bad that his child was dead.

More to the point, he didn't *want* that.

Chapter Twenty-One

⟳

I can't stop *worrying* about it. It's irrational, but I can't stop."

"Of course you can't," Eve said. "We've all been there."

Nora was hanging out with Eve in Maya's apartment—Maya herself had gone on a food run. It was two weeks after the three of them had initially retreated here—the day Nora confided in them about Jake and the pregnancy scare—and it had become a tradition of sorts. A couple nights a week, they'd bring dinner and drinks to Maya's and hang out and talk. It was nice.

Or it would have been nice, if Nora hadn't been freaking out. "I *haven't* been here, though," she said to Eve.

"Really? You've never had a pregnancy scare?"

"Not really. I mean, I've been a day or two late once or twice." And in those cases she'd always known what she would do. She'd been too young, or too buried in her education, to contemplate motherhood.

A baby was something she always vaguely planned on later. When she was older. More settled.

"Hello, hello, and welcome to Pregnancy Watch Day Seventeen." Maya hustled into the apartment carrying a pizza box and some shopping bags. "What did I miss?"

"You went to Grand View for pizza?" Eve asked, nodding at the box emblazoned with the name of a pizzeria in the neighboring town.

"I did." Maya set everything on the coffee table—Eve and Nora were on the sofa in her living room. "I also went to Grand View for this." She rummaged in her bag, produced a pregnancy test, and banged it down on the table like she was triumphant over a winning poker hand.

Nora could practically feel her blood pressure spike. "Whoa."

"Your period was due today, right?"

"Yes, but I wasn't going to test for another day or two." That's what she would have advised a patient. Save your money. Most of the time your period will come—hell, most of the time it will come on the way home from the drugstore.

It was science.

Or denial.

One or the other.

"Anyway, it's best to take those tests first thing in the morning when your HCG levels—that's the pregnancy hormone—are highest."

"Which is why I also got this." Maya produced a second test, and Eve giggled. Maya shrugged. "I figured I was already in Grand View for the pizza. It's not like you can stroll into the drugstore here and buy a pregnancy test without the whole town knowing your business."

"That's true," Eve said.

"Just take it," Maya said. "It's one of those early tests that's supposed to detect even before your period is due. If it's negative, it will ease your mind at least somewhat, won't it? And then you can take the other one first thing in the morning tomorrow to be sure."

"Well..." Nora wasn't sure why she was hesitating. Even though the doctor in her thought it was premature to pee on a stick at this point, the woman in her was like *Gimme that thing.*

"And if it's negative tomorrow, you can come back here for some of this." Maya produced a bottle of tequila.

Nora laughed and held out her palm. Maya slapped the test into it. "Go forth and pee. Think happy thoughts of tequila tomorrow."

"Tomorrow's Friday, though," Eve said. "Bar night."

"Well, I think we can all agree that a break from boys is in order." Maya made a face at Eve. "Or at least two-thirds of us can agree. All boys do is cause problems."

Nora left the door to the bathroom ajar so she could hear the conversation.

"Yeah, you're right," Eve said.

"You're such a liar—that's fake solidarity. *Yours* doesn't cause problems."

"That's because he got it all out of his system when we were teenagers."

"True."

Eve, Nora had learned, used to come to Moonflower Bay in the summers when she was a kid, and had had a romance with Sawyer and then not seen him again for a decade, until she inherited the Mermaid Inn.

"Have you heard from Jake?" Eve called to Nora.

"No."

"But has Jake heard from you?" Maya asked.

Also no.

It wasn't like they hadn't seen each other. He'd brought Mick by the clinic twice in the past two weeks. But both times he'd been on the way to a job and hadn't been able to stay very long. He hadn't suggested anything else, and she hadn't, either.

There had been times in recent months when Nora had felt like she and Jake had ESP. Like he could sense her thoughts, her wishes, without her having to verbalize them. Was that what was going on here? She'd thought after New Year's that they needed to cool it. Had he read her mind?

Or was this distance between them his idea? Had that weird moment outside on New Year's Eve been a bigger deal than she'd realized? She had to wonder. Jake wasn't an idiot. He would have sensed how warm things were between them before New Year's. And while it was okay for things—historically—to be hot between them, *warm* was uncharted territory. Warm was dangerous. She'd gone to his house with her needs and her emotions all over the place and her speeches about how he was her best friend, and maybe she'd scared him off.

So if he was pulling away because *he* wanted to pull away, and not just because he thought that was what *she* wanted, she could hardly blame him. He'd been up-front from day one about what he wanted—and what he didn't want.

"Anyway," Maya said, "it's a full moon tomorrow, so let's ditch the boys, do tequila here, then go to the lake."

Sounded fine to Nora. It wasn't like she had anything else to do now that she wasn't spending all her free time being sexed up.

Nora finished her business and sighed as she washed her hands, set the timer on her phone for three minutes, and thought about what Maya had said about boys causing problems. What Jake did, generally speaking, was *solve* problems. Decks, new housing, receptionists, paralyzing grief due to dead grandmothers—you name it, he solved it.

So no, Jake had not created this problem. That honor was 100 percent hers.

But she was getting ahead of herself. There wasn't a problem. A problem was statistically unlikely.

Probably.

She just didn't know the stats on how five-minute orgasms affected the likelihood of pregnancy. While female orgasm as a factor in successful conception had been debunked in many studies, most scientists thought oxytocin—the happy hormone—did play a role. And those had been five *very happy* minutes.

She rejoined her friends, setting the stick down on a Kleenex on the coffee table. But she thought better of it and moved to pick it up. "Sorry, this is gross."

Maya stopped her. "No, no, this is *great*." Eve elbowed her. "Well, not great. But dramatic."

They all leaned over and looked at the little window. There was a horizontal blue line. That was supposed to be there—it appeared immediately after peeing. What they were looking for—or *not* looking for—was another line, a perpendicular one that would make the image into a plus sign.

"I can't be pregnant," Nora said.

Maya patted her hand. "You're not pregnant."

"I *can't* be pregnant. I'm moving back to Toronto." If she had a baby whose dad was here, things would be messy. "I'm only here for another year and a half."

Maya snorted. "That's what they all say."

Huh? "That's what who says?"

"She's talking about me," Eve said. "I was only planning on being in town for a year."

"You might be following in her footsteps," Maya teased. "This town will do that to you."

"Oh, leave her alone," Eve said.

"I mean, I like it here, but I have plans that do *not* involve being here indefinitely. Which is why I *can't* be—" She squinted.

Was that...?

No. She tilted her head to get a better angle. *No.*

Maya whipped out her phone, turned on the flashlight, and aimed it, just as the timer on Nora's phone went off.

Just coming into focus, very faint but definitely *there*, was a vertical blue line.

Well.

Shit.

Where the hell was Nora? Jake was going to get whiplash from swiveling his head to look at the door every time someone came into the bar. She was just as likely to come in from the back as the front—it depended on if she'd left the Mermaid from the back or the front. Or maybe she would come from the clinic. She said she'd been working late nights to catch up on charting and billing.

He shouldn't have come.

But it sort of felt like if he *didn't* come, it would be odd. He had skipped last Friday to avoid seeing her. One Friday absence was not a big deal, but two would look weird. And in the meantime, he'd been more successful than he'd anticipated on the whole cooling-it mission. He'd barely seen her. He wasn't sure what he'd been expecting. Maybe for her to ask him to watch a movie. Maybe for her to suggest they jump each other. He had been worried about how he would respond to those kinds of suggestions. His thought had just been that they needed to reverse course a little bit. Become less...entangled in each other. He hadn't really thought through what that meant in practice. Did they have to stop sleeping together entirely? Were they done with zombies? Should he give her dog back?

But she hadn't asked him for anything.

Which made him feel...weird. He *liked* doing things for Nora.

Aww, damn, he missed her.

He missed his friend. His *best* friend. Even though his latest, most epic battle with the waves was behind him, he still flushed with pleasure when he thought of her thinking of him that way. *You're my best friend, Jake.*

"She's not coming."

"Who's not coming?"

Law snorted as he wiped down the bar. "It's a full moon. The girls are at the lake."

"But they usually..." *Come here first.* But he couldn't say that.

"Hey." Sawyer appeared and sat down. "What's happening?"

"Jake is mooning over Nora, who's not here because she's at the beach."

"Ah. Right." Sawyer looked for a moment like he was trying to hold back a laugh but then stopped trying, which resulted in a snort-snicker hybrid. He hopped off his stool. "Come on. Let's go."

"Where?"

"To the beach."

"Nah."

"Come on. You know even though I don't work Fridays I usually loiter on the pier in case anyone's wishing takes a bad turn."

"In the summer when tourists are here. Not in January."

"Dude," Law said. "He's trying to throw you a bone. Just go see your girlfriend. You know you want to."

"She's not my girlfriend."

"But you're sleeping together."

Jake sighed and looked at the ceiling.

"I *knew* it." Law chuckled.

There really was no point in hiding it anymore, not from these two, anyway. He looked around to make sure there were no old folks lurking and lowered his voice. "I *was* sleeping with her. Last time I checked that wasn't a crime. But for the record, I'm not anymore. And it *never* made her my girlfriend."

"Have you ever hung out with her and not slept with her?" Law asked.

"Of course. It's not like..." He'd been going to say that he *liked* her. It wasn't like he'd been using her for sex. But they wouldn't understand the nuance. They'd talked him into a trap.

"You're dating," Law proclaimed. "You're just not calling it that. Or doing it publicly."

"The thing is, in my line of work, I see a lot of heartbreak associated with pregnancy. People who've lost babies. People who wanted babies but waited too long."

Nora was standing on the pier with Maya and Eve, preparing to tell them what she had decided to do about the bomb that had exploded in her life.

"And you want a baby?" Eve asked gently.

"I think so. Someday."

"It's okay if someday isn't now, though," Maya said, just as gently.

Her friends were being so good to her. Maybe it was the pregnancy hormones, but she was overcome with affection for them—and gratitude. She sniffed. "I know. I just always thought there would be some future point at which I had my life together. But actually . . . I hired that receptionist today."

"You did? That's great!" Eve said.

"I hired a receptionist today for my medical practice—my successful medical practice in a town that I am growing surprisingly fond of. That kind of sounds like someone who has her life together, doesn't it?"

"Aww." Maya slung an arm around her shoulder.

"Mind you, I also live in a tiny pink room and appear to have lost custody of my dog to my baby daddy who I'm maybe kind of estranged from for reasons unknown."

"Well, one," Maya said, "you can't have everything. I don't think living in a tiny pink room and having your life together are mutually exclusive. And two, um, hello? Did you just refer to Jake as your *baby daddy*?"

"Yeah, I guess I did."

"Does that mean what I think it means?" Maya's voice was rising.

Nora took a deep breath. "It does. I decided this morning."

She'd known it all along, though, hadn't she? Even as she'd allowed her conscious, scientific mind to go through a rational decision-making process, somewhere inside she had known from the moment she'd seen that plus sign. It wasn't that she'd gone all gaga-gooey maternal. Not at all. She could only trust that that—or enough of that to get the job done—would come later. Maybe it was just that she was so fresh off a death that she couldn't, ultimately, let herself get too fussed over timing.

The timing was *bad*. There was no question.

But would it be better in a year? In three years?

She had thought of Wynd and her alpacas. *When the universe gives you what you want, are you going to complain that it's too early?* Those had been her exact words.

And Nora knew right now, better and more viscerally than she'd ever known before, that nothing was guaranteed. People got sick and stopped recognizing you. People died.

Time went fast.

"Oh my God!" Maya was squealing and jumping up and down. "Oh my God! You're really going to do it?"

"I'm going to do it." Nora's voice was shaky, but her intentions were not. "I have no idea how, but I'm going to do it. I also decided that..."

Oh, man. Why was this part so hard? Probably because she felt terrible about leaving Erin in the lurch. She wasn't looking forward to *that* conversation.

"What?" Eve said gently.

"I'm going to do it here. I'm going to stay."

The girls started shrieking—and Nora started panicking. It wasn't that she didn't feel sure in her decisions. She would miss Toronto and her family something terrible. But she had a sweet life here. As her own boss, she had flexibility. And she was betting the network of elders could be guilted into babysitting.

But more than that, she wanted her kid to grow up with access to its dad—assuming its dad wanted to be accessed. She wanted her kid to grow up by the lake.

Still, despite her elemental certainty that she'd chosen the right path, the *how* of it made her feel like hyperventilating when she thought about it too hard. How was she *possibly* going to do this?

"We'll help you." As if she had heard Nora's

unarticulated fears, Eve laid a hand on her arm, and Nora was overcome anew with gratitude for her friends. This phase of her life was supposed to be about her career, her finances—about getting over Rufus. She was beginning to see, though, that the unplanned dividend of her big move was these women.

"Totally!" Maya agreed. "We both have flexible jobs. And you know that whole it-takes-a-village saying? This town may have its drawbacks, but it's your village, lady."

"It's my village," Nora echoed. That felt right. That helped tamp down the fear.

"Yeah, this town really stepped in when Sawyer was younger, to help him with Clara," Eve said.

"You know who helped him *a lot*?" Maya said, looking at something over Nora's shoulder. "The Ramsey family. Jake." She lowered her voice. "Who is on his way over here right now."

Nora's stomach dropped as she twisted around to confirm that Jake was indeed approaching, along with Sawyer. "Don't say anything!"

"Of course not," Eve whispered.

"Even *I'm* not that much of a drama queen," Maya said.

"Hey," Sawyer said as they approached. Jake, of course, did not say anything. "Making wishes?"

"Not yet." Maya held up a small basket that contained their flowers.

Everyone was silent, the women no doubt because they were all—Nora included—processing Nora's big news and the men probably because the women were being so weird.

"Plotting something, then?"

Sawyer was teasing, but when Maya said, quickly, "No! Why would you say that?" more awkward silence descended.

Okay, she had to do something about this. She looked Jake square in the eyes. "How's Mick?"

"He's, uh, fine."

"Good."

"I can bring him by the clinic Monday if you like. I thought you might be busy catching up these first couple weeks back, so I didn't come very often."

"Yeah. Yeah, I was. But, uh, yeah, if you want to bring him by Monday, I'll try to take a break. Things are . . . still really busy, though." She was trying to let him off the hook.

No, that was a lie. She was trying to let *herself* off the hook. She had to tell him. She knew that. She just didn't want to face it yet. She needed to get . . . her village lined up before she did.

Jake nodded. He was staring at her really intently, but he didn't say anything else.

After a few beats of more of that awful silence, Eve said, "Well, girls, shall we get on with it?"

"Yep!" Maya held her basket up to Nora and Eve but spoke to Jake and Sawyer. "Skedaddle, boys. It's ladies' night at the wish factory."

Sawyer and Eve made moony faces at each other, which caused Maya to roll her eyes. Jake just stared at Nora until Sawyer, who'd already turned and started walking away, came back and shoved him to get his attention. Even then, he looked for a beat longer before he turned and trudged off.

Did he have ESP? Could he tell she was pregnant? No. That was just irrational panic. She needed to pull herself together.

"All right, *what* is happening?" Maya whispered urgently once the men were off the pier.

"You have to tell him!" Eve said. "I mean, you can't even hide a sneeze in this town, forget a pregnancy."

"That's not even what I mean," Maya said. "You two used to have a kind of ease in each other's presence. I used to think that was just because you were, like, vaccine-crusading pals, but we now know it was because you were getting it on. I get that you're 'estranged for reasons unknown' or whatever, but that was a *hella* weird vibe."

"I'm going to tell him," Nora said. "Of course I'm going to tell him. I want to give him a chance to be involved if he wants. I just want to wait until after the first-trimester ultrasound. What if something's wrong with the baby? Or I miscarry? Can he..."

"Can he go through that again?" Eve finished softly.

"Right." And really, how Jake was going to react to all of this was her biggest fear. Bigger than how she was going to manage the clinic or where she was going to live. "Maybe he can't go through this again, anyway, even if everything is fine medically. He didn't sign up for this."

"I don't really see Jake letting a kid of his go unacknowledged," Maya said.

Right. That was completely right. "But I guess if I'm going to ambush him with this news, I want to make sure it's actually news. However he's going to react, I don't want to...scare him more than I have to, you know?"

"I get it," Eve said.

"Yeah," Maya said.

"So you'll keep my secret?"

"Of course we will!" Maya sounded put out that Nora would think otherwise. "We would help you hide a dead body. This is nothing."

"Well, speak for yourself on the dead body," Eve said.

"But yes on the pregnancy. One hundred percent. I won't even tell Sawyer."

"It's freezing out here," Maya said. "Let's get on with this so we can go back to my place and have more tequila." She made a sad face at Nora. "And you can have some...milk? Kale smoothie? What do pregnant ladies drink?"

Nora took the flower Maya handed her and leaned over the railing. Maya and Eve came to either side of her. They all held their flowers out.

"You know, Eve," Maya said, "it's scientifically proven that if you donate your wish to someone else, it has a higher chance of coming true."

Eve laughed and handed Nora her flower. Maya did the same.

Nora was once again getting a little teary. Hopefully this was a temporary thing and not a pregnancy-hormone-induced preview of how the better part of the next year was going to go down.

"Three wishes!" Maya exclaimed. "Spend them wisely."

She should wish for a healthy baby, a place to live that ticked all her boxes, and...that Dr. Baker would still sell her the clinic for a good price. But all she could think of was:

Jake.
Jake.
Jake.

Chapter Twenty-Two

❦

*T*he answer to Maya's question about what pregnant women drank was electrolytes.

Nora dropped a tablet in water and took a deep breath. She was craving Gatorade like no one's business, but the doctor in her knew that she didn't need all the sugar that came with those kinds of drinks.

There was a knock on her office door. "Your first patient is ready in Exam Room One."

"Thanks," she called to Amber. "I'll be right out."

It was ten thirty in the morning, and her first patient was waiting for her.

Because mornings were no longer for working; they were for barfing. Had been for the past month.

"Take your time," Amber said.

She was pretty sure Amber was onto her. She had suddenly asked Jacques—the new receptionist—not to schedule any patients for the first ninety minutes of the day. That wasn't normal.

Also, it was hard to hide the sounds of her violent retching.

Jacques might not realize what was happening. Out at the front desk, he was farthest from the barfing. And he was very young and not medically trained like Amber was.

But Amber was being cool about it. "Did you see that there's a new midwifery practice forming in Grand View?" She handed Nora a brochure for Lambton County Midwifery. "I was thinking we should make contact with them. We might want to...make some referrals. Obviously, as a family doctor you're more than qualified to provide primary care to pregnant women and babies. I mean, your town square emergency delivery is legendary. But you know how this place can be. Some people might be more comfortable seeking care a little farther away."

Should she keep deflecting? Amber winked at her. She clearly already knew. Nora sighed and opened the brochure. "I've been driving to London, but it would be nice to have someone closer. I just never thought of myself as a midwife person."

Amber beamed and gave her a quick, affectionate squeeze on the shoulder before reverting back to professional mode. "They're fully licensed by the province. They have hospital privileges."

"Right." She referred women with low-risk pregnancies to midwives all the time.

Amber lowered her voice. "I'm guessing you're about eight or nine weeks?"

"Ten."

"Well, then you should be feeling much better soon, regardless of what kind of care you choose."

"And showing soon, too." Her pants were already tight.

"I can't help you there. You're just going to have to fess up." She grimaced. "And in this town... Well, I'm glad I'm not you."

She almost fessed up a week later when she threw up on Mick.

"Oh, shit, are you okay?"

Jake did his signature at-her-side-in-an-instant thing. It startled her. Made her realize how much she had missed his solid, quiet presence in her life.

But in answer to his question, no, she was not okay. She was mortified. "I'm fine. I have a bug."

"I'll take you home."

"I live across the street."

He looked at her like, *So?*

"I have patients."

"Patients you want to give your germs to?"

She pulled a packet of Kleenex out of her bag and started trying to clean off poor Mick, who was, she comforted herself, taking this all in stride. She should just tell Jake. She was going to have to soon anyway. The end of first-trimester hell—she vehemently hoped she would not be one of those unlucky women who were sick through their whole pregnancy—was in sight, and here was the perfect opportunity.

The problem was, things were starting to feel more...normal between them. Not sexy-normal. Her libido was in the toilet, but still. Things were less weird. He was bringing Mick around more often. He'd brought her some fish the other day. It felt like maybe they were getting their friendship groove back. Probably it was weird that they'd just stopped having sex, as if by silent agreement. Probably they should at least acknowledge that fact? Agree that the benefits phase of their friendship was over? But honestly, she was so tired and sick. And she didn't know how to have that conversation.

So she kept her mouth shut.

Which had an added benefit: it made her less likely to throw up again.

Jake couldn't shake the sense that something was wrong with Nora. She wasn't her usual self. He knew because he'd been watching her extra closely. She just seemed...heavier. Not her body, really, though she might have put on a few pounds, but her gait. Her way of moving through the world. She seemed less sparkly than usual, like all her silver icing had faded to gray.

It was probably her grandma.

It was probably grief.

He had handled this all wrong. He had been trying to put some distance between them. He'd honestly thought it was for the best. She made him forget Jude. When she was around, he wasn't himself. So if he wanted to protect himself—to protect the memory of his boy—he had to stay away. That was the theory, anyway. The problem was, try as he might, he *couldn't* stay away. She was too easy to be with. He *missed* her. He felt himself drawn back to her, almost against his will, like she was a planet he was orbiting. He'd started bringing Mick around more. Stopping into the Mermaid's cocktail hours. Putting himself in her path.

Also, he was worried about her.

Which was why, a couple weeks after she'd thrown up in the gazebo, he invited her to the cottage for dinner. Picked up his stupid phone and texted her. I never made you any of that panfried pickerel I promised. You want to come for dinner?

He was surprised when she accepted, given how weird things had been between them lately.

And even more surprised when she showed up looking like a million bucks. Gone was the dullness he'd noticed before. She looked rested and radiant.

He suppressed a sigh as he took her coat and steadied her while she stepped out of the boots he'd left on the other side of the outcropping. She was so gorgeous. It wasn't fair.

Well, if she was suddenly fine, maybe that made what he'd been planning to say obsolete. But hell, he'd just say it anyway. So as he was dredging the fish in flour and transferring it to an egg bath, he came right out with it. "I've been texting with Kerrie a little bit. She went to this grief counselor after Jude died, and she said it really helped her. I thought you might want the name."

She blinked rapidly. He'd offended her. He tried to change the subject. "You sure you don't want some wine? Or bourbon?"

"No!" She sounded a little manic. She blew out a breath, paused, and her voice sounded calmer when she spoke again. "You've been texting with Kerrie?"

"Yeah. Not much. Just . . . it was Jude's birthday recently, so we kind of reconnected."

"Oh," she said. "*Oh.*"

She probably thought this was why he'd pulled away from her. "Not like that," he hurried to say, even as he made himself carry on with the flour-egg-parmesan fish prep. "We've just been reminiscing about Jude a bit."

"Oh, well, that's good." She didn't sound like she meant it. But he didn't have much time to ponder it because she hit him with a doozy of a question. "If you hadn't had Jude, do you think you and Kerrie would still be together?"

"Probably not." He had never really thought about it, but once the question was posed, the answer was right there. "I think we would have grown apart. We got together so young, before we figured out that we wanted different things." That was the first time he'd verbalized that, but once again, as soon as he said it, he recognized its truth. His hand shook a little as he laid the first prepared fillet into a pan of oil.

"What things? How were they different?"

It was easier to talk about this stuff without looking at her, so he stayed by the pan to fuss over the fish. "Well, she was a hotshot lawyer. She commuted to Guelph every day, and I suspect she regretted that she couldn't get a job with a big Toronto firm. She would've rather we moved, but she let it go—probably because we *did* have Jude. She knew I'd never want to leave Moonflower Bay, and she knew it was important to me to raise him here. So she didn't force the issue."

"She loved you."

He turned. "Yes."

"And if Jude hadn't died?"

"We probably would have made it work for no other reason than we were both stubborn. But in a hypothetical world without Jude, I'm not sure there would have been any point to digging our heels in."

It struck him as funny suddenly, the way that thought announced itself in his head. A hypothetical world without Jude. He'd meant a world in which Jude had never been born. But a hypothetical world without Jude *wasn't* hypothetical. It was *this* world. He no longer had Jude.

That was a big thought. It was a fact. It was a fact he

confronted every day. But it was still intense to think it like that, so overtly.

He wondered why she was asking all these questions. She didn't seem like the jealous type. And that didn't seem like what was going on now. She seemed more curious than anything, but he wondered why now? They'd had ample time to talk about anything and everything.

They needed to clear the air. He couldn't stand any more of this weirdness between them. He was going to have to address the elephant in the room. He flipped the fish and turned to her. "Look, I need to apologize for a couple things. I'm sorry I—"

"No, you don't."

"I do. I'm sorry I busted out that stuff about the grief counselor. I was just worried about you. But mostly I'm sorry I haven't been around much lately. I know I've been distant. I need to explain..."

She was rummaging in her bag, her back half-turned. She wasn't listening to him at all.

When she straightened, she was holding a piece of paper. She slid it across the island to him.

"What's this?" It was a gray blob of some sort. It looked like a weather—

No. It looked like...

"I'm pregnant."

Nora wasn't sure what she'd expected. Incredulity, if she'd had to put money on it. Shock. Anger, even. She was, after all, ambushing him.

She hadn't been prepared, though, for utter and complete silence.

Which she felt compelled to fill, once it had stretched out to an uncomfortable degree. "I forgot my pills while

I was here for New Year's. I don't know what happened. I *had* them here. They were in my bag all along. I just was so...overcome, I guess. And we were keeping a really weird schedule. The days blurred together..."

This wasn't going well. This wasn't how she wanted to deliver the news, all tentative and full of excuses. She tried again. "I'm sorry. This is my fault."

His eyes were completely blank. "I may have almost flunked out of school, but I'm pretty sure it takes two to tango." His tone was blank, too.

"We agreed that the pill was going to be our method of contraception, and I failed to take it properly. It *is* my fault. But I've decided I'm keeping it. I'm not asking you for anything, though."

"Do you want to give me a little bit of credit here, Nora?"

There. There was some anger. His voice was low, but not the sexy-low she'd heard so many times. No, this was shaking-so-I-don't-go-postal low. He sounded like his control could snap at any moment. "I do give you credit," she said quietly. "I'm just trying to say that I know I'm ambushing you here. I know you don't want this."

"Well, we can't always get what we want, can we? If I could have what I wanted, I'd already have a kid. If I could have what I wanted, *this* kid"—he shoved the ultrasound picture back toward her—"would be obsolete. So yeah, this is pretty much the last thing I want."

It wasn't until the smoke alarm went off—Jake had continued standing at the kitchen island long after Nora fled crying—that he realized he didn't know *anything*. When was she due? Did she know if it was a boy or a girl? If not, was she planning to find out?

Was this why she'd been sick?

Well, of course this was why she'd been sick. He felt like an idiot for not seeing it.

The questions kept coming. Had she been eating enough through the morning sickness? Had she felt it kick yet? Did she have names picked out? Was she going to take a leave from work?

Why hadn't she told him right away? And, oh God, was she going to take the kid and move back to Toronto?

And one more question: What kind of man was he that he'd watched her face crumple and tears start flowing and just stood there? Let her stumble off the stool and, as her silent tears became sobs, flee?

Had she even taken her boots?

He had no answers to any of these questions.

He felt strange. Weak and shaky, like he was barely inhabiting his body. Like he was floating above it. It was a kind of panic, he supposed, but it was different from the waves. It was an emptiness. Just like he had no answers to all the questions that had been swirling through his mind, he had...no sensations in his body. He had been angry before. Shocked, then angry. Now he was just...blank.

Smoke was filling the kitchen. He should deal with that. That was a thing a person should do in this situation. He turned to the stove, grabbed the pan, and—

"Fuck!"

He burned his hand. Because that was what happened when you grabbed a hot pan with your bare hand.

Pain seared through him, yanking him back into his body, and as he jammed his hand under the cold water tap, it didn't stop. It started spreading, up through his arm and down into his chest. It radiated down his legs until they couldn't hold him up anymore. He slid to the floor of the kitchen with the sink still running and the smoke alarm still blaring. He was drowning. This *was* like the waves, except instead of being inside him, they were all around him. They were subsuming him. They were going to kill him. He couldn't breathe.

What should he do? What should he do?

Think. What did drowning people do?

Drowning people needed life preservers. Rescuers.

He stumbled out to the living room where he'd left his phone. It took him a stupid amount of time to get his fingers steady enough to type. I know this is a random question, and you don't have to answer it if you don't want to, but do you ever think about having kids again?

Kerrie replied with a photo. This is Sienna. She's eighteen months old. I should have told you. I'm sorry I didn't.

He sucked in a breath. The little girl looked a lot like Kerrie and a little like Jude. He hadn't cried, before, when he was drowning, but suddenly he had to bite back tears.

> *Jake:* You don't owe me anything. She's beautiful. Congrats.
> *Kerrie:* I got remarried. He's a good guy. I'm sorry I didn't tell you that, either.

He felt a little better. It was working. He wasn't going to drown after all. He took a deep breath. And another one. Don't be sorry. How would you have told me? Driven here and hiked into the cove?

He'd been kidding—or trying to, because although she was his life preserver, he didn't want her to know that—but she replied Maybe.

Jake: You don't owe me an accounting of your life.

Kerrie: I know. It's just weird to go through so much with someone and then just have them be gone.

Jake: Yeah.

He knew she meant the two of them, after they split, but he also kind of felt that way about Nora. She'd been his best friend. His lover. One minute she'd been having a five-minute orgasm, and the next she was practically a stranger. The *next* she'd been pregnant with his baby.

Kerrie: Don't feel pressured to say yes, but would you ever want to meet for coffee? We could meet halfway. In Stratford, maybe. You could meet Sienna. She's Jude's little sister. Or at least that's how I think of her.

He let the tears come. I'd love that. Can we do it soon? I think I really fucked something up, and I could use some advice.

Chapter Twenty-Three

Kerrie looked the same. She was a little fuller in the face, and her hair, which she used to highlight with blond streaks, was one solid color. But when she turned as Jake approached her table at the coffee shop in Stratford, her eyes were the same. Her smile was the same.

He hadn't been sure how to greet her. A handshake? A friendly nod? How did a person greet the ex-wife he hadn't seen in years? A person he had once shared everything with but who was now a stranger?

She settled the question for him by standing up and throwing her arms around him. She smelled the same, too, like the perfume she used to wear, kind of flowery and minty at the same time. He could still see the little pink bottle sitting on the bathroom vanity in their old house.

The sameness of her was a shock.

He wasn't sure what he'd expected. It was just that he

had storms inside him and he wondered if she did, too. Or if she *had*, past tense. She'd gone to a grief counselor, she'd told him, so she must have. He sort of felt like when you had such violent storms inside you, it should change you visibly. But she was the same.

She pulled back and studied his face. He remembered how much he used to love the dimple she had on her left cheek. It was still cute, objectively, but there was no longer any heat behind his appreciation of it. Whatever spark had brought them together had gone out a long time ago. He could smile at her, smell her perfume, and think of her only as...what? A fellow soldier, maybe. Like they were the sole survivors of the same bloody battle.

"Jake, this is my husband, Cody."

He hadn't even noticed there was a guy seated with her at the table. And he was holding a little girl with Kerrie's dark hair and Jude's big green eyes. He sucked in a breath and took the guy's outstretched hand.

"I know it's probably a little weird to bring my current husband to meet my ex-husband," Kerrie said. "But I wanted you to meet Sienna but then also for us to be able to talk. So Cody's gonna take Sienna to the park in a little bit."

Jake nodded, his throat tightening. He couldn't take his eyes off Sienna. She had a way of tilting her head that was just like Jude.

"I'm sorry for your loss, man," Cody said. "We talk about Jude all the time. Sienna has a picture of him in her room."

Kerrie opened a locket she was wearing around her neck and held it out to him. There were two tiny pictures inside—one of Sienna and one of Jude.

If Jake had imagined being undone by this meeting, he

had imagined it being the result of a magnified dose of grief, his constant, persistent companion. He hadn't imagined it being the result of kindness.

He swiped at the tears that were starting to fall.

"Actually, should we all go to the park?" Kerrie asked gently, and he could only nod.

The short walk to a nearby school playground allowed him a moment to get himself together. Kerrie, walking beside him, was silent, and Cody pushed Sienna in the stroller at a pretty good pace, which was putting them farther and farther ahead. Jake suspected he was doing it on purpose, and he appreciated it.

For some reason, it made him think of Jamila and his dad. Jamila and her prayers.

Of the way some people's happiness could depend on other people's loss.

Of the way some of those people had enough grace to acknowledge that. To honor it, even.

"How do I do this?" he said. He could feel Kerrie's attention on him, and she probably had no idea what he was talking about, so he gestured up at her husband and daughter.

"What's happened, Jake?"

"I accidentally fell in love, and she's pregnant."

Kerrie's delighted laugh drew his attention. She stopped walking, so he did, too. Thought about what he'd just said. *I accidentally fell in love.*

He hadn't articulated it that way before, even to himself. But as had been happening to him lately, he recognized the truth as it was coming out of his mouth, as he was surprising himself with it.

He loved Nora Walsh, the pixie doctor who was only staying in town for two years. He loved her zombies and her thoughtful questions and the clear-eyed, unflinching way she looked at the world. He loved the hair on her head and the brain inside it. He loved how much she loved the lake and his cove.

He loved her stupid, tiny dog named after the wrong band.

"Congratulations," Kerrie said. "That's wonderful."

"It doesn't feel wonderful."

"What does it feel like?"

"It feels like I'm betraying him."

"I know," she said.

He was startled by her easy agreement.

She went on. "Like, how can you just carry on and be happy when he's dead—right?"

He sucked in a breath. That was it. That was *exactly* it. "It's the same with you?"

"I used to feel that way, but not anymore." When he didn't say anything—he wasn't sure what to say—she kept talking. "Don't take this the wrong way, but you really need to talk to someone. That grief counselor I told you about or someone like her. I know when you're in it, it feels like the biggest, most unique thing that's ever happened to anyone. But what you're feeling is textbook. And there are things you can do, simple things, to help. You don't have to feel that way anymore."

"But what if I don't *want* to stop feeling it?" What if he didn't want to give up the waves?

"Ah." They had reached the playground. Sienna was laughing as Cody pushed her in a swing. Her delighted baby laughter was making her dad laugh, too. Kerrie led him to a bench on the far side of the play structure. "That's a problem, then, isn't it?"

He nodded.

"Let me ask you a question. Do you think I don't deserve

to be happy? That I don't deserve this?" She gestured at her family.

"Of course not." He bristled at the suggestion. What kind of monster did she think he was?

"So why is it any different with you?"

Because I let him die.

She knew his thoughts. She knew *him*. "He died, Jake. Kids die. It fucking sucks, but it's a thing that happens. It wasn't your fault."

How many times had he heard that phrase in the years since Jude died? It was a refrain in his life. Background noise.

She grabbed his upper arms. He let her turn him so they were looking into each other's eyes. "You were the best dad. You were a better parent than I was." He tried to interrupt, to protest that he wasn't better, just different, but she kept talking over him. "Jude was lucky to have you. *It wasn't your fault.*"

He wanted to argue with her, but she was in what he used to think of as lawyer mode. You couldn't win an argument with Kerrie when she was in lawyer mode.

"You've been a dad without a kid for a lot of years, Jake. Your girlfriend, or whoever she is, is going to have a baby. Do you want that baby to be a kid without a dad because you're too stubborn to get over yourself?"

No. Oh God, no. He couldn't breathe at the image her words conjured. *A kid without a dad.*

"Do you want that kid to have a stoic, silent dad who's too lost in his own guilt to do right by him, or do you want that kid to have a dad who's happy, who loves him and loves his mom? Who *shows* him what love is like?"

She was right. She was *right*. It sounded so *simple* when she said it like that.

He forced air into his lungs. It hurt like hell. It *sounded* like hell, like the dying gasp of a broken man, but it *wasn't* a dying gasp. It was the first breath of a new era.

He remembered, suddenly, Jude's first breath. He'd come out into Jake's arms—the doctor had positioned Jake to catch him—and had been utterly silent. They'd all paused for a moment, waiting for him to cry. It had seemed like an eternity, that liminal space between birth and breath. He'd looked at his tiny, slimy son, and thought, *Breathe*.

And then Jude had breathed.

Everyone else probably just heard the crying that came with the exhalation, but Jake was paying such close attention that he heard the inhalation *before* the exhalation.

His son's first breath.

He was there for his son's last breath, too.

Kerrie delivered her closing argument. "I know you have this twisted notion that by moving on, you're dishonoring Jude's memory, but I personally can't think of a better way to honor Jude than to love his little brother or sister."

He was at the top of his first breath, and like with Jude, what came out on the exhale was a sob.

His phone blew up on the drive home. He wasn't the sort of idiot who messed with texting while driving, so he didn't look at it until he stopped for gas on the Bluewater Highway before turning into town. He had a bunch of texts from Sawyer. He scrolled back to the first one. It's Sawyer. I heard you got a phone, you asshole. Call me. Or come to the station. I need to talk to you.

He wondered who had spilled the beans about the phone. Clara had kept his phone secret for so long. Nora? Why shouldn't she have, after the way he'd treated her when she'd told him she was pregnant? She needed *someone* to help her, and the way he'd acted had given her no indication that it was going to be him.

He kept reading. I'm home now. Come here. We're starting a new canoe.

Yep, Nora had told him. Probably everything. Or someone had. He still hated the idea of everyone in town talking about him, knowing his business, but it really couldn't be helped, could it?

There were two more texts, one from half an hour ago. I went to your house and let your damn dog out. Where the hell are you? And the last from a couple minutes ago. Listen, I know about you and Nora. She told Eve months ago, and today Eve told me. Get the hell over here.

He got the hell over there. Cheerfully, even. Well, okay, not cheerfully. But determinedly. Aside from the past couple of months, when he'd had his head in his ass about "cooling things off," he was a man of action. That was what Nora said she liked about him. So he needed to make a plan. And he needed to *show* her that plan, not tell her about it. And for that, he was going to need help.

When he got to Sawyer's, Law's truck was parked out front. Good. He went around back to the garage.

There was no canoe. There were just his friends, sitting in Sawyer's backyard.

"Lured me here under false pretenses, I see." He lowered himself into a lawn chair. "Is it time for another intervention?"

"It sure as hell is," Sawyer said. "Let's see. You and Nora. You like her. That's what you told us. You have shared values. I see you guys cracking up over inside jokes. You seem to have joint custody of her dog. And you're sleeping together."

"But it's not serious," Law said mockingly. "You're not dating."

"Right." Sawyer nodded sagely. "But oh, wait, you're helping her with her vaccine crusade, too. And making decks and shit for her. But I guess all that still doesn't add up to 'serious.'"

"You know what *is* serious, though?" Law asked. The two of them seemed to be performing a conversation, which was probably fair given that Jake usually didn't have much to say in these types of situations. They were saying his lines for him—or at least what they thought his lines would be. In another circumstance, it might have been funny.

"The fact that she's pregnant with your baby," Sawyer said, outright sneering at Jake. "That is pretty fucking serious. And what did you tell her when she told you?"

"He told her it was the last thing he wanted," Law said before Jake could answer.

He had to wince at that. He *had* said that. He was such an idiot.

"That," Sawyer said, "is incorrect. It was the *first* thing you wanted. And you had it. But you lost it."

Okay, enough. "What does *that* mean?"

"It means you had some shitty luck, mate, that's all. But this thing with Nora, and a baby, *is* what you want. It's exactly what you want. Maybe you're too chickenshit to reach out and take it, and that's one thing, but don't pretend it isn't a second chance at *exactly* what you want."

"You're right. It is what I want."

"And you know what—" Sawyer was still on autopilot when Jake's answer caught up to him. "Wait. What?"

"It is what I want. The baby. Nora. Nora, mostly."

Both men gaped at him. He couldn't help but smile. It felt strange on his lips, after the storms of the past twenty-four hours. Strange, but good. "I want Nora and the baby. I want us to be a family. But I need help."

It was so easy to say in the end. So astonishingly easy. So he said it again. "I need help. I need help *fast*. I need to get a couple things done before I talk to her, and I don't want to leave her hanging any longer than necessary."

"Anything," Law said. "Name it."

"Well, first, I need to find a grief counselor. Or someone in that vein. I saw Kerrie today, and she recommended someone, but she's in Guelph. I'll go there if I have to, but there must be someone closer. I googled and most sources said to ask your family doctor for a referral. But…" He shrugged. Allowed himself to crack another smile and was gratified when his friends did the same. "I'm not sure that's the best course of action in my particular case. I'm going to tell her about it, of course, but I need to take responsibility for this, to get this underway on my own."

"Amber will know," Sawyer said. "I'll ask Amber. What else?"

"I need someone to drive to Guelph to pick up something from Kerrie's house." Assuming she said yes. He would text her as soon as they were done here. He was pretty sure she would agree.

"I'll do it," Law said, and Jake was glad they hadn't asked any questions. He pulled out his phone. "I'll find someone to cover the bar and go tonight."

Jake thought back to when Nora had first come to the cove. She'd told him he was lucky to live in such a place, and he'd agreed. He'd felt lucky at that moment, that he had the cove and that she was there with him. It had been a strange sensation, something he hadn't felt for a long time.

He felt it again. He was lucky to have these guys in his life.

"Okay," Sawyer said. "That's covered. What else?"

"I need some help with the cottage."

"I have something to tell you."

The sisters spoke in unison, then both shouted, "Jinx!"

Nora laughed. "You go first." She would take any reprieve, even a momentary one, from having to deliver her dreaded news. Just because she'd decided to stay in Moonflower Bay didn't mean she wasn't full of mixed feelings. She'd decided to take a path that would close off another path. It was a sad thing. It was going to upset Erin.

"Dad found Grandma's will."

"Oh, good." There had been some confusion over the will. While Grandma was in the hospital and starting to fade, she had started insisting that she'd recently updated her will and that they needed to be sure they were using the new one. But then no one had been able to find it.

"It was in her breadbox with that pastry knife thing your friend there gave her."

"Pearl?" Nora chuckled. "And what does it say? Any surprises?"

"She left me her condo. Just me."

"Oh. Okay." Nora didn't know what Grandma had been planning to do with her condo to begin with. If she'd thought about it, she would have guessed it would have gone to her dad.

"There was a note about you and Alex not needing it." Their older brother Alex was a successful—and wealthy—anesthesiologist with a lawyer wife and no kids. "Which is strange, because she knew about our plan to buy a place together. So anyway, it's weird, but we'll just sell it and put the money into our shared pot. I talked to Alex, and he doesn't care." She snorted. "Alex, okay, but I can't imagine *what* Grandma was thinking saying you didn't need any money."

Nora laughed. She could. She could also imagine her grandma fitting right in with the meddling matchmakers of Moonflower Bay. Hell, for all she knew, she'd consulted Pearl. Maybe that was why the will had been in the breadbox.

"I had an agent out for an appraisal, and she thinks we can get six hundred grand for it. So that's it. Our fairy godmother has delivered. I know part of your whole 'Nora moves to small-town Canada' plan was emotional, or a time-out or whatever, but just be done with that part, okay? We've got our down payment, so just come home."

Oh boy. Nora sucked in a breath.

"What?" Erin said.

"I, ah, have a couple things to tell you."

Chapter Twenty-Four

❧

Nora was feeling better—but she also wasn't feeling better. The first-trimester morning sickness was gone, and she felt good physically. But getting through the rest of the week after she'd told Jake had been hard.

But she had done it. She'd seen all her patients. Jacques was really getting the hang of things. They'd had calls from some schools in the region asking about flu clinics for next season.

She had also met with a real estate agent and was about to make an offer on a cute little place near Art and Jamila's house. Eve had assured her she could stay at the Mermaid indefinitely, but Nora wanted to get her own place established before the baby was born in October.

Things were okay with Erin, too. She had been shocked by Nora's news, but she'd recovered quickly, and was currently at work trying to convince Nora that they should still buy a place together—but that it should be a cottage on the lake so the cousins could still grow up together on weekends and in the summer. Nora had told her she needed to get her main housing sorted out before she could worry about a second place, but Erin had resumed her habit of sending real estate listings. They were all sweet little lake cottages in and around Moonflower Bay. None of them were as sweet as Jake's place, though.

Erin was like a dog with a bone over the Jake question, but she'd finally let it go when Nora had sketched out the details of their last conversation. Now she probably had a Jake voodoo doll to go with her Rufus voodoo doll. Her mom was planning to take a short leave from work to come and stay for a few weeks after the baby was born.

And the baby. Her baby. She was having a *baby*!

She had a midwife in Grand View, and everything was looking good. She had an appointment for her twenty-week ultrasound and was trying to decide if she wanted to find out the gender at that point or if she wanted to be surprised.

It was all good. Mostly.

It was also...a lot. Thankfully, she had Eve and Maya by her side every step of the way. One of them was in the waiting room of the clinic at the end of every day—sometimes both of them. They'd have dinner for her, or they'd pick up pizza from the bar. She'd already told them to tell Sawyer and Law the news and had also decided that since she was starting to show, it was time to let the cat out of the bag more widely. So she stopped trying to hide the bump. In fact, she did the reverse: she wore formfitting clothing on purpose because she was anxious to get the big reveal over with.

The weird thing was that though it was clear everyone knew, no one said anything. When she went into the hardware store one morning for a light bulb, the old-timers stopped talking immediately—they had been yammering about something to do with human assembly lines? There was a weird, uncomfortable pause while they looked alternately at her belly and at each other. Then they started talking a mile a minute about stupid stuff, clearly overcompensating. She would have expected them to be over the moon about her news. She was staying. There was nothing like a kid to tie a girl down.

But no one said a word.

The other person who hadn't said a word? Jake. It wasn't like she'd expected a dramatic change of heart. She knew he was shocked and upset, and she respected that. But she kind of thought he would eventually be in touch to let her know what kind of involvement, if any, he wanted. But she hadn't seen him or heard from him in the few days that had passed since she'd dropped her bomb on him, not even in passing. She hadn't seen her *dog*.

Was Mick even her dog anymore?

She was heartbroken, was what it came down to. She was feeling better physically and accomplishing a lot, but she was heartbroken.

Still, as she had learned from Rufus, the way to deal with heartbreak was to keep going. To make a plan and execute it. And given that it was Friday night and she was locking the door to the clinic, right now her plan was to walk across the street to the bar to see her friends—strangely, neither Eve nor Maya had shown up in her waiting room today. But they were probably already at Law's and assuming she'd meet them there. Maybe Jake would be there. Maybe it would be awkward. Maybe it would be excruciating. But she wasn't going to let that deter her.

This was her town, too. She took a deep inhalation of the bracing early-spring air.

Despite her resolve, she didn't make it inside the bar. Art
and Jamila were standing outside, and judging by the looks
on their faces—serious for Art, teary for Jamila—they were
waiting for her.

She sighed. This was one big-ass item on the to-do list
that she'd been putting off. She was hoping that even if
Jake wasn't interested in the baby, his dad and stepmom
would be. She just didn't know how to make that happen.
How to ask.

"Nora." Jamila flashed her a watery smile as she approached. "We're so happy."

She blew out a breath. That was a relief. "I'm glad. I
hoped— Oof."

She couldn't get the rest out because Art had basically
tackle-hugged her. He held her for a long time. She held
him back. Let his strong arms bolster her. When he pulled
away, his eyes were bright. He was so like Jake, a man of
few words but many emotions.

He cleared his throat. "We want to show you something.
Would that be okay?"

"Of course. I just have to pop into the bar and tell Maya
and Eve not to worry about me."

"No you don't, because we're coming, too."

And there were her friends. Her generous, beloved
friends. She hadn't noticed them coming out of the bar
during the hug.

She narrowed her eyes. "What's going on?"

No one said anything. They just piled into Art's car—
Art and Jamila in front and Nora and her friends squished
into the back.

It was probably a surprise baby shower or something. She could be cool with that. That was the point
of staying here, right? As Maya had said, this was her

village. It wasn't long before they were parking behind Jake's truck.

"You guys. I don't think you understand. I can't just—"

"He knows we're coming," Art said quickly.

"He does?"

"He asked us to bring you here," Jamila said kindly.

"Hello, hello!" It was Eiko, opening the car door for Nora. "How are you feeling, Dr. Hon? You look wonderful."

"Doesn't she, though?" Pearl said—Pearl was here, too? "The pregnancy glow is real."

"Just run with it," Maya said, no doubt correctly intuiting that Nora was . . . what? What was she, even? Confused? Wary?

Scared out of her mind?

All of the above, actually.

"Trust us." Eve took her hand, which prompted Maya to take the other.

The whole clump of them—Eve and Maya holding her hands and Pearl, Eiko, Art, and Jamila walking beside them—escorted her to the outcropping. There, Law and Sawyer were waiting.

What the hell was happening?

"We're handing her over!" Pearl trilled. "The final item on the assembly line!"

"Handing me over? What?"

Sawyer and Law crossed their arms and clasped hands and made a "chair" for Nora to sit on.

"On you go," Eiko said.

Nora thought about how wary she'd been her first few days in town. How suspicious she'd been of anyone who was nice to her. *What's the catch?* she'd been constantly wondering.

Like that time she'd come home to find Jake building her a deck. Her hackles had gone right up.

But what had happened next? She had recognized her defensive impulse, paused, and thought about the fact that she was remaking her life. Asked herself what kind of person she wanted to be in that life.

"Trust," Eve said again, with so much warmth and affection in her voice.

Nora sat.

And let the men ferry her out into the lake and around the outcropping like she was Cleopatra or something.

Jake was waiting on the other side.

Of course he was.

Gah. Just seeing him made her feel better—and worse. Better because she loved him. She *loved* him.

And worse because she couldn't have him.

But hopefully, the baby could.

Law and Sawyer set her on the sand in front of him, and he smiled. "Everyone has been helping me with a remodel at the cottage. As you can imagine, the location makes it a bit of a challenge, so they made a human assembly line to help me get stuff in and out."

"And I'm 'stuff' in this scenario?" She couldn't help but smile, though.

He did, too, even as he winced. "You are. But you're the most important stuff." He ducked his head then, like he was shy. "Will you come see what I did?"

"Yes."

She wasn't sure what to say as they walked across the sand, but Mick saved the day by appearing out of nowhere, barking and wagging his butt. She bent down to pet him. She didn't pick him up—she'd been having a bit of dizziness lately—but she ruffled his fur and said, "I missed you."

"I missed you, too."

She shot Jake a quizzical look. "I was talking to the dog."

Ignoring this, he was the picture of chivalry as he held the cottage door for her and took her coat.

Inside, everything looked the same as it always had. "Where's this remodel?"

He pointed down the hall and to the left.

"Your mom's studio?"

"No." He nodded for her to go ahead of him. "The nursery."

And it was. She inhaled sharply. The walls were still covered with art, but it was bright, happy art—and he'd moved the painting of Jude in from the living room. The easels and paint-splattered tables were gone, replaced by a crib and a changing table and a rocking chair.

He steered her to that rocking chair, because her legs had lost their ability to hold her up, and somehow he knew. She plopped down unceremoniously and looked up at him.

"I'm sorry I reacted so poorly last week. I just..." He ran a hand through his hair. "I just never imagined getting a second chance. I didn't feel like I *deserved* a second chance."

"Jake. I—"

He held up a hand. "To be honest, I still don't. But I'm working on that." He cleared his throat. "I've got myself a therapist. A grief counselor. I'm going once a week for now."

Tears gathered in Nora's eyes. He was so strong. He'd always been strong, but to ask for help like that was maybe the strongest thing she'd known him to do. "Jake. I'm so glad for you."

He picked up a quilt that was hanging over the edge

of the crib. She recognized it as his mom's handiwork. It was full of shards of exuberant color—limes and aquas and purples.

"This was Jude's quilt. Kerrie asked if she could take it when she left, and I said yes. She had a daughter eighteen months ago. Sienna. Jude's sister. Sienna used the quilt, too. Now it's our turn—Kerrie gave it back with her blessing."

"Thank you," she whispered. Tears started to fall. Her kid had struck gold in the dad department. "I'm going to do up the nursery at my place—I'm buying a house, by the way—the same way. Maybe you'll loan me some art. I was reading this book about coparenting, and—"

"Hang on."

What? The heavy emotion that had been blanketing them had lifted a little, and he seemed...annoyed? Why was she having so much trouble recognizing emotions, both hers and his? Was that a pregnancy thing?

"Coparenting?" he said.

He probably didn't know the term. "Yeah, it's when two people who aren't together agree to—"

"For a smart woman, you are such a—" He cut himself off and huffed a frustrated sigh. "Okay. This is my fault. I'm doing this wrong." Before she could blink he was kneeling at the foot of her rocking chair. "Nora. I don't want to *coparent* with you." He said the word like it tasted bad in his mouth. "I mean, I will, if that's what you want. If you won't have me. But here's what I should have led with." He leaned forward, bracing his hands on the arms of the chair. "I love you."

Tears started. She swiped them away and gave him her full attention, because he wasn't done talking. "I fell in love with you even though I tried not to. You got me. Like the

zombie apocalypse. You just kept coming at me, and..."
He shook his head.

"Eating your brains?" She smiled through the tears.

"I'm still doing this wrong." But he smiled back.

"Nah. I think you're doing it exactly right. Keep going."

"I love you. I'm gonna love the kid in there, too."
He nodded at her belly. "I just...I thought I'd had my
shot. I thought loving you would somehow take away
from how much I loved Jude. The reason I disappeared
the morning after New Year's Eve was that I realized I'd
forgotten Jude's birthday. It was on the thirtieth, and I just
forgot it."

He sounded so disgusted with himself, it nearly broke
her heart.

"You make me *forget*, is my point. And even though it
would be easier, and a lot less painful, part of me doesn't
want to forget. But if that's the price I have to pay for you
and our baby, I'll gladly pay it."

Oh, her sweet man-god, whose heart was the most
beautiful thing about him. "I think," Nora said gently, "that
you're looking at it the wrong way. I can help you *remember*. If you tell me about Jude, I can help you remember."
She settled a hand on her stomach. "We can all remember
together."

He nodded. He was crying. They were both crying.

He lifted his hands off the arms of the rocker suddenly,
in a jerky sort of motion. It was like they'd moved of their
own volition before he got control of them again and put
them back down.

She thought she knew what was happening. She brought
her hands to her belly. "You want to touch?"

"Can I?" he whispered.

"Of course." She lifted her shirt up to expose the bump.

He put his hands on her, his big, rough, perfect hands, and it was such a *relief.*

He laid his cheek on her belly, too, and she tangled her hands in his hair. They stayed like that for a long time, breathing and listening to Mick's quiet snoring. While they were having the most significant conversation of their lives, he had fallen asleep.

"You know, this room was really a symbolic gesture," he said, his voice muffled as he spoke against her belly. The words tickled. "We can live in town. Or in Toronto, if you want to be near your family."

She extracted one of her hands from his hair and swatted his head. "Oh, shut up. You know this is my dream house."

"It is?" He sounded ridiculously pleased.

"They don't call it Paradise Cove for nothing, do they?"

"I guess not. But what about your sister? The house?"

"Turns out you guys aren't the only ones with meddling old people in your lives. My grandma left Erin her condo. She's going to sell it and get a place of her own, but she's been harassing me about cottages. She has this idea that they're all going to descend on Moonflower Bay in the summers." She snorted. "So you might have to, like, build a guest wing."

"I can do that." Rocking back on his heels, he grinned. "You gotta tell me everything that's been happening here." He rubbed her belly again. "I've missed a lot of stuff."

"Yeah, you missed all the barfing. Except that one time."

"No, like appointments."

"I'm using a midwife." He raised an eyebrow. "Oh, come on. It's not like I couldn't deliver it myself if I had to."

"That's true. So what happened at your last appointment? Did you hear the heartbeat?"

"Yeah." She smiled. "It was pretty amazing."

"What else?"

She thought back to the appointment, which had been routine. Except, actually...Heat started to spread inside her. "The midwife told me that in case I was wondering, sex is perfectly safe, and in fact there's some thinking that the hormones released by orgasm are good for the baby."

He licked his lips. "Are they now?"

"I mean, I don't know." She performed an exaggerated shrug. "I guess we just have to trust the medical experts here."

The Walsh repair.

It popped into Jake's mind as he helped Nora out of the chair. It was some kind of surgery stitch that her grandma had invented, if he remembered correctly. A method for fixing broken hearts.

Damned if Dr. Walsh Junior hadn't done it to him. Forced him to *want* things, to want them enough to hack through all the fear and habit that had accreted around him, calcifying his heart.

He cleared his throat. "I have one more thing to show you. In my room. Our room." He steered her across the hall. "We can redecorate it however you like."

"Are you forgetting that I'm the person who moved from Harold Burgess's hovel to the Barbie Dream Room? I don't care what the room looks like."

"Well, you might care about this." He had added a small cabinet to the far wall, across from the foot of the bed. He opened it to reveal a little TV and a DVD player. "Old-school, I know, but as you know, I'm a little behind the times on the whole technology front." He was getting rid of that damn phone ASAP, now that he had Nora back.

"You're not a Netflix guy, probably," she teased.

"Happily, it turns out that most of your weird zombie movies come on DVD." He pulled out a little drawer under the TV to reveal the collection that Clara had helped him order from Amazon with rush shipping.

"Oh, Jake. You know just how to romance a girl."

"I know." He wagged his eyebrows at her. "Now strip."

"Stop it. You're *slaying* me with the romance." She was stripping, though, and rather quickly, too. And laughing. He did the same.

How quickly they had gone from crying to laughing today.

Soon they were standing in front of each other totally exposed. And not just physically. He had told her his worst fears and she was still here, his beautiful, brilliant Nora.

And, not to get too caveman about it, but she was here with his baby inside her. Her previously flat belly was gently curved, and it made him *crazy*. It made him want to do wicked, wicked things to her, but then lay her down and rub her feet while she watched zombie movies. It was all very confusing—but in a good way.

He hardly knew where to start.

Except, wait. He did. He smiled. "I like your hair, Dr. Walsh."

"I like your hair, too, Mr. Ramsey."

Epilogue

Thirteen months later

When Nora told Jake about her ex-boyfriends, that night they were rounding third base—third base being talking about sexual insecurities while grilling fish—she had mentioned one dude who kept saying he needed her to "meet him halfway."

Jake had never really gotten that.

Nora needed someone to meet her more than halfway.

She worked a lot. She had an important job. She took care of the town of Moonflower Bay. She took care of their daughter. *They* took care of their daughter. Penny. Named after Dr. Penelope Walsh, of course, but maybe also a little bit after the Beatles song "Penny Lane."

So when Nora went back to the clinic three months after Penny was born, Jake met her more than halfway. He brought Penny in for feedings. He filled in at the front desk when Jacques was sick. He learned how to do the billing and did it during Penny's naptime so

Nora could come home sooner and they could have their evenings free.

He didn't even like to think of it as meeting her halfway, because that implied that there was a compromise being made. There were no compromises here. It was all his pleasure. It was, as Sawyer had shouted at him what felt like a lifetime ago, the first thing he'd wanted. He was good at it. At being a dad. At being a husband—they'd had what Nora called a shotgun wedding on a full-moon night by the lake before Penny was born. Eiko had gotten some crazy internet ordination, and they'd said their vows—"Standard, old-school. I'm not really a write-your-own-vows kind of girl," Nora had said—chucked some flowers into the lake, and that had been that.

The best part of every day was the end of it. After Penny's bath, they would all pile onto the bed and play two songs: "Hey Jude," and "Penny Lane." It had been the grief counselor's idea, and at first he'd felt weird about it, but now he loved it. Nora and Jake would sing and try to make Penny laugh.

Which she usually did. She laughed easily, his Pen. She embraced new experiences—she'd just started solid food this week, in fact—with gusto, delighted by nearly everything she encountered. Watching her reminded him that while being open to the world could have a cost, it could also have a payoff that was immeasurable.

She was laughing now, in fact. He blew raspberries on her belly while she screamed in delight.

"Hey!" Nora stuck her head into the room. "I thought we had to leave. I thought it was imperative that I get home by four so we could hit the road for the mystery trip."

"It was. It is." He planted one last kiss on Pen's chunky belly and snapped her into her new onesie.

"Is that..." Nora came closer. "Is that a Detroit Tigers onesie?"

"Sure is."

"Oh my God, are we going to a Tigers game?"

"Home opener versus Blue Jays."

"Are you *kidding* me?" She started jumping up and down. "Ahh!"

"Yeah, I mean, that was one of the whole points of moving to Moonflower Bay, right? And you haven't gone yet."

They dropped Mick at Jake's dad's house and managed to escape after only ten minutes or so of Dad and Jamila losing their minds over Penny—and hit the road. Nora made moony eyes at him the whole way.

That was the other thing about meeting her more than halfway. It paid off so profoundly. She was so ridiculously easy to please that it almost felt like cheating. Zombies and Tigers and trout melts by the lake all had the pixie doctor turning into a gooey pile of mush.

So yeah, the whole meeting-halfway thing wasn't work at all.

Leave it to Jake to think of this.

The Tigers were the one item in the new-life to-do list she hadn't gotten around to yet. But to be fair, she hadn't known that her new life was going to involve a husband, a kid, and a house you had to walk through a lake to get to, so she'd been a little busy.

They'd been in a cocoon since Penny was born, one made of sleep deprivation and endless feedings and the clinic and Jake's counseling, which she sometimes went to with him. Work. Good, important work, all of it. Which meant it had been a good, important cocoon they'd been in.

She wouldn't have traded it for anything. But an *outing* like this was a total thrill.

At the stadium, Jake hoisted Pen into a baby carrier. Nora tried to tug the diaper bag from his shoulder, but he wouldn't surrender it.

Nora had noticed, early in her friends-with-benefits phase with Jake, how easy it was to be with him. It still was. And she still marveled over it. She had been so adamant, when she got here, about not getting into a relationship, afraid that to do so would mean bending herself to fit into someone else's life instead of living her own.

But it turned out that if you fell in love with a guy who liked your hair and didn't mind zombie movies and never let you carry anything, you didn't have to worry about any of that.

"We're sitting *here*?" she asked as he led them to a spot about twenty rows up behind the catcher. He knew she was a center field aficionado—she had told him about how her grandma used to take them all to games, and they'd sit dead center.

So okay, maybe she'd spoken too hastily about Jake's magical powers to make her happy. The man had to have *one* flaw.

"Yup." He settled into his seat, extracted Penny from her carrier, and turned her around so she was facing the field. "Home base."

Oh.

"I was thinking," he went on, his eyes twinkling, "about the age-old question of what is home base. We talked about it so much, but we never figured it out. But in retrospect, it was obvious."

"It was?"

"Yeah." He gestured in front of them. "Home base is home base."

She laughed. "Literal home base."

"Yeah. First base is rolling around nearly naked in a pink room. Second base is talking about sexual insecurities while grilling trout. Third base is sex without a condom. So obviously, home base is sitting behind *actual* home base in Comerica Park with the world's greatest kid."

"I don't know why we didn't think of that before."

He shrugged. "Yeah, well, we aren't always the smartest."

She grinned. "I'm not sure I agree with that. You suddenly seem super smart. Can you work out the zombie metaphor thing, too?"

"No, I cannot. Some things just have to remain a mystery."

She swatted him on the shoulder. And kissed him on the cheek.

The jumbotron came to life as the music kicked on.

"It's starting," he said, shifting Penny to one arm and slinging the other one over Nora's shoulders. "Watch the game, Doc."

Don't miss Law and Maya's story in
SANDCASTLE BEACH

❧

Available Spring 2021

About the Author

Jenny Holiday is a *USA Today* bestselling and RITA®-nominated author whose works have been featured in the *New York Times*, *Entertainment Weekly*, and the *Washington Post*, and by National Public Radio. She grew up in Minnesota, where her mom was a children's librarian, and started writing at age nine after her fourth-grade teacher gave her a notebook to fill with stories. When she's not working on her next book, she likes to hang out with her family, watch other people sing karaoke, and throw theme parties. A member of the House of Slytherin, Jenny lives in London, Ontario, Canada.

You can learn more at:

> *JennyHoliday.com*
> *Twitter @JennyHoli*
> *Reader group: facebook.com/groups*
> */NorthernHeat*
> *Facebook.com/JennyHolidayBooks*
> *Instagram @HolyMolyJennyHoli*

Fall in love with these charming contemporary romances!

SUMMER ON HONEYSUCKLE RIDGE
by Debbie Mason

Abby Everhart has gone from being a top L.A. media influencer to an unemployed divorcée living out of her car. So inheriting her great-aunt's homestead in Highland Falls, North Carolina, couldn't have come at a better time. But instead of a cabin ready to put on the market, she finds a fixer-upper, complete with an overgrown yard and a reclusive—albeit sexy—man living on the property. When sparks between them become undeniable, will she be able to sell the one place that's starting to feel like home?

PRIMROSE LANE
by Debbie Mason

Olivia Davenport has finally gotten her life back together and is now Harmony Harbor's most sought-after event planner. But her past catches up with her when she learns that she's now guardian of her ex's young daughter. Dr. Finn Gallagher knows a person in over her head when he sees one, but Olivia makes it clear she doesn't want his companionship. Only with a little help from some matchmaking widows—and a precocious little girl—might he be able to convince her that life is better with someone you love at your side.

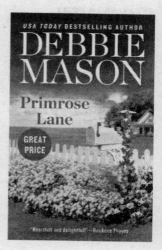

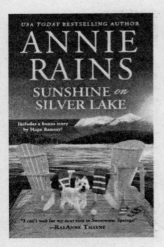

SUNSHINE ON SILVER LAKE
by Annie Rains

Café owner Emma St. James is planning a special event at Evergreen State Park to honor her mother's memory. Which means she'll need the help of the ruggedly handsome park ranger who broke her heart years ago. As their attraction grows stronger than ever, will Emma find herself at risk of falling for him again? Includes a bonus story by Hope Ramsay!

STARTING OVER AT BLUEBERRY CREEK
by Annie Rains

Firefighter Luke Marini moved to Sweetwater Springs with the highest of hopes—new town, new job, and new neighbors who know nothing of his past. And that's just how he wants to keep it. But it's nearly impossible when the gorgeous brunette next door decides to be the neighborhood's welcome wagon. She's sugar, spice, and everything nice—but getting close to someone again is playing with fire. Includes a bonus story by Melinda Curtis!

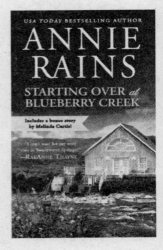

RETURN TO MAGNOLIA HARBOR
by Hope Ramsay

Jessica Blackwell's life needs a refresh. So while she's back home in Magnolia Harbor, she's giving her architecture career a total makeover. The only problem? Jessica's new client happens to be her old high school nemesis. Christopher Martin never meant to hurt Jessica all those years ago, and now he'd give anything to have a second chance with the one woman who always haunted his memories.

CAN'T HURRY LOVE
by Melinda Curtis

Widowed after one year of marriage, city girl Lola Williams finds herself stranded in Sunshine, Colorado, reeling from the revelation that her husband had secrets she never could have imagined, secrets that she's asked the ruggedly hot town sheriff to help her uncover. Lola swears she's done with love forever, but the matchmaking ladies of the Sunshine Valley Widows Club have different plans...Includes a bonus story by Annie Rains!

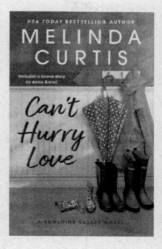

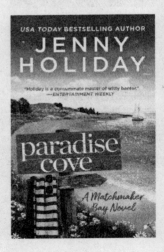